From Friends to Forever
by Karen Templeton
&
The Family He Wanted
by Karen Sandler

Baby By Surprise
by Karen Rose Smith
&
Daddy by Surprise
by Debra Salonen

A Kid to the Rescue
by Susan Gable
&
Then Comes Baby
by Helen Brenna

The Sheikh and the Bought Bride
by Susan Mallery

A Cold Creek Homecoming
by RaeAnne Thayne

A Baby for the Bachelor
by Victoria Pade

The Baby Album
by Roz Denny Fox

A KID TO THE RESCUE

"I know you don't like fighting, but do you ever at least fight yourself?"

Greg inched forward.

"Wh-what do you mean?" Shannon asked.

"I mean, say there's something you want that you know you shouldn't have. Say, cheese and pepperoni pizza. You know it's all wrong for you. It's never going to work. But you want it. It looks delicious." He planted his palms on the wall on either side of her head, then leaned in, nuzzled her shoulder and inhaled deeply as he skimmed the curve of her neck. "It smells fantastic. Do you fight with yourself over tasting it? Or do you just take a bite?"

"I–" She lowered her gaze to his mouth. The tip of her tongue darted out, moistening her lips, and Greg's hormones jumped to attention like a superhero to a beacon light in the night sky. "Fighting's wrong," she murmured. "Don't fight it. Taste it."

He bent his elbows, letting his body weight ease against her.

"Is that your utility belt," she muttered, "or are you happy to see me?"

THEN COMES BABY

Jamis shouldn't be here in the dark with a beautiful woman.

Not with the yearning for simple touch coursing through him. The need. The want for Natalie's warm hands on his skin. He should've been turned off by her too-good-to-be-true nature. Instead, he couldn't tear his eyes away from her lips.

Go, Jamis. For her sake. Get as far away as you can.

One of his favourite smells, wood smoke, emanated from her hair. He wished he could bury his face in those long blond curls and breathe her in.

"Why are you hiding on Mirabelle?" she whispered.

No one had ever asked him that. "I'm not a nice man, Natalie. The world is a much better place with me out of the way, unable to harm."

"I think you're wrong. I think inside here," she said, pressing a fingertip to his chest, "there's a good man hiding away."

All the characters in this book have no existence outside the imagination of the author, and have no relation whatsoever to anyone bearing the same name or names. They are not even distantly inspired by any individual known or unknown to the author, and all the incidents are pure invention.

First published in Great Britain 2010
Harlequin Mills & Boon Limited,
Eton House, 18-24 Paradise Road, Richmond, Surrey TW9 1SR

ISBN: 978 0 263 87982 7

23-0710

Harlequin Mills & Boon policy is to use papers that are natural, renewable and recyclable products and made from wood grown in sustainable forests. The logging and manufacturing processes conform to the legal environmental regulations of the country of origin.

Printed and bound in Spain
by Litografia Rosés S.A., Barcelona

A KID TO THE RESCUE

BY

SUSAN GABLE

THEN COMES BABY

BY

HELEN BRENNA

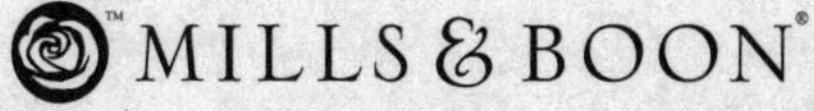

A KID TO THE RESCUE

BY
SUSAN GABLE

Susan Gable's love of reading goes back to her pre-school days, when books arrived at her house through the Weekly Readers Book Club. Both her parents are voracious readers and they passed that on to their daughter. Susan shared her love of books (and Weekly Reader!) as an elementary teacher for ten years, then turned to writing after a year of home-schooling her son caused her to nearly lose what was left of her mind.

Dedicated in loving memory:
Of Susan Harmon, who always believed there'd be another book. Sus, you're missed so very much. Storytelling's not the same without you.

And of Deandra Francis May,
who left her family way too young. Dee, we're never letting go. You'll stay in our hearts forever.

Special thanks to: Stacey Konkel, Esquire, for answering my numerous family law questions.

Jack Daneri, Esquire, for answering a million criminal law questions and being a good sport that a romance author, not a thriller writer, consulted him with legal questions.

Holly, for always encouraging me to keep fighting.

Jen and Diana, tireless CPs, always there to lend encouragement and tell me where I'd gone off track. Di, thanks for making me laugh.

Victoria and Wanda, for making this book so much stronger.

Tom and TJ. Living with a writer is never easy. Thanks for understanding when I disappeared into the office and appeared to have forgotten your existence in favour of my imaginary friends. Do we have any clean socks?

CHAPTER ONE

FOR THE UMPTEENTH TIME, Greg Hawkins glanced at the observation window—the one that reflected into the room he used at Erie University's Children's Center—and wished he had superpowers.

Nothing spectacular, mind you. Just the ability to see and hear through walls. To know who was staring at him this time.

At least a goldfish in a bowl could stare back.

"*Kerpow! Kerpow!*" At the far end of the table, one of Greg's kids wiggled in his chair, banging his fist on the cluttered surface and sending colored pencils rolling in all directions. "Mr. Hawkins, how do you spell kerpow? I want to write it big."

"Kerpow, huh?" He jotted it on a scrap of paper and passed it down the table, sneaking a covert look at his watch as he did. They were more than halfway through the session and Julie still wasn't here. It wasn't usually a good sign when one of his kids was late. Especially this late. Without a parent calling him.

Just three weeks earlier they'd lost Scotty, a member of the group, and Greg didn't think any of them—not him, not the kids, nor their parents—were ready to deal with another setback. Hopefully there was another explanation.

"Okay, guys, quick five-minute break. Take a stretch,

look at what everyone else has been doing." While the kids got up from their chairs, he pulled out his cell, checking for messages.

"I need a drink of water," Cheryl announced as she headed for the door.

"And I have to go to the can," Michael said, following on her heels.

"Hold it. Earlier I let you get a drink—" he pointed at Michael "—and you—" he moved his finger to Cheryl "—go to the bathroom. What's going on?"

Cheryl turned in the doorway, hands behind her back. She shrugged her shoulders, but her face had gone white. That concerned him. Guilt, or not feeling well? Michael, meanwhile, danced in place, attempting, no doubt, to convince Greg of the urgency of the situation. "Got a drink before, now I have to take a leak. In one end and out the other, right?"

"Thanks for the biology lesson, professor. Be back in five. We have work to finish." Greg flipped his phone closed. No messages.

While the other three kids milled around the room, and the unseen eyes on the other side of the observation window watched, he doodled a clock, hands racing around the face, springs exploding from the side. Time. The enemy of all.

The enemy of his program.

The new university dean was on a mad cost-cutting rampage, and had made it clear that Greg's art therapy program was near the top of the chopping block. She believed his program would be better run through one of the local hospitals, or cancer centers, or even one of the social services organizations.

And being that the university provided him with

space he'd otherwise have to purchase or rent, utilities, an umbrella of insurance, grad students to do the grunt work… A serious amount of money would be needed to fill the gap if he couldn't find someone else to take on his program.

He was funded through the end of the summer semester. Unless he convinced Dean Auld otherwise, time was up in August.

"All right, you guys, back to it." The kids didn't need much encouragement and returned to their places and drawings.

Except the two who'd left the room and were still missing in action.

It was the action part that had him worried. Michael and his sidekick Cheryl, ever faithful though of late slow moving, were undoubtedly up to trouble.

He didn't need superhero powers to sense it. Being the uncle to almost a baker's-dozen kids—one of his sisters was due in two months with nephew thirteen—and having been a boy himself, he just knew it. He had a soft spot for Michael, in part because the boy shared his name with Greg's dad. But soft didn't mean he'd give the kid a free pass.

Sticking his head out the therapy-room door, he scanned the hallway. Big surprise, Cheryl wasn't at the water fountain on the corner. He couldn't see Michael, either. "You guys keep working. I'll be right back."

Greg turned toward the mirrored window, crossing his fingers Dean Auld wasn't behind it. "Watch them," he said, exaggerating the words in case the observers didn't have the speaker turned on. At the very least, they could make themselves useful.

At the men's room, a quick search revealed Michael

wasn't there. He rapped on the women's door next. "Cheryl? Are you in there?"

"Yeah, Mr. Hawkins. Sorry, but after I got a drink, I had to go to the bathroom again. I'll be right out." Suppressed giggling followed her confession.

Crap. "Do you know where Michael is?"

"Uh, no. Didn't he come back to the classroom yet?"

"If he had, would I be asking you?"

"Oh, right. I guess not."

"You have two more minutes. If you're not back by then, I'm coming in there after you."

"You wouldn't!" she shrieked. "This is the girls' room."

"Try me. You could be sick in there. It would be my duty to be sure you're okay."

"I'll be back to the classroom." Cheryl's voice was more subdued this time.

"If you see Michael on your way, tell him he's pushing it if he wants to keep working with me. I don't tolerate nonsense like this."

A loud gasp echoed in the bathroom. He didn't often threaten to kick kids out his program.

Satisfied she'd roust Michael, Greg hustled to the classroom, resisting the temptation to open the observation-room door and find out exactly who was in there. Low voices reached him as he passed.

Back inside, he walked around, praising the other children. Stopping at Cheryl's empty chair, he studied her four-panel page. An honest-to-goodness strip in the making, it had real potential. There was definitely art talent there, not that this was about talent. Still, he loved to nurture it when he found it.

The Dastardly Duo skittered in the door and into their seats next to each other, both out of breath. "Sorry,

Mr. H.," Michael said. "Didn't mean to take so long. I went for a stroll. Needed to stretch my legs, you know?"

Greg narrowed his eyes, but opted to let it go. No fire alarms had gone off; there hadn't been a flood coming out of the bathroom. "Cheryl, this looks great. I love your use of color here." He pointed to the first panel, where a flying dog carried a basket of treats toward a building labeled Cleveland Clinic—where Cheryl had had her tumor removed three months earlier.

She looked smugly at Michael, then beamed up at Greg. "Thank you." She elbowed the boy. "Come on. Show him."

"Are you crazy? No way."

"But it's great. I want him to see."

"No."

"Yes." Cheryl grabbed Michael's Penn State baseball cap and yanked it off his chemo-bald head.

"Cheryl! You know we don't touch people's caps in here," Greg scolded, reaching for the hat, then stopped, staring at the crown of Michael's head.

"See? Now if someone at school steals his hat, it won't matter. Because they'll think it's cool. Isn't it cool? Don't you love it?"

He had to admit, the superhero about to kick the snot out of a cancer-cell bad guy drawn in black Magic Marker actually looked good. Maybe Cheryl had a future as a tattoo artist. "Not bad, Cheryl. Still, I don't think Michael's mother is going to be happy when she sees this. What's wrong with working on paper like everyone else?"

"Michelangelo painted the Sistine Chapel ceiling," offered one of the others from the end of the table. "That's not paper."

"He didn't paint someone's head and besides, that was a commissioned work," Greg said.

"Does 'commissioned' mean someone asked for it?" Cheryl said. "'Cause Michael asked me to do this. And he paid me." She yanked a rumpled five-dollar bill from her pocket and displayed it proudly. "Now I'm a professional artist, Mr. Hawkins, just like you."

Greg swallowed his chuckle, turning it into a cough. Then, recalling that he was being watched, he pasted a stern look on his face. "Go to the bathroom, Michael, wet some paper towels and clean that off. With soap." Thank God they only used water-based art supplies, nothing permanent.

"Awwww, come on. At least let my mom see it first. Maybe it will make her laugh. She hasn't laughed in a long time." Michael made sad, puppy-dog eyes at him, a technique the ten-year-old had perfected with hospital nurses.

"You can't pull that face on another guy, kid. It only works on women."

"Damn. Well, it was worth a shot."

"Language, mister."

"Leapin' lizards, Batboy, it was worth a shot."

Greg struggled to keep a straight face at that one. Then the idea of what Michael's mom would say chased the fleeting humor away. "You seriously think your mother is going to laugh when she sees your head?"

The boy shrugged. "Like I said, it's worth a shot, don't you think?"

"Put your hat back on. Save the surprise for after you're out in the car, okay?"

The boy's grin returned as he crammed the cap back on his head. "You're cool, Mr. H. Thanks."

Greg wasn't sure Michael's mother would thank him.

If nothing else, it would remind her that despite her child's illness, he was still a kid. All boy and then some, despite his second bout of cancer. "Now, all of you, finish your work. On the *paper*. We've got ten minutes left."

The door flew open, crashing into the wall as Julie came barreling into the room, causing the drawings taped nearby to flutter upward, then slowly fall back into place. The group stared at her, pencils, crayons, markers, poised midstroke.

"Woo-hoo! Guess what, everybody? I did it." She waved a piece of paper in the air. "I kicked cancer's butt! I'm in remission."

"All right!" Greg caught the girl as she launched herself into his arms, lifting her up in a celebratory hug as a wave of relief washed over him. A win. Not a loss, but a win. Exactly what they needed right now. He glanced over her now-curly-haired head at her mom, who leaned against the door frame. He smiled.

Happy tears glistened in the woman's eyes, but didn't spill over. "Thank you," she said.

He just nodded, then set Julie back on her feet. "That means I owe you a special certificate, doesn't it?"

"Yes, you do. And you hafta make me a character in your next comic book, too."

While the rest of the kids hugged her—no more work was getting done today, that much was obvious—Greg thumbed through a folder he kept in his briefcase, looking for her certificate. He kept one prepared for each kid, showing it to them when they were down and needed some extra motivation. A lump filled his throat as he flipped past Scotty's to find the right one. It featured Julie in a flowing purple cape, one fist raised victoriously, booted foot on the "head" of a cancer-cell villain with black *X*'s for eyes—because he was dead. Using a calligraphy marker, he inked in the date, then blew on it before presenting it to the girl with a flourish.

"There you are. I knew you could do it. And so can the rest of you. Say it with me…"

Voices blended together as they all shouted, "Captain Chemo kicks cancer's butt!"

"KICKS CANCER'S BUTT?" Shannon Vanderhoff raised a skeptical eyebrow at the social worker as they watched the commotion from the dimly lit observation room. "See? That proves my point. This man, this *comic-book artist*—" she let the phrase drip with as much scorn as she could muster "—encourages violence in children. Ryan hardly needs more violence around him. Besides, my nephew doesn't have cancer. I'm not sure why you wanted me to see this."

"Greg Hawkins isn't *just* a comic-book artist, Ms. Vanderhoff. He's got a master's degree in art therapy. And he doesn't only work with cancer kids. He's had amazing results with children who need empowering. Children like Ryan."

Shannon turned to the opposite window, moving closer and leaning her forehead against the glass. In this other room, set up like a mini preschool with a wide variety of toys and books on short shelves, Ryan sat at a low, kidney-shaped table. A social-work grad student was vainly trying to coax the boy into helping her assemble a wooden puzzle. "Really? Children like Ryan? So, he's worked with kids who've watched their father kill their mother? How many?"

"Well, I don't know if Greg's worked with kids exactly like Ryan. I just meant emotionally traumatized kids."

In the room, Ryan shook his head at the young blond woman, pushing the puzzle to the far end of the table. He rose from his chair and wandered to the bookshelves. Without being choosy, he pulled out a picture book and plunked down in a beanbag. He held the open book close to his face, effectively shutting out the student who'd followed him.

Shannon closed her eyes and drew in a deep breath. Breathe in, take what life hands you; hold it, accept it; breathe out, let it go.

The mantra had worked well for her up until almost two and a half months ago, in early February, when six-year-old Ryan had come to live with her. Neither one of them quite knew how to deal with what life had handed them this time.

His mother, her sister, dead.

His father, her brother-in-law, sitting in jail, awaiting trial.

Ryan, the nephew she'd only had personal contact with twice in his six years, living in Shannon's computer room, both of them struggling to come to grips with it all.

The social worker gently laid her hand on Shannon's shoulder. "You look completely exhausted."

Exhausted didn't begin to cover it. Shannon worked nights as a hotel auditor, doing bookkeeping. Finding a reliable babysitter hadn't been easy. And she wasn't getting much sleep during the day, since she had to take care of the boy. Single parenthood wasn't for the weak of body or spirit.

"I'm worried about you as well as Ryan. Please, speak to Greg. I think he can help. What have you got to lose by talking to him?"

Lose? "Absolutely nothing." Shannon straightened

up, moving from beneath the woman's palm and returning her attention to the scene in the art room. Parents who had come to claim their children had joined in the celebration and were exchanging hugs and high fives.

"Great. I'll go tell Greg you want to speak with him." The door to the observation room closed before Shannon could get another word out.

She took the opportunity to get a better look at Greg Hawkins, who'd spent most of the time in the classroom with his profile to her. Now he faced the window full on, talking animatedly to one of the parents.

She'd expected a geek—scrawny, thick glasses, pants hiked halfway to his armpits. What else would a comic-book artist look like?

Not like this. He was gorgeous, with features that could accurately be described as chiseled, high cheekbones that gave his face an angular appearance, a strong chin and a wide smile that put an extra spark in his—blue? green?—hard to say with the distance and window between them—eyes. Dark brown hair. He looked fit, too, in a blue striped shirt with its sleeves rolled up to his elbows and a pair of khakis.

He probably made superheroes jealous. And geeky alter-ego personas would sell out their identities for half the charm and confidence this guy oozed.

The social worker had reached his side, and after a few murmured words, Greg looked up at the window. Shannon almost took a step back, convinced he was gazing through the mirrored glass and actually seeing her. He nodded, to her or the young woman standing next to him? After a quick glance at his watch, he made his way through the throng, offering more nods and comments as he went. Several of the children were tugging on his arms, looking up at him with pleading expressions on their faces. The positive response—"Yes" was easy enough to lip-read—made the kids jump up and down, then he disentangled himself and headed out of the room.

Only a few moments later, he entered the narrow observation room. "Hi," he said, hand outthrust. "I'm Greg Hawkins. I understand you wanted to speak to me about…?"

"Shannon Vanderhoff. About my nephew." She briefly shook his hand, then gestured in Ryan's direction. "Miss Anderson seems convinced you can help him."

"But you're not so sure?"

She sighed, looking over at Ryan, who once again sat in a chair at the table, face propped in his palms so that only his sandy-blond hair showed. "Mr. Hawkins, no offense to you, but your specialty—"

"Comic books?"

"Yes, comic books. Superheroes. Big-busted women in tight clothes, weird creatures and people fighting. I don't think that's what my nephew needs. He's seen enough violence, thank you."

"Abused?" he asked. "Because I've worked with a number of abused kids. My program, which doesn't focus exclusively on using comic-book formats, gives kids back some sense of control in their lives."

"I don't know if I'd classify Ryan as abused. No one ever hit him, at least, not that we know of. I don't think his father meant him to see what he saw."

"Which is?"

"No one knows exactly what happened, except maybe Ryan. But in the end, my sister was dead. The police believe Ryan saw his father beat and strangle his mother."

Greg whistled softly. "Poor kid. That's hard to swallow. Watching your mom die, and not being able to do anything about it, that's got to make you feel kinda helpless."

"That's how I feel right now, too." Shannon splayed her hand across the glass. "I haven't been able to help him so far. I'm taking him to a therapist twice a week, but it doesn't matter because he won't speak. He won't play for play therapy. He barely sleeps, barely eats."

"And what about you?"

She turned to him, moved by the compassion in his eyes. Which she could now see were blue. "Me?"

"Yes. Have you talked to anyone? Are you eating? Sleeping?"

"As much as can be expected, I suppose."

Greg snapped his fingers. "I remember now. I saw this on the news. Philadelphia, right?"

"Yes. The media turned my sister's death into a circus. I was glad to get Ryan away from there. Here in Erie he's not so much a news story. I detest the idea of hauling him back there when the trial starts."

The man appeared pensive for a moment. "Listen, the parents and kids from my group are all going out for lunch to celebrate Julie's remission. Why don't you and Ryan come with us? Maybe you can both eat, we can talk, and you can check out some of my references. Let them tell you if they think I've made their kids more prone to violence or if they suddenly want to wear skin-tight outfits and try to fly off the garage roof." He smiled at her. "I'll even spring for the pizza and pop. So what have you got to lose?"

What was it with these people and their asking her what she had to lose? Most of the time she stood to lose nothing. Because Shannon didn't believe in keeping things, holding on to things. You couldn't lose what you didn't try to keep.

But Ryan…

Ryan was different. If she didn't do something, it was Ryan who stood to lose himself. Someone had to reach him.

"Pizza, huh?" She shrugged. "Sure, why not?"

"Your enthusiasm underwhelms me."

"Try not to take it personally, Mr. Hawkins. Look, I never had much use for superheroes. I don't believe in heroes or white knights of any sort. I believe in not expecting too much out of life, and being content with what you have." She pointed to Ryan, waited for the art therapist's gaze to follow. "But for that little boy in there, for him, I want more. So I'm willing to entertain the notion that superheroes and comic-book artists *might* just offer him some hope. Convince me."

CHAPTER TWO

PAULA'S PARLORS was actually two restaurants connected by an open archway between the pizza parlor and the ice-cream parlor. It was a big hit with Erie-area kids, as Greg knew quite well. They'd bumped three tables together, which though they now held sixteen people, still weren't as large as the dining-room table at his parents' house. That could accommodate twenty.

Greg watched the boy seated next to him. The kid wrinkled his nose at the slice of pizza on his plate.

"Looks weird, doesn't it?"

Ryan darted a glance at his aunt, who'd ordered the small artichoke hearts and goat cheese pie. She was currently at the far end of the table with her own food, talking to Cheryl's mother.

Julie, on Greg's other side, piped up, mouth full of half-chewed pepperoni pizza. "What the heck is an artichoke heart? Eeewww. Sounds gross."

"I'll bet you'd rather have this, huh?" Greg leaned across the table and grabbed another slice from the closest "normal" pie.

At a slight nod from the boy, Greg slipped the pizza on his plate, exchanging it for the gourmet slice that no six-year-old in his right mind would eat. Hell, Greg wouldn't eat it, either. Not even if it was served by his brother Finn, who was an accomplished chef. Come to think of it, it sounded exactly like something Finn would concoct.

"Aunt" Shannon certainly had odd taste in pizza.

If you discounted the puffy bags beneath her eyes that she'd tried, in vain, to cover with some kind of makeup, she was attractive enough. Not in the superheroine sense, but more the girl next door. The kind the superheroes always fell for. Shoulder-length burnt-sienna hair. Milk-chocolate eyes. If he had to guess he'd estimate her to be around his own age, somewhere in the early to mid-thirties.

She carried herself with quiet, easygoing grace, someone comfortable with herself and her life.

Except when it came to her nephew.

She glanced up and caught Greg studying her. With a nod to Cheryl's mother, she picked up her plate and headed back to their end of the table. She did a double take as she slid into her chair. "Ryan, you ate that whole slice of pizza already? Wonderful. Do you want anther one?"

The kid ducked his head, pleading with Greg from beneath his lowered eyes.

"Wait a minute," Shannon said, hand hovering over the artichoke pie. "There were only two slices of this left. How come there are three here?"

Ryan's expression turned beseeching.

"He, uh, decided he wanted the pepperoni instead. We traded it in," Greg explained. "Artichoke's sort of an acquired taste."

"And how will he acquire the taste if he never tries it?"

Greg shrugged. "You've got a point."

"There are so many wonderful, interesting foods. It's a pity more people don't try to expand their horizons." With a sly grin that animated her face for the first time since they'd met, she lifted the metal pan and offered it to him. "How about you, Mr. Hawkins? Ever tried artichoke pizza before?"

"N-oo. Can't say that I have."

"Well, I think you should set a good example for the children. Try it. Just a taste. If you don't like it, you don't have to eat it."

Julie giggled, then covered her mouth with her hands. Her mom also chuckled. Ryan's eyes widened. The challenge was passed from kid to kid around the table, like a lightning-fire version of the telephone game, until all conversation stopped and everyone turned to look at him.

She'd thrown down the gauntlet.

With a wink at Ryan, Greg took a slice. He slowly lifted it to his mouth, pausing to dart a quick glance with raised eyebrows at each of the kids, who all shook their heads, several of them calling out, "Don't do it!"

Like a connoisseur checking a fine wine, he inhaled deeply. "Smells okay," he reported. Not as tasty as pepperoni, or sausage. But he wasn't about to admit that.

He chomped a third of the piece, chewing with an exaggerated motion, rocking his head back and forth as if considering the flavor. He swallowed. It was edible, better than some things he'd had—Finn's frog leg gumbo experiment, for example—but not something he'd go out of his way to order in the future. "Not *baaarrg!*" He clutched his throat, gurgling, thrashing in his chair, the wooden frame creaking as he sagged back.

Julie giggled.

"It's like kryptonite," he gasped. "I'm getting weak. Weak." His shoulders dropped, his head lolled to the side and he let his tongue hang out.

As laughter rang in all directions, he heard a cluck of disapproval. Opening his eyes, he found Shannon shaking her head. "Great example. Thanks. Very helpful."

He would have laughed himself if he hadn't noticed Ryan covering his face. *Stupid move, Hawkins*. The kid had watched his mother die. He hurriedly straightened up. "Okay, okay, I'm just kidding. You knew that, right, Ryan? Really. It's not bad." To prove his point, when the boy lowered his hands and warily peeked at him again, he took another bite.

Shannon leaned closer, bringing with her a scent of flowers that should have clashed with the smell of garlic sauce and Parmesan in the air, but strangely didn't. "To quote you," she whispered, "your enthusiasm underwhelms me, Mr. Hawkins. How about it, Ryan?" she asked louder, moving away from Greg. "You want to try this?"

The child clamped his palm over his mouth.

She pursed her lips and shot Greg a dirty look.

He just shrugged, finishing up his slice.

You could lead a kid to an artichoke pizza, but you couldn't make him eat it.

Shannon Vanderhoff appeared to have a lot to learn about six-year-old boys.

LATER THAT AFTERNOON, on the other side of Paula's, the Old-Fashioned Ice-Cream Parlor part, Shannon watched as Greg, in true Pied Piper fashion, led a parade of kids around the black-flecked Formica tables to the make-it-yourself sundae bar along the far wall. No wonder he got along so well with children.

He *was* one. Only taller.

Still, Ryan eagerly held a bowl aloft, letting the man

scoop ice cream into it. Her nephew had eaten more in one afternoon than he usually did three days put together. That scored points for Greg Hawkins.

One of the moms at the table sighed, prompting Shannon to look at her. "If only I weren't married," the woman mused, watching Greg with the children. "That is one yummy man."

Nods of agreement went around the table, then all eyes turned to Shannon. The silence stretched uncomfortably, a quiet bubble in the clamor around them. She shrugged. "He's not the comic-book geek I expected, that's for sure. But he's not what I'm interested in. I want to know how you feel about him as a therapist working with your kids. Do you think the whole superhero thing is too much? Does it make your children more prone to fighting with other kids, or jumping on the furniture? Stuff like that?"

"I wish Cheryl had the energy right now to jump on the sofa."

"She had the energy to decorate Michael's head," the boy's mother retorted, unsuccessfully trying to stifle a chuckle. "Honestly. I just never know what they'll come up with next."

The women all chimed in with their opinions of Greg Hawkins. None of them had anything even slightly negative to say about him.

"He really helped Julie fight. It's hard to teach kids visualization. The comic-book drawings are a concrete first step. At the cancer center, they say visualization and positive attitude can make the difference in beating the disease. I think Greg has had just as much to do with Julie's remission as the medical doctors." The mother's eyes got shiny as they welled with tears. "I've been so scared. Now I'm just really relieved."

One of the other women wrapped an arm around her, giving her a squeeze. When one of the kids shouted "Mom, look at my sundae," they broke apart and Julie's mom wiped the back of her hand across the corner of her eye.

Ryan cradled his bowl, walking carefully back to the chair at Shannon's side. Gobs of whipped cream and chocolate syrup topped the small mounds of vanilla ice cream. Rainbow sprinkles turned it into a party in a bowl.

Shannon's throat tightened. The whole thing seemed normal. Average. Which made it feel surreal, because nothing had been average or normal for Ryan—or her—in months.

The boy dug into the creation, drizzling syrup from the end of his spoon before cramming it into his mouth. He licked dark smudges from his lips, then dipped back into the sundae.

"It's yummy, huh, sport?" Greg was busy with his own chocolate ice cream with…chocolate sprinkles, syrup, chips…and even chocolate whipped cream.

"Like chocolate much, Mr. Hawkins?" Shannon asked. "I thought chocoholism was an exclusively female disorder."

His grin lit up his eyes and revealed tiny dimples at either end of his mouth. "There is no other flavor for ice cream. And when presented with such a spread of chocolate accoutrements, well, why not take advantage of them?" From beneath the pile of napkins he'd brought with him, he pulled out another spoon. "Want some? I'm excellent at sharing."

Shannon hesitated.

"They don't have any artichoke ice cream. I checked. Please, don't tell me you don't like chocolate. I have a deeply held distrust of people who don't like chocolate. Allergic, I can excuse. But to not like chocolate..." He shook his head. "Suspect behavior."

"I like chocolate."

"Phew. That's a relief."

She accepted the spoon from him, then hesitated. There was something...intimate...about eating from the same dish, and it felt odd.

He shoved the bowl closer to her. "Go on. Have some. Or else I won't believe that you really like chocolate. After the artichoke pizza, that's a second strike, so to speak."

"I thought *I* was interviewing *you*, Mr. Hawkins."

"Greg. And you are. You now know that I am a discriminating person when it comes to new clients."

"And you accept them based on their ice-cream preferences?"

The smile faded from his face. "All kidding aside, Ms. Vanderhoff—"

"Shannon."

"Shannon. I take art therapy very seriously. Even if, at moments, it appears I don't. It's not a game. It's not frivolous, even if we use crayons or pudding finger paint."

Ryan made a gurgling noise, and Shannon glanced over at him. He had his spoon poised at his mouth but was staring at Greg with wide eyes.

"You like the idea of finger painting on the tables with pudding, huh, sport?"

The boy nodded.

"Well, maybe we'll have to try that sometime." He returned his attention to Shannon. "So? Are we going to work together?"

She dipped her spoon into his sundae, savoring the

various textures against her tongue and the roof of her mouth. "Mmm. This is very good."

"You didn't answer my question."

"Because I don't have an answer yet, Mr. Hawkins."

"Greg."

"I'm going to have to think about it."

"Fine." He leaned forward in his chair, pulling a black leather wallet out of his back pocket. "Here's my card. Call me when you decide." He stole a peek at his watch, then snatched the bill from the table as he stood. "Sorry, everybody, but I have to leave. My sister's wedding is this summer, and I have to get measured for a tux."

The table clamored with good-byes and best wishes for his sister. He made his way around to everyone, butting fists with each of the kids, admonishing them all to "fight the good fight."

Fight the good fight.

Another reference to violence. And while it might be appropriate for sick kids struggling to survive, Shannon didn't think it was appropriate for Ryan.

Maybe there was another art therapist in Erie. One that didn't come with Greg Hawkins's other "specialties."

GREG FORCED HIMSELF to stand still on the platform while the woman from the tux shop ran a tape measure up the inside of his thigh. It wasn't so much her actions that were making him uncomfortable, or that two of his brothers, Finn and Hayden, were snickering at his obvious unease. No, he was uncomfortable and on his way to being pissed off because his sister Elke, who insisted on supervising every last detail of this wedding right down to the tux measurements, had brought her best friend and maid of honor with her.

His ex-girlfriend, Denise.

The one he'd broken up with a month ago.

Hayden came behind him and leaned in. "She's eyeing you like a Doberman eyes a T-bone. She's hungry, and you're the main course."

"What are you whispering about, Hayden?" Elke demanded. "Is there a problem?"

Her groom, Jeremy Kristoff, who'd been doing his best Invisible Man act over in the corner since his measurements had been completed, looked heavenward. Something told Greg the man regretted not whisking Elke off to Vegas or anywhere else for an elopement. Not that any of his sisters would ever agree to anything less than the traditional church wedding. In his family, tradition ran deep.

"Absolutely not, Elke," Hayden assured her. "Nothing to sweat. Everything's cool. Don't go all Bridezilla on us, okay?" He walked over to prop himself against the counter, raising his eyebrows at Greg, gesturing with small jerks of his head at Denise.

Greg ignored him. And her.

When the attendant pronounced him finished, jotting down the final measurements on a slip of paper, he stepped off the platform, pulling on his mocs, and headed for the door. "Hate to measure and run, but—"

"Wait. You can't leave yet. We haven't decided what you're going to wear." Elke grabbed him by the arm.

"Whatever you decide is fine with me. It's your wedding, I'll wear what you want." He planted a kiss on her cheek.

Beaming, Elke glanced around at the rest of the

men in the wedding party. "Thank you, Greg. That's very refreshing."

"Traitor," Finn hissed.

"You can't go by him. He draws guys in tights all day long. He doesn't have any fashion sense at all," Hayden said, now taking his own place up on the platform. "Have you seen the Captain Chemo costume he had made?"

"Come on, Greg," chimed in the best man, Jeremy's brother. "You can't actually mean that. So, if she decides we're wearing purple cummerbunds and frilly shirts—and pink bow ties—you're cool with that?"

"You're not going to pick something like that, are you, Elke?"

"Of course not. I want this wedding to be amazing, not tacky."

Greg shrugged. "See? No problem."

"You still have to put down a deposit," Denise piped up.

"I can come back next week. Or even take care of it by phone now that they have my measurements. It's not like they're going to run out of order forms." Greg untangled the grip his sister had on his bicep and headed for the door again, shrugging into his denim jacket. "Sorry, but duty calls."

On the sidewalk of the strip mall that hosted Erie Bridals and Tuxedos, the April sunshine glinted off cars' windshields and into his eyes. Greg heaved a sigh of relief, a feeling that was short-lived as a voice called from behind him, "Greg, please. Give me a minute."

Great.

He turned to face her. "What is it, Denise? Really, I've got a lot to do. Deadline next Friday." Not to mention he had to figure out a way to convince Shannon Vanderhoff that he should work with her nephew. Ryan was just the kid to get his program some media attention and make Dean Auld sit up and take notice. Reconsider keeping him at the university.

Besides, he really could help the boy, despite what Ryan's skeptical aunt thought. It was a win-win situation.

"We're going to be able to get through this wedding okay, right?"

"Of course. We're both adults. We both care about Elke. This wedding means a lot to her, and I'll be damned if I'll do anything to mess it up."

"Of course not. I don't know why I even asked that." She waited a beat. "So, how's everything going?"

"Fine." He could see in her face idle chitchat wasn't what Denise had in mind. "Spill it. What is it you really want?"

"I—I just miss you, that's all." She stepped in, grabbed the edge of his jacket with one hand and used the other to smooth his tie against his chest. "Don't you miss me?"

No. Greg swallowed a groan. If he told her the truth, she'd end up back in the store in tears, upsetting Elke. "Denise, sweetie." He took her hand and eased it off his body. "It's over. It didn't work. We gave it a good shot. We had some fun. But now you have to let it go. Let *me* go."

"Let go? Excuse me, aren't you the guy who advocates fighting for what you want? Isn't that what you told me about getting that promotion? Isn't that what you tell those kids you work with?"

"Uh..." Nothing like having his own words, his own philosophy, bite him in the ass. "Well, you've got me there." Sweat beaded on the back of his neck. "But this is different."

"Why? Because you say so?"

"Yes. Because we're just not right together. And somewhere out there is a terrific guy for you."

Her lower lip quivered, taking on that little pout he'd once found cute, but that had quickly grown old. The persistence he'd admired so much was also wearing thin.

"But, Greg, *you're* a terrific guy. I love you."

The *L* word. In his opinion, it was a word women—particularly this woman—tossed around altogether too easily. He'd seen real love in action. His parents had been married for forty-six years and survived raising twelve kids and losing one of them. The love they'd shared had seen them through all sorts of trials.

And so far, he hadn't found a woman he could love like that. Or one who could love him that way, either.

Just as he opened his mouth to wiggle his way out of this jam, a car screeched to halt behind his Tracker. The passenger's door opened, and a man burst out. The driver aimed a camera out his window over the vehicle as his companion raced toward Greg.

"I am Trash Man, evil polluter of the earth!" The guy's costume consisted of a black garbage bag with a slot for his head and arms. Stuck all over his body was a wide variety of junk—Starbucks coffee cups, Oreo packages, a pizza box, an open diaper that Greg hoped was unused. The bitter scent of stale coffee competed with the overwhelming smell of apple and cinnamon emanating from the round air freshener stuck to the center of the man's chest. He wore a black Zorro-like mask across his face. "I am the world's next supervillain. Draw me or suffer the wrath of trash!"

Greg struggled to contain his laughter but couldn't. "Forget it. Even supervillains shouldn't smell quite like that."

"All right, then will you at least sign my comic book?" Trash Man reached into a brown paper bag stapled at his hip and pulled out a comic book in a plastic sleeve.

Greg recognized it immediately. *Y-Men,* issue 23. "Hey, that's my virgin issue."

"I know." The young man's hands trembled as he passed it and a pen over.

"You sure you want me to do this?" Greg asked. "I mean, this is in great condition."

"Yes, sign it."

"To Trash Man?"

The kid flushed around the edges of his mask. "And devalue it? Are you kidding? Just sign it, please."

"You're putting this on eBay tomorrow, aren't you?"

His mouth dropped open and he gawked at Greg. "No way, dude."

"Okay. Just checking." Greg scrawled his name on the cover and handed it back. "Now, do me a favor. How the hell did you know I'd be here?" This was the third "ambush" by overzealous comic-book fans in the same number of weeks.

Trash Man grinned as he tucked his treasure away. "*Bwa-ha-ha!* A supervillain never reveals his secrets." He turned and ran back to the car, leaping inside. The driver, who'd caught the entire episode on his small video camera, slid back into place. No doubt the scene would be on YouTube before the end of the day. Tires squealing, the car peeled out of the parking lot, leaving a black patch of tread on the pavement.

Beside him, Denise stared. “You live the oddest life, Greg.”

He turned, and discovered the entire bridal party, along with the employees, clustered around the store’s front door, watching through the glass. “Yeah. And I wouldn’t have it any other way.”

SHANNON HEARD the gurgle of water leaving the tub in the bathroom. A few minutes later, the boy came out, cotton pajamas plastered to the spots on his chest he’d forgotten to dry, and his sandy-blond hair sticking out in twenty different directions. “Hey, buddy, you forgot to comb your hair.”

He smoothed it down with his hands.

“That’s not enough.” Shannon went into the bathroom, tossing Ryan’s discarded clothes in the hamper before grabbing the comb. The boy was nowhere to be seen when she came back out. “Ryan? Come on, I’m just going to comb your hair. I’ll be careful, I promise.”

A rustling noise from his bedroom gave him away.

Shannon walked into the room that had formerly been her home office, and actually, still was. She’d put a futon against the far wall, and that served as Ryan’s bed. He had a two-drawer unit inside the closet for his dresser.

Ryan had tucked himself into the corner of the futon, arms tight across his dawn-up knees. A couple of the books they’d borrowed from the library lay beside him. He shook his head as she approached with the plastic comb.

“I’ll make you a deal. You tell me not to comb your hair, and I won’t do it tonight.”

The boy’s counselors had assured Shannon that Ryan

would most likely speak again, in his own time. They'd urged her to be patient. Still, she couldn't resist coaxing him on occasion.

He turned his head toward the wall.

"Okay. Your choice." Shannon moved the books out of the way and sat beside him, then very gently began to tame his wavy hair.

The doorbell rang.

"That's weird. Did you order takeout?"

The boy rolled his eyes at her attempt at humor.

"Well, I'm not expecting anyone." Shannon handed Ryan the comb. "Why don't you finish it yourself. Maybe it won't bother you so much that way."

Shannon descended the stairs, brushing against the jackets hung on a rack in the entryway. She peered through the peephole—and drew back as if the door was on fire.

Hell's bells and Lucifer's toenails.

Patty Schaffer. Which meant Lloyd had to be out there, too.

Ryan's paternal grandparents. The ones whose calls Shannon had been avoiding.

Patty pounded on the door, and the voice that reminded Shannon of a canary on steroids called, "Shannon? Open up. We're here to see Ryan, and we're not leaving until we do. Even if we have to camp out on this doorstep until you run out of groceries."

She left the safety chain on the door, but cracked it open. "Ryan's just getting ready for bed. He's in the process of settling down. I don't think seeing you right now is a good idea. He has trouble sleeping, and—"

"And that's why he needs to see us. We're his family. We can help him. We've been driving for hours from

Philly. The least you can do is allow us a few minutes with our grandson before we have to find a hotel." Patty sniffed. "Hopefully we'll find someplace better than the last hotel. It's been over a month, Shannon. You have no right to keep that boy from us."

"The last time you visited, Ryan shut down for almost a week. Since I'm trying to get him to come out of his shell, I'd like to avoid a repeat performance. And technically, as his legal guardian, I do have the right." But morally, ethically, how could she? Shannon eased the door shut and slipped off the safety chain, opening the door wide.

"Don't get too used to it." Patty, a huge wrapped box in her arms, pushed past Shannon and began up the stairs. "I don't think you're going to be guardian much longer. You should be hearing from our lawyers soon."

A tiny dart of pain pierced Shannon's chest. They were going to apply for Ryan's custody? She heard the familiar whisper of emptiness and struggled to draw a deep breath as Lloyd followed his wife without a word.

Breathe in, take what life hands you; hold it, accept it; breathe out, let it go.

Was she going to have to let Ryan go? Already?

Another voice clamored in her head, drowning out her mantra. Greg Hawkins. And he was exhorting her, fight the good fight.

She'd never fought for anything, always doing as her daddy taught her and not holding on to things. Or people.

But Ryan was just a fragile little boy. He needed her right now.

She shoved her hand in her back pocket and fingered

the card the art therapist had given her, and which she'd carried like a talisman for some unfathomable reason.

Maybe it was time to call in a superhero.

CHAPTER THREE

PATTY SCHAFFER entered into the jail's visitation room, head held high enough to balance a book on it without mussing a strand of her recently dyed auburn hair. She strode to the space indicated by the guard, second from the end.

She eased into the stiff chair and waited. Moments later her son, Trevor, in his bright orange inmate jumpsuit, appeared on the other side of the Plexiglas. He'd lost weight; she could see it in his face. He perched on the edge of his seat, then picked up the phone. "Mom."

"Trevor. You're not eating enough. I've left you a check for the commissary. Don't use it all on nasty cigarettes, okay?"

"Thanks. Dad didn't come?"

The *again* was unspoken but plain in his eyes. Trevor, their only child, had always sought his daddy's approval. The fact that Lloyd wouldn't visit him while he awaited trial was a point of contention between Patty and her husband. Lloyd's resumption of the duties he'd passed to Trevor several years ago at Schaffer Furniture, their regional furniture-store chain, added to his resentment toward their son. "You know how stubborn he can be."

Trevor nodded. "I do."

"Maybe if you'd tell him what happened that night—"

"Mom, you know better than to even ask me about that. Especially here." He jerked his head to indicate the confines of the space, then at the guard behind him.

"But if he just knew you didn't mean to—"

"Did you see Ryan?"

"We did." Patty shook her head. "If you could only see that woman's apartment. Cold. Practically empty if you ask me."

"Is he talking yet?"

"No." The child had barely looked at her. Though she hadn't been highly involved as a grandmother to this point—she had a very full life of her own, what with all her volunteering for various charity groups, the traveling she and Lloyd did and all her friends—she'd expected more from her only grandson. Some sign of affection. She'd even bought him a remote-controlled car the salesclerk had assured her would be a hit with a six-year-old boy.

Trevor leaned onto the table, slumping. With disappointment, Patty presumed. "I did what you asked me to."

"Oh?" He shifted closer to the glass. "Did he react when you reminded him about the promise he made me?"

Patty waved the ruby fingernail of her free hand. "Not really. But don't worry. I could see in his eyes he remembered. He's your son. Of course he wants to make his daddy happy. He misses you."

"I know all about sons wanting to make their fathers proud, Mom."

"Your father is sensitive, Trevor, but he hides it well. This isn't easy on us, either. Some of your father's golf buddies have snubbed him since your arrest."

"Maybe if he'd called in a few more favors from

some of the golf buddies, I'd be out on bond and with my son." Trevor leaned closer to the clear barrier, laid his palm against it. "Mom, I want Ryan back here. I want him with you. I still can't believe Willow did this. Her damn sister saw Ryan even less than you and Dad did." Censure flooded Trevor's blue eyes, then they narrowed, turned demanding. "Get my son back."

Patty's hand appeared delicate, tiny, against Trevor's on the other side of the glass. Her baby might be full-grown and way bigger than she was, but he needed her. If she and Lloyd hadn't been out of the country at the time of their daughter-in-law's death and Trevor's arrest, if only she'd been more of a hands-on grandparent, things might have happened differently. "We're working on it," she promised.

GREG DIDN'T MIND being observed when he knew who was in the other room.

He'd been thrilled to get the call from the woman who once again stood behind the mirror. He *needed* to work with her nephew, but there was also something about Shannon Vanderhoff…something about the small boy in her awkward care…that spoke to him.

A thin layer of chocolate pudding now coated the yellow worktable. Ryan, wearing an old Y-Men T-shirt that had holes in the armpits and splotches of pudding where the child had leaned against the table, drew squiggly lines in it.

"That's great, Ryan." Greg made the same design as the child had, dragging his finger through the sludge.

The boy giggled.

Greg heard a very faint sound from the other side of the window.

Ryan reached out, tracing more shapes, then wiping the "slate" smooth, he did it again.

Greg, his shirtsleeves rolled up to his elbows, began to sketch funny faces in the pudding. After a few more minutes—this was the warm-up activity, not the main event—he announced, "Okay, sport, it's time to clean up. I've got some other stuff I want to do with you today. We can do this again another time, okay?"

Ryan nodded. Together they proceeded to scrape the pudding off with paper towels, then sprayed the table down with blue fluid. Once everything was clean, he spread out an assortment of paper, colored pencils and a new sixty-four-count box of crayons. "I'm going to make a picture of my family," he told the child. "My family is really big, so I'm going to use a big piece of paper. What paper would you use to draw your family?"

The kid leaned back in his chair, turning away from the table.

"Okay, you think about it. No rush."

Greg's pencil began to flash across the paper. While he sketched, Ryan pulled a brick-red crayon from the box, holding one end in each hand. With a twist of his wrists, he snapped the crayon in half.

Greg ignored it, and kept drawing even as Ryan broke a few more crayons. Eventually, getting no response, he picked up another and began to actually work on a picture.

Great. Now the silent boy was communicating with him, which, in his case, was the major point of art therapy.

Minutes crept by. Greg tossed out occasional words of praise and encouragement, but mostly the only sounds in the room came from the scratch of his pencil on the paper, the soft taps of the crayons touching the page or being dropped on the table. Greg kept moving after his piece was finished until the boy pushed his paper forward and set down his final crayon.

"Are you done?"

Ryan nodded.

"Me, too." Greg lifted his paper. "See all the people in my family? This is my mom and dad, and these are all my brothers and sisters. This is Alan, Bethany, Cathy, Derek, Elke, Finn, me, Hayden, Judy, and Kyle and Kara. These last two are twins. That means they were born together on the same day. This isn't even my whole family, if you can believe it. Some of my brothers and sisters are married and have children of their own. And I had another brother, Ian, but he's in heaven now." Greg laid his drawing down as Ryan grew somber. The child pointed to something in his own drawing. Someone up in the right corner, near the sun and clouds.

A female, judging by the long yellow hair. "Is that your mom?"

Ryan nodded.

Greg scanned the rest of the picture. On the left side was another figure—basically a head with arms and legs sticking out of it—with lines drawn across it. Bars. Easy enough to guess who that was. Near his jail-celled father were two other people holding hands.

In the middle of the page, the boy had drawn himself, contained inside a lopsided circle.

And way off in the bottom corner, a final figure had brown hair and, sprouting from its arm, a tiny triangle with green specks. Greg pointed to it. "Is this Aunt Shannon?"

Another nod.

A wave of sorrow for the child flooded Greg as the

symbolism sank in. Still, he forced a chuckle. "This is the artichoke pizza from the other day, isn't it?"

The edges of the boy's mouth pulled up slightly.

"That's funny. This is a terrific drawing, Ryan. You did a great job. So great that I'd like you to work on another picture for me, okay? And while you do, I'm going to take this and have a chat with Aunt Shannon, okay? I know she's going to love this. Why don't you draw something cool for Aunt Shannon's refrigerator?"

At Ryan's gesture of consent, Greg headed out the door and barreled into the observation room.

Shannon turned from the window. So far, she was impressed with the man's results. "You got him to crack. That's the first time he's almost smiled since he's come to live with me." She paused. "I'm really sorry about the broken crayons. He's not usually destructive."

"I'm not worried about a couple of broken crayons. The kid has emotions that are stuck inside him. Breaking the crayons said he's mad. He didn't want to draw his family. But he did. And I am way more concerned about this—" he thrust the drawing at her "—than I am about broken crayons."

She took it, turning the paper around to examine it. The hard edge to his voice surprised her. He'd been nothing but soft-spoken with Ryan.

The art therapist reached over the paper, pointing. "This is his mother, in heaven. Notice that she's the only person on this paper who's smiling. This is his father, in jail. That's positive. Shows that Ryan understands where his father is, and hopefully isn't afraid that his father is going to come after him next."

"We've talked about that. Well, I have. I've tried to assure him that he's safe."

"Who are these two people, holding hands outside the jail?"

"Ryan's paternal grandparents. Patty and Lloyd."

"Interesting how he kept them close to his father." Greg pointed again. "This figure in the middle, this is Ryan. Notice that he's inside a circle? Isolated?" He reached farther over. "See this, way down here? That's you, Aunt Shannon. Far away from this little boy who feels like he's all alone in the world. The kid just narced on you. He's complaining. You're not bonding with him, and I'd like to know why not."

"That's absurd. I've taken him into my home. I've spent the last three months with him damn near Velcroed to my side. I've damn near lost my job because of missing work to take care of him. Of course I'm bonding with him."

"That's not what Ryan says in this picture."

"I read to him every night. We watch TV together." Shannon's stomach felt heavy, as though she'd eaten a fast-food meal instead of something decent. "How is that not enough?"

"Well, despite all that, he's not getting the message that you want him." Greg narrowed his eyes. "You do want him, right?"

"Of—of course I want him. What kind of question is that?"

"Ryan's not feeling it."

"Do you have any suggestions?" Shannon turned back toward the window, watching Ryan work. Her nose started to tingle, and she fought against the tears welling in her eyes. Basically, she sucked as a guardian. That's what the art therapist was saying. Ryan wasn't progressing because of her.

Maybe he would be better off with Lloyd and Patty.

Maybe his time with her was already over, and she should just let him go with his grandparents.

"Yes. I suggest we move our sessions to your home, where I can observe Ryan in his own setting."

"Okay. We can do that. Just let me know what supplies I should have on hand."

"Don't worry about supplies. However, I have one more request." The man moved to stand beside her.

"Oh?"

"Yes. That you draw right alongside him."

"But—"

He held up his hand. "No buts. It will let him know you value this therapy, and him. Look, Ms. Vanderhoff—"

"I thought we'd gotten to first names? I mean, if you're telling a woman she sucks as the caregiver to a six-year-old, I think you can at least call her by her first name."

The lines in his face softened, and he lowered his hand. "Shannon. I'm not saying you suck as Ryan's caregiver. I'm saying for whatever reason, this child feels like he's all alone in the world. We have to fix that. If he can't bond with you, who can he? He needs you. He won't start talking again if he feels isolated. Getting him back in school next year won't happen, at least not in regular classes. And I don't think you want that for him, do you?"

"No." She sighed. "All right. If it's that important, I'll sit and I'll draw. But I'm not drawing any superheroes."

Greg's dimples appeared with his smile. "No superheroes. I think I can live with that. Let's compare calendars and see when we can start at your house."

OUTSIDE THE ROW of garden-apartment buildings, Greg pulled his Tracker into one of the spots labeled Visitor Parking Only. "Elke," he said into his Bluetooth earpiece, "I'm here. I have to go. Tails, no tails, whatever you decide, really, it will be fine. Just make sure I have something to cover my ass—uh—assets, and I'll be happy. Really. You're making yourself crazy for nothing."

"Denise said the same thing," Elke murmured.

Greg groaned. "Elke, come on. You promised me when I started dating her that if it crashed and burned, you'd be okay with it. Actually, I think you said you'd support me. I'm not seeing that support when you bring up her name every time we talk and drag her along for wedding stuff when she shouldn't be there."

"I know, but she's been so sad since you guys broke up. She's my best friend, and I'm the one who's had to pick up the pieces."

"That's usually how it works when a couple breaks up, Elke. The woman's best friend has to pick up the pieces."

"And the guy sails off, trauma free. End of story."

Trauma free? No, not completely. One more attempt at love that fizzled. It had been a loss for him. And if there was one thing Greg hated, it was losing. Anything. "Gotta go, sis. Love ya." Greg pressed the button on the earpiece, effectively cutting off the conversation, then he removed it, leaving it next to the empty Baby Ruth wrapper in the cup holder. From the backseat, he gathered up his supplies.

At apartment 7A's front stoop, he used his elbow to stab the doorbell. He heard footsteps on stairs inside, then the lock was released.

"Mr.—Greg," Shannon said as she opened the door. "You're very prompt. Thank you. Come in."

There was a short corridor, a private foyer, inside the

doorway. Several coats hung on a rack on the wall, with two pairs of sneakers on a rug below them. Greg toed out of his mocs, set the supplies down and tossed his jean jacket—demanded by the unseasonably cool early-May weather—on one of the hooks. Then he followed Shannon up the stairs to her second-floor apartment.

Ryan already waited at the table in the dining area. He offered Greg a half smile in greeting.

"Hey, sport. How you doing today? You ready to draw some more with me?"

The child nodded.

"Did you hear Aunt Shannon's going to draw with us this time?"

Affirmation.

"Can I get you something to drink before we start?" Shannon asked.

"No, thanks. I never drink and draw."

Her eyebrows scrunched together.

Greg laughed. "I don't like to risk spilling on the work. I learned that lesson early on the hard way. I was inking my third issue, and spilled some juice. Bad news. At least now if I do it, I'm the illustrator, too, but back then, it was someone else's hard work on the panels I'd wrecked. That nearly cost me my career in comics." As he spoke, Greg spread the supplies across the oval tabletop. "So grab a seat, Shannon, and let's get busy."

As they settled in, Greg checked out the apartment's partially open-floor layout. The living room, which flowed into the dining area, contained a black sofa and one slightly battered black recliner. A low table against the wall supported a nineteen-inch television. Aside from a clock, the walls were bare.

She made the Amish look materialistic.

The kitchen counters were likewise pristine, except for a hand-grinder salt-and-pepper shaker next to the stove and a silver toaster that seemed like something his parents might have received for a wedding gift—forty-six years ago.

The disconnect came from the set of gleaming copper pans that dangled from a rack over the breakfast bar, a set like Finn owned. Made some sense. A woman who enjoyed artichoke pizza would probably enjoy other foods that required more serious cookware than a paper plate in the microwave. Maybe he should introduce her to his brother.

A quiet tingle—a Spidey sense—told him maybe not. Actually, it screamed *no damn way.*

Kind of weird to feel that possessive of a woman he barely knew. But then, there was something intriguing about her. Too intriguing to consider introducing her to Finn.

The drawing Ryan had made at their last session was held up on the pale green refrigerator by a magnet.

"Okay, Shannon, since you didn't draw last time, I'd like you to do a family picture for me."

"Fine." She took a sheet of paper and a pencil.

Greg inched his chair closer to the boy's. "Ryan, today you and I are going to have some real fun. We're going to draw superheroes."

Shannon made a small noise, a cross between a growl and a groan, in the back of her throat. Then, catching his raised eyebrows, she studiously bent over her picture, flicking away nonexistent bits of dust from the surface.

"I love superheroes. They're so much fun. Do you have a favorite superhero?"

Eyes wide, Ryan nodded slowly.

"Great. Why don't you draw him for me." Greg flipped to a blank page in his sketchbook. "And while you do that, I'm going to draw some pictures of my favorites, too." While they worked, Greg kept up a running monologue, chattering away about superheroes, drawing techniques, whatever came to mind.

"I'm done," Shannon announced a short time later. "Here's my family picture." She held it out to him.

For a quick pencil sketch, she'd actually done a hell of a job. Ryan's face, right down to the smattering of freckles across the lower bridge of his nose, filled the right side of the paper, and on the other side, cheek almost pressed to the boy's, was a fairly accurate self-likeness of Shannon, including her perky nose.

"This is well done." He showed it to Ryan. "Check this out. Isn't this great?"

The boy flicked a quick thumbs-up to his aunt.

"You've got some talent there you didn't tell me about."

The woman shrugged. "No big deal."

"But, this is just you and Ryan. I wanted you to draw your whole family."

Pain flickered in her eyes, today more the color of dark chocolate. Then she blinked and it was gone. "That is my whole family now."

Ouch. Okay, *that* could be why she was keeping the boy at such an emotional distance. "Sorry. My bad. My family is so ginormous, it's hard for me to even imagine a family of only two people."

"Yes, how many brothers and sisters did you name last time? You mentioned a pair of twins, too?"

"I'm one of an even-dozen kids. The last two are a set of fraternal twins, a boy and a girl."

"Wow. Your mother must be either a saint or insane."

"Just a woman who loves kids and considers each one a blessing." Greg shoved another piece of paper at her. "All right, while we finish up our stuff, I'd like to see a picture of your family from when you were Ryan's age. Not just faces this time. Whole bodies. And draw your people doing something. Something your family liked to do together back when you were six."

For several minutes she just let the pencil tip hover over the paper. Then, she leaned over, forearm shielding her work like an elementary-school kid afraid her neighbor was going to copy her spelling test.

Shannon didn't want him to see what she was up to. She might have agreed to draw with Ryan, but she'd never agreed to actually let the man inside her head through her artwork.

Meticulous gray shapes took form on the paper. Precise. She used the eraser to fix any errors. Once she had the people complete, all she had to figure out was the setting. What innocuous activity could she have her "family" doing?

The image of the old beige car, Betsy, flashed into her mind, and just as quickly Shannon dismissed it. That was hardly an innocuous memory, and she didn't feel like explaining the night when her seven-year-old self had wept for hours after her father had given away their car to "someone who needed it more."

That had always been Daddy's response. Someone else always needed it worse than they did.

Clothes, food, dolls, even pets, it didn't matter what it was. The only thing that mattered was that Daddy placated his demons by giving it away.

There'd been moments as a child when she'd wondered if he'd go so far as to give her or her older sister, Willow, away. But she'd been equally certain that her mother, who always supported Dad in his donations, would have drawn the line there. Shannon had only been eight when that certainty had died with her mother.

So Shannon sketched in a lake behind her people, and a few trees, some clouds. Made it into an idyllic summer day.

They'd never gone to a lake.

Adding a few details here and there, she watched the man at her table, working with her nephew. His pencil flew across the page with an ease she both envied and despised. A flying superhero was taking shape, rescuing a cat from a tree. Superguy's cape flapped in the breeze, and a crowd of people stared adoringly at the kitty's savior.

Uh-huh. Why not just draw a fireman with a ladder? A real hero who might actually rescue a stranded pet?

Still, at least the guy wasn't bashing anyone. There were no kerpows or whammos.

It was some time later when she realized Greg was talking to her, holding up Ryan's picture. The entire top part of the paper featured Ryan's version of a flying superhero—a roundish head with long legs that grew from it, with an almost-triangle sticking out from the back of the skull—the cape, obviously. Straight stick arms poked out in the front of the hero's head.

And down in the corner, waving its arms, was another figure, this one tiny.

"It's—it's terrific, Ryan. I love the blue cape. Good job."

Greg beamed at her. "See, we agree on the color. Excellent choice, sport. Now, Aunt Shannon, let's see yours. You've been acting like it's a national-security secret over there. We want to see. Right, Ryan?"

The boy nodded emphatically, his hair askew.

"Well, all right. Ta-da!" Shannon held up her drawing. Ryan clapped his hands.

The art therapist studied it carefully, but joined in the applause. "Very nice. The scenery is an especially nice touch." Greg picked up Ryan's drawing, then hers, tucking them into his sketchbook. "Let's get cleaned up, then Aunt Shannon can walk me to my car."

With no observation room for them to chat in, Shannon presumed that was the man's subtle way of giving them some privacy to talk about Ryan.

Greg got down on one knee to say goodbye to the boy. "I'll see you again soon, okay? But I'm leaving you your own sketchbook. That way if you want to draw more before I come back, you can."

Ryan threw himself against Greg, wrapping his arms so tightly around the man's neck that Greg swayed off balance. His strong forearms went around the small torso, and he enveloped the child in a return hug.

Shannon swallowed the bitter taste in her mouth. Ryan had never hugged her like that.

Greg rose to his feet, giving Ryan a final pat on the head. Shannon followed Greg down the stairs, holding his stuff as he slipped his shoes and jacket on.

Outside, he stopped on the concrete porch, leaning against the black metal railing. He pulled Ryan's picture from the sketchbook. "See this?" He pointed to the figure at the bottom corner. "That's Ryan. This picture illustrates how inadequate he feels. The superhero is huge, and yet he doesn't see the boy who needs help. So, Ryan's still feeling overlooked. The kid is starved for some physical affection. That wasn't a hug he was giving me, it was a near strangulation. Do you have a counselor, Shannon? *For yourself?* If not, I'd suggest you get one."

She snorted. "Yeah. Right. With all my spare money. My savings are rapidly dwindling because of all the time I've taken off from work. If it weren't for your discounted fee to help Ryan, we wouldn't be able to afford you, either. I can't tell you how much I appreciate that." She nudged the sketchbook. "What did you learn about me from my drawing?"

He exchanged the papers. "You made every figure the same size. Length of hair is the only thing that varies. That's despite the fact that two of these are your parents, and the other two are you at six and your sister. So, you should have been smaller.

"What does this tell me about you? It tells me that you thought you could scam me. I'll bet this lake doesn't even exist, does it?"

She smiled. "No."

He shook his head. "You, Shannon Vanderhoff, are a control freak. And that's affecting your nephew."

"A control freak? I'm not a control freak. I'm totally Zen. I take what life hands me, I accept it, hold it, embrace it, then let it go. Nothing is ours to keep."

He arched one eyebrow. "Would you repeat that?"

"Breathe in, take what life hands you, accept it, hold it, embrace it for a moment, then breathe out and let it go. Nothing is ours to keep."

"Oh, Shannon." He stared at her with his soulful eyes. "And you wonder why you're not bonding with him?" His fingers caressed her cheek. When he let them skim along her jawline, then linger beneath her chin, she had a fleeting moment of wondering what his mouth would feel like on hers—strong and assertive, like him? Gentle and caring, also like him? Would he be as playful, as skillful, in his lovemaking as he was with his drawings?

"Ahem." Shannon glanced down at the new arrival on the bottom of the porch steps.

"I'm looking for Shenandoah Vanderhoff?"

"Yes? I'm Shannon Vanderhoff."

The young man in dark pants and a collared polo shirt passed her an envelope. "Shannon Vanderhoff, you are served." He turned and strode down the sidewalk.

"Served?" Shannon opened it, skimmed the first page. Her knees began to tremble, and she swallowed hard. "Well, my lack of bonding with Ryan may not be an issue for much longer. Like I said, nothing is ours to keep."

She passed the documents to Greg, letting him read them.

Lloyd and Patty had done it. They'd filed for custody.

CHAPTER FOUR

SHANNON DROPPED DOWN to the top porch step, the concrete cool through the seat of her jeans. Closing her eyes, she dragged in air until her lungs could hold no more, battling the pain.

Let it go, let it go, let it go, she silently chanted as she exhaled. But her chest remained tight, the pain unrelenting. She sucked in another long breath.

"Oh, no you're not," Greg said, his voice stern.

A hand closed on her elbow and he hauled her to her feet.

Her eyes flew open. "Hey! Not what?"

"Quitting. Just like that. Without even a hint of a fight."

"I'm not quitting."

"Sure looked like it to me. Sounded like it, too." Accusation blazed in his blue eyes.

Shannon lowered her head. "I'm preparing myself for the inevitable."

"That's what I said. Quitting. There is nothing inevitable here. Your sister chose *you* to be Ryan's guardian if something happened to her. Listen—" he tucked the envelope under his arm and took hold of her other elbow as well "—that little boy up there needs you." His voice softened. "And I think you need him, too. He's the only family you have left. Remember your first drawing? You can't let him go without a fight."

"I don't know how. And what if I lose?"

His fingers tightened their grip, and he shook her gently.

Her head snapped up and she glared at him. "Cut that out." She circled her arms up and over his, a neat little self-defense trick, disengaging his hold on her.

He grinned slowly as he held up his hands, inching backward.

"What are you smiling about?"

"There's fight in you. Just takes some provoking to bring it out."

She shook her head. "You are…exasperating."

"So I've been told." He held out the papers. "Well, Shenandoah Vanderhoff, what's it going to be? Quit or fight for Ryan?"

The memories of so many other losses—her mother, her father, Willow—taunted her. "What if I lose?" she whispered.

Greg raised her chin with one finger, making her meet his gaze. "You don't go into a fight expecting to lose. You go in with your fists high, knowing you're going to win."

"I can't afford a lawyer. Lloyd and Patty can afford great lawyers. You should see the dream team they've got defending Ryan's father."

"Leave that to me. Are you free for lunch on Sunday?"

"Lunch? On Sunday? What's that got to do with a lawyer?"

"Trust me. I'll pick you up at eleven-thirty. Let me help you. And Ryan."

If anyone could teach her how to fight, it was this man. "All right. But on one condition."

"Okay."

She propped her hands on her hips. "Don't *ever* call me Shenandoah again."

Greg chuckled. "That's the spirit. I'll see you Sunday. Fight the good fight." He offered his closed fist in the gesture she'd seen him do with his kids.

After a moment, she lightly bumped knuckles with him. "Fight the good fight," she repeated.

The phrase left a sardine taste in her mouth.

DAWN HAD JUST LIGHTENED the May sky, making it easier to navigate the parking lot as Shannon trudged toward the sidewalk. Living only a few minutes from the hotel where she worked 9:00 p.m. to 5:00 a.m. as a night auditor—at least for now, considering how annoyed her boss was over her frequent requests for time off—had its advantage.

She eased the key into the lock, creeping into the apartment just in case Mrs. Kozinski, the older neighbor woman who babysat Ryan overnight while Shannon worked, was sleeping. Most mornings she was up and raring to go when Shannon came home. The strong aroma of fresh coffee as she climbed the stairs indicated this day was no exception.

Mrs. K. met her at the top step, stainless travel mug in hand, expression way too chipper for the crack of dawn. She'd obviously had more than one cup of caffeine already. "He's awake, too, dear. Neither one of us slept much last night, I'm afraid. Which could be good for you. Maybe he'll sleep now." The woman often crashed on Shannon's bed during the night, more times than not with Ryan at her side instead of in his own bed. Shannon had gone through too much to find a reliable sitter to quibble over the fact that she let Ryan sleep in her bed.

The television played softly, illuminating the living room with flickering shadows. Mrs. K. leaned over the back of the couch to tousle Ryan's hair. "See you Tuesday night, Ry. You, too, dear." She saluted Shannon with the mug, then headed down the stairs.

On the couch in front of the TV, Ryan turned his bleary eyes toward Shannon. "You're supposed to be sleeping," she said softly, wagging a finger at him. "Come on. I have to get some rest, and so do you. Let's go."

Before Ryan, she hadn't headed directly for bed after coming home from work. She'd eaten dinner—or rather, breakfast—and unwound before hitting the sack. But she'd had to adapt, trying to grab some sleep in the early-morning hours, when the boy was usually still asleep.

It hadn't been working too well for either of them.

After tucking him into the futon in the second bedroom, Shannon stumbled into her room, pulling the shades and drawing the curtains, then peeling off her clothes. After yanking on a nightshirt and matching shorts, she slid between the cotton sheets, exhaustion quickly overtaking her.

The creak of the door and a crack of light coming in from the hallway roused her some time later. Faint footsteps scuffed across the rug, and the double mattress shifted as Ryan slipped in on the other side.

Too tired to return him to his own bed as she usually did when he snuck into hers, Shannon tugged her sleep mask on and rolled to her side, letting sleep reclaim her.

GREG RAPPED on the apartment door a third time, then checked his watch. 11:35. He'd told her eleven-thirty, right?

His mother wasn't happy when people were late for Sunday dinner.

While contemplating his next move, the door inched open, and a freckled face appeared in the space just above the doorknob. "Hey there, sport. I was starting to think you guys had stood me up. Aunt Shannon's probably still getting ready, right?"

The boy shook his head, then opened the door wider. He still wore navy pajamas. The boy's hair splayed in multiple directions, and he boasted a faint chocolate-milk mustache.

"Shannon?" Greg called as he entered the apartment. "We're still on for lunch and a lawyer, right?"

At the top of the stairs, Greg paused. On the dining-room table, a half-full glass of chocolate milk sat beside the remains of a bowl of soggy cornflakes. Drips of chocolate and stray flakes dotted the tabletop; the open cereal box lay on its side. The only noise in the apartment came from the television in the living room. "Where's your aunt?"

Gesturing for Greg to follow him, the kid went to a door and pushed it open, pointing inside the cavelike room.

Concern knotted the muscles along his neck. Shannon had her issues, but being a neglectful guardian wasn't one of them. "Shannon," he called softly. "Are you okay?"

No response. The hair on his arms stood up and he tripped over scattered clothes on the floor in his hurry to reach her bed. Using the light from the hallway as a guide, he fumbled at the nightstand before turning on the small lamp.

Shannon lay on her back, left arm sprawled out, right hooked up over her head. A comforter tangled at her waist. The gentle rise and fall of her chest reassured him—until he noticed that the thin nightshirt she wore left no need for X-ray vision. He could see the swell of her breasts and the rosy outline of her nipples quite clearly without superpowers.

And what breasts they were. His palms tingled with the urge to see if they fit his hands as perfectly as they promised.

Feeling more than a bit voyeuristic, he forced his gaze higher, to her face. A royal-blue satin mask covered her eyes, so only her nose and mouth showed, coral-pink lips slightly parted.

He wrestled with the asinine impulse to lean over and wake her with a kiss, but the realization that a six-year-old stood in the doorway quickly subdued it. This woman, with her nothing-lasts attitude, was not what he needed. She was the antithesis of that woman. Kissable lips and cuppable breasts be damned.

"Shannon, wake up. It's late."

When she still didn't stir, he grabbed her left arm and tugged. "Shannon, come on. Wake up."

Everything exploded. She bolted upright and wrenched away at the same time, ripping off the mask while shrieking at the top of her considerable lungs. Her features distorted as she shrank from him.

He held his hands out. "Easy, it's just me. Greg. Ryan let me in and—"

A sound rumbled behind him, a cross between a cry and a growl, something a wounded animal might make. The next moment, a small body leaped onto his back, hammering him with little fists. Teeth sank into his shoulder, and fiery pain radiated outward from the spot.

"Ow! Whoa there, buddy. It's okay. I'm not hurting her."

Greg seized the child, dragging him around and wrapping him in a bear hug to bring him under control. "Everybody take a deep breath, here." Ryan wailed, keening his distress. He squirmed, freeing his arms, then flailed, reaching out toward his aunt, who was still wild-eyed herself.

"He thought I was hurting you," Greg explained.

Understanding dawned, and she held open her arms. Greg released the boy.

She gathered Ryan in an embrace, rocking him on the bed. "It's okay. I'm okay. I was just scared. As any woman would be if she woke from a sound sleep to find a man standing over her." Shannon narrowed her eyes at him over Ryan's head.

"The door was unlocked and Ryan let me in." A defensive note crept into his voice. "You should keep your door locked."

"It *was* locked. The babysitter must have left it open this morning."

Greg eased himself down on the edge of the bed, rubbing the spot where teeth marks undoubtedly remained. "Sport, I would never hurt your aunt. Or anyone. I'm sorry I scared you guys. Man, Ryan, that was brave. I'm proud of you." Inwardly, Greg wanted to cheer. A sure sign of progress. Progress they desperately needed.

Ryan twisted his head from Shannon's chest. His tears had stopped, and his expression was quizzical. A far cry from the daggers Shannon was now launching in Greg's direction.

"Yep," he hastily continued, "totally brave to defend your aunt like that when you thought she was in trouble. Way to go." He held out his hand, and Ryan slapped him a weak high five. "Now, why don't I help you get ready? That way Aunt Shannon can get herself together before we're late for our lunch."

Ryan scrambled from the bed and was out the door in the blink of an eye.

"Ah, the resiliency of youth. They bounce back better than RubberMan." Greg rose to follow him. "Can you be ready in fifteen minutes? The cook where we're going can be temperamental about people who don't arrive on time."

Tossing aside the covers, she swung her feet to the floor, giving him an eyeful of lean, long legs. Then she stood and raised her hands over her head, interlocking her fingers and stretching in a way that pulled the nightshirt tight against her chest.

Greg's own clothing suddenly felt snug. He dropped his gaze to his toes. *Down, boy.* No sense in starting something that wasn't going to work out, setting himself up to lose.

Still, the attraction was getting harder to ignore.

She grabbed some clothes from the closet and brushed past him. "We'll talk about this later."

"I can hardly wait," he muttered.

SHANNON LET HIM SUFFER in silence during the ride. The man was unbelievable. Praising Ryan for attacking him? What was next? Martial-arts lessons? Fights with broomsticks in her living room?

And yet…Ryan had not only cried but cried out. A tiny step in the right direction that might force her to forgive Greg for scaring the snot out of her.

Besides…she needed him. Much as it pained her to admit it. She hadn't needed anyone or anything in a long time, and the idea didn't sit well.

He swung his Tracker off the country lane onto a tree-flanked dirt driveway. "I thought we were going to lunch. Where are we?"

"Home," Greg said. "Well, not that I live here anymore. But this is where I grew up. Welcome to the Hawkins's nest."

"You're taking me home for Sunday dinner?"

Numerous vehicles edged the driveway as they drew closer to the cedar-sided house. Greg parked. "Best Sunday dinner in town. Lunch and a lawyer is what I promised, and that's what you'll get."

"Just how many people show up at your house for Sunday dinner?" Shannon asked as she got out of the car.

He shrugged. "Depends. Mom likes to gather the tribe at least once a month if she can. Not everyone's here. Alan couldn't make it, and I don't see Bethany's SUV, either."

Ryan ran past Shannon, falling in step with Greg and lifting his hand, which the man took in his as if it was the most natural thing in the world.

"So, the rest of your brothers and sisters will be here?" She did a quick mental calculation. "That still leaves eight sibs."

"Along with significant others, kids and assorted strays they might have brought along." He winked at her.

She slowed her pace. "I—I don't know about this. I wouldn't want to intrude on family time. Besides, I didn't bring anything. It's rude to show up empty-handed. You could have warned me."

"And risk you not coming? Not a chance. Don't worry about not bringing anything. There'll be plenty to eat, I promise you. My brother Derek's kids are here for Ryan to play with. They're eight, six and three. There's a trampoline out back and a pond…all sorts of great kid stuff. But the rule is you have to have an adult watching you near the pond, and on the trampoline. Okay, sport?"

Ryan beamed up at Greg, nodding enthusiastically. Shannon winced. The child was setting himself up for more pain. The poor kid would be crushed without Greg in his life. Or when Ryan left to live with Lloyd and Patty.

Ryan had already lost his mother. And, God and the justice system willing, his father. Shannon didn't want him to know the pain of losing more.

So until she learned how to fight well enough to keep Ryan with her, she was stuck with Greg Hawkins. That the idea appealed to her made her all the more nervous.

They entered the house through a massive three-car garage. Only one car was parked inside. The rest of the place was filled with bikes lying on their sides, in-line skates, scooters and scattered sporting equipment. The door opened into a laundry room–mudroom combo that boasted two washers, two driers and a long double row of hooks. "You can leave your jackets and your purse here," Greg said.

She hesitantly followed Greg into the empty kitchen, where she was immediately struck with kitchen envy. A large island with a six-burner cooktop, a double-wall oven. Of course, with a family the size of the Hawkinses', this kitchen was a necessity. It wasn't as though they were cooking for one or two. Her cheeks flushed.

The scents of roasted meat, garlic, onion and tomato sauce lingered in the air.

"Uh-oh," Greg said as laughter and conversation, punctuated by occasional shouts and high-pitched shrieks, came from the next room. "They started without us. My ass is grass now. Oops." He glanced down at Ryan and grimaced. "Sorry. Pretend I didn't say that, okay, sport?"

He leaned in to Shannon and whispered, "That's one plus of a kid who's not speaking—he won't repeat your faux pas or naughty words." Herding Ryan ahead of them, he grabbed Shannon by the elbow and pulled her into the dining room.

An overwhelming number of people sat at an enormous table filled to overflowing with dishes and food. A toddler sat in a high chair drawn up near the table, banging a spoon on her tray.

As she and Greg were noticed, the room slowly quieted down. Shannon blushed under everyone's frank and open appraisal.

Greg finally cleared his throat as he steered her toward the end of the table. "Sorry we're late—"

"It's my fault," Shannon said. "I, uh, I work nights, and I overslept this morning. I'm sorry."

A man with salt-and-pepper hair—heavier on the pepper—and the same strong jawline as Greg sat at the head of the table. He put down his fork and smiled at her as he climbed to his feet, extending his hand. "Hello there."

"Dad, this is Shannon Vanderhoff and her nephew, Ryan. Shannon, this is my dad, Michael."

"Nice to meet you, Mr. Hawkins."

"And this is my mom, Lydia."

Lydia Hawkins had beautiful short silver hair, piercing blue eyes and didn't appear old enough—or worn enough—to have birthed and raised a dozen children. "Greg's told us a little bit about you. Perfectly understandable that you might oversleep. Working nights and acting as a single parent is a tough gig."

"Not as tough as mothering a brood of twelve, I'm sure."

"I can certainly offer you some tips, if you need them."

Shannon nodded. "I do."

"Everyone, this is Shannon and Ryan. Shannon, this is everyone else. They're not as important as food right now, so you can meet them all later."

"Welcome, Shannon!" "Says you, Greg!" "Nice manners. Emily Post you're not." "I'm important, right, Dad?" A cacophony of calls overwhelmed her as Greg led her down the length of the table. He bopped one man on the head as they passed, glared at another in response to eyebrow waggling in Shannon's direction.

Ryan clung to her hand.

Soon enough, they were seated and being passed roast beef, lasagna, garlic bread and other assorted foods. Nothing gourmet, but simple, tasty fare. Ryan enthusiastically gulped down his lasagna and bread.

While they ate, Greg not only kept up three different discussions, but also pointed to each person around the table in order, giving Shannon their name and a brief tidbit of information. Her head swam. "You should provide name tags."

He chuckled. "Don't worry. There won't be a quiz."

It was easy to see where Greg had gotten his good looks. There wasn't an ugly duckling in the entire family. And all the Hawkins men had the same angular jaw, obviously inherited from their father.

So how come the grins two of his brothers were

flashing at her from the opposite end of the table didn't make her pulse quicken the way Greg's smile did?

The children pushed away from the table first, asking to be excused before carrying their plates into the kitchen. A boy a few years older than Ryan returned. "You done eating? You can play with us if you want."

Ryan turned uncertainly to Shannon, who glanced at Greg, equally unsure. "They'll just be in the family room for now."

"Okay, Ryan. Go ahead."

"Show him what to do with his plate and silverware, Jack."

Ryan slid from his chair, trudging out behind Greg's nephew, plate balanced in both hands. At the doorway, he stopped, shooting Shannon a long look.

She nodded, jerking her head toward the kitchen, and the child left somewhat reluctantly.

"Don't worry, he'll be fine," Greg said.

"I know." Shannon chased a grape tomato around her salad bowl with the tip of her fork. Some of the adults also began leaving the table.

Attempting to remember who was who just gave her a headache. There were too many people, too many names.

"Hi, I'm Elke." A young woman whose brown hair flashed honey highlights in the sun streaming through the sliding glass doors plonked down at the vacant chair on Shannon's right. "I'm Greg's favorite sister."

"No, she's not. Kara's my favorite sister," Greg said. "You are my nosiest sister. Listen, Shannon, don't let her grill you. Five minutes alone with Elke, and she'll know everything about you. Don't say I didn't warn you. Elke wanted to be an interrogator for the FBI, but even they couldn't stand her."

Elke stuck her tongue out at him, then propped her chin in her palm and turned her complete attention to Shannon. "So, tell me about yourself, Shannon. How did you find yourself in the company of my loser baby brother who still plays with crayons?"

The snort of laughter Shannon stifled made her choke. Vinegar from the salad dressing burned her nose.

"Now see what you've done." Greg whacked Shannon between the shoulder blades.

"I'm sorry," Elke said. "It's not like I meant to—"

Shannon held up her hand. "I'm fine," she managed to say between coughing fits. Her eyes watered. "Really."

She dropped her napkin on the table and pushed back her chair. "I think I'm done, though. I'm sure I can figure out what to do with my dirty dishes."

"Are you kidding me? Are you trying to get me in more trouble with my mom?" Greg jumped up, taking the plate from her and stacking it on his own.

Shannon risked a glance at Greg's mother and discovered the woman's narrowed eyes turned in their direction. "Sorry," she murmured. "You know, this family stuff is far more complicated than I remembered."

Greg's laughter drifted over his shoulder as she followed him from the dining room. "No, it's not. There's one thing to remember—If Mama ain't happy, ain't nobody happy."

"She was strict with you?"

"With twelve kids, you're either strict and structured or mowed over by absolute chaos."

In the kitchen, Greg joined the process already in motion as one woman rinsed dishes, another loaded them into the side-by-side dishwashers. One of the guys packaged the small quantities of leftovers, while another—not a Hawkins, judging from the jaw—scrubbed the face and hands of the protesting toddler from the high chair.

Elke came in with an armload of serving dishes and joined the fray. Shannon fidgeted by the island.

She straightened up as she was flanked by the two guys from the opposite end of the table.

"So you're the Shannon we keep hearing about," one of them said, his wide grin revealing a long, deep dimple in his right cheek. "Nice to finally meet you." He held out his hand.

"I'm sorry, but I don't remember your name," she admitted as his grip enveloped her fingers.

"Finn, living inspiration for my brother's superheroes, at your service." He brushed his lips over her knuckles before the other brother elbowed him out of the way.

"I'm Hayden." He took her hand and picked up where Finn had left off, placing a chivalrous kiss on the back of her hand. "And I'm in love. Greg neglected to mention how beautiful you are."

Shannon's cheeks warmed, and she gently disengaged her hand from his grasp. "I'm flattered, I think. Do you always fall in love so easily?"

"He's superficial," Finn said.

"Back off, bozos." Greg wedged himself between his two brothers and hip-checked first one, then the other, widening the space. "She doesn't need either of you slobbering all over her."

The other guys exchanged a look, eyebrows lifting. "So, it's like that."

"It's not *like that*." Greg took Shannon by the elbow. "Come on. It's time to meet with that lawyer I promised you. Cathy," he hollered across the kitchen, "you ready?"

The woman nodded. "Just let me get my stuff. I'll meet you in Dad's office."

Shannon once again found herself following Greg through the house. The living room featured vaulted ceilings with exposed beams, a towering stone fireplace and two sets of sliding glass doors that opened out onto a wraparound deck. They went down a short flight of stairs to a slate-floored foyer that had an enormous coat closet and a suit of armor…

A suit of armor?

Greg didn't give her time to ask, just barreled down the next staircase. She scrambled to keep up.

"This is the rumpus room," he said. "We did a lot of rumpusing down here growing up." She glanced around, taking in another fireplace along with a Ping-Pong table, a Pac-Man game table, a pinball machine and a dartboard sans darts hung on the wall.

Passing an efficiency kitchen just off the rumpus room, he led her down a short hallway, then into a room with a built-in bookcase behind a large desk. Greg grabbed two padded folding chairs from behind the door and opened them in front of the desk. "Sorry about the chairs. Dad doesn't often hold meetings in here."

"What does your father do?"

"He's a lawyer, too. But he does big corporate stuff."

"So your sister followed in Dad's footsteps?"

"Yep. Along with my brother Alan. And Kyle's in law school now."

Cathy came in, laptop cradled in her arms. She had lighter hair than Greg, though the hint of darker roots suggested the chestnut with honey highlights hadn't come from the Hawkins gene pool. She radiated confidence and professionalism that immediately gave

Shannon the sense that she was in good hands. "Goodbye, Greg," Cathy said. "I'll take it from here."

"I thought I could stay."

"No. You're burning time. Don't let the door hit you on the way out. I promise not to bite your friend."

Greg paused in the doorway. "If she does bite you, you let me know, and I'll take care of it."

Shannon nodded. The family's good-natured ribbing intrigued her. Her family—back when she'd one—had never been this…comfortable…with one another.

"Let's get started," Cathy said once Greg had closed the door behind himself. "My brother tells me you have a custody fight on your hands. He's told me some of what's going on, but I want to hear it from you. Give me all the details."

Shannon launched into a summary of how Ryan came to live with her, ignoring the sympathetic glances from Greg's sister. Cathy's fingers danced over the laptop's keyboard as she took notes.

"How long have you lived in Erie?"

"About six months."

"And how long have you worked at your present employment?"

"About five months."

Cathy asked her numerous other questions, from the jobs she'd held in the past to the relationships she'd had with men in the past five years. She dug into corners of her life Shannon hadn't expected, like the status of the rest of her family, whether or not she'd ever done drugs and what skeletons would drop out of her closet if someone rattled it long enough.

"What kind of support system do you have here for Ryan?"

"Support system?" Shannon shrugged. "I have a babysitter who stays with Ryan at night while I work."

"Friends? Distant relatives?"

Shannon shook her head. "That's it."

"No, it's not. You've got Greg Hawkins, talented art therapist, on the job. You've got a social worker. You've got Ryan's other therapist, Dr. Lansing. Plus, you are now plugged into the Hawkins-family support system. When the other lawyer asks you about it, that's what you say. And you say it confidently."

"Okay."

"The first thing we do is file for a change in venue. We want this heard in Erie, not Philadelphia. Since Ryan lives here with you now, we'll try to convince the court that this is where his custody should be decided."

"Can you tell me my chances of keeping custody?"

Cathy leaned back in her chair. "There are never any guarantees in a courtroom. I fight to win, but never make promises. Now let me ask you a question. Is losing an option?"

"What?"

"Is losing an option? Can you accept your nephew living with the people who raised the man who murdered your sister?"

"No," Shannon murmured.

"I'm afraid I don't believe you. Try again."

Shannon straightened. "No."

"Better, but I think you're still holding back."

"No," Shannon ground out, "I do *not* want Ryan living with the people who raised the man who *murdered* his mother."

Cathy smiled. "Now, *that's* what I'm talking about."

Great. Another Hawkins coaching her on fighting

tactics. She'd have a few choice words with Greg when he took her and Ryan home.

And he probably wasn't going to like what she had to say.

GREG MET THEM as they came out of the office. Ryan grabbed at Shannon immediately, tugging on her arm.

She glanced from the boy to Greg.

"He wants you to go outside with him. The other kids are bouncing on the trampoline, but I wouldn't let him go on it until you said he could."

"Thanks." She turned to his sister. "And thank you."

"You're welcome."

"Ryan, why don't you show me the way to the trampoline?"

Greg started to follow them, but Cathy laid her hand on his arm, holding him back. "You guys go ahead. I'll be right there."

Shannon waved her agreement as Ryan hauled her down the hallway toward the rumpus room and the doorway that led to the backyard.

"What's up, Cat?"

Cathy clutched her laptop to her chest, shot a quick look down the corridor, then spoke softly. "I'm walking a fine line here between attorney-client privilege and big-sister privilege. So just shut up and listen to me for once in your life. I told her no men until the custody trial is over. Now I'm telling you. Not that woman, ever."

"Not that woman? What's that supposed to mean?"

Cathy scowled, her disgust rumbling in her throat. "Don't play stupid with me, Gory."

Greg rolled his eyes at the nickname she'd dumped

on him as a baby, when she'd decided that just because everyone shortened Gregory into Greg didn't mean she couldn't chop his name up another way. Gory had so much more pizzazz, she said.

"No men for her. No *her* for *you.* Got it?"

"And even if I was interested, which I'm not saying I am—"

Cathy snorted.

"But if I was, why not?"

"Her track record of revolving-door relationships. Any judge is going to hate it, and I personally don't like it for my little brother. Not for *you,* anyway. Maybe Hayden. She's the first woman you've ever brought home for Sunday dinner."

"That's just because I knew you'd be here, and—"

"Keep telling yourself that. But I'd have met her at my downtown office, like any other client, if you'd asked." Cathy hefted her laptop over her shoulder.

"Why Hayden and not me?"

"Because Hayden's methods would work perfectly for her."

"I find that hard to believe." Hayden's "methods" mandated an end date for every relationship he started. In fact, one of his exes had been known to say that a relationship with Hayden was like a gallon of milk—it came with an expiration date.

And yet, most of his exs still adored him. How he managed it, Greg would never fully understand.

"You don't work that way, Gory."

Shannon didn't know it, but she'd been damned with faint praise. As to her assertion that he didn't work that way… No, he didn't. "Can she beat the grandparents and keep custody?"

Cathy shrugged. "I'll do my best, but you know how the courts can be, Gory."

"You have to win. That kid needs her. And she needs him just as much."

And his needs…well, he'd just have to keep his needs—his *wants*—under control.

CHAPTER FIVE

"You didn't have to give my mother the bracelet off your arm," Greg told her as he drove them home. They'd lingered at his parents' far longer than he'd expected, and now the sinking sun struck him full in the face. He lowered the visor. "What would you have done if she'd admired your shirt?"

He'd been admiring the shirt—and the cleavage beneath it—ever since she'd come out of the bathroom at her apartment wearing it. A midnight-black, clingy, wraparound thing with a V-neck, it provoked all sorts of thoughts he wasn't supposed to be having at a family dinner.

He hadn't sat at the dining-room table with a quasi-boner since Thanksgiving the year he was thirteen, and Cathy, then twenty, had brought home her smokin'-hot college roommate for the holiday.

Apparently, Finn and Hayden had also appreciated the sweater, judging by their ridiculous behavior. And after Cathy's lecture, Greg still hadn't been able to keep his eyes off of Shannon. But as a bonus, thanks to his sister, he felt guilty about it.

"Would I have given her the shirt off my back, you mean?" Shannon chuckled.

Even though that was where he'd been going with the

comment, the next image to flash across his brain was Shannon, peeling off the second-skin shirt to reveal…

He cleared his throat. "Don't be silly. I just meant you really didn't have to do that. My mother certainly didn't expect it. She wasn't sure how to handle it."

"Her son gives discounted services to me. Her daughter is doing pro bono work on my behalf. So it's okay for you guys to give things away, but not me? She liked it, and I wanted her to have it."

"Pro bono and discounted work isn't the same as giving away something that belongs to you."

"The bracelet made me happy for a while, and now it will make your mom happy for as long as she has it. No big deal."

Greg eased the Tracker into a parking space near her apartment. "It was a gracious gesture. You scored points with Mom, that's for sure. Oh, and I didn't thank you for taking the heat for us being late."

"It was the least I could do, seeing as it *was* my fault." Shannon turned and glanced into the backseat, then she groaned softly. "He's sleeping. That figures."

Ryan slumped against the door, dead to the world, mouth slightly open.

"Too much trampoline, I'd wager."

"Or maybe he's worn out from fighting with your nephew." She sighed. "Scrapping, as your brothers euphemistically termed it, is precisely what I've been concerned about."

"Shannon, it was hardly a fight. It was boys being boys, and besides, Jack shouldn't have mocked Ryan for not talking. That was wrong. Don't blame Ryan for sticking up for himself."

"I don't blame Ryan. I blame you."

"Me? *Me?*" He clenched his jaw shut so he didn't gape at her.

"Yes, you, you. Who praised him this morning when he attacked you? You did. Who's been filling his head with all this superhero nonsense? Why, I believe that would be you, *Mr. Hawkins*."

"Obviously you don't know progress when you see it, *Miss Vanderhoff*. What you're seeing now is a kid who feels more comfortable around you, around people. A kid who's starting to come out of his shell. A kid we're finally empowering." Closing the front door with a restraint he didn't feel, Greg stalked around the car, gingerly opening the back door. Once he freed the child from his seat belt, Greg hoisted the slumbering boy to his shoulder, praying Ryan would stay asleep.

Shannon brushed past him on the sidewalk to unlock the apartment door and let him in. Without a word, he carried Ryan upstairs to his room, laying the child on the futon. He removed the boy's shoes and socks, finagled him out of the pint-size windbreaker, then draped a blanket over him.

In the doorway, Shannon raised her eyebrows. He waited until he was close enough to respond in a harsh whisper, "What? You've never seen a guy put another guy to bed before? I tucked Derek in only last week after he tied one on because… Never mind. Suffice it to say I know how to pull off shoes and throw some covers over a sleeper."

He crooked a finger at her, then headed back down the stairs. In the foyer, he spoke normally again. "I'm taking you and Ryan to the zoo tomorrow. We're making progress, and we should capitalize on that.

Are you working tonight?" Greg pulled out his Treo, checked the calendar.

"No, thankfully I'm off tonight and tomorrow night."

"Good. I've got a couple of appointments in the morning, but I'll pick you up around noon, okay?" He slid the phone back into his pocket.

"Yes sir, Mr. Bossy."

"Did you see my family today? Pushovers get nowhere in that house."

"It was…interesting, that's for sure. To have that many people related to you…interesting."

A glimmer of longing flickered in her eyes, kicking Greg in the gut. How lonely must her life have been? He couldn't imagine taking on the world without his brothers at his back, having his sisters to torment and share their insights into the opposite sex—even if they were lecturing him about his love life—or without his parents there.

Shannon had only the little boy asleep upstairs, a child who also, for all intents and purposes, had lost both of his parents. And people were trying to take him away from her.

The impulsive urge to wrap her in his arms and shelter her made him step closer. The air in the foyer grew heavier, warmer, and she retreated, leaning against the wall.

"I know you don't like fighting, but do you ever at least fight yourself?" He inched forward.

"Wh-what do you mean?"

"I mean, say there's something you want that you know you shouldn't have. Say double-cheese and pepperoni pizza. You know it's all wrong for you. It's never going to work. But you want it. It looks delicious." Greg planted his hands on the wall on either side of her head, then leaned in, nuzzled her shoulder and inhaled deeply as he skimmed the graceful curve of her neck. She smelled of coconut, sunshine and summertime. He pulled back to meet her eyes. "It smells fantastic. Do you fight with yourself over tasting it? Or do you just take a bite?"

"I—" She lowered her gaze to his mouth. The tip of her tongue darted out, moistening her lips, and Greg's hormones jumped to attention like a superhero to a beacon light in the night sky. "Fighting's wrong," she murmured. "Don't fight it. Taste it."

Greg bent his elbows, easing his body weight against her, sliding his knee between hers to widen her stance so he could settle between her thighs.

Her eyes fluttered shut, and she lifted her chin, arching her neck with a sigh. "Is that your utility belt, or are you just happy to see me?"

"Shh." Once more he nuzzled her neck, this time trailing light, teasing kisses up the slope. He nipped her chin gently, just enough to surprise her eyes open, then he slowly brushed his lips over hers. A moment of testing, then he slanted his head and took full possession of her warm, lush mouth.

True to her nature, she offered no resistance, opening for him, eagerly welcoming his probing tongue, giving back just as enthusiastically.

And the inner war began in him, the voices of reason that sounded very much like his sisters'. Cathy, telling him Shannon wasn't for him and to keep his distance. Elke, pleading with him to stop before it was too late, reminding him that kissing—hell, devouring—Shannon Vanderhoff was a very, very bad idea.

Bad idea or not, she felt perfect pressed against him.

The heat index in the foyer climbed until it well surpassed an Erie summer day, headed toward Phoenix in July. The faintest flavor of hazelnut coffee and Finn's German chocolate cake made her all the sweeter.

Shannon's heart thudded faster, her pulse audible in the rush of blood in her ears. His mouth *was* as talented as his quick-sketching fingers. She tipped her hips a fraction of an inch, increasing the friction of the impressive package hidden beneath his snug jeans. Jeans she'd been admiring the fit of while he'd been bouncing on the trampoline with her nephew.

Ryan.

Who was sleeping upstairs. Who was counting on her to save him from Patty and Lloyd.

Reluctantly Shannon placed her hands on Greg's firm chest, and pushed.

He broke off the kiss, pulling back just enough so she could see his blue eyes, heavy-lidded and full of heat. "What?"

She shook her head. "We can't do this. You were right. It's all wrong. Ryan's upstairs. And I can't afford to do anything that will make me a bigger target for Lloyd and Patty's lawyers. One of the things your sister said was no men until after the custody fight. I'm pretty sure that means you, too."

Greg shifted, skimming his lower body against hers. Shannon struggled not to respond in kind, putting on her best poker face.

He stepped away from her, leaving her cold, wanting. Needing to grab him and haul him back to her.

"You learn too fast," he said. "I kinda hoped fighting yourself would take longer to master."

"Progress." She forced a smile. Under other circumstances, she'd have embraced the temporary gift Greg represented. There would have been fun times and, judging from this steam-her-socks-off encounter, incredible sex. But she had to face the new reality of her life, and that meant fighting. Even herself.

The concept still didn't sit well with her. In fact, she viewed it even less favorably now.

"Progress. Yeah, great." He cleared his throat. "I'll pick you and Ryan up at noon."

HEADING TOWARD MIDNIGHT, Greg stopped the flight of his pencil long enough to really examine the panel he was sketching, one where the hero confronted a flame-throwing villain on a city street while horrified onlookers watched. He tossed down the pencil in disgust, then pushed back from his drawing table and rose to pace the length of his third-floor studio. Again.

Two of the bystanders in the crowd bore a significant resemblance to Shannon.

A man's ego could only take so much, and his wasn't sure what to make of her late-in-the-game rejection. Up front, he could understand. But in the midst of one of the most mind-blowing kisses he'd ever experienced?

The signals she'd been sending had said she'd been just as caught up in the heat as he'd been.

The hardwood floor creaked beneath his feet as he drifted from one end of the spacious room to the other, past the shelves of comic-book memorabilia, past the superhero wall mural featuring some of his brothers. He turned at the brick fireplace in the middle of the street-facing wall and headed in the opposite direction.

At a rap on his door, he stopped and listened as footsteps climbed the short set of stairs to his refuge and workplace. Finn appeared at the top and held out a long-necked amber bottle. "Heard you pacing up here. Repeatedly. Brought an ale to chill you out."

Greg snorted. "There's beer in the minifridge. But…thanks." He took the bottle from his brother, who, along with Hayden, lived in the big old house on West Tenth Street. Greg had purchased it five years ago and renovated it, using sweat equity from all of his brothers, even their father. The girls had pitched in, too, and now the house was quite respectable, considering three bachelors lived in it. The former attic had been converted into Greg's workspace, a studio complete with a drafting table, a light table, space for his computer and scanner—every bit as much an artist's tool as his pencils and inks—a half bath…and plenty of room to pace.

Finn twisted the cap off his own brew, then wandered to the oversize chairs in the corner, slumping into one of them with his leg draped over the arm. "What's going on?"

"Nothing." Greg plopped into the chair opposite Finn, skittered the bottle cap across the short table between them. It teetered to a stop on the edge.

"And a fantastic-looking nothing she is, too."

Greg paused with the bottle to his mouth, glaring at his brother over the rim.

Finn laughed. "You couldn't take your eyes off her all during dinner. And don't think it's just Hayden and me who noticed. I think even the kids picked up on the sparks you two were throwing. And Mom was watching you watching her."

"Shit."

"Yeah. I think you stepped in it this time, little brother."

"There's nothing to step in. It's a business thing. The kid needs my help. They both need my help."

"And so superhero Greg rushes in to save the beautiful woman in distress, right?"

Greg flipped Finn a one-finger salute.

"No, thanks. You're not my type. However, if you're saying that you're really *not* interested in Shannon, I'll take her phone number."

"Like hell you will."

Finn arched a dark eyebrow at him.

"She's off-limits until the custody hearing. Cathy said so. No men. It could hurt her chance of keeping the boy."

His brother said nothing, just stared at him.

Greg slumped deeper in the chair. "Shit."

Finn leaned over and clinked his bottle against Greg's. "You're screwed." He got up and started to leave, stopping at the top of the stairs. "Let me know if it gets to the point that Hayden and I should start thinking about new digs, huh? Don't evict your own flesh and blood without notice." The stairs groaned as Finn went down.

"Finn?"

He paused, peering through the railing spindles at Greg. "Yeah?"

"I still haven't found anyplace else to host my program. I need that kid to start talking, to help me keep my program at the university. Need the PR he can bring."

"I wouldn't tell her that." The door slammed behind his blunt statement.

Greg took another pull of the beer, glanced over at the sketch with Shannon's face appearing twice in the crowd. "I am so screwed," he muttered. Why was he drawn to a woman who wouldn't keep him even if they did start something? Why hadn't he felt like this with Denise? She wanted him. She was fighting to get him back.

While Shannon, the pacifist, the Zen take-it-and-leave-it woman, held him at arm's length despite a sizzle that had damn near set fire to the coats on the hooks near where they'd kissed.

God sure had a warped sense of humor.

SHANNON WATCHED from the fence as Greg swung Ryan onto one of the horses on the Erie Zoo's merry-go-round. The man had an easy rapport with the boy she envied. He was a natural with kids.

While she was still…awkward.

The tension between her and Greg today had made her even more awkward. Neither of them had brought up the night before, but it hung heavily between them.

Greg fastened the safety belt around Ryan's waist, then the boy shoved him on the shoulder. Greg said something Shannon couldn't catch, nodding, then came off the ride to stand beside her. He leaned over, propping his elbows on the weathered wood. "He wants to ride alone. Said he's not a baby."

Shannon gaped at him. "He *said* that?"

"Not in words. But I understood him, loud and clear."

The calliope music started, and the carousel slowly chugged into motion. Shannon waved to Ryan as he circled past. Without the child to engage with, she and Greg stood there in uncomfortable silence for three or four rotations. Unable to stand it any longer and desperate to clear the air between them, she blurted, "We should probably talk about last night."

Greg jerked upright. "No, we probably shouldn't. I should have trusted my first instinct. I'm sorry. Won't happen again."

"Which is too bad. I found it rather…nice."

"Nice?" He slapped the center of his chest like she'd wounded him. "Nice? Nice is when I kiss my sister. Or my mom. What happened between us last night was smokin'. Set-off-the-fire-alarms hot."

Her skin began to tingle and her pulse kicked up a notch. "That, too. I'm still new to this idea that I have a child to worry about. Someone I have to put ahead of what I want. Scares me to death if you want to know the truth."

"I can imagine. But you're doing great. Everything's going to work out."

"Thanks." They turned back just in time to wave to Ryan as he went by again, and then the ride began to slow.

"You go get him," Greg said. "I'll wait here."

Ryan had already unfastened the seat belt by the time she reached him. She grasped him by the waist, and he threw his arms around her neck. For a moment, she just held him, warm and sticky from cotton candy. A memory surfaced of Willow, laughing as she opened her mouth wide, letting pink cotton candy dissolve on her tongue.

Willow's son was her sister's legacy. Shannon squeezed Ryan tighter, until he squirmed and struggled in her embrace. She slid him to the ground.

A mother with a baby on her hip and a toddler by the hand shook her head. "He's a big boy. Shouldn't he be in school?"

Ryan froze, then looked up at Shannon. She squeezed his shoulder. "Are you the truant officer?"

"Uh, well, no," the woman sputtered.

"Then I guess it's none of your business, right? For all you know, he's a genius who completed his high-school courses yesterday, and we're celebrating before he starts college tomorrow. Come on, Ryan, let's go see how many more of the animals you know the scientific classifications for. I've seen enough of the species *Annoyus buttinski*." She took Ryan by the hand, leaving the woman standing on the merry-go-round platform with her mouth hanging open.

Greg chuckled softly as she stormed out of the gate with Ryan in tow. "Excellent," he murmured, scrambling to keep up with her as she raced from the children's section of the zoo. "Way to tell that woman off. *Annoyus buttinski*. I love it."

Shannon tried to glare at him, but ended up dissolving into laughter herself. Ryan slipped his other hand into Greg's and, as the three of them walked around the swan pond, he jumped, lifting his feet and making them swing him. Sunlight glinted off the rippling water, and for a brief moment, all seemed right in Shannon's world. For a moment, she allowed herself the fantasy of a normal life—something she'd never even considered before. Life with a man, a child…children. A family. A big family.

For keeps.

Greg checked his watch. "Okay, sport, we've got to go now, so we have time for our art before I have to get to another appointment. Okay?"

The fantasy melted like cotton candy in the rain, like fantasies always did. Which was why Shannon didn't often indulge in daydreaming.

Or hope.

As they approached the parking lot, she heard hushed voices and scuffling, then three men in… Shannon blinked. Yes, three men in formfitting spandex costumes, one red, one green and one blue, burst out from behind a van. Two more people pointing small handheld cameras also appeared.

Greg stopped in his tracks, muttering under his breath.

"We are the ABC Men!" the guy in red said. "I am A." He pointed to the giant letter *A* on his chest, then propped his fists on his hips, striking a pose Shannon assumed was meant to be superheroish.

Ryan giggled.

"I am B Man!" B Man wore blue spandex—*B* for blue?—that emphasized his jiggling beer belly. Also *B* words. He, too, struck a pose.

"And I am C!" said the green-clad guy. They all wore small color-coordinated masks.

"We are the defenders of the preschool set," A announced. "Wherever there's a bully throwing sand in a sandbox, wherever a kid is unfairly put in timeout or wherever a little boy—" he gestured to Ryan "—won't eat his vegetables, we'll be there." A folded his arms across his chest.

Several other families in the parking lot watching the spectacle clapped, sending the ABC Men into sweeping bows. Then they all clambered into the open sliding door of the van, followed by their camera crew. As the van carefully pulled out of the zoo parking lot, the "superheroes" waved to the kids.

Greg shook his head. "How do they keep finding me? And why? Wanting a comic book signed, I can understand, but what the heck was the point of that performance?"

Shannon poked him in the back. "Is this a normal occurrence for you?"

He jingled the keys in his hand. "It started a few weeks before I met you and Ryan. Seems to happen about once a week or so. But things have been slow lately, so I thought they'd stopped."

"Hmm…interesting. Who knew we were coming to the zoo today?" Shannon helped Ryan into the backseat of the Tracker. He smiled broadly at Shannon, warming her all over. "You thought that was funny, huh?" She tapped his freckled nose as he nodded. Shannon buckled him, then did the same for herself in the passenger's seat.

"Nobody except us. They never show up at my house or work. Which is why I haven't worried about it too much. But it's getting kinda weird and tiring, even for me."

"They're probably college kids." Frat boys who'd had too many keggers, judging from B. Shannon tapped her fingers on the armrest as Greg headed down Thirty-eighth Street. "That's why you haven't had any incidents lately. They've been busy studying for finals. Maybe this was their last hurrah before they head home for summer vacation."

"Uh-huh. Erie University has a popular summer semester, plus there's all the college kids who live in Erie who come home for the summer. I don't know that I can expect a break."

"Guess you'll have to wait and see."

"Guess so." He shook his head again. "The ABC Men for preschoolers." He chuckled. "At least they're semicreative. Maybe *Sesame Street* would be interested in booking them."

Back at her apartment complex, Ryan, head held high and chest puffed out, helped Greg carry the art supplies inside. Once at the table, Greg took a large sheet of paper and folded it into fourths, then opened it. He used a black marker to trace the folds. He did the same thing for two more sheets of paper. "Comic books are just ways to tell stories with pictures. That's what we're going to do today. We're all going to draw the story of our trip to the zoo in these boxes."

The reason for the trip to the zoo became clear. Greg had been building a shared experience to use in Ryan's session. It had been an actual field trip, for educational purposes, not a fun outing.

Why did that make her feel hollow?

"So, in this panel—" he pointed to the upper left box "—we'll draw something that happened first. Then here—" the upper right box "—we'll put what came next." Greg continued demonstrating the sequence of the boxes. "So, think of something you'd like to draw first."

The phone rang. Shannon pushed back from the table. "Sorry. I'll be right back."

The wall phone over the counter was the only one she had, so Shannon was able to watch Ryan carefully choose a pencil, examine the tip as he'd seen Greg do on numerous occasions, then begin drawing.

The woman on the other end of the line identified herself as Ellen Kelaneri, with the Philadelphia D.A.'s office. Shannon's stomach tightened. "Yes? Is there something wrong?"

"No, no, Miss Vanderhoff. We just wanted to know if we could send some people up to interview Ryan now."

Shannon glanced at the boy who was happily drawing away. "Not yet. But maybe soon."

"His testimony is critical to the case against his father."

"Uh, you know, this phone connection isn't very good. Can I call you back in a minute?" Shannon gestured at Greg, motioning like she was writing. He tossed her a crayon, and she jotted down the phone number on the paper she was supposed to use for her zoo-trip comic. "Okay, I'll call you back shortly."

After hanging up, she crossed back to the table, glancing down at Ryan's drawing. "You're doing a great job." She turned to Greg. "Can I borrow your cell phone? That was an important call, and I couldn't hear anything on the connection."

Wordlessly, he passed her his cell, the slightly raised eyebrow telling her he understood.

"Uh, it's long-distance."

"Unlimited calling is a wonderful thing. No sweat."

"Okay. I'll be back in a few. Keep drawing, Ry." Shannon smoothed her nephew's wavy hair, then leaned over and impulsively pressed a kiss to the top of his head. He twisted around to scowl at her, indicating she was interrupting his work. "Sorry."

Out on the front porch, she dialed the D.A.'s office. "This is Shannon Vanderhoff. Sorry, I couldn't talk with Ryan in the same room. What do you mean, his testimony is critical? Last time we spoke, you said you thought it was a slam-dunk case against my brother-in-law, and you weren't even certain Ryan would have to testify."

"Miss Vanderhoff, we have a fairly strong case against him, but Ryan's testimony will be the nail in his coffin, so to speak. Juries can be fickle. Your brother-in-law claims he remembers nothing of that night and that there's no way he killed his wife. That an intruder must have done it."

Shannon snorted. "Ah, yes, the unknown intruder. The not-me argument."

"Exactly. There's no evidence of a break-in or

anyone else at the scene. The physical evidence points to him. But Ryan's testimony…that would make our job so much easier."

"I'm not interested in making your job easier. I *am* interested in healing my nephew, and seeing that the son of a bitch who killed my sister spends the rest of his miserable days behind bars. But Ryan still isn't speaking."

"Trevor Schaffer's defense attorney is pulling out all the stops to rush this case to trial. Please, call us as soon as Ryan starts talking."

"I'll do that." Shannon snapped the phone closed. What if Trevor got off? What would happen to Ryan then? The idea of her nephew testifying against his father made her queasy, but the idea that the man could get off and regain custody of Ryan made her downright want to vomit.

Shannon headed back inside, setting the phone on the table near Greg's elbow. "Now, where were we?" She grabbed another sheet of paper and a pencil. "Okay, drawing our trip to the zoo. This is going to be fun." Greg eyed her curiously, questions about the phone call or her sudden newfound zeal for his art therapy, or maybe both, plain to see.

The wall phone rang again. "Oh, honestly." Shannon tossed down her pencil and went back around the island.

And nearly hung up as she recognized the voice this time. But Cathy had warned her to be gracious and polite. Shannon forced a smile to add enthusiasm to her response. "Hi, Patty. What can I do for you?"

"I'd like to speak to my grandson."

"He's in the middle of something right now. How about I have him call you back later?"

"No, that won't work for me. I have things to do later. I want to talk to him now, please."

Please? Maybe their lawyer had warned them to be polite, too. "All right. But not too long."

"It's rather tedious to keep up a one-sided conversation…I assume he's not talking yet?"

"No, no, he's not."

"Oh, okay." Was that a note of relief in Patty's voice? "So I won't keep him long."

Shannon covered the mouthpiece. "Ryan? Grandma wants to talk to you."

The boy's shoulders slumped. He shook his head, pointing at his drawing and Greg.

"I know. But she promised to keep it short. Come on, buddy. She's your grandma. And—" Shannon swallowed hard and forced the words past her clenched teeth "—family is important." But not all family was created equal. Shannon felt better about using the term to apply to Mrs. K., Ryan's babysitter, than she did about using it with Patty and Lloyd. Even if they were his blood relatives.

Ryan slid from the chair and trudged over.

"Okay, here he is. I'm putting him on now." Shannon handed the receiver to the boy, who dutifully held it up to his ear. The canary-on-steroids chirping spilled out, but Shannon couldn't make out what Patty was saying.

For a minute or two, the only sound in the room was the faint scratch of Greg's pencil on the paper as he continued drawing casually keeping an eye on Shannon and Ryan.

Then the boy slammed the receiver down on the island countertop. He looked up at Shannon with wide eyes and trembling lower lip, then turned and dashed to the table, pausing only long enough to grab a black crayon and scribble across his paper before he raced from the room. The bedroom door slammed a moment later.

Torn between going after him and demanding answers from the woman on the phone, Shannon hesitated.

"I'll see to Ryan." Greg's long strides quickly covered the length of the apartment's hall.

Shannon snatched up the phone. "Patty? What did you say to him?"

"Nothing. Why?"

"Nothing my rear end. Nothing doesn't make a kid go running."

"I have no idea what would upset him. I told him we'd seen his father, and his daddy was asking about him, that's all. And that hopefully he would get to come live with us soon."

"And you don't see how either of those two things would upset him? Buy a clue, Patty." Shannon wrapped the phone cord around her finger until the tip turned red. "Goodbye." After fumbling to free her hand, she forced the hand piece into the cradle so hard the ringer jangled.

In Ryan's doorway, she pulled up short. The boy had wrapped himself like a monkey around Greg's body. The man sat on the edge of the futon, rocking gently, patting Ryan's heaving back. "It's going to be okay, sport. You know, Aunt Shannon and I could help you a lot better if you'd talk to us."

Ryan shook his head hard.

"You know we're not going to be mad at you, right? No matter what you say?"

No, she wasn't going to be mad at Ryan, but she sure as hell was mad at his grandmother. She moved to sit next to Greg, reached out toward Ryan's back, hesitated, then at Greg's nod of encouragement, she too stroked the child. "Ryan?"

In a flash, her nephew scrambled from Greg's lap to hers, wrapping his arms around her neck and his legs around her waist, squeezing so tight it became difficult to take a breath.

A blinding flash of white-hot panic froze her for a moment, the depth of the child's need overwhelming her.

He'd chosen her over Greg. He wanted her.

Nose tingling, and cold fear giving way to warmth, she enveloped Ryan in her embrace. "It's okay. I've got you."

Shannon didn't know how long they sat there, but Ryan's quivering body slowly settled, and the sniffling sounds muffled against her neck—her now moist and icky neck—eventually stopped. Greg left, returning with a handful of tissues. Shannon eased Ryan from her, taking the tissues and mopping his face, running one over the sopping-wet crease near her collarbone. "Ryan, are you upset because Grandma Patty wants you to live with her and Grandpa?"

The little boy nodded, wiping his arm over his face.

"Do you want to live with them?"

He shook his head fiercely.

"All right. We already have a lawyer. Remember Greg's sister Cathy?" At Ryan's affirmation, she continued, "Well, she's going to help us." Shannon cleared her throat, but still had to force out the words that were like a foreign language. "We're going to fight." She held up her closed fist.

Greg smiled at her over Ryan's head. "And I'm going to help, too." He held up his fist. "What do you say, Ryan?"

Ryan bumped his knuckles against both of theirs.

The team was forged.

CHAPTER SIX

PATTY STARED at the wireless phone she'd replaced on the mahogany night table. How dare that woman?

The maid, a load of freshly washed towels in her arms, bustled toward the master bath.

"Would you believe it, Rosa? That woman told me to buy a clue. *Buy a clue*. What on earth is that supposed to mean?"

Rosa shrugged. "I don't know, Ms. Patty. I'm gonna put these towels in the bathroom. You ready for me to draw your bath?"

"That will be fine. While I'm soaking, make sure the black-and-white linen dress is ready for this evening."

Trevor's call—she knew it was him by the prison's name on the caller ID—came as she was fastening the black-pearl-and-diamond earring that completed her ensemble. She'd be so stunning at the Philadelphia Art Museum's charity dinner that no one would dare look at her with pity in their eyes, or whisper things behind their hands, stopping when she drew near. Whispers that compared her son to Scott Peterson, or O. J. Simpson. *Ignorant, small-minded people*. "Hello, Trevor."

"Mom."

"I trust you're well."

"I'm in jail, Mom. What do you think?"

She sighed. "That's no excuse to speak to me that way."

There was a momentary silence. Then Trevor said, "You're right. I'm sorry. Live in a cage long enough, and eventually you're reduced to acting like an animal."

"You're *not* an animal." The comment came out more sharply than she intended.

Trevor's laugh was equally sharp. "Loyal to the end, Mom. Glad to know I can count on you to have faith in me."

"You'll be out of there before you know it. Your father got an update from Harvey Lowenstein. They're doing everything they can to speed your case to trial."

"Good. Yesterday you said you were going to call Ryan. Did you?"

Patty glanced at her thin diamond-encrusted watch. Lloyd would be home to pick her up in five minutes, and he hated to be kept waiting. "I did. Frankly, I only knew he was actually on the phone by his breathing. Unnerving, I must tell you. And he slammed the phone down in my ear. Almost ruptured something, I think. And—"

"So he's still not talking?"

"No. And that woman…"

"What about her?"

"She had the nerve to tell me to buy a clue. What does that mean?"

"It means she's not the person we want raising Ryan, Mom. Get him back before she ruins him, will you?"

"These things take time, Trevor. I'm doing the best I can."

"He's your grandson, Mom. *My* son. Make sure your best is good enough." Trevor hung up.

Once again Patty found herself staring at her wireless phone, marveling at her son's rudeness. Jail had eroded Trevor's manners.

No matter. He'd shape up again once he'd been exonerated. Why, even knowing Ryan was with them would probably help his disposition.

Family meant everything to Trevor.

As she tucked a clutch purse under her arm and hustled from her room, Patty vowed to push the lawyers harder.

"I'm SORRY TO BOTHER YOU, but I just didn't know who else to call." Memorial Day weekend behind them, the two weeks since the zoo excursion had passed with little incident—and no progress. Actually, after Patty's phone call, Ryan had regressed to the point that coaxing a smile out of him took a lot of effort. While cradling the phone against her shoulder, Shannon crumbled the last piece of feta cheese. She stirred it into the mixture already in the long casserole dish. "They want me to come in early tonight to make up some of the time I've missed, and Mrs. K. just called. She's not feeling well and can't sit with Ryan tonight. She thinks it was something she ate."

Greg didn't respond right away.

"I can't lose my job. What's a judge going to say about that?"

His quick, blown-out breath echoed through the phone. "I don't mind watching Ryan for you. It's just that I'm already watching Derek's children tonight until about eight. He's got a dinner meeting. If you're willing to drop Ryan off at my place, I can bring him back to your apartment after Derek picks up his kids, or when Hayden gets home and can take over for me, whichever comes first."

"That's fine, thanks. Give me your address and directions." Shannon jotted down the information. "I really appreciate it. I owe you one."

"Remember that." He hung up, leaving Shannon staring at the phone. There'd been an uneasy edge to his voice, one she hadn't heard from him before.

After packing up a few items, she got Ryan from his room where he'd been playing a learning game on her computer. She planned to send him back to kindergarten in the fall, so she was trying to make sure he kept up with his letters and numbers. He deserved every advantage she could give him because of the emotional blows he'd suffered—and those yet to come, if he had to testify against his father in court.

Ten minutes later, she parallel parked in front of a charming old house, complete with a wraparound porch. Narrow driveways separated the homes in the neighborhood. Kids next door drew chalk art on the sidewalk while a bored teenager sat on the stoop, cell phone glued to her ear.

Greg's front door was opened by a little girl—his six-year-old niece Katie, if Shannon remembered correctly. "Uncle Greg said let you in and he'll be right down. He's working up in his lair."

"His lair, huh? Is that like the Batcave?"

Katie giggled. "Uh-huh." She turned to Ryan. "We're watching a movie in the theater room. Come on." She took his hand and began to pull him from the foyer.

"Just a minute. Let's get your coat off first." Shannon set her armload on the seat of an oak bench, next to a slumped-over stack of newspapers. As she reached to help Ryan with his windbreaker, he scowled at her, unzipped it and thrust it at her.

"Sorry," she murmured. "Of course you can do it yourself." She crouched, meeting him square in the eye. "Listen to me. I don't care what Jack says to you today. I do *not* want you fighting with him, do you understand?"

Ryan looked down at his toes.

She lifted his chin with her finger. "Ryan? I mean it. Physical fighting is never the answer. When I told you we were going to fight, I was speaking about the legal system. The justice system. I'm not actually going to have a wrestling match with your grandparents to see who gets custody of you."

The corners of Ryan's mouth edged up.

Shannon chuckled. "I know, it's an appealing image. But that's not the way to solve problems. That's make-believe. Just like the superheroes are all make-believe. You understand the difference, right?"

The boy nodded.

"Okay then. No fighting with Jack or anyone else, no matter what they say. It's very nice of Greg to keep you, so you have to behave. Right?"

This time Ryan's nod was exaggerated. *Yes, Aunt Shannon, can I go play now?* was easy enough to read in his expression.

She tapped the tip of his nose. "Go on. Have fun."

Finally dismissed, Ryan scrambled after Greg's niece.

"Oh, hey, where's the kitchen?" Shannon called after the girl.

"Straight down this hallway." Katie's words echoed off the walls, then their small feet pounded up a wooden staircase.

She grabbed the loaded bag she'd set on the oak bench, then headed down the hallway, which was two-tone beige with some sort of painted texture.

The cozy kitchen wasn't what she'd expected. A small desk next to the refrigerator overflowed with papers, but that was the only messy thing in sight. A square wooden chopping block served as a kitchen island, and Shannon set her bag there, drawn to make a closer investigation of the backsplash over the black-and-stainless stove.

A Tuscan village perched on a hill in the distance. In the foreground, as if on a windowsill, sat assorted glass bottles, one filled with black olives, another with some spiced oil. A bunch of deep purple grapes and some other bottles occupied a shelf above the sill. A tree branch dangled across the top left portion of the frame. She reached out to touch the tiles.

"You like it?" Greg asked from the doorway, making her jump and yank back her hand.

"I do. It's beautiful."

"Thanks. Took me about a day and half with all the details."

"You did it yourself?"

"I did."

"Wow. I didn't know your art skills were so versatile."

Greg laughed. "Yes, I do more than sketches and comic-book art. But don't ever tell my kids that I paint on anything other than paper, okay? Especially not Cheryl. Not after that incident with Michael's head the day we met."

"Ah, yes. The Sistine Chapel argument."

"Right. Now, what brings you to my kitchen? This isn't exactly where I expected to find you. Can I get you a drink? Coffee? Tea? A beer?"

"No, thanks. Actually, I brought you something. I

hate imposing on you, and don't want you to have to feed Ryan, so I brought dinner. Enough for all of you. Luckily I was making a big batch to freeze." She opened the canvas bag. "Just pop it in the oven at 325 for about forty-five minutes."

"Uh-oh. Um..." He peeled back the tinfoil on the top of the glass dish and peered in while she pulled out a few more dishes. "Hey. That almost looks like mac and cheese."

"I prefer to call it five-cheese pasta."

He wrinkled his nose. "And is one of those five cheeses goat cheese?"

She laughed. He was so cute when he did that. The man had no inhibitions about appearing "funny," and she found that appealing. The view on the wall might be faux, but the man was real. "I guess you'll have to try it and find out. Ryan and I have made some culinary compromises. He eats this. That should be all you need to know."

"But, but...mac and cheese is supposed to be glow-in-the-dark orange."

"Don't you have enough color with your artwork, without needing artificial ones in your food? There's plenty of color in real food. If you look closer, you'll see that there's some cheddar in there, and it's orange."

"Well, okay. Thanks. We'll try it. I just won't tell Derek's kids about the goat cheese."

"Good idea." She dug in her purse. "Now, here's a key to my apartment—"

"Awesome. Already we're exchanging keys. I like how you think." He took the key ring from her fingers, giving her a wink that turned smoldering. Cute Guy was gone, replaced with the hot, handsome man who could actually be a superhero.

Shannon blushed, then groped for something to say. "S-smart aleck."

It was as if she'd flipped a switch, activating every nerve in his body and triggering a flood of hormones. Greg set the keys on the cutting block and stepped even closer to her. The rise of scarlet up her neck and in her cheeks clued him that she'd felt it, too. "What is it about you—" he stroked the back of his fingers over her cheek "—that makes me forget common sense, forget that we agreed not to go here for Ryan's sake, and just makes me want to kiss you senseless again?"

She grabbed his wrist and forced his hand away from her face. "I—I… I have to get to work," she stammered, backing away from him. "That's a spare key, so you can lock the door behind you when you take Ryan home. I'll—I'll see you in the morning. Thanks again."

The sway of her ass in the clingy black dress pants as she hustled out of the kitchen sent a further surge of testosterone through him. He parked himself in the archway to watch her stride the length of the hall and didn't move again until the front door closed behind her.

He wanted to see her in the morning, all right. But not exhausted after a long night's work. He wanted to see her heavy-lidded and languid, silky hair spread out across a pillow, rousing from sleep after a long night of lovemaking, to start the morning off with another round.

Damn, he had it bad.

Lust. It's just lust. Nothing that a long cold shower wouldn't cure. At least, temporarily. Unfortunately, with four kids running around the house that was out of the question right now.

So he'd have to deal with it.

The house phone rang. Greg went to the desk,

fumbling through the piles of junk mail before locating the wireless handset. Caller ID said Blocked Caller, but that would be typical of most of his brothers. "Yell-ow."

"No, blue." At the sound of familiar feminine giggling, Greg's gut lurched.

"Denise." He sighed. The phone call worked better than a cold shower, as his libido—and its physical manifestation—shrank. "What's up?"

"Not me, that's for sure. I've had a really bad day at work. So much that I'm in need of chocolate-cream pie. I thought I'd see if I could pick one up at the bakery and swing by your place. I could use someone to help me eat it. If I eat the whole thing myself, I'll just be more upset."

Chocolate-cream pie with graham cracker crust and whipped cream on top happened to be his favorite. As Denise very well knew. "Sorry, Denise. I've got plans tonight."

"Yeah, I know. Elke told me you're babysitting for Derek. That's okay, I don't mind the kids. Besides, they're not staying that late."

"Elke doesn't know everything. Actually, I've got an overnight babysitting gig. Even if I didn't, Denise, the answer would still be no."

"Overnight? Who are you babysitting overnight?"

"It doesn't matter—"

"It's for her, isn't it? The one with the kid who doesn't talk? Elke told me you had them to Sunday dinner a few weeks ago, and couldn't keep your eyes off her."

"Sorry you had a crappy day, Denise. I have to go now." Greg disconnected the call, vowing to answer no more Blocked Caller numbers, his brothers be damned. He immediately dialed another number. He felt like an ass, racing from Denise to Elke, but he had a few choice words for his sister before his ex got to her first. "Elke," he snapped, before she'd even finished saying hello, "I want you to stop discussing me with Denise. Enough already."

"What are you talking about, Greg?"

"I'm talking about the fact that Denise knew all about me babysitting for Derek tonight, and about Shannon and Ryan coming to Sunday dinner."

"So? She's my best friend. I tell her all sorts of stuff about my life."

"Discussing *your* life is fine. The parts where I come in are now off limits, got it?"

"Geez, I don't know what you're so mad about."

Greg took a deep breath and dropped his voice to a low, silky tone. "Elke? You know your wedding this summer? Unless you want me showing up in the Captain Chemo costume, I suggest you stop talking to Denise about me. Do I make myself clear?"

"You wouldn't!"

"Don't try me!"

"That's just wrong."

"Yes, it is." Overhead, an ominous thud shook the ceiling. "Gotta run, Elke. See ya on the funny pages." At the funny farm was more like it lately. He tossed the phone on the desk and headed for the stairs to investigate. By the time he hit the landing, the sounds of shushing, interspersed with childish giggling, reached him. Super Uncle instincts kicked in—they were up to trouble.

He stopped at the top of the stairs and folded his arms over his chest, as Jack hoisted his three-year-old sister, Lila, to unlatch the hook and eye on the door to Greg's studio. Ryan glanced over his shoulder, twinkling eyes going wide beneath the black mask he—like the rest of the gang—wore.

Greg shook his head, putting his finger over his mouth. "Just what do you think you're doing?"

"Ack!" Jack fumbled with the toddler, and Greg raced forward to catch her. He set Lila on the floor.

"Geez, Uncle Greg, you scared me. I almost dropped Lila!"

Greg stepped in front of his door. "You didn't answer me, Jack. What are you doing? You know this room is off limits. The lock is up here to keep short people like you out. And read this sign. What does this say?" He pointed to the red street sign bolted lower on the door, eye level to any six-year-old, Ryan and Katie included.

"Stop," Katie said.

"Stop," Lila repeated, nodding solemnly.

"Stop," Greg agreed. "But what do I find? A bunch of rugrats trying to break into my secret lair. You know better. Just for that, you're all banished from the second floor tonight as well. You're stuck watching the old television in the living room."

"Aw, Uncle Greg, we just wanted to show Ryan all the cool stuff you have in there," Jack said.

"Exactly why you're not allowed in there without me. That's *my* cool stuff." He snapped thc elastic on the back of Jack's head. "What's with the masks? You're all burglars?"

"'Course not!" Katie squeaked indignantly, propping her fists on her hips. "We're superheroes!"

"Superheroes don't break and enter. They leave that for the villains. Now, downstairs, all of you. Git!"

The three older kids scrambled down the stairs. Greg

descended behind Lila, who clung to the banister and took one precise step at a time.

There were just too many people in his life these days who didn't know where the stop signs were. As he headed back to the kitchen to put the five-cheese pasta in the oven for his masked gang of sure-to-be-starving-soon superheroes, his thoughts wandered back to Shannon, and the impulse to kiss her.

Hell, even he had a hard time observing the boundaries.

The good stuff always lay just on the other side.

GREG LOOKED OVER at the boy on the sofa. Apparently an evening of racing around his house playing superhero—the little TV hadn't held as much appeal as the wide screen in the theater room—had taken its toll. The movie they'd brought from his house when they'd returned to Shannon's apartment for the overnight portion of his babysitting gig had barely started, and already Ryan had crashed. The holes in the black mask he still wore revealed shuttered eyelids. Opting to let sleeping kids lie, Greg pulled a crocheted blanket from the back of the sofa and covered Ryan.

At the table, Greg opened his portfolio, pulling out some sheets of vellum, and tried to pass the time usefully, working on the latest issue of *Y-Men* he was sketching. But he hadn't worked outside his studio in a while, and it felt odd. Not to mention the fact that he was in her place.

An intense need to know more about her tormented him. He headed for her room. Once inside, he sat on the edge of the bed, giving the mattress an experimental bounce. The satin mask she'd worn the morning he'd scared her lay on the bedside table, along with a stack of hardcover library books. The top book was about changing your thoughts to change your life, using the wisdom of the Tao. Very Shannon. But the other two… *The Zookeeper's Wife: A War Story* and the biography of Charles Schulz, creator of the Peanuts…

Interesting. Not what he'd expected from her. Fascinating that a woman who seemed to so actively dislike comic books was reading the biography of one of the most famous comic-strip artists ever. But then she often caught him by surprise. A woman of contradictions. He'd love to know the why behind that reading choice.

And why he couldn't stop thinking about her.

He jumped from the bed to prowl the perimeter of the room, socks scuffing against the low-pile carpet. There was nothing on the top of her dresser, not a hairbrush, not a bottle of perfume or makeup, not a piece of jewelry. His sisters had always had cluttered dresser tops, overflowing with all sorts of girlie crap. But Shannon's austere lifestyle even reached her bedroom.

Greg's chest tightened.

Finn would have a field day with that reaction, but the truth was, he hurt for her. For both her and Ryan.

Enough mushy stuff. He eased open the top dresser drawer, hoping to learn more about her.

And came face-to-face with Shannon's secrets.

Or at least her lingerie.

Another surprise. Because there was nothing austere or Amish-like about the woman's taste in undergarments. He'd expected white cotton briefs. What he found was…not.

Matching bra and string-bikini sets. One was eggshell with eyelet details and a scalloped edge along the waistband. Another was midnight black with embroidered hot-pink flowers and a cream bow between the cups.

A soft pink set lay beneath the others.

It wasn't his chest that tightened this time.

He'd give his left hand—his drawing hand—to see her in the black.

"What are you doing?"

Greg jumped, slamming the drawer shut while heat flamed his face. "I'm not—nothing—" Realization dawned. "Ryan? What did you say? Did you talk? You're talking!" Heart hammering, Greg forced himself to slowly head for the boy. "That's terrific! Your aunt Shannon is going to be so happy, Ryan."

"I'm not Ryan. I'm SuperKid." The boy propped his fists on his hips, striking a pose like the ABC Men at the zoo. "You're not supposed to be opening Aunt Shannon's drawers. She doesn't like that."

Great. The kid starts talking and my ass is grass because the first thing he's going to say to Shannon is that I was pawing her underwear. That would score points with her. Scratch the possibility of ever seeing her in the sexy lingerie. "SuperKid, huh? That's cool. Should we call Aunt Shannon at work?"

Ryan shook his head. "She doesn't like it when Mrs. K. calls her at work."

Apparently Aunt Shannon had a number of dislikes, and Ryan knew all of them. "Okay. We'll wait and surprise her in the morning. Let's go watch the rest of the movie, huh, sport?"

He held out his hand, and the boy accepted it. Greg felt like celebrating with a touchdown dance. For whatever reason, the boy was speaking.

With any luck, Ryan's success story and the promo they could get out of it would be enough to save his program at the university after all. The dean loved positive press relating to the school. Not to mention it would look pretty bad to dump a program that heroically helped kids.

SHANNON TRUDGED UP the apartment stairs. The extra hours, while great for the paycheck, had taken their toll. She wanted nothing more than to crawl into bed and sleep. A pair of large, bare, masculine feet hanging over the end of her sofa brought her up short.

Ryan, the usual occupant of the couch, didn't have feet that size.

It wasn't that she'd forgotten Greg was spending the night in her apartment. But the reality of finding him on her couch at five-twenty in the morning was something else.

Did it mean she was developing a foot fetish if she admitted that those bare feet, so strong, so unabashedly male beneath the hem of his dark denim jeans, were sexy?

Shaking her head, she crept into the living room. Greg sprawled on his back, one arm dangling onto the floor. A picture-book version of *The Ransom of Red Chief* by O. Henry tented across Greg's chest. Ryan's favorite. They'd checked it out four or five times since he'd come to live with her.

Shannon gingerly plucked the book from Greg's torso, wincing at the crackling of the plastic library cover as she closed it and set it on the end table behind his head.

In sleep, without the distraction of the twinkle in his eye or the quick grin, the angles of his face—the high cheekbones, the sharp jawline—demanded exploration. She reached out.

No touching! Though her fingers yearned to caress him, she had to keep her hands to herself. A pity. Shannon fled the temptation, searching for Ryan instead.

She found him where she'd least expected to, in his own room, in his own bed. Score another point for Greg Hawkins. He knew how to get kids to sleep where they belonged. A black mask lay on the floor near the bed. Shannon picked it up, setting it on the computer desk on her way out.

She went to her own room, closed the door, and went through her morning ritual of darkening the room. It was odd to slide between the sheets knowing Greg was only a few feet away in her living room. She had no idea what time he had to head off to work, but that wasn't her problem. She had to grab what rest she could before Ryan got up.

She inhaled deeply and exhaled slowly, let her muscles relax, willing herself to sink into the mattress, into sleep.

It seemed like only minutes later that a harsh whisper woke her. "Shannon? I come in peace, okay? Let's not have a replay of our first bedroom scene, huh?"

She cracked open one eye, blinking against the light he'd turned on. "You're like Ryan."

He paused at the side of the bed. "I am?"

"Yeah. Cuter when you're asleep. Go 'way." She rolled onto her side, giving him her back. "Thanks, though," she mumbled.

"But I have amazing news. Ryan spoke."

"Wh-what?" She sat up. "He did? What did he say?"

Greg laughed. "A lot. Did you know he can recite all of *Red Chief?* Come on." He held out his hand.

She let him pull her out of bed, grabbing her bathrobe

as they passed the closet. Greg led her into Ryan's room, her heart hammering with excitement.

Greg leaned over the futon and shook the boy. "Ryan? Hey, wake up, sport. Look who's home. Aunt Shannon. Say good morning to her."

Ryan knuckled his eyes.

Shannon knelt on the floor. "Ryan? Hey, buddy."

He blinked a few times, glancing from one to the other. Then he shook his head.

"No what, Ryan?"

He tossed back the covers and bolted from the bed, then the room. The bathroom door slammed a moment later.

Shannon raised her eyebrows as she got to her feet.

Greg shrugged. "When a guy's gotta go, there's no time for words." He headed for the door. "I know what will get him talking."

She followed him as far as the bathroom, then waited there while Greg dashed to the living room. The toilet flushed, then water ran in the sink. A moment later Ryan reappeared.

"Sport, c'mere! Look, I have *Red Chief*. Let's read it to Aunt Shannon, huh?" The plastic crinkled as Greg waved the book.

Ryan turned his big eyes toward Shannon, gazing up at her. He slowly shook his head, then returned to his room.

"That's not talking." Shannon's stomach tightened. "What the hell kind of a game are you playing?"

"I swear to you, that kid was talking last night. Actually, I wasn't sure he was going to shut up once he got started. I don't get it." Greg dragged his hand over his face. "I don't get it."

"Maybe it was just a dream."

"It wasn't a dream. Dammit, that kid talked to me last night!"

"Well, he's not talking now. And I have to get some rest. Thanks for babysitting. I really appreciate it. But like Ryan, I'm going back to bed now."

"Ta-da!" Ryan, who'd obviously not gone back to bed, jumped into the hall, the black mask she'd put on the computer desk in place over his eyes.

Shannon pressed her palm against her chest, a lump swelling in her throat. So that's what he sounded like. It had been so long she'd forgotten.

"I'm SuperKid," Ryan pronounced. In a firm, *strong* voice.

Shannon wanted to sink to her knees and thank the universe. But she had to play it cool. Ryan's psychiatrist had advised her not to make a big deal of the fact that he didn't talk, so she couldn't make too much fuss that he now was. "SuperKid, huh? I wondered whose mask that was on the floor." She bent over and gave him a hug. "Now, how about I make us a special breakfast? What do you want?"

"SuperKid needs to be strong." Ryan flexed a nonexistent bicep. "So he can fight the good fight. How 'bout red-and-green eggs?"

"Seems like a plan to me." Amazed at just how normal Ryan sounded, Shannon headed for the kitchen. Well, the therapist had said he'd talk when he was ready. Apparently, he was right.

"Red-and-green eggs?" Greg asked.

"Tomato-and-spinach omelet," Shannon explained. "Ryan, take that mask off and go wash your face and hands so you're ready to eat."

"SuperKid doesn't take off his mask." Ryan set his feet wide and propped his fists on his hips.

"He does if he wants to eat at my table."

"Uh, Shannon," Greg started, "I think—"

"That's enough playing around." Though thrilled at Ryan's miracle, she was tired. She went over, pulled the mask off and handed it to him. "Go on. Put this away and get ready."

Ryan's shoulders slumped as he turned away.

"You want some red-and-green eggs, too?" she asked Greg.

"I don't think you understand what's going on with Ryan."

"And you do?"

"I believe so, yes."

Shannon lit the flame under the sauté pan and flicked some butter into it. "Enlighten me, Mr. Know-it-All." She stifled a yawn with the back of her hand.

Greg folded his arms across his chest. "No. I think I'll let you figure it out for yourself."

"So you're staying for breakfast?"

"Absolutely. I wouldn't miss this for the world."

"Red-and-green eggs?"

"As long as the green isn't artichoke, I'm game."

Shannon made short work of turning out three omelets. Greg poured orange juice. Ryan slouched in his chair, chin propped on his hand. When Shannon set his plate in front of him, he nodded.

Like he had every other morning.

"Ryan?" Knowing nagging and cajoling hadn't worked to get him to talk in the first place, Shannon searched for something that would entice him to respond. "Did you have fun at Greg's house last night?"

A halfhearted nod.

"What did you do?"

A lazy shrug.

Shannon shot a worried glance at Greg, who simply raised his shoulders and one hand. Saying very clearly in the silent language she'd become adept at decoding, *Don't look at me.*

"Did you have fun with Katie and the other kids?"

Another nod.

"Did you get into a fight with Jack this time?"

Indignant head-shake.

"Ryan! Why won't you talk to me? You talked to me just a few minutes ago. I'm sorry if I hurt your feelings about the mask."

Ryan shoveled eggs into his mouth.

Shannon pushed her plate away, no longer hungry and more than a bit apprehensive that she'd done something to derail Ryan's miracle.

Greg left the table, returning with the black mask. He slipped it on Ryan's head, carefully adjusting it so the boy could see. "There you go, SuperKid."

"Thank you," Ryan said, sitting up straighter.

"Tell Aunt Shannon what we had for dessert last night."

"We made chocolate-chip cookies," he said around a mouthful of omelet.

"Don't talk with your mouth full," Shannon murmured. There was something she hadn't expected to tell him anytime soon. "Cookies, huh?"

"Yeah. Me and Katie got to scoop the dough out of the bucket. Jack took them off the tray when they were cooked."

"Impressive." Shannon's mind whirled. What did it

mean that Ryan—or rather, SuperKid—would only talk with the mask on?

The implication made her stomach queasy. "G-Greg? Can I see you in the other room? Ryan, finish your breakfast. We'll be right back."

She didn't wait to see if Greg followed her, but darted to her bedroom. When the door closed, she spun to face him. "What did you do to him? You broke him."

CHAPTER SEVEN

"WHAT DO YOU MEAN, I broke him? Don't be ridiculous. I helped fix him. He's talking, right?"

"*Ryan* is not talking. SuperKid is talking. Not only did you push my nephew into multiple personalities, but thanks to you, his other personality is a superhero."

Greg's mouth dropped open like a ventriloquist dummy with no ventriloquist. Then he started to laugh, and for a moment, Shannon wanted to forget she didn't believe in using violence to solve problems and slug him. "I don't see what's funny."

"Oh, Shannon. Ryan doesn't have multiple personalities. He's pretending. The mask and the superhero persona make him feel safe. Empowered. Trust me, this is a great first step. Eventually he won't need the mask to talk to us."

"How do you know for sure?"

"Didn't you ever pretend as a kid?"

Head reeling, Shannon perched on the side of the bed. "Doesn't mental illness tend to run in families?"

"What? Was someone in your family mentally ill? Ryan's mother?"

"Just answer the question. Does it run in families or not?"

"It can," he said. "But I'm telling you, Ryan hasn't

disassociated into multiple personalities. He's using SuperKid as a safe haven to start talking to us."

"You'll forgive me if I don't take *your* word for it. I'm calling Dr. Lansing's office this morning as soon as they open. Hopefully he can see Ryan today." Shannon opened the night-table drawer, searching for the psychiatrist's card.

"Great idea. He'll tell you the same thing I have."

"Then I guess I'll owe you an apology." But right now, she wanted firm answers. From someone with more letters after their name than Greg.

LATER THAT AFTERNOON, Greg paused as he reached the beach, shielding his eyes with his hand. Wind blew in off the lake, stirring up small waves out beyond the break wall. A golden retriever with a stick in its mouth towed its owner past him.

Shannon sat on a blanket halfway to the water while Ryan, jeans rolled up to his knees, hopped around in the damp sand at the water's edge. The boy wore the mask.

Greg resisted the urge to pump his fist in victory. If Ryan was wearing the mask—in public, no less—then the shrink must have confirmed what he'd told Shannon. He trudged across the shifting beach surface, cursing under his breath as the sand seeped into his shoes. He flopped down beside her on the blanket.

"I see you got my message."

"I did. You really should get a cell phone." Greg untied his shoe, removed it, then dumped the sand out.

"I don't need a cell phone."

"If you had a cell phone, you could have called me from here and told me what Dr. Lansing said. You could have called me from Dr. Lansing's *parking lot*. So, spill it. What *did* he say? When do I get my apology?"

She glared at him, which made him want to laugh. If Shannon were a superhero, one of her powers would be vaporizing beams shooting from her eyes.

"I'm sorry," she said. "You were right."

"That wasn't so hard, was it?"

"Remember when I said you were exasperating?"

"Yes."

"Clearly I understated things."

Greg surrendered, letting himself laugh out loud. "My sisters would agree. So, details. What exactly did Dr. Lansing tell you?"

She wrapped her arms around her knees. "Ryan's fine, just like you told me. In fact, Dr. Lansing repeated you almost word for word. This is a positive first step. That the mask and the SuperKid persona make him feel safe. Empowered. I believe that's the term you and the social worker both used to get me to try the art therapy, right?"

Greg emptied his other shoe. "It was. To prove what a terrific guy I am, I'm not going to say I told you so. Still, with your dislike of superheroes, I'm surprised you're letting him run around the beach with the mask on."

"According to the psychiatrist…and you…he won't be a superhero forever. Eventually he'll be just a boy again. But if it makes him feel safe right now, after all he's been through, who am I to take that security away?" She lowered her head, her fluttering hands smoothing the blanket.

"You didn't have a very secure childhood, did you?"

She looked back up, her expression softening. "What gives it away?"

"I'd like to take credit for seeing it in your art, but no. It's in your demeanor. Your lifestyle. Your whole just-let-it-go attitude."

"Really?"

He nodded. "Yeah. Does it have anything to do with that mentally ill family member you mentioned this morning?"

She focused on Ryan. Waves lapped at the shoreline and gulls keened overhead, filling the silence.

"Would it be easier to talk about it if you had a mask on?"

Startled, she returned her attention briefly to him before watching the boy again. "Hmm. Yeah, I guess it would." Her fingers picked at the hem of her jeans. "My father. I don't know if he was ever diagnosed, but considering his behavior, I think maybe he was mentally ill. Bipolar or obsessive-compulsive." She shrugged.

"What kind of behavior?" he asked gently, bracing himself. He'd heard all sorts of stories from the kids he'd worked with.

"He gave away everything I ever cared about. Toys. Books. Clothes. There was always someone he knew who needed it more. We didn't *need* it. He even gave away our cat.

"My mother ran interference the best she could. Mostly she supported what he did. He was teaching us to be good people. To be givers. To help others. But..." She paused. "My mother died when I was eight. Dad got worse after that."

"Damn." He wanted to ask how her mother had died but didn't dare interrupt as she opened up to him.

"Yeah. Willow split the minute she turned eighteen

and didn't look back. My father died a month before my high-school graduation. I was already eighteen, so I finished school living with a friend's family, and then I followed in my sister's footsteps and left town."

That explained her lack of attachment to things. Or people. His admiration for her rose another notch. In her childhood, she'd learned it was better to just let go before she got too attached. Yet here she was, doing her best to parent and keep Ryan.

"You're an amazing woman, Shannon Vanderhoff."

"Not so amazing. You do what you have to. Enough about me," she said. "What about you? I guess you had a secure childhood, huh?"

"What do you think?"

She averted her gaze again, intent on the swirl she was drawing in the sand with her fingertip. "I think you're a lucky guy."

"Yeah. I think so, too." He reached out and stroked her face. The soft, smooth skin made him want to know if the rest of her felt the same. He had to taste her again. "Very lucky." He shifted closer, leaned in…

"Aunt Shannon! Lookit."

Greg retreated as Ryan charged for the blanket, cupped hands held in front of him.

"Hey, Uncle Greg! Look."

Shannon raised an eyebrow. "Uncle Greg? When did you become Uncle Greg?"

"Last night. Apparently it's something he picked up from Derek's kids." He shrugged. "No biggie. I'm uncle to so many, what's one more?"

They oohed and aahed over Ryan's green beach glass. "You know," Greg told him, "some people make jewelry out of that stuff." The slivers of old glass, once part of a bottle, had been tumbled smooth by the water of Lake Erie.

"Cool! SuperKid will find more. Here, hold this." The boy dumped the pieces into Shannon's hand, then scampered back down to the waterline.

Greg shook his head.

"Amazing, isn't it? Almost like nothing had ever happened." Shannon propped her chin on her knees, drawn up to her chest.

"What's wrong? You know he's okay, so shouldn't you be happy about it?"

"I am. But now that he's talking again, I have to call the D.A.'s office and let them know. I hate the idea of them asking him questions about that night."

"I can understand that." Greg peered at her more closely. The bags—more like steamer trunks—were parked beneath her eyes again. A few thin, red lines crisscrossed the white of her eyes, making her a perfect candidate for a Visine commercial. "You're exhausted."

"I'm running on about an hour and half's sleep, and it's been quite a day. Who'd think happy events would be emotionally draining?"

"Do you have to work tonight?"

"Yes."

"And do you have a sitter?"

Shannon's shoulders lifted, then fell. "I haven't heard from Mrs. K. yet."

"Tell you what. How about you let Mrs. K. have another night to recover from whatever bug she's got. I'll take Ryan with me, and you can go home to peace and quiet and get some sleep. I'll bring him over just before you go to work so you can say good-night to him, and I'll stay with him again."

"You don't have to do that."

"No, I don't *have to*. But I want to."

"Why?"

"Why? What kind of a question is that?"

She let her legs drop down, her body slumping. "An ungrateful one. I'm sorry. I guess I just wondered what we'd done to merit your going well above and beyond the call of duty. I mean, you don't babysit for your other clients, do you?"

He shook his head. "No, not usually. You really want to know why?"

"Sure."

Greg edged closer, catching a fleeting and tempting whiff of her coconut scent as he whispered, "I like Ryan. I like *you*."

She mustered a weary smile. "Despite my better judgment, I like you, too. For a comic-book artist, you're not half-bad, Greg Hawkins. But you probably shouldn't let your sister know you're coming on to me with flattery and favors."

"I won't tell if you won't."

She pressed her lips together with her fingers.

"Okay. Let's round up SuperKid and get out of here, huh? The sooner you go home, the more sleep you can get."

Shannon called Ryan over. The boy dragged his feet through the sand on his way, as if he knew beach time was over. His initial protests while Shannon dried his legs and brushed sand off him with a towel quickly subsided when she told him he was going home with Greg again.

"What do you say we grab some pizza for dinner?"

The boy narrowed his eyes behind the mask. "Not

artichoke pizza, right? Artichoke pizza makes SuperKid weak."

Greg laughed, ruffling the boy's hair. "No, I was thinking more like pepperoni."

"How about sausage?"

"That'll work, too."

"All right!" He wiggled impatiently as Shannon tied his sneakers.

"Wasn't that water still cold?" Greg asked. Though almost June, Lake Erie generally didn't warm up until July.

"Not for SuperKid," Ryan assured him.

"Of course. What was I thinking?" Greg extended his hand, then pulled Shannon up from the blanket. She shook out the towel and the quilt before folding them. They made their way toward the dune that led down to the parking area.

There was a rightness to their being together.

Like they were a family.

A family? What the hell was he thinking? Especially now that he knew just how deep her emotional wounds ran, how hard it would be for her to overcome her let-it-go tendencies. He stumbled, sliding down the last few feet of the dune. See what that kind of thinking got him? Off balance and shoes full of gritty, irritating sand.

A clear warning if ever there'd been one.

Shannon dumped the towel and blanket in the trunk of her battered old Taurus. The car probably didn't even have air bags. "Are you holding this thing together with duct tape and twine?" he asked.

"No, chewing gum and rubber bands. Hey, it runs fine. It gets us where we need to go. Who wants more than that?"

"As long as it's safe, I suppose."

Shannon stooped and hugged Ryan. "Behave for Greg, okay? I'll see you later, before I go to work." She straightened. "Thanks again. You're a lifesaver."

"So don't I get a hug, too?" He held open his arms.

She hesitated a moment. He'd only been joking, but she stepped into his arms and he wrapped her in an embrace. Once again the scent of coconut filled his nose and a sense of well-being centered him.

Weird. Completely opposite to how he'd felt only moments before.

Was he supposed to cave in to his attraction, or stay the hell away from her?

She patted him on the back, then pushed away, and the friendly hug was over long before he wanted. Greg held Ryan's hand and they waved as she backed out of the parking space. Then he swung the boy into his Tracker and buckled him in. "Okay, sport, let's go run some errands, then we'll get some sausage pizza and head home."

SuperKid gave him a thumbs-up.

HAYDEN MET HIM at the front door. That wasn't a good sign. Greg had barely gotten in the house, juggling two pizzas and a six-pack of dark ale, not to mention herding a mini-superhero who didn't want to be herded because he was more interested in watching the next-door kids shoot hoops, when his brother descended.

"Man, I'm sorry! I couldn't get her to leave. She was on the front porch when I got home, and just wouldn't take no for an answer. That is one determined woman, dude."

The woman in question hustled down the hallway, a

pie carefully cradled in her extended hands. "Greg! You're home. Look what I brought. I figured since you were too busy to share a chocolate-cream pie with me last night, I'd just bring one over tonight."

Ryan stepped out from behind him. "Chocolate pie? With whipped cream?"

Hayden crouched down. "Well, hey, Ryan. I didn't know you were coming over again. Gimme five."

The boy slapped palms with him.

Denise stopped short. "I didn't know *he* was coming over again, either. And I thought he didn't talk?"

"Hayden, take Ryan and dinner into the kitchen, will you?" Greg stifled the urge to throttle her. Even Hayden possessed enough instinct not to draw attention to the boy's dramatic recovery. Obviously she didn't.

"Sure." His brother collected the pizza boxes, balancing the six-pack carefully on top, then took Ryan by the hand, leading him around Denise. "Let's go, little man. You can help me find some paper plates."

Ryan stared over his shoulder at Greg, who nodded at him. "I'll be there in a minute, sport."

"Why are you babysitting that boy again? There *is* something going on between you and his aunt, isn't there?"

An upset, potentially angry female with a pie in her hands. Not a good combination.

Greg gently took the pie from Denise and set it on the bench in the foyer. "We're friends. Friends do favors for each other. Like you bringing this pie over. Thank you. But I thought I'd made myself clear. I don't know how to say it any plainer, Denise. We are *over.* A chocolate pie is not going to get us back together."

"Maybe you don't know it yet, but I do. There's something going on between the two of you, and I'm telling you now, she's not the keeping kind. That kid and his aunt will break your heart. And when they do, don't come running to me for comfort. Because I'm not waiting around for you. This is your last chance."

"Good," he murmured.

"What?"

"I said, food. I'm hungry, and my dinner's getting cold in the kitchen. Plus, Ryan doesn't know Hayden that well, so I should probably go check on how he's doing." He sidled toward the door.

Her lower lip quivered. "You always said you admired my determination. My loyalty. How I never give up."

"I did. I do. But I've discovered that there's a very fine line between persistence and stalking. You're crossing that line." He cleared his throat, shifting his feet in place.

"Really?"

"Yes. Really. I'm sorry. I don't mean to hurt you, Dee. You've been Elke's best friend since I was in kindergarten."

She tilted her chin up in defiance of the tears he could see gathering in her eyes. "You didn't hurt me. But you're not getting this." She snatched up the pie along with her purse. "And I might still be Elke's best friend, but *we* are *not* friends. Don't expect any more favors from me." Lips tightly pressed together, she looked at the pie, then at him.

He flinched, bracing himself.

She laughed, a cold, hollow sound. "You're not worth it. I'm not wasting this by tossing it in your face, no matter how tempting."

When the door clicked shut behind her, Greg heaved

a huge sigh. Hopefully she meant it this time. He headed for the kitchen, where Ryan knelt on a chair at the table, busily chowing down on a slice of pizza. Hayden raised one eyebrow in question, and Greg shrugged. "Well, guys, there's no chocolate pie for dessert. Maybe we'll just go get some ice cream instead."

"Chocolate?" Ryan asked, mouth smeared with red sauce.

"Is there any other kind?"

"Artichoke," the boy said, then giggled.

"Artichoke ice cream?" Hayden shook his head. "You have some strange taste, little man. We should hook you up with Finn."

The running joke between him and Ryan made Greg smile. And despite his protests to Denise, despite his love of chocolate, despite the conflicting signals he was getting, Greg had to admit, he'd developed a hankering for something different.

For a woman who liked artichoke pizza.

IN THE 2:00 A.M. DARKNESS of the apartment-complex parking lot, Shannon leaned her head against the steering wheel.

Breathe in, breathe out, let go.

She repeated the mantra a few more times before heading into the apartment. The light over the table shone down into the foyer, and she heard a chair shift as she climbed the stairs.

"Shannon?" Greg rose from the table, which was spread with papers and art supplies. "What's wrong? What are you doing home?"

"What are you doing *up?* I figured I'd find both of you guys sleeping."

He gestured at the comic-book pages. "I've had a bunch of business meetings lately, so I'm behind with this."

"Business meetings?"

"Yeah." His shoulders slumped.

"Try not to sound so excited. They didn't go well?"

"No, they didn't."

"Is there any way I can help?"

His wry smile was tempered with sadness. "Got a hundred thousand dollars you could lend me?"

"Absolutely. Let me just write a check. You don't mind if it bounces, do you?"

He chuckled. "Exactly my problem, too. Enough about my troubles. Now, you answer my question."

She set her purse on the kitchen island. "I got fired."

"Oh. That sucks. What happened?"

She sighed. "I fell asleep at my desk. First time that's ever happened. And I even had a nap today, thanks to you."

"I'm so sorry."

"It's just a job. I'll get another one. I was checking into doing something else anyway. A day job. Especially if Ryan's talking now. I couldn't keep this up."

"Just let it go, huh?"

"Exactly."

"I don't think Cathy's going to be happy. But I'm sure she'll spin it to your advantage. You're searching for a job that makes it easier for you to care for Ryan." Greg gathered up some of his papers, putting them into a large leather folder. He blew on another page, the ink still glistening. "The woman from the district attorney's office called."

"She did?" Shannon leaned against the counter.

"Yeah. The detectives are coming up on Saturday

to take Ryan's statement. I volunteered my workroom at the university for it, that way you can watch through the window."

"Through the window? I can't be with him?"

Greg shook his head. "She said if possible they like to talk to the kids alone. They're bringing their shrink, too."

"Great. I can hardly wait. Why Saturday?"

Greg shrugged. "The sooner the better, she said. Apparently the defense attorney is fast-tracking the trial. Probably to try to get it done before Ryan recovers and starts talking. Well, we fooled them." He punctuated the statement with a thin brush in the air. "Saturday is the soonest they can come. Eleven thirty. That's when I finish up with my second group of cancer kids on Saturday mornings."

Shannon shivered, then rubbed her arms, pacing a short circle in the kitchen. "What if he gets off, Greg? What if Ryan can't tell them what happened? What if he tells them something that doesn't fit the evidence?"

"Hey." He stopped packing his plastic supply case and came over to grip her by the shoulders. "Stop it. Take one step at a time, right?"

"Yeah. But..." The implications struck her hard. Not only could she potentially lose Ryan to his grandparents, an even worse case scenario would be losing Ryan to his father.

To the man who'd murdered her sister.

Greg pulled her into an embrace, stroking her hair. She tucked her face into the curve of his neck, inhaling deeply. The faint, clean scent of soap mingled with warm, musky man. She wished she could just lose herself in him. To forget all the problems she faced and just...enjoy. She lifted her head....

And found a hunger smoldering in his blue eyes, mirroring her own. "We're not supposed—"

"Shh. I've been wanting to do this all day." He slid his hands into her hair, cupping her head, holding her firmly.

Shannon shut her eyes as he closed the gap between them. Without hesitation, he crushed his mouth to hers, his tongue seeking entrance, which she gladly granted.

He walked her backward until she bumped into the counter. She fitted against him so perfectly. Pulling gently on her hair, he forced her head back, grazing his teeth over her neck, sending shivers of pleasure coursing over her.

She flexed her hips, and denim brushed denim as she arched into him like a demanding cat, needing more attention. He ground his erection over her sweet spot, and she gasped.

"Like that, do you?" he growled into her ear.

"Oh, yes," she panted. "More."

"I…want…you." He punctuated each word with a grind, while his nimble fingers opened the top buttons of her blouse and slid into the cup of her bra.

"No kiddi—oh." She moaned as he stroked her nipple to attention.

He changed up the rhythm, faster, slower, faster, then almost nonexistent, and her mind went blank. She clutched his back. "Don't stop!" she hissed.

His mouth fastened on hers again, his fingers, his body, all driving her closer and closer to the goal.

Almost, almost, almost…

She shuddered against him, an orgasm claiming her. After a few moments, the high was replaced with blessed languidness. She sagged weakly.

Greg supported her, pulling his lips from hers to stare at her with surprise. "Did you just…"

"Oh, yeah." Shannon blew out a long breath. "I did. And it was good."

His expression turned smug. "Cool." He waggled his eyebrows. "If you thought that was *good,* just wait. I can provide *great* if we're both naked." A slow grin lit up his face. "I think we just found your superpower. Besides vaporizing men with your laser-beam glare, I mean."

"Superpower?" Still dazed, she wasn't following.

"Oh, yeah. Remember those ABC guys? I dub thee Lady O. But I envision you with a much sexier costume than those guys." He fingered the eyelets along the edge of her bra. "Something skimpy. And I can't wait to see you in it. This was hot—" he cleared his throat "—especially for you. But I want more."

"Actual sex?"

"That's a start, yeah."

"Greg," she began, fumbling for the right words, "if you want more than that, I'm not sure we should go there."

"You just went there."

"I did." She stroked her finger over his high cheekbones, delighted to finally get the chance to touch them. "You're a terrific guy, Greg. You're great with kids, you're talented, you're compassionate…"

"Geez, why does that sound like a post-hookup kiss-off when we haven't even hooked up yet?" He slid his hands along her waist and pulled her to him again.

"I just want you to know what you're getting into. I don't generally get involved with guys like you."

"Comic-book artists?"

"No. Guys with forever in their eyes."

"And here I thought it was lust."

Shannon chuckled. “Oh, that was there, too. But tell me you’re not looking for what your parents have. What you grew up with.”

“I…um—”

“Precisely. I can’t give you that.”

The sound of Ryan’s bedroom door opening made them both jump. They moved apart faster than a speeding bullet, Shannon frantically fastening the top buttons of her blouse.

The bathroom door closed.

Greg adjusted his jeans. “I think you sell yourself short. You’re not the same person you were just a few months ago. And I’ll bet that scares the crap out of you, doesn’t it?”

Hell, yes, it scared the crap out of her, but she wasn’t about to admit it.

“Precisely,” he said in response to her non-answer.

For a moment, they just stared at each other across the narrow kitchen. “I’ll see you Saturday morning?” Shannon asked, moving into safer territory.

He glanced away from her, but not before she’d caught a flicker of…anxiety? guilt?…on his face. What was that about?

“Yeah. Saturday morning.”

CHAPTER EIGHT

SHANNON CLUTCHED Ryan's hand as they walked into the Children's Center. A dull ache throbbed in the back of her head, and a flock of gulls, like the ones in the campus parking lot, had apparently taken up residence in her stomach.

She didn't want to put him through this.

But there was no choice. Willow deserved justice, and that meant her sister's son had to tell what he'd seen and heard that horrible night.

They climbed the stairs to the second floor, and headed down the corridor that led to Greg's art therapy room. She'd arrived ten minutes ahead of schedule, wanting to show Ryan the observation room, to assure him she'd be nearby if he needed her.

Shannon came to an abrupt halt, processing the commotion outside the room. The unnaturally bright light, the crowd of people. She edged closer.

The light came from a television camera. A reporter held a microphone up to Greg, who was animatedly talking, gesturing.

The gulls wheeled and careened in her stomach.

"…not just cancer kids," Greg was saying. "My program helps many children who need empowering. Victims of child abuse, kids whose parents are going through a divorce, those who've lost a parent or sibling. This program is important."

"Have you tried to find another organization to sponsor your program?" the reporter asked.

"I have. They already have their budgets in place for this year, so they can't take on anything additional, even if they love the idea."

"Do you have any cases that stand out for you?"

"Yes." Greg caught Shannon's eye, looking straight at her. "A child who became mute because of a traumatic experience. If we're lucky, maybe his aunt will tell you about it."

The reporter followed his gaze.

With one hand, Shannon pulled the mask from Ryan's head, eliciting an indignant squawk from the boy. She shoved it into her back pocket, grabbed him by the arm and forced her way through the throng of gathered parents, some of whom she recognized from their excursion to lunch the day she'd met Greg. "Excuse me, let me through."

"Ma'am? Could we ask you some questions about your experiences with Mr. Hawkins's art therapy program?"

"Absolutely not." Shannon kept her body between Ryan and the camera. The media had hounded them in Philadelphia, going so far as to film Willow's funeral from across the street. Whisking Ryan away to Erie had the added benefit of making him anonymous again. She wasn't about to blow that by feeding the vultures for any reason. "I'm sure these other fine folks would be happy to sing Mr. Hawkins's praises."

"Please, Shannon," Greg pleaded as she barreled past.

"No!" She shoved Ryan into the observation room and slammed the door behind them.

The kids working in Greg's room all glanced up at the mirrored window as the wall rattled. Another cameraman was filming the children and their drawings.

Hands tightly clenched, Shannon paced. Greg had let her walk into an ambush.

Ryan's wide eyes stopped her. She crouched down. "I'm sorry if I scared you. I don't like reporters." She pointed to the window. "See the kids working in Greg's room? That's where the lady is going to talk to you. I'm going to be right here. So even though you can't see me, you'll know that I'm close by, right here, okay?"

The boy just stared at her.

Shannon pulled the mask from her pocket and slipped it on his head. "There you go, SuperKid."

He didn't say anything, just moved closer to the window. For the next few minutes, they watched the children clean up the art supplies and tables. Some parents wandered in, collecting their kids. Eventually the room cleared out and the commotion in the hallway died down. Shortly after that, Greg escorted a woman and two men into the room. Shannon recognized one of the men as Detective James.

The other man began setting up a video camera on a tripod, pointing it at the table. Greg rapped on the window and gestured for her to join them.

"Ryan, I'm going into Greg's room now. You stay here and watch me through the window, okay?" At his nod, she left.

"Ms. Vanderhoff." Detective James extended his hand. "Nice to see you again. This is Dr. Martin, a psychiatrist who works with us. She'll be the one questioning Ryan. And that's Detective Evans. He was assigned to the case after you left Philadelphia with the boy."

After the introductions and assurance that they had Ryan's well-being firmly in mind, Shannon returned to the observation room, her heart in her throat. Greg followed on her heels. She pretended he didn't exist.

Ryan was plastered to the window. Shannon stooped to his level. "They're ready for you, Ryan."

He shook his head and yanked off the mask, thrusting it at her. She grabbed both his hands in hers. "Ryan, remember we talked about this? These people are the good guys. They're police detectives. They're here to see that your mom gets justice. This is how we fight the good fight, remember? Through the justice system? They need you. Your mom's counting on you."

Tears welled up in the boy's eyes and Shannon fought the urge to scoop him up and run away with him. Her nose tingled and she blinked hard several times.

But she slipped the mask back on his head. "Superheroes are all about truth and justice. Isn't that *right*, Greg?" She growled his name, annoyed that she needed him to back her up.

He cleared his throat. "Absolutely."

"You can do this," she told Ryan. "Just go in there and tell the truth. No one's going to be mad at you. You're not going to get in trouble, whatever you say. There's nothing to be afraid of."

"SuperKid isn't afraid." The faint quiver in his voice said otherwise.

"Of course not." She willed her hand steady as she extended her closed fist.

Ryan bumped his fist into hers less than enthusiastically.

"I'll be right here, watching, okay?"

He nodded.

"Okay, sport, I'm going to take you in there and get you settled," Greg said. "Then I'm going to be in here with Aunt Shannon."

Shannon got to her feet as Ryan took Greg's hand. "You told them about..." Over the top of the boy's head, she gestured to her face, mimicking the mask.

"I did. They weren't thrilled with it, but..." Greg shrugged. "It's not like they have a lot of options right now."

Greg accompanied Ryan into the other room, providing him with paper and crayons. Something familiar for him. The doctor shook Ryan's hand. The other adults did their best to fade into the background. Greg tousled Ryan's hair and left.

Shannon turned on the speaker, facing the window. Warm-up chitchat started as Greg came back into the observation booth.

"Shannon, about the reporter—"

"Don't talk to me."

"I needed the press. You know how much this program means to me. I'm in danger of losing it. The *kids* are in danger of losing it."

She snapped her head around to glare at him. "*I'm* in danger of losing it right about now. And the only kid I care about is in there. So *shut up* and let me hear what's going on."

The doctor took her time getting Ryan comfortable. She complimented his drawing, and the mask, turned the talk to superheroes, the differences between telling a lie and telling the truth...

At first, Ryan answered nonverbally. Then with one or two words. Finally he offered short sentences.

Greg grunted. "She's skilled. Ryan's in good hands."

Eventually the questions veered to the night of Willow's death.

Shannon took a deep breath, willing all the strength she could through the glass to the little boy on the other side.

"Did you hear anything that night, Ryan?"

He nodded but didn't look up from his drawing. "Ryan heard yelling. It woke Ryan up. They were fighting."

"About what?"

He shrugged.

"Did they fight a lot?"

"Sometimes." Ryan deliberated on which crayon to choose from the box, then pulled out gray. "But not so loud."

"Then what happened?"

"Ryan's mom was crying. He went to see why."

"Where?"

"To their bedroom."

In the observation room, Shannon reluctantly turned to Greg. "Why is he using the third person? He's never done that before."

"He's distancing himself as far as possible from the events of that night. It's okay. It's a coping technique."

Ryan described how he'd snuck to his parents' room and stood, unnoticed, just inside the door. How he'd seen his father strike his mother, several times, until she'd fallen. The boy went silent and stopped drawing.

"What happened next, Ryan?" the doctor asked gently.

Shannon closed her eyes and leaned her forehead

against the window. Greg placed his hand on her shoulder, giving it a squeeze.

"Daddy got on top of her." Ryan's voice was barely discernible through the speaker.

"He's switched to first person," Greg whispered. "He's lost his distance. He's in the memory now, in that night."

That made Shannon feel even worse.

"On top of her how?"

"H-he, like, sat on her."

"Where on her body? On her feet? Her knees? Can you show me?"

Shannon opened her eyes to see Ryan point to his chest. "Here."

"Did Mommy say anything?"

Ryan shook his head. "But her fingers were, like, waving around, and her feet were kicking the air. She kept kicking and kicking…"

"And then?"

"And—and then…she stopped."

Shannon covered her face with her hands, stifling the cry that threatened to escape. The image of Willow, struggling to get air, to break free from her husband while her son watched, was horrifying.

Greg tried to pull her into his arms, but she shook her head, pushing him away. "Don't touch me. I—I have to stay strong. For him." She inhaled slowly, forcing herself to watch Ryan in the next room. If he could be strong and brave, so could she. Falling apart could wait until later.

Much later.

"What did you do, Ryan?"

"I—I just stood there. I was scared. Daddy got up. He looked scared, too. And mad. Really mad. He kicked her, but she didn't move or cry anymore. He called her bad names."

"Did he see you in the room?"

"Yeah," Ryan said.

"What happened when he saw you?"

"I—I wet my pants." The child started to cry. He pulled off the mask, threw it on the floor, then put his head on the table.

Shannon bolted for the door, but Greg grabbed her by the wrist. "No, Shannon! Let them finish." He jabbed the speaker on the wall, and despite her struggles, wrapped her in a strong embrace against his chest, preventing her from seeing into the art room.

She stood rigidly in his arms for a few moments, then gently banged her head against his shoulder over and over. "I want to hurt him," she said. "If he were here, I think I could hurt him. I hope they fry him. Bastard! I hope they fry him!"

Tears streamed down her face in spite of her best efforts to stop them. She looked up at Greg. "What kind of person does that make me?"

"A human one." He wiped at her cheeks with his thumbs. "Just human." Cradling her head in his palms, he leaned down and tenderly kissed her. Short but, oh, so sweet.

"What was that for?" She ran her hand across her nose after he released her.

"Distraction. The bathroom is down the hall on the left. You might want to, uh, you know, fix your face? It's probably better that Ryan not know his story got to you."

She straightened up. "Right. Listen, when they're done with him, will you take him outside to the playground? I have a few questions for them."

"If that's what you want, you know I will."

Halfway down the corridor, she once more came to an abrupt halt. She *had* known he'd do it, even before she'd asked.

So that was what it was like, to have someone you could depend on.

But then she remembered how he'd tried to throw them under the bus with the reporter.

More proof that the only person you could ever really count on was yourself.

TWENTY-SOME MINUTES LATER, Shannon emerged from the Children's Center through the back door. She headed for the playground that served the university's day care as well as the local community. With classes not in session and most of the students gone for the summer, the campus was largely deserted. Ryan, who had the entire playground to himself, lay on his belly on the edge of the swinging bridge, drawing in the sand with a stick.

Greg sat on a nearby bench, bent over with his elbows propped on his knees. In his hands, he toyed with SuperKid's mask.

Shannon dropped onto the end of the bench.

Greg didn't look at her, just kept fiddling with the elastic band. "Get your questions answered?"

"Yes." She now knew that Ryan's account coincided with the physical evidence. An autopsy had determined Willow's death to be caused by compression asphyxiation. Trevor claimed he'd been under the influence of sleeping meds and unable to remember the events of that night. However, toxicology tests hadn't revealed the presence of any drugs. Ryan's interview, despite the superhero persona and partial third-person narration, would help the case. "They're hoping Ryan will be able to tell the story again without the mask and without slipping into third person." Ellen, the A.D.A., would want to interview Ryan herself, soon, since she hadn't been able to make the trip to Erie with the detectives this time.

"Yeah, well…" Greg sat up. "I wouldn't expect that in the next few days. Actually, I don't think Ryan plans on talking to us at all right now. Not even through SuperKid. He wants nothing to do with this." He handed her the mask.

"So, what do we do now?" Shannon reluctantly tucked the black plastic into her purse. She'd grown rather fond of her pint-size, freckle-nosed superhero.

"We go back to the drawing board. Literally. We keep doing more of the same, supporting him, strengthening him, making him feel secure. And we hope." Greg laid his hand on her knee, patting it twice before squeezing it. "How are you holding up?"

"Okay. As long as I don't think about what he said in there."

"I'm sure… Look, Shannon, about the reporter—"

"Really, Greg, I don't want to talk about that."

"Well, I do." He released her leg and shifted on the bench, turning sideways to face her. "I didn't mean any harm. I'm just trying to save my program here."

"I didn't know it was in danger."

Greg grunted. "Remember those business meetings I told you about the other night? The ones that didn't go so well? My need for a hundred thousand dollars?"

Shannon nodded.

"Well, the new dean wants to put her own stamp on the university. She has the same distaste for 'comic-book artists' as you do. Did." He grinned. "Hopefully by now I've changed your mind. But it means I'm out so *her* pet project can move in. Shannon, I love doing comic books. I get paid for having more fun than any adult should. But my true calling is art therapy. Helping these kids. Individual therapy can continue easily enough without this space. But my group sessions… I have to have a place for those. An office of some sort. That means rent or a mortgage. Utilities. Insurance. A hell of a lot of things I don't have if the university kicks me out."

"I'm sorry. It's a worthwhile program, Greg. There's no doubt about that. But to ask me to discuss Ryan on camera… Do you have any idea how much media attention surrounded Willow's murder? An upper-middle-class man, whose family owns a chain of furniture stores in the Philly area, murders his wife with his child in the house? The news ate that story like your brother's chocolate cake."

"I know. I remember."

"But you set me up to walk into that anyway?"

He shrugged. "I didn't think. I was so caught up in my own stuff that I just didn't think about how you might react. I'm sorry." He offered his hand. "Forgive me?"

She pressed her lips together and was silent for a while. "Okay," she finally said, taking his hand. The physical awkwardness between them tingled. They stared at each other for a moment, then Shannon yanked her hand back. Forgiving him—or at least giving lip service to forgiving him—was one thing, going *there* again was something else entirely.

"I don't think you should be alone today." Greg glanced at his watch. "I have someplace to be this afternoon, but

I'd love you and Ryan to come with me. It might be just the thing to keep your mind off this morning."

"Uh-oh. Where?"

"The Children's Cancer Institute is sponsoring a picnic at Waldameer this afternoon. Captain Chemo is putting in a guest appearance, and I'll be signing *Captain Chemo* comic books as well as presenting a donation check from myself and my publisher. There will be food, and you can take Ryan on the rides." He cleared his throat. "There'll be reporters there, too. The woman from this morning is meeting me to continue the story. The newspaper is also sending someone."

Shannon looked across the stretch of grass at the boy who halfheartedly dangled a stick over the edge of the bridge. Much as she hated the idea of taking him anywhere near reporters, an afternoon at the local amusement park might be just the thing to perk him up.

Not to mention keep both their minds off the picture he'd painted for the detectives.

"All right. We'll go. But no pointing us out to reporters. I don't want you talking about him, either. Not even in general terms. All I need is for Lloyd and Patty to get wind of that. They'll call it 'exploiting the child' and add it to their list of strikes against me, I'm sure."

"Deal."

GREG'S FACE ACHED as he smiled for what he hoped was the final picture by the newspaper's photographer. He, Captain Chemo and Randolf Kendal, the president of the Children's Cancer Institute, posed in front of the Waldameer train.

"Okay, great. That's it, we're done. Thanks." With a wave, the photographer trotted to the park's exit.

Mr. Kendal folded the check and tucked it into the pocket of his jeans. "Thanks again, Greg. We appreciate all the support you've given the institute. I'm sorry we haven't been able to help you out in return. I promise, we'll see about getting your program into our next budget. That doesn't mean it will fly, but I'll do my best."

As Kendal left, Captain Chemo, aka Hayden, gave Greg a slap on the shoulder that appeared friendly but left his ears ringing. Then his brother leaned in to hiss, "Next time you design a superhero you might want me to impersonate, let's go more with a Zorro instead of the traditional, huh? Maybe a contemporary hero who wears jeans and a trench coat? These damn briefs are giving me a wedgie. And the tights are hot."

"I didn't hear you bitching when those two blondes were checking out your six-pack in that spandex." No fake abs of steel for Hayden, who worked out three times a week.

"There is that. Captain Chemo has scored four numbers today. But seriously, Gory, am I done?"

"Almost. Come say goodbye to the kids still in the picnic area." As they sauntered back to the pavilion, small boys ran up to Hayden to shake his hand. Captain Chemo also posed for several pictures, including one Greg took with a cell-phone camera at the request of a group of giggling teenage girls. Captain Chemo was immortalized with his mouth gaping open as he yelped.

The girls ran off, grabbing the phone from Greg as they darted past.

"What's the world coming to?" Hayden asked. "Would you believe one of those girls reached under my cape and pinched my ass?"

Greg bit the inside of his lip. "Sorry. I've heard

costumed characters are often abused, but I didn't think anyone would disrespect Captain Chemo."

"Where's the nearest phone booth? I am so out of this gig." Hayden scratched his head with his purple glove. "Hey, where *does* a Superhero change his clothes these days? Cell phones have made phone booths extinct."

After Hayden bid goodbye to the kids still hanging out at the picnic area with their parents, Greg did the same, then walked his brother to the restroom and waited until he emerged as himself once again, Captain Chemo tucked securely into a gym bag. "Just leave that in my Tracker on your way out."

"No problem. See you at home later."

Greg scanned the passing crowds, searching for Shannon and Ryan, who'd wandered off shortly after the arrival of the reporters and had been missing ever since.

"Or maybe I won't see you at home later."

"What?"

"Greg, you might be eighteen months older than I am, but you're still way behind when it comes to women. I've never seen you so, I don't know, entranced, before. What is it about this one?"

Greg shrugged. "I wish I knew."

"Is it because she needs a hero?"

Greg laughed. "I promise you, the last thing Shannon is looking for is a hero."

"She might not be looking for one, but you're sure playing the part. Cleverly without wedgie-inducing spandex, I might add. You're babysitting for the kid, spending way more time with them than I've ever seen you with a client, you got Cathy to rep her for the legal stuff..."

"Bye, Hayden. Thanks for playing Captain Chemo

today." Greg cuffed his brother on the shoulder to repay the shot he'd taken earlier.

"Next time, make Finn or Kyle do it," Hayden called after Greg as he trotted into the thick of the park.

He waved a hand over his head without turning. If Shannon had a cell phone, he could call and meet up with them. Instead, he was reduced to searching Waldameer end to end.

He found them standing in front of the Tilt-a-Whirl, Ryan tugging on Shannon's hand while she, pasty white, shook her head.

"Hey, guys. What's going on?"

Ryan dropped Shannon's hand and grabbed his, pointing at the ride.

"That's a great idea. Greg can take you on it, and I can sit on that bench over there and watch." She turned pleading eyes on him. "If I ride that thing one more time, I swear, I'm going to puke. I don't do well with rides that go in tight circles."

"Well, we certainly don't want you puking. Ewwww, gross, right, Ryan?"

The boy nodded. Greg once again rescued the damsel in distress. Maybe Hayden had a point. But hell, what man didn't want to feel needed? Important? He was definitely making a difference for Shannon.

But he'd been riding a Tilt-a-Whirl ever since he'd met her. The episode in her kitchen had left him reeling. He'd brought her to orgasm without even touching her…and he wasn't sure what to make of that. Had it been their chemistry that night, or would any source of friction have worked for her?

In other words, had she actually needed him at all?

As they spun, Ryan gripped the safety bar, closing

his eyes. The boy didn't appear to be enjoying himself, making Greg wonder why he'd had a fascination with this particular ride.

When the cart stopped, Greg held the boy's elbow as they staggered down the steps. At the bottom, Ryan broke free and ran to the bench were Shannon waited. He threw himself down and draped his arm over his face.

Greg raised an eyebrow at her.

She shrugged. "Beats me. He's done that every time he's gotten off the thing. I think they should call it the Tilt-and-Hurl."

"Not the best marketing strategy."

"Probably not." Shannon shook Ryan's leg. "How about we go on something that doesn't spin? What about the log flume?"

Ryan sat up, cocking his head to the side. Not an enthusiastic response, but not abject uninterest, either. And considering the experience Ryan had had earlier in the day, better than what Greg dared hope for.

"That sounds like fun. Can I come?" he asked.

Ryan nodded. He slid from the bench, holding his hand out to Greg. Instead, Greg swung the boy up onto this shoulders, eliciting a gasp and squeak from him. Holding on to his wrists, Greg headed for the log flume, passing a variety of stands that tantalized the nose with the scents of French fries, funnel cakes and hand-squeezed lemonade.

Once they got in line, he put Ryan down. The late-afternoon sun slanted into the park from over the lake. As they waited, a pair of youthful voices, one male, one female, called for Greg's attention. "Mr. H.! Yo, Mr. H.!"

Cheryl and Michael waved at him. Greg returned the gesture. Then Michael leaned over to whisper in Cheryl's ear. A wide grin filled her face, and the pair darted off.

"Uh-oh," Greg said. "That can only mean trouble." The Dastardly Duo had already narrowly missed being thrown out of the park for flying paper airplanes off the skyride. Kids their age often roamed the small family-friendly park without being tethered to their parents, who were probably sitting on a bench in the shade somewhere, exhausted from trying to keep up with them. It was almost a rite of passage in Erie, the first time your parents let you wander the park without them.

He kept an anxious eye out for the pair as they moved forward in the line but didn't see them. Soon Greg stepped into the back of the boat, with Shannon in front of him, and Ryan in front of her. As the ride climbed the first hill, she settled against his chest. He tightened his thighs around her, ignoring the pang of desire the position inspired. The wind fanned her hair, making it fly in his face.

At the top of the peak, the chain released the boat and it dipped free into the trough. "Look how pretty the lake is from up here," Shannon said.

The sloshing water rushed them along the turns and drops of the ride. When they hit the top of the final drop, Ryan shrieked.

They hurtled down the plunge, landing with a big splash that only dampened them. But then two blasts of water slammed into them. Shannon took the brunt of the hit, but enough nailed Greg's arms and face. Loud shouts came from the viewing area, where quarter-fed water cannons allowed guests to drench flume riders.

"We got you!" Michael yelled. "Score! We soaked you, Mr. H.!"

"You sure did!" Greg yelled back. "Just wait!"

Michael poked Cheryl, and the pair vanished into the crowd. As their log headed back into the carousel, Shannon wrung out the bottom of her T-shirt.

Ryan was miserable when Greg helped him out. Bedraggled hair framed Shannon's face, and…

God help him.

Her cream T-shirt had gone translucent and skin-tight. Beneath it she wore a pink bra with delicate decorations on the edge and thin, pink ribbons trailing down the middle.

One of the bras he'd admired on his late-night snooping session.

The heat that flashed through him was enough to evaporate all the water in the ride.

Hell, all the water in Lake Erie.

"Sir!" one of the ride attendants hollered. "You've got to get off the platform! Please keep moving!"

Shannon grabbed him by the hand and pulled him along with Ryan off the rotating surface to the more stable platform at the base of the stairs to the exit.

The unsteady sensation when he staggered onto the nonmoving floor reinforced the point.

Attraction to Shannon made him off balance. Mostly.

To the point that he kept forgetting the boy's needs. The custody battle. Shannon's track record for revolving-door relationships.

Somehow he had to find a way to maintain an even keel.

To keep the volatile chemistry between them in check.

CHAPTER NINE

"THE END." Shannon closed *The Ransom of Red Chief* and struggled up from the futon. Ryan knuckled his eyes, then rolled over and reached under the pillow to pull out another book. "No, it's time for you to go to sleep now. We've got to get on a normal schedule."

Ryan tapped on the cover of the book *Are You My Mother?* Shannon gently took it from him and placed both library books on the small bookcase she'd bought at the local consignment store. She knelt alongside his bed and tucked the blankets firmly around him. The story about the baby bird searching for its mother had obviously struck a chord in her nephew.

Shannon brushed back his hair, leaning over to kiss his forehead. "I'm not ever going to take your mom's place, Ryan. But I'm going to do my best to do all the things for you that she would. Your mom is watching you from heaven, and she's so proud of what you did today. She knows—and so do I—how hard it was. But you told the detectives the truth, and that's what matters." Shannon lightly tapped the tip of his nose. "Being brave and telling the truth? That makes you a real hero in my book, Ry."

His exhaustion-bleary eyes didn't buy it.

"I mean it. You're a real hero." She opted to change the

subject before either of them started thinking too much about what he'd said earlier. "Did you like Waldameer?"

A slow nod.

"Me, too. We'll have to go there again."

Ryan's mouth edged upward, and he spun his index fingers in circles.

"Maybe. No promises about the Tilt-and-Hurl." She ruffled his hair. The kid had been a mess of contradictions all day. Even the things he'd seemed to enjoy had become issues afterward, when he'd slumped into a deeper funk. Getting soaked on the flume ride had been the final straw for Ryan. Greg had received a phone call that had thrown him into a foul mood as well, and he'd quickly agreed to take them home.

"Go to sleep," she told Ryan. "See you in the morning." She blew him another kiss, then stood, turning on the train night-light he'd selected during their shopping trip to the secondhand store. She pulled his door shut.

In her bedroom, she faced a confusion of scattered furniture. She'd moved her desk out of Ryan's room and into her own to make it easier to use after he'd gone to bed. She'd started work for a company that employed virtual assistants, including bookkeepers. This way she could make her own hours, and even work from home during the day while keeping an eye on Ryan.

It beat night shifts, hands down.

But now she had to put the computer pieces back together with the miles—or so it seemed—of wires that connected everything. Monitor to computer. Computer to printer. Computer to Internet connection. The project also served to keep her mind from straying to the images of Willow that had haunted her all day long.

Before that, though, she needed the furniture in a

workable layout instead of the crowded jumble she currently had going on in the bedroom.

About an hour later, finally satisfied, Shannon started reassembling the computer. A soft sound made her freeze. She tilted her head. There was another gentle knock on her apartment door.

Shannon glanced at her alarm clock, but it just blinked a red 12:00, reminding her in its not-so-subtle way that she'd forgotten to reset it. She scrambled down the stairs, praying it wasn't another ambush visit by Patty and Lloyd. After the day she and Ryan had had, that would be the proverbial last straw.

She peered through the peephole.

Greg.

She flipped the lock and undid the chain, opening the door. "Hi. This is a surprise."

He pulled his hands from his pockets. "I just wanted to check on you. Make sure you're doing okay. Mind if I come in?" He didn't wait for an answer, just brushed past her and up the stairs.

"Why no, not at all." Shannon closed the door and followed him. He paced the length of her living room as restlessly as the new polar bear at the Erie Zoo had paced the perimeter of the exhibit's pool. Coiled energy radiated from him. "What's with you?"

He stopped, but bounced lightly on the balls of his feet. "Nothing. Like I said, I just wanted to see how you were making out after today. Ryan's sleeping?"

"Yes. Amazingly enough."

"And you?"

"I'm not thinking about it."

"Is that how you do it?"

"Do what?"

He waved his hands. "What you do. That whole let-it-go thing. You just don't think about it? How does that work?"

Shannon stared at him. The edges of his eyes were red. "Have you been drinking? Or something else?"

"What? No." He shoved his hands back into his pockets and resumed stalking the small space.

"Greg." Shannon eased onto the couch, patted the leather cushion next to her. "Sit. You're making me anxious."

"Sorry." He dropped onto the end of the sofa, facing her, one leg pulled up. He drummed his fingers on his knee.

"So, are you going to tell me what's going on?"

"I need to know how you do it. Let it go."

"Why?"

He shrugged. "Why not?"

Shannon shifted closer to him, took his twitching fingers into her hand. "What happened, Greg?"

He blew out a quick breath and stared up at the ceiling. "I got a phone call today."

"While we were at the amusement park?"

"Yeah. Turns out one of my former cancer kids, one who 'graduated' from my program a few years ago and was in college now…well, she relapsed." His gaze met hers. "Captain Chemo didn't kick cancer's butt this time. Cancer kicked hers. She died this morning out in California."

"Oh, Greg. I'm sorry."

He pulled free and jumped to his feet. "So how does it work? How do you let go of people like they never existed? 'Cause I'm not so good at that." He rubbed the center of his forehead. "It hurts, dammit, and I hate it. I don't want to feel this. Teach me how to cut off my feelings."

His words kicked her square in the chest. He thought she was cold? Unemotional? That she pretended the people who'd mattered to her never existed? "It's not like that. It's about acceptance. You accept that all things are temporary. You enjoy and embrace them while you have them. You cherish the memories you keep. Even pain is temporary."

"Thank God for small favors," he muttered, raking his hand through his hair.

"Surely you've lost one of your cancer kids before?"

"I have. And every damn time it kills a part of me." He prowled stiff-legged around the sofa, into the dining area where he stopped in front of the long double window that looked out over the parking lot. He leaned his head against the pane.

Shannon followed. She extended her hand toward his shoulder but stopped, dropping it back to her side. "Your empathy's part of what makes you so strong at what you do."

"You think?" His warm breath fogged the glass.

"Only someone who hates to lose can teach someone else how to fight for their life. Or for what they love."

"Or want?" He turned to face her, and before she could process the husky timbre to his voice, she was in his arms. His mouth crushed against hers, demanding. Mingled with desire, she could taste his need, his pain.

Her body answered with need of its own, her soul seeking to soothe its own pain. What better relief could she find than with him?

His hand trailed along her back to cup her butt. Heat from his palm radiated through the thin sweatpants she wore. The teasing caress became demanding as he pulled her flush against his body. His mouth trailed up her jaw toward her ear. "No more fighting this chemistry between us," he murmured, then nipped her lobe. "I need this. I need you. I'm going to have you tonight, Shannon."

"Not in front of this window you aren't." She reached behind and took his hand from its place on her bottom. "No more fighting. Embrace the gift." She led him from the room, flicking off the lights as they passed the switch.

She let him go ahead of her into the bedroom, then pulled the door shut, turning the lock. After switching off the overhead light, she reached for the sole remaining source of soft illumination, the bedside lamp. He grabbed her wrist. "No. I want to see you."

Before she could answer, he lifted the hem of her T-shirt, pulling it up over her head and tossing it to the floor.

Greg's mouth went dry.

She wore the black bra with the hot-pink flowers and tiny ecru bow in the center. The swell of her breasts rose over the embroidered edges, every bit as amazing as he'd imagined the night he'd pawed through her drawer. He sent a silent whisper of thanks to the Dastardly Duo and their water bombs at the park for forcing her to change her clothes, right down to her underwear.

"Beautiful," he said, reaching behind her with one hand to unclasp the bra. He slid the straps down her arms, exposing her breasts. "Even more beautiful."

The pain of the day forgotten, he bent, exhaling gently over one salmon-blush nipple. When it peaked in response and Shannon sucked in a quick breath, Greg drew the tip into his mouth.

She threaded her fingers into his hair, moaning softly. He continued to caress and tease.

Until the needy sounds she made deep in her throat spurred him onward. He shoved her sweats over her hips, sending the tiny black panties with them, letting both slide into a puddle of fabric around her feet.

Greg lifted her in his arms, carrying her to the bed where he unceremoniously deposited her in the middle.

"Hey! No fair. You still have clothes on."

"All's fair in love, war and the bedroom." A slow, predatory grin lifted the corners of his mouth. He pulled out his wallet, tossing two condoms on the bedside table.

"That's good to know." She scrambled off the bed, placing her palm square on his chest. "Since I plan to do this." She nimbly unbuttoned his shirt, then traced the exposed skin, lightly brushing the dark hair across his pecs. He shrugged out of the sleeves, adding the shirt to the growing pile on the floor.

She showered kisses along his abs while fumbling with the button and zipper of his jeans. Kneeling in front of him, she tugged them inch by painstaking inch down his legs.

Damn, he wanted her.

She paused when she had the pants just below his boxer briefs. "Hmm…"

"Hmm? That's not what a guy wants to hear when a hot, naked woman has just dropped his drawers."

"It's just not what I expected."

"Shit."

She laughed. "I expected boxers with a superhero print."

"My Y-Men briefs are in the wa—wa—" Greg lost

the ability to speak as she yanked down the underwear in question, immediately taking him into her mouth. "Ho—holy hotness," he croaked a minute later.

Her laughter vibrated around him, through him…

Warming a spot a lot farther north than he expected.

He needed her. More than just physically.

He grabbed her by her arms and hauled her up, claiming her mouth with a fierce kiss while walking her backward until she bumped into the bed.

They tumbled down together, him settling between her legs. She arched against him, slick against his skin. He groped blindly on the night table for a condom, made quick work of getting it on.

She reached between them, taking him in hand and guiding him. She raised her hips as he eased inside, and drew a deep breath, closing her eyes.

When he'd buried himself to the hilt in her warmth, she raised a hand to his chest.

He recoiled, withdrawing. "Am I hurting you?"

"No. Come back."

He obliged, once more slowly sinking as far as possible.

"Don't move," she purred, as he prepared to withdraw again.

"Don't move?" he croaked. His erection pulsed in the silkiness of her body, *demanding* he move. His arms trembled with the effort of holding himself up, holding himself still.

And yet, it was perfect. The two of them linked as he'd never felt before. A moment, suspended in time.

One moment, one night, was never going to be enough for him. But he'd learned enough from her to try to leave tomorrow's worries for tomorrow. If he had to seduce her over and over again, well…it wouldn't exactly be a hardship.

Besides, he was used to fighting for what he wanted. Needed.

"Is this some kind of kinky Zen thing?" he finally whispered.

"Yes," she whispered back, not opening her eyes. "Kinky. Zen. Shh." She clamped her muscles around him, causing waves of pleasure that made him grit his teeth.

She caressed his chest. His heart pounded beneath her palm.

Sweat beaded across his forehead.

She rocked ever so slightly. He followed her lead, moving just enough to control the need.

"Greg." Sweet chocolate eyes stared up at him.

He wanted to melt into them, into her. "Shannon?"

"Embrace the gift. Now."

He lowered himself against her, groaning into the curve of her neck as he began the rhythm. "I thought you'd never ask."

Male ego demanded he make good on his great-if-we're-both-naked promise.

He drove her higher, faster, harder, until they were both panting and soaked with sweat. Choked-back moans rumbled deep in her throat, egged him on, made him hold tightly to control when she pulsed her pleasure around him. He slowed to a languid pace.

The second time he pushed her over the edge, she clutched his back and gasped his name, making it even harder to maintain his tenuous grip on control.

When he slowed once more, her eyes slowly fluttered opened. "You—you haven't?"

He shook his head. "Third time's the charm."

She chuckled softly. "Superheroes are *so* jealous of you."

He stilled, then bent his arms, leaning down to brush his lips over hers. "Any guy with an ounce of sense is jealous of me right now. Because I'm here with you."

She met his tentative thrust enthusiastically. "One more time, Superlover. But this time, fly with me."

He'd never been with a woman so damn responsive.

She *did* make him feel like a friggin' super man.

"Now," she said, a few minutes later, as the first ripple of her orgasm gripped him. "Now, now, now!"

Forget flying. He let go and fell with her.

Fell hard.

Shannon didn't think she'd ever move again. Every muscle in her body felt like an overcooked strand of pasta. Eyes closed, she let the afterglow run its glorious, mind-numbing, soul-soothing course, only vaguely aware of Greg's moving from the bed, returning, then pulling her to his side, settling her head onto his chest, wrapping his arms around her.

He stroked her hair. She mustered enough effort to purr, content to just be held in his warm embrace.

But the sweat evaporating from her body made her shiver. He shifted again, dragging the blankets over them.

For a few more minutes she floated, listening to the steady thud of his heart, anchored only by his arm draped around her shoulders.

Then he had to go and talk, his voice not only in her ears, but rumbling through his chest, her pillow. "I just noticed. You brought the computer and desk in here. That's terrific. You're acknowledging Ryan deserves his own space."

Ryan. Willow.

Images she didn't want, images she'd banished for most of the day, flashed through her brain. The afterglow vanished. She groaned. "Your pillow talk could use work, comic-book boy."

"Comic-book *boy?* A few minutes ago I was Superlover."

"A few minutes ago you knew when to be quiet." She sat up, the blankets falling away along with her failing grip on her emotions. "Just as well, though. I'm going to hit the shower. Do you still have my key?"

He nodded.

"Then you can lock the door behind you on your way out."

His blue eyes flickered his hurt. He quickly narrowed them. "Here's your pants. What's your hurry?"

She shrugged, heading for the closet. "I have no idea if Ryan will sleep all night or not. We're trying to get back on a 'normal' schedule. I think it would be best if he didn't find you here, naked, in my bed. Don't you?" She pulled on her satin robe, tying the belt.

"Don't hide behind the kid. If you want me to leave, I'm going." He slid out of the bed and jumped into his jeans. "My pillow talk might need work, but your kiss-off needs more."

"I'm sorry, Greg. I'm not…I can't…" Her lower lip started to tremble, and she bit it. Better he think her a bitch than to melt down in front of him. Bitches got respect. Blubbering women were just…weak. "I really need a shower." She fled, doing her best to keep quiet in the hallway. Once in the bathroom, she started the water, but waited until she heard the main door open and close before she climbed in.

Steam billowed around her. She bowed her head, the

hot water pounding her neck. The day's pain, from putting Ryan through telling his story, to the images of her sister's death, rose up. Shannon did her best to stuff it back down, to wrestle it into submission.

It didn't work. Even sleeping with Greg had only temporarily held it at bay.

So she let it come.

As though she stood behind Ryan in the doorway of Willow and Trevor's room, Shannon saw her sister, trapped beneath the bulk of her husband, feet kicking, hands twitching…

Then stopping.

The breath, the life, crushed out of her.

While her little boy watched.

"Oh, Willow." Shannon turned into the spray, allowing the water to mingle with her tears. "I'm sorry. I'm so sorry. I wish…"

I wish I'd said something about my misgivings the first time I'd met Trevor, or when I realized you'd confused material comfort with security…

I wish I'd been there for you…

I wish I'd fought to keep you closer…

Sinking to the floor of the tub, Shannon drew up her knees, resting her forehead against them. She wrapped her arms around her legs. The water cascaded over her, picking up her tears, then gurgled down the drain. She tried to envision her pain going with it.

Wishes wouldn't change anything.

CHAPTER TEN

AFTER USHERING RYAN into the entryway of the center, Shannon shook the water from her umbrella and folded it. With only a few summer classes in session, the building had a deserted air. The *squeak-squish-squeal* of their damp sneakers on the floor echoed along the hallway as they headed to Greg's workroom.

He'd canceled their session earlier in the week—something had come up involving to his sister's wedding, or so he'd said—and then he had insisted they meet at the center, not at her apartment.

She'd hurt him. She knew it. She was less sure how to go about fixing it.

Ryan stopped in the doorway, shaking his head.

"It's okay, Ryan. It's just us today. No detectives." Shannon nudged him forward, setting her purse and umbrella on the counter beside a pile of crumpled Baby Ruth wrappers. Maybe she should have brought chocolate as a peace offering.

Greg turned from the window that overlooked the playground. "My next client is here," he said into his cell phone.

His client. Ouch. She'd been seriously downgraded. She'd gone from friend to lover then back to client in two easy steps.

"Keep me in the loop. I'll talk to you later." He snapped his phone shut and tucked it in his pocket, then sank to one knee in front of Ryan. "Hey there, sport. How's it going today?"

Ryan shrugged.

"You ready to work?" Greg held out his closed fist.

Ryan rapped knuckles with him.

"All right." Greg stood, finally acknowledging her. "Shannon."

"Greg. Listen…"

He held up his hand, palm out. "Let's get right down to it, shall we?" Gathering supplies from the shelves, he spread crayons, pencils and markers on the table, motioning for them to take a seat.

Shannon sank into the small chair, accepting the sheet of paper Greg slid over to her. No matter how she tried, she couldn't get him to make eye contact.

"We're going to fold our paper in half like this, and then again like this." Greg demonstrated, then helped Ryan make the folds. "Remember how we used pictures to tell the story of our zoo trip?" That lesson had come after the one Patty had interrupted with her "good" news about Ryan living with her and Lloyd.

Ryan nodded.

Shannon felt invisible. Which made it hard to apologize, or make amends to him.

"We're going to do that again today. I'll tell you what story we're going to draw in a minute. Right now, though, let's do this." Greg used a black marker to further define the panels on the paper. Ryan watched and duplicated the process. "That's right," Greg said.

Shannon prepared her paper, fighting the urge to write

I'M SORRY in big red letters on it, fold it into an airplane and fly it at him. Pointy end right into his forehead.

Maybe that would get the message to him.

Most guys would have been thrilled to have the incredible, mind-blowing sex they'd had, with no strings attached.

Her mistake for sleeping with a man who couldn't appreciate temporary gifts.

Someone who expected more.

"Ryan, the last time you were in this room, you told a story to the detectives. The story of what happened the night your mom died."

Shannon jerked her head up so fast her neck muscles seized.

"Aunt Shannon and I heard you from the observation room." Greg pointed to the mirrored window. "Today we're each going to draw that story."

Shannon shot out of her chair, knocking it over. Ryan and Greg stared at her. "Can I see you in the hallway?"

"No." Greg shifted closer to Ryan, lifted the boy's chin in his hand. "Ryan, look at me. You've already told this story. You're just telling it again in a different way. The cat's out of the bag already. Okay?"

Ryan lowered his eyes, but gave a nearly imperceptible nod.

"Attaboy." Greg offered him a box of crayons. After Ryan took it, he moved to the far end of the table with his paper.

Greg extended a pencil to her. "You, too, Aunt Shannon. Draw what Ryan told you about that night."

Stomach churning, she snatched the pencil from him, then righted the kid-size chair. She plonked herself into it and dragged her paper back from the center of the table.

Hands clammy, she adjusted her grip on the yellow wood, then set the tip to the page in the first box.

The images came unbidden to her brain. Graphic, horrifying visions. The very ones that had made her banish Greg, driven her to the shower to weep out her pain, her frustration. To try to let it all go.

Try as she might, she couldn't make the pencil move.

She glanced at Greg, whose fast-sketching fingers were already covering the paper with images. She cleared her throat.

He ignored her and kept drawing.

At the far end of the table, even Ryan was busy recreating the scene from that night.

If he could do it, she could. He was just a little boy. She was an adult, who excelled at dealing with pain.

She rolled the pencil along her fingers, then put the tip to the paper again. When she began to move it, the point snapped.

Greg handed her another one. She caught his eye as she took it. *Don't make me do this,* she mouthed to him, shaking her head.

He raised his eyebrows and glanced at Ryan, then back, as if to say what she'd already told herself.

So Shannon began, making ever-so-soft strokes that left behind almost invisible lines. The first panel wasn't so bad. She drew Ryan, in his bed, sitting up, rubbing his eyes. Hearing noises from another room.

Pins and needles tingled in her right hand as she moved on to the second panel. Shannon stretched her fingers a few times, but the sensation only got worse. The image of Ryan in the doorway began to take shape. The boy's form loomed in the foreground of the picture, taking up most of the space. In the background, she sketched a tiny version of her sister, tears streaming down Willow's face.

The tingling spread to Shannon's left fingers as well.

Ignoring it, she started the third panel. A giant hand appeared. Shannon stole a few quick peeks at Greg's hand for a model. But she couldn't imagine him ever raising a fist against a woman. Or a child.

The lines appeared darker now. Shannon's feet got into the tingling act. She curled and released her toes inside her sneakers as she sketched Willow's face—the target of the giant hand.

Shannon paused to rub her chest.

Greg got out of his chair. As he passed behind her, he leaned over to examine her paper. He grunted. "That's not bad. You might have a future in comics."

"Thanks but no thanks," she said, her voice breathy.

He stared at her for a moment, then strode to Ryan, crouching beside the boy. Greg made quiet comments Shannon couldn't catch, gesturing at the child's picture, then patting him on the shoulder.

The point of Shannon's pencil hovered over the empty fourth panel. The final box in her story strip.

There was only one image that could go here.

The pins and needles in her right hand had progressed. Or stopped. In any case, Shannon couldn't feel anything. She set the pencil down and flexed her fingers a few times, then massaged her hand.

She would finish this, damm it.

She picked up the pencil and drew furiously—until this point snapped, too.

Greg and Ryan both glanced over at her.

"I'm sorry, I'm sorry." She snatched another pencil

from the center of the table, and continued drawing Trevor's back.

A wave of dizziness made the room—and her head—spin. The pencil rolled across the paper as she pressed her fingers to her temple.

"Shannon?"

The pictures on the walls blurred. A tight band circled her ribs, and her heart pounded. Shannon tapped her fingertips on her breastbone. "I—I can't breathe."

Greg was beside her in a flash. "What's wrong?"

"Can't…can't…breathe."

"It's okay."

"Not…okay."

Through her hazy vision, she could see he'd gripped her right hand, but she couldn't feel it. "What's…happening?"

"You're breathing too fast, Shannon. Take a slow, deep breath."

"Can't. Get. Air."

Greg's own heart thudded as he planted himself on the table in front of her. Had he pushed her too far? The exercise was supposed to reassure Ryan that his story was already out. Who knew Miss Control Freak would crack like this? "Yes, you can."

Ryan ran to hover next to her, anxiously glancing from his aunt to Greg.

"You're scaring the crap out of Ryan." Greg leaned closer, putting his face next to hers. "Hell, you're scaring the crap out of me. Listen to me, Shannon. You have to slow your breathing. Just like that day out on the porch. Remember? Breathe in deep." He squeezed her fingers hard. "Do it!"

She gasped, panting.

He transferred his grip to her shoulders. "Shannon. You have to get control. Close your eyes and listen to me."

She shut her eyes.

"Breathe in. More. Good. Hold it. No, hold it. Okay, let it out slowly. Good. Again. Breathe in slowly. Hold it. Exhale. That's it." Over and over, he repeated the process until her muscles relaxed under his fingers, and her chest rose and fell in a more natural pattern.

Tears spilled from her closed eyelids, and he wiped them away with his thumbs, his anger at her easing with every tear.

"Don't cry," said a soft voice to Greg's left.

Shannon's eyes flew open, and she turned to her nephew, whose lower lip trembled as he reached out to pat her shoulder.

"Ryan?"

"Don't cry, Aunt Shannon."

Greg leaned back on the table, making room so Shannon could scoop the child into her arms. She embraced him tightly, rocking in the chair.

"It's okay," he said. "It's okay." He patted her on the back.

"Yes, my brave boy. You're right. It *is* going to be okay." After a few moments, she eased him forward on her lap so she could look at him. "I know I told you this the other night, but I mean it. You're a real hero to tell this story for your mom."

Ryan leaned into her, snuggling beneath her chin. "Don't cry," he said again. "I love you."

Shannon smoothed his hair, then kissed the top of his head. "I love you, too. We're going to get through this together." She looked at Greg. "I'm sorry," she said.

The tightness in Greg's abs loosened. "For what?"

"The other night. This is what I didn't want you to see."

Always go with the smart-ass remark when you don't want them to know how much they hurt you. "You hugging Ryan?"

"Me falling apart. I hate blubbering."

"I know. You're a control freak."

The affront in her expression faded. "I suppose I am. I didn't want you to think I was weak."

"Weak? You're one of the strongest people I've ever met, Shannon."

"And me?" piped Ryan. "I'm strong!" He made a muscle to prove it.

Greg chuckled, tweaking the boy's arm. "Yeah, you, too, sport. It must run in the blood." He hopped off the table. "What do you say we clean things up? I think we've accomplished all we needed to for today."

"But I didn't finish my picture," Ryan said.

"Trust me, sport. You did enough." Enough to make him start talking again. Of course, it had been Shannon's tears that had moved the child to finally speak again—this time as himself, not SuperKid.

God knew the tears had moved Greg. Every time he thought he had her completely figured out, she surprised him.

Like her declaration of love for the child.

Granted, it was a response to Ryan's own declaration, and she'd probably been in shock that he was speaking again.

But Shannon "keep-the-world-at-arm's-length" Vanderhoff had used the *L* word.

Only a fool would take hope from that.

Damn, damn, damn! Who was he trying to kid? Besides himself?

His heart was gone. Melted into fondue by both the woman and the boy.

At least melted things couldn't break.

The fight to convince her that she needed him as well as Ryan had only just begun.

AMAZING, THE DIFFERENCE a month could make. Shannon leaned on the railing of the Hawkinses' upper deck, watching below her as Ryan climbed the ladder of the pool's slide. He yammered away at Jack, who was right behind him.

These days her nephew was silent only when he fell asleep.

The Hawkinses' annual Fourth of July picnic was in full swing. The sliding glass doors to the kitchen were wide open, and people milled about in both directions on the deck that wrapped around three-quarters of the house.

Smoke seeped from the closed grill, where Finn, beer in one hand and spatula in the other, kept watch. Though she'd finally mastered the Hawkins-family basics, Shannon couldn't keep track of all the new folks she'd been introduced to. She turned her attention back to the pool.

Greg stood at the bottom of the slide, arms open. Water on his wide shoulders glistened in the sun. "Come on, Ryan. I'll catch you."

The boy hesitated only a split second before launching himself down the water-greased blue plastic with a shriek.

True to his word, Greg caught him as he hit the water. "Way to go, sport." He bounced up and down with the boy in his arms, making miniwaves as he carted Ryan to the edge of the pool and set him back on the wooden deck. Ryan shook like a dog, making Katie, now soaked, squeal, then he ran to get back in line at the ladder.

Greg glanced up and caught her watching him. With a broad grin, he spread his arms wide in her direction. "Come on, Shannon. Jump. I'll catch you."

She laughed. "I don't think so."

And yet, a quiet voice inside her said if ever she was going to jump, he was the one to jump to. To count on.

Greg made a face at her and slowly submerged himself, then popped up, water sluicing down his abs.

A flash of heat ignited deep in Shannon's belly.

They hadn't been intimate since the disastrous night she'd put him out of her bed and hurt his feelings, but sparks continued to arc between them anytime they got close. So they did their best to keep their distance. Neither of them mentioned that night, leading Shannon to believe Greg had truly forgiven and forgotten. She'd been promoted back to friend. He'd been there for her in every other way, from continuing his sessions with Ryan, to taking them both out for ice cream—chocolate, of course—to painting a wall mural in Ryan's bedroom at her request.

A mural that wasn't finished, but due to be unveiled soon, he assured her.

Greg had insinuated himself into her everyday existence almost as much as Ryan had. It comforted her at the same time it made her uneasy.

Waiting for the other shoe to drop, no doubt.

Shannon decided to wander. Finn had made her a gourmet burger with feta cheese and spinach and she loaded her plate with potato salad and corn on the cob.

Chatting with various Hawkinses as she ate, Shannon enjoyed the laughter, and the occasional ambush by either a child or one of the Hawkins boys—though the youngest was twenty-four, their mother insisted they were all still boys—with a water balloon or water pistol.

Even some of the grown-ups took turns on the trampoline.

When the sun set, Hayden started a bonfire, while the kids collected sticks. Shannon stuck a marshmallow on the end of Ryan's, showing him how to hold it just far enough from the fire to toast the white surface golden brown. Three marshmallows later, Ryan took off with Katie and a bunch of the other kids to catch fireflies along the edge of lawn where the woods began.

On the far side of the bonfire, Lydia Hawkins leaned back in the circle of her husband's arms, the pair laughing softly at some private joke. Michael nuzzled her cheek.

That's what forty-six years together looked like.

A sense of longing filled Shannon.

"About time I caught up with you alone," a familiar deep voice said in her ear, sending a tingle of awareness down her spine. "Can I hold you tonight? Please? I'm not asking for anything more. Just that."

She nodded, and Greg led her to a lounge chair, sinking down onto it. She settled between his legs, resting against his chest.

Overhead, stars flickered in the sky. Wood smoke mingled with the scent of the citronella torches. The fire crackled and popped; laughter and the low hum of conversation floated on the light breeze.

Shannon closed her eyes, relaxing into Greg's body, into his warmth. He held her loosely around the waist, as though afraid to grip her too tightly, skimming his fingers along her arm.

She took a deep breath and held it.

After a moment, Greg whispered, "You can't hold your breath forever, babe."

But she wanted to. It was a perfect moment. Instead of savoring it and letting it go, she wanted to hang on to it.

Forced by the laws of biology to exhale, she let the air out slowly.

The logs in the fire shifted, sending a cascade of red sparks into the air. In the distance, a child giggled.

Another perfect moment.

And that, Shannon supposed, was the problem with trying to hold on to any one moment. You'd end up missing the next one, be it better or worse.

"Time for the fireworks," someone called.

Greg nudged her from the lounge despite her protests. "Come on. We can see the university's display from the deck." The kids were gathered, and they all made their way up. Greg ushered her to the railing, where he fitted his body to her back again, wrapping his arms around her waist. Ryan, Jack and Katie appeared, slurping red-white-and-blue ice pops in various stages of melting.

Greg pressed her against the railing as the first burst of color lit up the night sky. Every nerve in her body leaped to attention, craving him. The children oohed and aahed, except for the youngest ones, who covered their ears.

By the time the display ended, Ryan was slumping in a chair, head wobbling. Shannon sighed. Much as she didn't want to leave, it was time to take him home and put him to bed.

Greg was one step ahead of her. He scooped the sleepy child into his arms. Ryan rested his head on Greg's shoulder.

"I'm taking these guys home, Mom," Greg told his mother when they passed her in the kitchen.

"Worn out, is he?" Lydia stroked Ryan's back. "I'm glad you could come."

"Thanks for having us. It was wonderful."

"You're welcome anytime. I mean it." Greg's mother folded Shannon into a warm hug.

Shannon stood stiffly for a moment, then put her arms around the woman and hugged her back. She was soft and squishy and smelled of wood smoke. More than twenty-five years had passed since Shannon had felt the warmth of a mother's embrace.

"If you need anything, you let us know," Lydia said as they disengaged. "We'll all be thinking about you next week."

Greg groaned. "Aw, Mom. You weren't supposed to mention the trial. I thought I'd been clear about that."

Shannon forced a smile. "No, it's not a problem. Really. Thank you. We can use all the good wishes we can get."

Back at her apartment, Greg carried Ryan in and laid him on the futon, which was currently in her bedroom. Ryan's room had been off limits to everyone except Greg for the past two weeks while he worked on the mural.

Shannon removed Ryan's shoes and clothes, wrestling the limp body into a pair of pajamas while Greg leaned against the door frame. When she looked up at him, he smiled.

"What?"

"That's an advanced parenting skill, in case you didn't know. The less skilled of us call it quits after taking off the shoes and socks. You've come a long way."

Shannon covered Ryan, then stooped to press a kiss against his sticky cheek, catching the faint taste of cherry. Tomorrow she'd not only have to make sure he got washed, but the bedding as well. She followed Greg into the hallway, turning out the light and closing the door behind her.

"Hey." Greg hesitated, then pulled her lightly into his arms. "Sorry about my mom."

Shannon shrugged. "I can't ignore it much longer. Trevor's trial starts next week, and I'm going to have to take Ryan down there and watch them put him on the witness stand, where he can tell the story *again*." Ryan had now told it to the A.D.A. several times as she prepped him for the case. But this time would be different. This time his father would be in the room. Along with a defense attorney who'd get to cross-examine the child. "The very idea makes me sick. But we don't have a choice."

Greg stroked her hair. "You know I'm going with you, right?"

Shannon's relief was so strong, her knees wobbled. She looked up at him. "You are?"

"Yeah. For one thing, I'm not about to let you and Ryan drive all the way to Philly in that piece of crap you call a car."

"Oh. Thanks. I think."

"And for another…" He framed her face with his hands. "I promised I'd be there for you. I know it's still a foreign concept, but we're a team."

"A team, huh?" Fear nagged at her. What happened when he decided he didn't want to be on their team anymore? Or worse, when something happened to take him out of the game completely? Well, for now, she'd embrace the help. The support. "Which one of us is the sidekick?"

"Neither. We're both equal." He lowered his head, brushing his mouth over hers, just a tease before he broke away from her, putting his hand on the doorknob to Ryan's room. "I want you to see the mural. If you don't like it, I'll paint over it and try again. You haven't peeked, have you?"

Shannon rolled her eyes. "No, I promised I wouldn't, and I haven't."

"Good. Wait a sec while I get everything ready." He opened the door just wide enough to slip through. It clicked shut behind him. Light soon trickled beneath the door, illuminating Shannon's bare feet.

A moment later Greg reappeared. "Okay, close your eyes." He radiated eagerness, like one of his kids showing a parent the latest masterpiece, but there was also a hint of uncertainty in his expression. "Close them."

She dutifully shut her eyes, extending her hand. He led her into the room. The soft squish of the carpet yielded to the stiff texture of a canvas drop cloth. He stopped her, moving behind her and placing his hands on her shoulders. "Okay. Open your eyes."

She did.

Summer had a permanent place on Ryan's wall. A large weeping willow on the bank of a river dominated the scene. Beneath the tree, propped against its trunk, a woman and boy read a book together. *The Ransom of Red Chief.*

The boy had unruly sandy-blond hair and a smattering of freckles across his nose. The woman…

It was like looking in a mirror. Only…better. He'd somehow infused her with a beauty, a glow, she knew she didn't possess.

Two thin branches dangled from the tree, one touching Ryan's shoulder, the other Shannon's, giving the impression the tree was embracing them.

The Giving Tree, another much-borrowed library book about a tree that loved a little boy, leaped to Shannon's mind. "Oh, Greg, it's wonderful."

"Look closer." He moved to the wall, pointing. "Here."

Deftly woven into the bark, hidden until he'd called her attention to it, was a delicate face.

Willow.

Right down to the freckles she'd passed on to her son.

While the symbolism of the tree hadn't escaped her, actually seeing her sister's face…

"I found her picture on the Internet. I hope you don't mind."

Shannon reached for but didn't touch the surface, letting her fingertips skim the air over the image. "It's…amazing."

"So why are you crying?" He brushed her cheeks.

"Be-because." She sniffled. "It's…my sister. It's magic."

"That means you like it?"

"Oh, yes, Greg." She tipped back her head, staring up into his soulful blue eyes. "Thank you." Her gratitude was for so much more than the artwork.

He leaned down. "You're welcome." His lips once again connected with hers, a slow, resonant kiss.

The kiss intensified, along with her hunger, her need… She struggled to push him away.

He arched an eyebrow.

"I—I don't want to hurt you again."

"Let me worry about that."

"Are you sure?"

"Someone's got to take the first leap of faith, right?"

So under the spread branches of the willow tree, on the paint-spattered drop cloth, beneath the image of her sister—and with her nephew sleeping in the next room—Shannon thanked him properly.

Without clothing.

When their bodies were joined, Greg stilled overtop of her. "You won't get rid of me so easily this time, Shannon. Fair warning. I fight for what's mine."

Mine. The note of possession rang through her head, through her heart.

"Is that forever I see in your eyes?" Greg murmured.

Shannon smiled, blinking back tears. "Maybe. At least next week anyway."

He laughed, then began to move. "Let me love you, Shannon."

"Oh, yes, Greg." She wasn't so sure about forever. Didn't know how to measure it, how to hold it, how it could possibly be that anyone or anything could stick long-term.

But right now—tonight—was as close to it as she'd ever been.

CHAPTER ELEVEN

SHANNON KNELT on the cool marble floor of the courthouse, adjusting Ryan's superhero tie—a gift from Greg to bolster the boy's courage. She smoothed his suit jacket. "Remember, who do you look at when you're sitting in the chair, telling what happened?"

"You."

"Right. We'll be there the whole time."

Greg and Shannon had been carefully instructed as to what they could and couldn't discuss with Ryan regarding his testimony. Ellen Kelaneri, the A.D.A., had practiced with Ryan, taken him into the empty courtroom and let him sit in the witness chair. They'd done everything possible to prepare him for this moment. Tammy, the victim/witness advocate, a grandmotherly woman whose sole task was to be there for Ryan, had also spent hours with him. He knew they were the ones to turn to when he had any questions. Both had a great rapport with Ryan, and Shannon trusted the women completely.

But she still wanted to grab him and run. She took Ryan's hand and placed it in Tammy's. Until he was called to the stand, he'd be waiting in the victim/witness room, a place with games and a television that had been part of their tour.

"Okay," Shannon said. "You're going to do great. Remember, your mom is watching, and she's so proud of you. And so am I."

"Me, too, sport." Greg leaned down, offered his fist.

Shannon bumped Greg's knuckles, then Ryan slowly added his hand, completing the trio.

Greg took her by the elbow, hauling her to her feet and propelling her toward the courtroom doors. "Don't turn back," he warned. "Let him be."

As Greg steered her down the aisle, Shannon caught sight of Trevor. Her whole body went cold. Wearing a navy pinstripe suit, the man who'd murdered her sister leaned forward on the table, doodling on a pad.

Almost directly behind him, in the spectator section, Patty sat with her hands folded over the designer purse that no doubt matched her shoes.

"Come on, Shannon." Greg moved her forward, then into a seat near the front of the prosecution's side of the room.

Time crawled by as a variety of witnesses were called. Shannon closed her eyes when the medical examiner displayed pictures. Pictures of Willow, pasty white in death. Pictures of bruises.

Shannon toyed with the button of her jacket.

Finally Ellen said, "The prosecution calls Ryan Lloyd Schaffer."

Trevor straightened and turned to stare at the back of the courtroom, as Tammy brought Ryan in. As they passed through the opening in the wooden railing that divided the room, Ryan stole a glance around Tammy at his father, then quickly looked down at his shiny new black dress shoes.

Shannon gripped Greg's hand. He gave it a reassuring squeeze that did nothing to calm her.

Ryan settled into the witness chair, nodding in response to the quiet questions Tammy asked him.

Trevor launched to his feet. "Not one word, Ryan! You promised me. Not *one word*."

With a hoarse cry, Ryan slid from the chair, vanishing below the waist-high panel around the witness stand.

The judge slammed his gavel. "Mr. Lowenstein, control your client."

Shannon half rose from her seat, struggling to see what was happening with Ryan. Greg gripped her forearm, restraining her.

"The prosecution calls for a recess, Your Honor."

Bang, bang. "This court will be in recess until the witness is prepared to resume." The jury filed out of the room again, after which the judge turned to the defense. "Mr. Lowenstein, there will be order when we resume, and your client will keep his mouth shut, or he will be removed. He will not make faces at the child, stare at him or do anything else to disrupt the testimony he's about to give. Understand?"

"Yes, Your Honor," Trevor's defense attorney said.

Tammy carried Ryan, wrapped around her in his clinging-monkey pose, back through the courtroom, down the aisle.

Fists clenched at her sides, Shannon got up and followed the woman out of the courtroom, Greg hot on her heels. Tammy led them to the victim/witness room down the hall. They'd barely gotten inside when Shannon peeled Ryan from her. "Ryan. It's okay. Come here."

With a sob, the boy threw himself into her arms. Shannon sank into a chair, cradling him.

"Remember, you can't discuss the case with him," Tammy said.

Shannon glared over Ryan's head at her.

"Easy there," Greg said. "She's on Ryan's side, remember?"

"Sorry," Shannon muttered, rocking back and forth as Ryan's tears gushed down her neck. She murmured soothing nonsense, assuring the little boy that everything was going to be okay.

She wanted to rip Trevor's liver out through his nose. *Not one word.* No wonder the child hadn't spoken for months. The bastard had made him promise not to say *one word.*

And Ryan had taken it literally.

Tammy extended a box of tissues to Shannon. Gratefully pulling out several, Shannon mopped at Ryan's face. "Hey, you're wrinkling your tie. You're going to make a mess of your superheroes."

Ryan shrugged.

"Oh, no, Ry. We're not going back to you not talking. No way. I will not let that happen. Look at me." Shannon forced his chin up. "You can do this. I know you can. Because you are an amazing kid. Brave. A real hero, remember?"

Ryan shook his head, then lunged forward, hiding his face in the curve of Shannon's neck again. She sighed.

"Give him to me." Greg held out his arms. "Come here, sport."

Ryan went to Greg, leaving Shannon's lap cold. She glanced down at the yellow-and-black fabric flower pinned to her lapel. The petals were crushed and drooping.

Sort of like all of them.

Greg sat in a chair and pulled a white handkerchief from the inside pocket of his suit jacket. He wiped Ryan's nose, holding the handkerchief while the boy honked. He folded it and tucked it away.

"Heroes come in all shapes and sizes, Ryan. They all have different powers. You have the power today to stand for justice. To stand for your mother. Quitters don't win, Ryan. Are you just going to quit?"

The kid shook his head.

"That's my boy. Of course you're not. You're going to fight the good fight. You're going in there, and answer all the questions the attorneys ask you. You're going to tell the truth." Greg rumpled Ryan's hair. "Then we can blow this taco joint and go get some pizza. What do you say?"

"A-artichoke."

Greg chuckled. "Anything but."

Shannon propped her hands on her hips. "Hey. I like artichoke pizza."

"We know," Greg said.

Ellen came into the room to check on her star witness. Greg slid Ryan off his lap, handing him over to the prosecutor, who took him to the sofa on the other side of the room for a private conversation. Ryan's head bobbed repeatedly, then he bumped fists with her.

Shannon and Greg headed back to the courtroom.

Hopefully the second time would be the charm.

PATTY SHIFTED to the edge of her seat as her crying grandson was carried past her. The boy's aunt and the man who'd been the child's art therapist—and then some, according to her P.I.'s research—followed right behind.

Patty hissed at her son, who turned in her direction. "Why did you do that? You made him cry."

"He'll get over it, Mom."

"But what will the jury think?"

"I'm more worried about what they'll think if Ryan doesn't keep his trap shut."

The lawyer glared at them both.

Trevor ignored him. "Who's that guy with Willow's sister? Her boyfriend? I don't like the way he looks at *my* son. You know, if you'd moved faster on the custody case, Ryan would be with you and Dad by now, and I wouldn't have to worry about it."

"They transferred the venue to Erie, Trevor, and that complicated things. Your father has no connections in Erie. Plus, her slick lawyer got the judge to postpone the hearing until your criminal case was decided." Patty opened her purse, digging for a compact and checking her makeup. The media would be waiting on the front steps as soon as court was done for the day. She could only imagine what they'd be asking after Trevor's outburst.

About ten minutes later, Willow's sister and the dark-haired art therapist came back into the courtroom. Before long, the jury was reseated, the judge had called things to order again, and Ryan once more walked down the aisle. Patty tried to wave to him, but he stared straight ahead as the court lady led him to the chair. The polyester suit he wore didn't fit quite right, and the tie was hideous. Once he was in her care, Patty would have to go shopping immediately. What had his aunt been thinking? If she dressed him like this for a court appearance, Lord only knew what his everyday clothes were like.

Ryan kept his eyes glued to Shannon as he answered the preliminary questions.

His comments didn't seem to make much of an impact. Until he mentioned seeing Trevor hit Willow.

Patty stiffened in her seat. He was lying. Trevor would never hit a woman, let alone his wife. He'd loved Willow.

Their wedding had been a fairy tale. Ryan had come along just over a year later. Lloyd had given Trevor more responsibilities at the stores then, figuring their son had settled down and was ready to take the reins.

"Daddy sat on her," Ryan said on the witness stand. "Right here." He pointed to his chest.

"What happened then?" the woman prosecutor asked.

"Mommy kicked her feet and waved her hands, but Daddy didn't get off her."

"Then what happened?"

"Then she stopped."

A low murmur passed through the courtroom. Patty pulled her jacket closed against the sudden chill. Surely Ryan was mistaken. Trevor hadn't simply crushed the breath from his son's mother.

Had he?

Patty shook her head as the prosecutor asked more questions. Trevor propped his elbows on the table, forehead in his hands.

There had to be an explanation for what her grandson described.

She tried to catch Trevor's eye, but he studiously avoided her.

Her son wouldn't look at her.

Just like when he'd been Ryan's age, and the Waterford vase in the living room had shattered. Or when he'd taken his daddy's BMW joyriding at fourteen and put it in a ditch.

Patty's shoulders slumped. On the stand, Ryan's voice trembled, a note of panic lacing his reply to a question she hadn't heard. Several of the female jury members wiped their eyes, and Patty's heart sank.

She was afraid she wasn't going to be able to get Trevor out of this one.

But as his lawyer approached the witness stand to cross-examine Ryan, Patty made a vow. No matter what happened to Trevor, she would do right by her grandson.

THE AMOUNT OF STUFF needed to take three kids to the beach for the day blew Shannon's mind. Two trips to the car transferred most of the "essentials." Now she sat on a blanket beneath the umbrella Derek had forced on her, watching as Ryan raced after Jack and Katie at the water's edge. An assortment of buckets, shovels and small trucks were scattered nearby. A cooler filled with bottled water, juice boxes and their picnic lunch served as a table to hold the bedraggled Beach Barbies, complete with Surfer Dude Ken and his board, which Katie had insisted on bringing as well.

Only a few other intrepid beachgoers had already staked out their beach real estate, but then, it wasn't quite ten in the morning. Ryan had been up at 6:02 a.m., swim trunks already on when he'd bounced into her bedroom and peeled her sleep mask off.

Muffled ringing sent Shannon digging through the quilted beach bag, beneath the bottles of suntan lotion, towels and clothing the kids had shed immediately upon arrival. She flipped open the cell phone she'd finally succumbed to purchasing to keep in touch with the attorneys. "Hello?"

"Just a heads-up," Ellen said. "The case is in the

jury's hands now. It could be hours, it could be days, but I'll call you as soon as they deliver the verdict."

Despite the summer heat, Shannon shivered. Ryan's fate lay in the hands of those twelve strangers. "Okay. Thanks, Ellen."

"I just wanted to tell you again how much I admire your attitude. It's a refreshing change. Most victim's family members hang on every word of the trial and have to be here in person when the verdict's read."

With a shriek of laughter, Ryan kicked water at Jack, then turned to run from the older boy.

"Ryan deserves as much normalcy as possible. If I'm in Philadelphia, holed up in your courtroom, how's he going to get that?" Six days ago, they'd left the city as soon as Ryan had been allowed, and Shannon had no intention of returning. It wasn't going to make any difference to Trevor if she sat in the front row and stared imaginary holes in his head. It wouldn't influence the jury's decision.

And it certainly wouldn't make her sister happy to know Trevor had messed with Ryan's life once again.

"Besides, if I want to see Trevor in handcuffs, I'll just turn on the news tonight."

"Excellent point. I'll call you when I know something."

After disconnecting from the A.D.A., Shannon hesitated a moment, then punched Greg's number. If he was with a client, she'd leave a message.

"You're calling me from the beach?" he said by way of greeting. "Ain't technology grand?"

"Yeah, great."

"Everything okay?"

"The A.D.A. just called. The jury's got the case."

"Oh. She have any clue how long it might take them to decide?"

"No."

"So now we wait?"

"Now we wait." Shannon talked to Greg for another minute or two, then returned the phone to the quilted bag. Then she pulled it out again and set it on the blanket next to her.

Then she tucked it into the pocket of her denim shorts and got up to meander to the water. She spent some time splashing around with the kids in the small waves, before heading back to their blanket, Katie in tow. The girl chattered as she dug a hole in the sand. The hole became the ocean, and she stuck Ken's surfboard into it, perching the figure on the board.

Shannon pulled out the phone, opened it. Nothing.

She snapped at Ryan when the boy squeezed his juice box, squirting sticky apple juice down her leg. Mortified at his crestfallen expression, she quickly apologized.

Just as quickly, he wrapped his arms around her neck in a hug, then scampered off with Jack to find sticks for a sand fort.

Damn, her nerves were shot. How long could it take for twelve people to agree Trevor was guilty?

"Excuse me, miss, but is this spot taken?"

Shannon shaded her eyes, glancing up at Greg. "What are you doing here?"

"Thanks, I'd love to join you." He flopped down on the blanket, stretching out on his side and propping his head on his palm. "I was in the neighborhood. Thought you could use some company. No word yet?"

She shook her head. "Not yet."

"Where's your phone? You did remember to charge it last night, right?"

"Yes, I charged it. I'm not a complete idiot, you know."

"Just a partial one?" His broad grin took any sting from the words.

"Yes. Just a partial one."

"No, you're not an idiot at all. And look at you, taking care of three kids at the beach. Three. When I first met you, I wasn't sure Ryan was going to survive, what with you pushing artichoke pizza on the poor boy. And here you are today, taking care of three kids. Though I did notice you didn't bring Lila."

Shannon laughed. "I'm not ready for a toddler."

A few minutes later, Greg's brother Derek showed up, and Katie and Jack came running to launch themselves into his arms.

Ryan hung back, sad eyes following every move Derek made with his kids. Finally Greg peeled off his shoes and socks, rolled up his jeans and took off down the beach with the boy on his shoulders.

Shannon watched wistfully. The man had the father thing all over Trevor. Had Trevor ever played with Ryan on the beach? Somehow Shannon doubted it.

Had he ever been in tune with someone else's feelings enough to know what they needed, the way Greg seemed to know what Ryan needed? What she needed?

Also doubtful. Trevor was as self-centered as they came.

Derek sat on the edge of the blanket to help work on the sand fort and a new castle for the Barbies.

"What brought you out here?" Shannon asked.

"Just wanted to check on you. Single parenting is hard enough. Takes a while to master dealing with multiple kids."

"Daddy, did you take the afternoon off? Can you stay and play, or is it just lunchtime?" Katie danced a sand-encrusted doll over her father's leg.

"We'll see, honey. I might be able to sneak away for the rest of the afternoon." The bond between Derek's children and Ryan had grown tighter when they'd discovered they'd all lost their mothers.

"Hey, did somebody here order sandwiches?"

Shannon turned to find Hayden strolling toward them with a large plastic bag in his hand. Greg trotted back, swinging Ryan down from his perch on his shoulders. "All right, you brought lunch. Smart thinking."

Before she could say *What's going on?*, the three Hawkins brothers had the cooler opened and were feeding not only themselves but the kids as well.

Busy with her own sandwich—turkey with alfalfa sprouts on whole-grain bread that she'd packed at home—Shannon's mouth was full when the next Hawkins arrived.

Greg's mother, Lydia, carried a bag of homemade brownies, which her sons quickly appropriated. She was followed by Judy and her toddler and baby, Bethany and her nine-year-old son, and Elke, who popped by with the excuse that she needed her mother's input on the final seating arrangement for the wedding.

The beach was literally crawling with Hawkinses. "We're going to need a way bigger blanket," Shannon muttered. She pulled out her cell phone yet again, setting it to vibrate before she tucked it back in her pocket. With all the commotion of the impromptu family reunion, she wasn't sure she'd hear it ring.

She scanned the crowd for Greg, and fixed him with an evil eye. Eventually he looked over at her, and she crooked a finger at him. He handed a blue Frisbee to Ryan and slunk to her.

"You beckoned, m'lady?"

"Greg, what's going on? Surely your entire family didn't show up just to make sure I didn't lose one of Derek's kids. Did they?"

Greg shrugged. "I don't think so."

"So why are they here?"

Greg glanced down at the blanket, pulling off a speck of lint and tossing it aside. "I, uh, well… I might have called Hayden and told him that the jury has the case. And he probably called Derek, who called Elke, who… Well, let's just say that the Hawkins-family grapevine runs fast and furious. We *all* have cell phones."

"They all came because I'm waiting to hear the verdict?"

Greg nodded. "We thought you might need some company. Support. That's how families work, Shannon. In a pinch, you've got people you can count on." He started to tick off on his fingers. "Finn couldn't get away from the restaurant right now, but said his money's on guilty. Dad's taking depositions out of town this afternoon and Cathy's in court herself. But they both sent text messages to keep the faith. The twins are God only knows where, and they're the only ones who didn't send a message." He ran another quick count. "Wait, I forgot Alan. He said he hopes they fry Trevor's sorry ass."

Shannon scanned the beach. The laughter, the camaraderie, the knowledge that they would always be there for one another.

She got to her feet quickly and took off, headed away from the group.

"Shannon! Hey, wait." Greg caught her as she skidded down the dune toward the parking lot. "What's wrong?"

She turned to him, wiping at her eyes. "I—I got sand in my eyes. I was going to the bathroom."

"Liar." He pulled her into his arms.

She let him hold her, drawing solace from his embrace. Until her phone vibrated. Then she shoved him away, scrambling to get to the thing. "Hello?"

"Jury's back. I'm on my way into court right now. I'll call you as soon as I can." Ellen hung up, leaving Shannon gaping at the phone in her hand.

"Well?" Greg asked.

"She's just going into court now to hear what they decided. Crap." Shannon trudged back up the dune. At the top, she paced a short circuit.

"Not much longer," Greg said, following her. "Don't lose your cool now."

"My cool?" She stopped, hands clenched. "I lost my cool months ago. He murdered my sister, and I want him to pay. I don't want him to be able to get anywhere near his son ever again."

Unable to contain her nervous energy, Shannon trotted down the beach. As she passed, various Hawkinses fell silent, staring at her. "Soon," Greg called out to them. "The jury's back. We'll know soon."

She headed along the tide line. The cool water lapped at her toes. After she'd put enough distance behind her, she turned toward the trees, planting herself on one of the weathered picnic tables that dotted Presque Isle.

Greg sat next to her, taking her hand.

The comfort in his touch coursed through her. Mr. Reliable. In the four months she'd known him, he'd become a constant in her life.

Ryan didn't need his services anymore. But she counted Greg as one of the most fortunate things to come out of the horror Ryan had faced.

The idea of letting Greg go didn't fill her with the peace she normally associated with letting go.

It filled her with dread.

They waited, together, the sound of the rolling waves and the distant laughter of children carrying on the breeze.

Shannon set the phone on the table and stared at it, willing it to ring.

Instead, it chattered against the wood, rattling along the surface. She snatched it up. "Well?"

"Guilty." Triumph laced the A.D.A.'s voice. "We nailed the bastard."

Shannon slumped over, head resting on the table, her shoulders shaking. "Thank you," she said softly.

Greg gripped the top of her arm, and Shannon sat up again. Worry etched lines in his face, and his hands flew in the air. She stuck her thumb up, and he pumped his fist in victory.

"It was my pleasure," the A.D.A. said. "I'll let you know the details of the sentencing hearings when I have them. You should consider making a victim-impact statement. For yourself, and for Ryan."

"I'll think about it. Thanks again." Shannon closed the phone and put it away.

Greg yanked her from the bench and spun her around. "Woo-hoo! How's it feel to win?" he asked when he'd set her down again.

"I could get used to it," she said.

She could get used to a lot of things, it seemed. Not the least of which was the presence of this man.

And his huge family.

Maybe a lifetime really was within her grasp.

But first…one more court case. Ryan was safe from his father.

Now she had one more fight to win. She rolled her neck, and danced in the sand on the balls of her feet, smacking one fist into her palm. "Bring on the next loser."

Greg laughed. "I've created a monster."

No, the monster was safely headed to prison, where he belonged.

One victory down, one to go….

CHAPTER TWELVE

GREG ADVANCED TOWARD CATHY on the steps of the Erie County Courthouse with his hands palm out. "You talking to me today?"

"No."

"I said I was sorry."

"Sorry doesn't cover stupidity of that magnitude."

He scanned the pedestrian traffic on the far side of the street, watching for Shannon. "It looked worse than it really was."

"What it looked like, Gory, was you making out with my client in front of an open window. At night. With the lights on in the apartment. I don't appreciate being blindsided like that." Cathy sighed. "I told you specifically to stay away from her. And I've watched you grow closer and closer, despite my warning. I'd been planning to spin your relationship with her as a positive thing, a stable influence on her and Ryan. Positive male role model, and all that. But I didn't think you'd be so idiotic as to get photographed, in her apartment, with Ryan just feet away, with your hands on her ass."

"Do you think it hurt her case?"

"Who knows? The Schaffers have a lot of cards in their favor, money being a big one."

Across the street, Greg spotted Shannon in the laser

lemon jacket and black skirt she'd worn for the criminal trial. The colors attracted the attention of more than a few men, who gave her long legs and great rear appreciative stares as she passed. He waved to her, getting a charge out of the envious glares he got from her sidewalk admirers when she waved back. *That's right, suckers, she's with me.*

"Rumor has it you bought a ring."

Greg's hand froze midwave. He slowly lowered it, turning to face his sister. "Who narced?"

She shook her head. "Two rules if you want to keep something private. Don't make out in front of lit windows at night, and don't tell Hayden."

He cursed under his breath. "When I get my hands on him…"

"He's worried. Seems to think you've totally lost it over her. When are you planning to pop the question?"

"Tonight. I figured to ask her when she's riding the victory."

"And if she says no?"

"Then I plan to ask her every day for the rest of my life until she changes her mind."

"In this state, that's considered stalking." Cathy checked her watch, then glanced at the opposite sidewalk, tracking Shannon's approach.

"I love her, Cathy."

His sister's well-groomed eyebrows inched upward.

"And I love Ryan, too," he added quickly as Shannon drew nearer. "I can't bear the idea of being without either of them. Why is that such a problem with the family?"

"It's not a problem with the family. Geez, don't be so defensive. Her track record isn't outstanding when it comes to stability and commitment, but I think she's changed a lot since Ryan—and you—came into her life."

"Does everyone feel that way?"

"Almost everyone showed up to wait with her for the criminal verdict, right? That should tell you all you need to know, Gory. Even Hayden was there, and he's afraid he's losing his best friend to a woman. You'll have to cut him some slack."

Slightly breathless, Shannon bounded the final few yards to their side. "Sorry. I meant to be here sooner, but Mrs. K. was running late."

"No problem. We've got time. Shall we?" Cathy gestured toward the courthouse entrance.

The blast of air-conditioning was a welcome relief from the summer heat. The women's purses and Cathy's briefcase rode the X-ray machine while they passed through the metal detectors. Outside the courtroom, Greg stopped. Family court proceedings were closed except to participants, and he'd already done his part by testifying about Ryan's progress and Shannon's ability as a guardian.

Of course, he'd come across biased as hell when the Schaffer's lawyer produced the picture of them together in her window, him feasting on her neck like some sort of vampire wannabe.

"You ready for this?" he asked Shannon.

With a broad smile, she held out her fist. "I'm ready, Coach."

"You've fought well, my Padawan." Instead of bumping knuckles, he took her hand, unclenching it and raising it to his lips. "I'm proud of you. Now get in there and show them that the good guys win with grace. No making faces at Patty, okay?"

She laughed. "I'll try to resist the temptation to gloat."

Cathy had the door open. "Shannon?"

"See you in a bit." Greg leaned in to give Shannon a quick kiss.

Amazing how such a friendly little public display of affection from him could zap right through her. Shannon turned and, head held high, she followed Cathy into the small courtroom.

Lloyd and Patty were already seated behind their table, their Ivy League lawyer at their side.

But all the high-priced attorneys in the world couldn't beat a single Hawkins, and Shannon had one at her side, one waiting outside the door and the rest of them pulling for her.

The judge kept them waiting a few minutes, but soon enough, the proceedings were under way.

Judge Victoria Otis leaned forward, propping her arms along the edge of the desk. "I want to say up front that this has been a difficult decision. As you all know, I've waded through reams of reports from various professionals, and listened to several days' worth of testimony.

"Ms. Vanderhoff, you've done an exemplary job of taking a child so severely traumatized that he was mute, and helping him recover to the point that he appears to be functioning very well."

Shannon fought the urge to peek at Patty, to see how the woman was taking that. She smiled at the judge, dipping her head slightly.

"However, I also have to consider your past pattern of behavior. Anyone can find themselves in a crisis situation in a new place. But when I examine your record, it is indeed a pattern. New living places every few years. New jobs even more frequently. Relationships that don't last. You never stay in one place long enough to put down roots.

"Stability is absolutely essential for a child."

Uneasily, Shannon tucked her hands into her lap to hide their trembling.

"Your financial situation is another source of concern for me. Ryan's grandparents, on the other hand, have lived in the same house for decades. They run a highly successful chain of stores and can provide for their grandson's every need. Though they're older, they're reasonably healthy." The judge folded her hands. "This decision has kept me awake for the past two nights. I'm charged with determining what's in Ryan's best long-term interests.

"Therefore, it is my decision that custody of the minor child, Ryan Schaffer, shall be awarded to his paternal grandparents, Lloyd and Patty Schaffer."

Cathy quickly reached over and grabbed Shannon's hand.

Her whole body went numb.

"In the interest of not prolonging the pain for either Ryan or Ms. Vanderhoff, transfer of physical custody shall take place no later than 9:00 a.m. tomorrow morning. I highly recommend that the parties work together to arrange visitation between the boy and his aunt. The bond they've forged should be honored, and both of them will benefit from continued contact in the future." The judge banged her gavel.

Lloyd and Patty rose from their seats, pumping hands with their lawyer.

Shannon sat and stared blankly, heart hammering against her chest wall so hard she could feel it.

Lloyd paused in front of the table. "We'll be by your apartment tomorrow morning to pick him up."

Shannon glanced up at him, nodding once. Trevor's father had the grace to appear apologetic.

Sympathetic.

"Don't bother sending any of his things," Patty said. "He and I will go shopping tomorrow afternoon."

"Patty," Lloyd said sharply. "Don't rub salt. I'll meet you outside." When his wife hesitated, he jerked his head in the direction of the door. "Go on."

Shannon wanted to bowl Patty over and bolt for the door herself, but couldn't make her muscles cooperate.

"I'll make sure you get to see him, Ms. Vanderhoff," Lloyd said softly.

Cathy tapped Shannon's leg, urging a response.

"Thank you," she replied woodenly.

Lloyd's shoes clipped a hasty retreat.

She felt as if someone had autopsied her without waiting for her to be dead, scooping out all her insides.

A huge, hollow shell was all that was left.

"I'm so sorry," Cathy said.

Shannon shook her head. "You did your best. I didn't give you good material to work with." *Breathe in, hold it, breathe out.*

Let go.

She fisted her clammy hands in her lap and blinked hard. Her chair scraped against the floor as she pushed back from the table and abruptly headed for the door.

"Shannon," Greg cried as she stepped out of the courtroom.

"I don't want to see you right now." She hurried down the hallway as fast as she could in the pumps she rarely wore.

"Let her go, Greg," she heard Cathy say behind her. "She needs some time to process this."

"Shannon, wait."

Shannon whirled on him. When he got close enough, she poked him in the chest. "Fight, you said." Poke. "The good guys win, you said." Poke. "But I was right all along. Letting go hurts less." Her voice shook. "Just stay away from me. I'm going home to try to teach a little boy who trusted me—who trusted *you* and the legal system—another lesson in losing and letting go. I don't want to see you again. Got it?"

"Shannon, please…"

She turned her back on him.

Somehow she would get through the next twenty-four hours.

After that…she'd figure out how to get through the rest of her life with pain she suspected wasn't temporary.

"BUT I DON'T WANNA GO live with Grandma Patty," Ryan said as Shannon crouched in the foyer to retie his sneaker.

"I know." He'd only told her about twenty thousand times since she broke the news to him yesterday afternoon.

"She smells funny. And she looks at me all pinchy, like *I* smell. Like this." Ryan scrunched up his face, eyebrows drawn together, freckled nose thrust up in the air, and proceeded to look down at her.

The impression was so totally Patty, she'd have laughed if her heart wasn't breaking. "I know, pal, but we have to do what the judge said."

"That judge is stupid! Let's ask another judge."

"I wish we could, buddy. But we can't. It doesn't work that way."

"Don't make me go, Aunt Shannon." Ryan threw himself against her, wrapping his arms around her neck.

She fell back against the wall, hugging the boy who'd come to be her world. "I have to, Ry. Otherwise the police will put me in jail. And you'd go live with Grandma Patty anyway."

"We could run away. We'll take Uncle Greg with us, too."

Tears spilled over her cheeks. "We don't fight physically, and we don't run away. Those aren't ways to solve problems." But it was tempting.

"Don't you want me?"

Shannon sniffled. "Of course I do. I fought for you." She pushed the boy from her arms so he could see her. "I love you, Ryan. Don't *ever* doubt it. No matter what happens when you leave here, you're my boy. I'm going to miss you terribly."

Ryan framed her face with his hands. "Don't cry, Aunt Shannon."

Which made her blubber like a damn fool. She dragged him back into her embrace, her tears falling into the curve of his neck.

He patted her on the shoulder, and for a split second she considered taking him and running, just as he'd suggested.

But Patty and Lloyd were already waiting outside.

Shannon climbed to her feet. "Wait here, Ry. Just a minute." She ran back up the stairs and dashed into the bathroom, blowing her nose and splashing cold water on her face. No way in hell she'd give Patty the satisfaction of seeing her like this.

Back in the foyer, she cleared her throat and took Ryan's hand. She squeezed it. "We've been through worse," she assured him—or maybe herself. "We can get through this. Grab your backpack." The backpack held a few items. His night-light. A box of crayons and some paper. A picture he'd drawn of them at the beach.

They stepped out onto the porch—and found Greg leaning against the metal railing. She glared at him.

"I wanted to say goodbye to Ryan, too."

Ryan launched himself at Greg, who swung the boy up, holding him tight against his chest. After a moment, hc set Ryan on his feet, then went to one knee in front of him. "I'll miss you, sport. Hey, I brought you a present." Greg reached for the book sitting on the top step.

"The Ransom of Red Chief!" Ryan exclaimed, hugging it.

"Yep. Your very own copy."

"Thanks, Uncle Greg."

Greg cleared his throat, his voice suspiciously unsteady when he said, "You're welcome." He put out his fist. "Fight on, SuperKid."

"I'm not SuperKid anymore. I'm just Ryan."

"Well, I think you're a super kid, no matter what."

Ryan bumped fists with him, and Shannon had to look away.

A car door shut in the parking lot, and Lloyd sauntered down the sidewalk. "Time to go, Ryan."

"I don't wanna."

"We've been through that, Ryan," Shannon said.

"I'm not going." Ryan stomped his foot.

Lloyd gently took Ryan by the wrist and picked him up, ignoring the boy's struggle. He took the backpack in his other hand. "He'll call you." Lloyd turned and headed back to the car.

"Aunt Shannon! Uncle Greg! I don't want to go—please!"

Shannon could no longer see for her tears. A huge fist squeezed her chest, and she found it difficult to breathe.

Another car door slammed, muting Ryan's gut-wrenching cries. Then a second door closed.

The car started, and gravel popped as they backed out of the parking space.

Shannon stood waving, even though she didn't know if Ryan could see her, until the car vanished around the corner.

Then her knees buckled, and she crumpled into a heap on the top step, sobbing.

Greg rushed to hold her.

She wanted to let him. To take refuge in his embrace and have him kiss the pain away. But if it hurt this much to lose Ryan, she wasn't about to let herself love Greg. *'Tis better to have loved and lost than never to have loved at all.*

Bullshit.

Loving and losing hurt like hell. Letting go had never hurt like this.

"Get…away." She flailed at him the way Ryan had flailed at Lloyd. "Don't touch me."

"Shannon, please—"

She scrambled to her feet. "This is all your fault. I feel like I'm dying. Bond with him. Fight for him, you said. That sure worked out, didn't it?"

Greg extended his hands to her. "I'm sorry, Shannon—"

"Sorry doesn't help." She dashed into her apartment, locking the door behind her. She ran up the stairs and threw herself down on the leather sofa, pulling the blanket over her head. In the dim light that filtered through, she tried to take a deep breath.

A key scraped in the lock, and footsteps pounded up the stairs. The warmth of a body settled beside her. She sniffled. "I want my key back. Don't think I'll be needing a babysitter anytime soon."

Greg dragged the blanket away. His chest tightened at the sight of her splotchy face and Rudolph-neon nose. "I didn't think we'd lose him."

"We?"

"Yes, we. I love you, Shannon. And I love Ryan, too. I didn't think it would end this way."

"Love?" She narrowed her eyes.

"I love you," he repeated. "Why is that so hard to believe?"

"Love is apparently highly overrated, comic-book boy. Love sucks. Love hurts." She thumped her chest. "I've got nothing to give you. Not when it comes to love. I'm empty."

"I know it hurts, Shannon, but—"

"No buts. You've got a whole huge family. Ryan was all I had left. Now he's gone. And I want you gone, too. I'm letting you go, Greg. Time's up." She turned her face toward the back of the couch.

"Let me help you through this."

She struggled off the sofa, feet tangled in the afghan. She kicked it away. "What part of 'it's over' don't you get? Do I have to draw you a picture?"

He rose slowly to his feet. She needed time. In a few days, the worst of it would have passed, and they could take this up again. He wasn't about to give up on her. The near-violent reaction to losing Ryan only meant she had a far greater capacity to love than either of them had suspected. "I'm going."

But I'm not quitting on you.

"Leave the key."

Greg dug in his pocket, setting the key on top of her television. "If you need anything, call me."

She turned away from him again, giving him her back.

"Okay." He descended the stairs deliberately, gripping the banister, feet heavier with each step. Out on the porch, he shielded his eyes, looking up at her dining-area window. The glare of the morning sun prevented him from seeing anything. "I'll be back," he vowed. "This isn't over."

SHANNON'S APARTMENT was too damn quiet.

Too empty.

Just like her.

The second merlot of the night had blunted the edge of the pain, but didn't make it go away. After three days, she'd expected things to be easier. That's how long it had taken her to let go of Willow. For the most part, anyway.

Shannon leaned against the doorway to Ryan's room, long-stemmed glass in hand. Several sealed boxes lined the floor, near the closet.

She'd tried to take them to the Salvation Army because someone out there needed all those little shirts and shorts and such. But she just hadn't been able to do it. She set the glass of wine on the bookcase and hefted the first box, tucking it into the corner of the closet. She piled the other two on top and shut the door. Out of sight, out of mind.

Too bad she couldn't put the mural out of sight as easily.

Shannon went to the wall Greg had spent weeks

painting. She touched Ryan's face, then skimmed her finger over the tree trunk to trace the same freckled nose on her sister. "I'm sorry, Willow," she whispered.

She turned away from the mural, picking up her glass and slamming back the rest of the dark red wine.

Inspiration struck. Where were her keys? She plucked them from the kitchen island.

Barreling down the stairs, she bolted from her apartment. Somewhere in the dusky summer, kids were shouting and laughing, pounding a basketball. She ran down the sidewalk, then took the steps to the basement laundry room two at a time. On the far side of the washing machines, she opened the door to the maintenance closet using the key provided to all tenants. Mostly so they could access things like a plunger in the event of a bathroom-plumbing emergency.

She'd had one of those when Ryan had overdone it with the toilet paper. Or maybe it was the toothbrush that had fallen in the bowl and gone unreported.

Shannon gathered what she needed and lugged her booty back to her apartment, dropping everything in Ryan's room. She pushed the futon against the closet doors, then spread the tarp. After a quick trip to the kitchen to refill her glass, she went to work, prying the lid off the paint can with a screwdriver. The boring beige used to neutralize and refresh the apartments between tenants suited perfectly. She poured some into a tray and picked up the roller.

She started on the outside edges, obscuring the river first, then the upper branches and leaves of the tree.

Erase it.

The field grew smaller. Flecks of paint rained onto her as she covered the mural.

Let it go.

She closed her eyes when she got to the magical portrait of Willow, deftly hidden in the bark. God only knew how long it had taken Greg to create the incredible image. It took her all of five seconds to coat over it.

Only the woman and the boy remained.

She set the roller in the tray and slugged back another shot of merlot.

For a long moment, she stood in front of the wall, dripping paint onto the drop cloth. Images came back to her. Ryan as SuperKid. Searching for beach glass on the shores of Lake Erie. Riding the Tilt-a-Hurl. Cuddling up with him on the sofa and reading *The Ransom of Red Chief.*

She raised the roller.

Her lower lip trembled. Tears welled in her eyes. "No more crying. Let *him* go."

She took a deep breath, held it for a moment, then let it out.

The content boy and woman vanished.

Leaving a blank wall in their wake.

CHAPTER THIRTEEN

GREG CAREFULLY REMOVED the last picture—one Ryan had made—from the wall and added it to the pile on the top of the shelving unit.

Several cardboard boxes, overflowing with colored pencils, markers and boxes of chocolate pudding, cluttered the tabletops. The room was forlorn and barren: naked walls, empty storage units, everything shades of brown and beige despite the late-afternoon sunshine filtering in the windows.

It reminded him of an elementary-school classroom the day before summer vacation started.

Only today, there was no presummer excitement.

No, in his case, summer was just about over, and the fall term loomed ever closer. He'd gone past his deadline to clear out of the room at Erie University—July 31—by one day.

He, who never missed a deadline. At least, not a comic-book deadline.

He crouched to get a broken crayon from under the edge of the shelves. Cadet blue, a color that couldn't make up its mind if it was more blue or gray.

He could relate.

Hayden bounded into the room. "These the last boxes?"

"Yeah."

"Okay." His brother scooped up two, balancing one in each arm. "You ready then?"

"I suppose."

"Don't be such a mope. There are no endings, only beginnings."

Greg snorted. "Don't quote your code at me. I've got nowhere for my groups to meet. Individual therapy isn't always as helpful as group." His cancer kids, for example, benefited from the group experience, the support and camaraderie.

The insurance premiums alone were killing him, never mind rent and all the other stuff he needed for his group practice. He'd been forced to start charging more and, as a result had lost a couple of his kids whose parents just couldn't afford the higher fees. He'd felt horrible, but he had to pay his own bills as well.

The paperwork for his nonprofit organization—the Erie Foundation for Art Therapy—had finally been approved, but funding it was a whole different matter.

"Something's going to break. Keep the faith, huh?"

"I'm trying. Head on down," he told Hayden. "I'll meet you at the car."

"It's your call." His brother paused on his way out. "Seriously, Gory, it's the university's loss. *Anybody* who cuts you loose is crazy."

Greg understood who Hayden meant by *anybody*. He nodded.

"Don't be long, man. We've got places to be and beers to drink." Hayden headed out.

Greg laid the pile of drawings on top of the final box and hefted it. He hesitated in the doorway.

So many memories here. So many kids, so many drawings…

He took a deep breath, held it for a moment, then exhaled. *Let it go.* Just like Shannon had taught him.

He might be able to let go of the room, the university. But letting go of the freckle-faced boy he'd said goodbye to a week ago wasn't as easy.

Neither was letting go of the woman who'd stood behind the observation glass and watched him, like a fish in a bowl.

A woman who'd learned to stand up for herself. To love. And let herself be loved.

And who'd lost so much more than he'd ever imagined possible.

The enormity of it made him feel even more like a chump. This was a room. A place. A small component of his program. Plenty of therapists ran their own practices. This was just a setback. He'd overcome it.

He flipped the lights off.

In the parking lot, he set the final box on the backseat of his Tracker. He peeled the Erie University Staff parking sticker off the back window, then tossed it to the floor.

"That's the spirit," Hayden said from the passenger seat.

As they pulled out from the parking lot, a cape-and-costumed figure seemed to materialize on the sidewalk. The superhero wannabe snapped to attention and raised his hand in salute.

No cameras. No crowd. No gawkers.

Just a comic-book geek giving him a send-off.

Greg saluted back, then stuck his hand out the window to wave as they drove away.

"You figured out how they know where to find you yet?" Hayden asked.

"Nope." And for the moment, he didn't care. His "stalkers" had become part of his routine, which was an odd comfort. After all, he must've still "had it" to be worthy of so much attention.

Hopefully Shannon felt the same way. He didn't relish the idea of her actually taking out a restraining order against him.

But he couldn't give up on her.

He turned toward her apartment complex.

Hayden groaned. "No. No way. We're supposed to be meeting all the guys at the Marina for beer. Elke and Jeremy are getting married next Saturday. We have to finalize the bachelor-party plans. Time lines, the route for the bar crawl."

"Just a quick stop. To check on her. It's been a week today."

"Dude, you remember how much you hated that Denise wouldn't get it through her thick head it was over? You're doing the same thing she did."

"I am not."

"You're suffocating her. Man, if there's ever a chance, you've gotta back off. Give her a chance to miss you. She can hardly miss you if she's busy dodging your calls and slamming her door in your face."

Greg sighed. She'd been doing exactly that for the past week. She'd made it abundantly clear she wanted him out of her life.

Just as he'd done with Denise.

"Don't be pathetic. She knows where to find you if she changes her mind. Man up."

Stomach churning, Greg turned down a side street

before they reached her complex, making a giant U-turn around the block.

Maybe sometimes you had to call it quits.

SHANNON MADE A FINAL correction on the newsletter she'd crafted for a client, then attached it to an e-mail and sent it winging off through cyberspace. She composed an official e-mail for another client, sent that off as well.

Then she clicked open the Internet. "Just the news," she promised herself. But the news was boring. And before she realized it, she was on YouTube, typing in Greg's name.

The red, green and blue ABC Men appeared, flexing and posing. Shannon paused the video when it cut to Greg's face.

She missed that face. And the man it belonged to.

After a moment of studying the high cheekbones, the angular jawline, she put the action into motion again, stopping next on the shot of Ryan giggling at the ABC Men's antics.

She missed *that* face, too.

Somehow, she'd lost her ability to put them behind her. Greg hadn't broken Ryan, but the two of them had broken her.

The two weeks since losing Ryan to Patty and Lloyd had been more like years.

Like a junkie in desperate need of a fix, she played several more videos, including one featuring a villain called Trash Man, then surfed to another Web site, one she'd discovered after compulsively Googling Greg and visiting page after page in the early morning hours. Her fingers flew over the keyboard, typing in the password.

A map of the area appeared, with a stationary blip.

College kids with a love of comic books had created a new game with Greg in the unwitting starring role. It had an element of geocaching, a game where a treasure is buried with a GPS unit, combined with an element of homemade reality TV. Someone had planted a hidden GPS unit on Greg's Tracker one day when he'd been signing comics at a local store.

Ironic. They were tracking his Tracker.

And she'd joined the online geeks' group with the name Mysterious Lady O in order to weasel the password to the Web site that displayed Greg's movements and location. Pathetic? Maybe. But there was comfort in knowing where he was, in watching the blip move around Erie.

At the moment, the blip wasn't even in Erie. Greg was somewhere south, almost in Crawford County. Which made her even lonelier.

She should have told him about the GPS unit, but he'd quit calling her a week ago.

Mr. Fight-the-Good-Fight had given up more easily than she'd expected. And she wasn't about to call him. She'd seen his exasperation at Denise's attempts to rekindle a romance. Besides, she didn't *want* Greg's attention.

At least, that's what she kept telling herself. *Liar!*

With a sigh, she closed the Internet and resumed working. She'd returned the computer to the extra room, positioning it so she had her back to the wall behind the futon. Despite painting over the mural, she could see it every time she looked at the space.

Shannon moved on to some bookkeeping entries. A while later, the doorbell rang repeatedly, followed by rapping on the door. In the foyer, Shannon peered through the peephole, seeing nothing.

The banging started again.

She opened the door, confused. "Yes?"

"Surprise! I'm home!" Ryan barreled over the threshold and threw himself at her, knocking her backwards.

She squatted, bracing herself with one hand while wrapping the boy in an embrace with the other. "Ryan! Ohmygosh. Ohmygosh." The warmth of the small form fitted against her was the return of sunshine after a long winter. Shannon basked in that glow until Ryan started to squirm.

"I flew in a airplane and rode in a yellow taxi cab. Did you know cars look like ants from the sky?" He wiggled out of her embrace.

She wanted to haul him back and never let him go again. "Do they?"

"Yep. I was like a superhero, way up in the clouds."

The sounds of scraping brought Shannon's attention to the man dragging an oversize suitcase up the porch steps. In the other hand, Lloyd carried the backpack Ryan had left with.

"Are you surprised?" The boy jiggled in place like an eager puppy.

"Very," Shannon said. "I didn't expect a visit quite this soon." There'd been no time to get over the first loss. Like a barely healed wound suddenly deprived of its scab, she was going to bleed again when he had to go back. But for now, he was here. With her. That would have to be enough.

She got to her feet, stroking Ryan's unruly hair. "But it's the best surprise I've ever had." She peered over

Lloyd's shoulder to a cab parked at the end of the sidewalk. "Where's Patty?"

"Patty's home with the mother of all migraines, having realized what I told her all along." He offered Shannon a weary smile as he heaved the luggage inside her foyer.

"Oh? What's that?" Uneasiness stirred Shannon's stomach. Why was Ryan here? Why hadn't Lloyd called ahead?

"I gotta go to the bafroom," Ryan announced. "Bye, Grandpa Lloyd. Thanks for bringing me home!" He scrambled up the stairs, and the bathroom door slammed a moment later.

"That boy is pure energy," his grandfather said, running a hand through his white hair.

The back of her neck prickled. "Why don't you come upstairs? Tell me what's going on."

"I can't stay. A friend of mine flew us out here. He's at the airport, refueling his plane and filing the paperwork for our return flight. I have an important business meeting tomorrow, and need to get back." He unzipped a compartment on the front of the black suitcase, pulling out a manila envelope.

"What's this?" She took it hesitantly, her hand quivering.

"Paperwork. Have your lawyer go over it, sign it, notarize it and send back our copies."

"What's going on, Lloyd?" Shannon's heart thudded against her ribs. *No, don't hope. Don't care. It'll just hurt more later.*

"My wife has realized there's a reason folks our age don't have kids. We're too old. Especially for a ball of fire like that one." He grabbed the suitcase. "Let me just take this up the stairs for you. It's heavy. Wheels aren't any help at all on stairs."

Shannon followed, envelope clutched to her chest, Ryan's backpack over her arm, the lump in her throat making it hard to speak. "So, that means what?"

"That means, we made a mistake in trying to take Ryan from you in the first place."

Shock stopped her dead in her tracks. She tried twice before she managed to choke out, "You're giving me custody?"

"Where do you want this?" Lloyd gestured to the suitcase.

"I…uh…in Ryan's room, please."

He popped out the handle and wheeled it down the hallway.

Shannon climbed the remaining stairs, then waited for him to reappear. When he did, she fired off her question again, resisting the urge to scream. "You didn't answer me. You're giving me custody? After all the lawyers, that whole big legal fight, just like that?"

"We'd like to visit, of course."

Words finally failed her. She tried to process it. Ryan was staying. With her. Her knees trembled, and she sniffed to quell the tingling in her nose.

"Um…are you okay? You do still want custody, right?"

"Oh, yes. Hell yes."

"Visitation terms are spelled out in the documents. I think you'll find it fair."

"I—I'm sure I will."

"All right." He strode back to the top of the stairs, then paused. "I'm sorry our son…I'm sorry about your sister."

Shannon swallowed hard, managing a wobbly nod.

Lloyd descended to the landing, then turned and slowly climbed back up, stopping on the first step. "I almost forgot." He hauled his wallet from the back pocket of his pants. "This is to help with Ryan's expenses. School will be starting soon, and we know that little boys grow like weeds. Or in case you need to buy a big container of migraine medicine." He smiled.

She almost refused. But something in Lloyd's eyes—something she'd seen in her own father's eyes, a need to help—made her take the blue check.

He held out a second check. "And this one is for Mr. Hawkins. Patty found out about his new art therapy foundation, and she plans to make him her new pet project. The difference he made in Ryan really impressed us both. Here's Patty's card. She'd like Mr. Hawkins to call her so they can discuss potential fund-raising events." He smiled wryly. "One thing my wife knows besides spending money is how to raise it for charity."

Fingers still trembling, Shannon accepted the second check, too. "I—I know Greg will be very appreciative. As am I."

Lloyd shook his head. "We're the ones who appreciate everything you've done—everything you're doing—for our grandson. I can't imagine what kind of shape he'd be in if not for you and Greg Hawkins. You know, you're all that boy talked about. Aunt Shannon this, Uncle Greg that..." He flipped his wrist and checked his watch, then swore softly. "I have to run. You call if you need anything, okay?"

"Okay." Shannon stood at the top of the steps, manila envelope and checks still in her hands when the apartment door closed.

She ran to the window overlooking the parking lot to confirm it really had been Lloyd Schaffer in her apartment. Not some impostor toying with her emotions.

A shriek from Ryan's room shook her out of her trance. "My painting! What happened to my painting?"

He met her in the doorway, planting his fists on his hips. "Who ruined the picture Uncle Greg made me?"

Dropping the backpack on the floor in front of his closet, right next to the suitcase, she set the envelope and checks beside the computer. Sinking onto the futon, she held her hand out to Ryan.

He crossed the room in starts and stops, dragging his sneakers on the rug. When he stood before her, she lifted him to her knee. "I'm sorry about the painting. It made me sad to see it."

"Really?"

"Yes." She cleared her throat. "Looking at the painting just reminded me of everything I'd lost. Your mom, you…"

"I'm not lost now. I'm back."

Shannon smiled, blinking back tears. "You sure are. I'm going to call Cathy to check those papers, though. We need to make sure everything is in perfect order. We don't want to count our chickens before they're hatched." She wouldn't survive losing him again.

Once had been enough.

Ryan crinkled his freckled nose. "Huh?"

"I just want to make sure they can't change their minds again, Ryan. I want to make sure all the t's are crossed, and everything is legal."

"So we don't have to see a judge again?"

"Exactly." She narrowed her eyes. "Now, you want

to tell me what happened to change Grandma Patty's mind about keeping you?"

Her nephew shrugged. "I dunno. She said I was a handful."

"A handful, huh? Sounds like there's a lot more to the story than that."

Ryan slid from her knee to the floor, digging in the backpack. "Well, she was mad when the police came."

Shannon pressed her lips together, waiting a beat before asking, "Why did the police come?"

"I called 911, like you showed me."

"Ryan, I told you, that's only for emergencies."

"It *was* a 'mergency. I wanted to come home."

Home. Her apartment was home. What a beautiful word.

"Okay. What else?"

He shrugged again, tugging a yellow truck from the bag. "I had a few accidents."

"What kind of accidents?"

"It wasn't my fault. Grandpa Lloyd even said so."

"What wasn't your fault?"

"At dinner in this special place where I had to wear a tie—it wasn't nice like the one Uncle Greg gave me, it was a boring tie—I tried to do what Grandma Patty said. I put my napkin on my lap. But then I had to go potty, and the white thing on the table got stuck on my belt, so when I got off my chair to hold Grandpa Lloyd's hand so we could go to the bafroom, *smash!*" He gestured wildly. "Everything fell on the floor and everybody looked at us. Grandma Patty's face got all red."

I'd have given a million dollars to see that. Shannon battled a laugh. *Smash, kablam, kerpow!* "That sounds like an accident to me."

"Right. Just like when I broke the TV."

She leaned forward. "What happened to the TV?"

"Me and Grandpa were playing a video game. I tried to make the ball go down the little thing and knock the pins down, and *whoops*. The thing flew outta my hand, and crashed into the giant TV set. It made sparks! Grandpa Lloyd said bad words."

"I'm sure he did." She bit the inside of her lower lip.

"The video-game thing is in here." Ryan patted the suitcase. "Grandpa said to take it with me."

Shannon made a mental note to make sure the "thing" didn't go flying out of Ryan's hand in her apartment. She couldn't afford a new TV. "That was very nice of him."

"Yep. It was." He dug into the backpack again, pulling out the book Greg had given him as a going-away present.

The puzzle pieces clicked into place. "Ryan?"

He glanced up at her. "What?"

"Are you sure those were all accidents?"

His eyes widened, and Shannon could all but see a tarnished, crooked halo appear over his head. "Uh… yeah. Well…the police weren't."

"When you called them so you could come home?"

"Yeah, and when I called them 'cause I saw a stranger in the garden. I didn't know Grandma Patty *wanted* him there. A whole bunch of cop cars came that time. They let me turn on the lights."

"Grandma Patty had a lot of headaches while you were there?" Squad cars screaming up to her house might have contributed to at least one or two migraines.

The boy wrinkled his nose. "She *always* had a headache. You can't play trucks and not make noise, you know."

"Oh, I know." The child had fought the only way he could. In a *Ransom of Red Chief*-inspired way.

And the little imp had won.

He'd accomplished what she hadn't been able to. Fine role model she'd turned out to be. The kid had rescued both of them. Her from an empty, lonely life, and he'd saved himself from Grandma Patty, who'd meant well. Or so Shannon now chose to believe.

Torn between praising him for his courage and ingenuity, and scolding him for being mischievous, she took the book from him and returned it to his bookcase, propped open on the top shelf in a place of honor.

"Can we go see Uncle Greg now? I want him to know I'm home. Maybe we can go to Paula's Parlors. You can have artichoke pizza, and me and Uncle Greg will have pepperoni."

"We can go to Paula's. We should have a celebration. This is the best day I've had in two whole weeks." And it would be even better once she'd gotten Cathy to read the papers and assure her that they really said what Lloyd had promised.

"Cool! A party. Can we invite Jack and Katie, too?"

"Oh, sweetie. I don't think so."

Ryan's shoulders drooped. "Why not?"

"Because." Shannon couldn't figure out how to explain to a six-year-old that she'd dumped the family that had welcomed them into their midst. Dumped the man he'd claimed as an uncle.

The man she'd fallen in love with.

In a preemptive strike.

Ryan once again propped his fists on his hips. "You made him mad, didn't you? Because you wrecked the painting."

"Greg doesn't know I wrecked his painting."

Ryan's mouth gaped. "Oooo, he's going to be really mad when he finds out."

More likely, he'd be hurt. Again. His hard work, his thoughtful gift, gone. "All the more reason not to call him."

Ryan shook his head. "You need to tell him you're sorry. I miss him."

Out of the mouths of babes.

"I don't know if a simple 'I'm sorry' is going to be enough to fix this."

Fate—and a six-year-old's ingenuity—had returned Ryan to her. Returned her hope and her faith.

Was it too much to ask for Greg as well?

If she didn't try, she'd never know.

"We need a plan."

SEVERAL HOURS LATER, Shannon chewed her thumbnail as Cathy read the paperwork at Shannon's table. Ryan played his new video game in the living room—with the controller securely fastened to his wrist.

Finally Greg's sister flipped the packet closed. "I'll want to go over it again, but on first read-through, this is solid. Bring it by my office Monday, we'll make a few minor changes, and you can sign. We'll have one of the staff witness and notarize it."

"Thank God." Shannon exhaled slowly, and it had nothing to do with letting go, and everything to do with the biggest sense of relief she'd ever known. And the greatest joy she'd ever known.

Ryan was well and truly hers.

To keep.

The magnitude staggered her. She leaned against

the kitchen counter. From here on out, she and Ryan were a team.

The only thing that tempered her joy was Greg's absence. The man who'd taught her—and Ryan, apparently—to stand up for what she wanted should be here with them.

Celebrating.

But she'd destroyed her chances with Greg, just as she'd destroyed his mural.

All because she'd been too scared of losing him to hold on.

How stupid was that? So stupid, in a horror movie, she'd have been one of the idiot women who went, unarmed and in her underwear, into the dark basement after several other people had gone missing.

Cathy pushed back her chair. "Congratulations, Shannon, it's a boy. And he's all yours."

"Woo-hoo!" Ryan called from the living room. "No more stupid judges."

The two women laughed.

"I don't know how to ever thank you," Shannon said.

"Don't thank me for this one. Thank Ryan. Or should I say Red Chief?" Cathy checked her watch. "I have to run. Tomorrow's Elke's wedding, so tonight is not only the bachelor party, but the kidnapping of the groom *from* the bachelor party."

Elke's wedding. The whole Hawkins family gathered together. Shannon had eagerly anticipated going with Greg. "Kidnapping of the groom?"

"Family tradition. Basically the women stop the party dead in its tracks so the groom isn't too hungover for the wedding. But because the men know we'll be coming, the challenge is to find them. They don't tell us where the party is, and they keep it moving from place to place."

"Really?" Wheels turned in Shannon's head. A plan began to take shape. She needed the rest of the Hawkinses, especially the women, back on her side if she'd ever stand a chance with Greg. "So you have to be able to locate them?"

"Exactly."

"Do you know if Greg's using his Tracker tonight?"

"They rented a Hummer limo, but believe it or not, they can't all fit in it. So, yes, I think Greg is a designated driver. Why?"

Shannon pointed at Cathy's laptop on the table. "Does that thing have wireless Internet?"

"Yes. I use a wireless phone card. I can get Internet anywhere over the cell-phone network."

"Perfect." Shannon resisted the temptation to rub her hands together like a plotting supervillain. "If I help you with your mission, can I get the Hawkins women to help me with mine?"

Cathy's eyes narrowed. "I guess that depends on exactly what you have in mind. You're persona non grata with the Hawkinses right now. I'm here because of professional obligation." Her expression softened. "Okay, and because of my brother. I'm trying to get the lay of the land here. He's been miserable."

"Cathy, I know I've hurt Greg." Not that she'd intended to. But the reality was, she had. She'd seen it in his eyes when she'd told him to leave. Heard it in his voice when he'd called to check on her, or pounded on her door, begging her to let him in. Her stomach sank. This was going to be a long shot.

"I'm *really* sorry for that. I can only claim temporary insanity over losing Ryan, and throw myself on your mercy. The truth is—" Shannon swallowed hard "—I've realized how empty my life is without him. Without all of you. A smart kid and an even wiser man taught me I have to fight for what I want. I want your brother to give me another chance."

"Do you love him?"

She wiped her palms on her jeans. Nodded. "Yes. I do."

Cathy studied her for a moment, examining her with the strip-her-down-to-the-bare-essentials gaze of a lawyer. She jerked her head downward. "All right then. Let's go to my parents' house, and you can fill in the details on the way."

CHAPTER FOURTEEN

GREG TOOK OUT his cell phone, flipped it open, then stopped. Disgusted with himself, he snapped it shut and put it away. He leaned his elbows on the scarred wood of the bar's edge, toying with the once-frosted mug that had thawed long ago. He swirled the dregs in the bottom.

A roar erupted from the men gathered in the corner, shooting darts at a life-size cardboard centerfold covered with balloons.

"You're a freakin' downer," Hayden said, dropping onto the stool next to him, a bottle of ale in his hand. "Sitting over here, crying in your root beer."

Greg snorted. "Get the hell out of here. I'm not crying."

Hayden leaned over and sniffed Greg's mug. "But you are drinking root beer."

"Hello, designated driver, remember? Besides, it looks like ale if you don't get too close. Even kicks up a head."

"What's got your boxers in a bunch tonight, Gory? No, wait, let me take a wild guess. Shannon?"

Greg lifted one shoulder. "Cathy called earlier. Ryan's back with Shannon, where he belongs. Apparently the kid drove his grandmother insane until she returned him. Kudos to him." He lifted his glass in salute, then slugged back the last mouthful of soda.

At least someone had fought for what they wanted, and won.

This giving-her-space crap was for the birds.

Greg slid off the bar stool. "I'm going over there."

Hayden grabbed him by the arm. "Oh no you're not. Not tonight, anyway. You're my designated driver, Root Beer Boy."

"I'm sure if you, Derek and Finn tried, you could squeeze into the Hummer."

"I'm not sitting on anybody's lap. Especially when they've been drinking all night."

"Call a taxi."

"You are *not* ditching us tonight." Hayden released his grip. "Look, Gory, tonight and tomorrow are for family. Besides, maybe now that she's got the boy again, she'll come crawling back to you."

"You think?"

Hayden shrugged. "Maybe. You won't know if you don't give it a chance. She dumped *you*, bro. It's only fair that she does the crawling."

Greg didn't care about fair. He just wanted her back. Still, he was obligated tonight.

And tomorrow.

"Fine. But if I don't hear from her by Sunday afternoon, I'm going after her. I'm not going to wait around and lose her because I'm too proud."

Hayden's bushy eyebrows climbed his forehead. He groaned, shaking his head in disgust. "You are so whipped."

"Someday, Hayden, you'll meet a woman, and immediately there'll be this connection. It might be vague and hard to pin down at first, but you'll feel it. And then we'll see who's whipped."

Their father sauntered over and dropped an arm around each of their shoulders. "You boys about ready to mount up? Time to move this party and keep a jump on the women. You've outdone yourself this time, Hayden. I think Jeremy may just become the first groom in recent family history to outsmart the ladies. Love the loophole. You should have been a lawyer."

"Thanks, Dad," Hayden said, puffing out his chest.

Greg slapped him across the breastbone, forcing him to deflate. "Don't get too excited yet. It's still early. Besides, if we do outwit them, just think how pissed Elke's going to be at you tomorrow."

"True," their dad said. "I wouldn't want to be you, son, if we do win this one. You know what will happen." He stepped into the center of the room, cupping his hands around his mouth. "Mount up, gentlemen. Time to take this party on the road."

"Aw, we didn't get the centerfold naked yet," someone yelled from the corner.

"Bring her with us," Hayden shouted. He'd designed the "lady" and commissioned Greg to create her.

The group left the bar with a partially balloon-clad cardboard centerfold tucked under Derek's arm. He stashed her in the far back of the Tracker.

"Push that down so I don't get a ticket," Greg ordered, after looking in the rearview mirror and discovering a wardrobe malfunction had uncovered one breast. The last thing he needed was some sort of obscenity violation.

That would go over well for a guy who worked with kids.

A guy whose new nonprofit needed funding.

As they pulled out of the bar's parking lot, Greg glanced in the direction that would take him to Shannon's.

Hayden twisted in the passenger seat and slugged him in the arm. "Knock it off. No pining until Sunday. Tomorrow, we sell Jeremy into bondage to our big sister. Tonight, we party and mourn the loss of another bachelor."

From the backseat, Derek and Finn added their agreement.

Greg rubbed his shoulder, where a knot was undoubtedly forming. He wasn't in the mood to party.

And he was mourning that tomorrow he'd attend Elke's wedding stag, when he'd anticipated being there with Shannon.

With a ring on her finger, and him the next Hawkins in line to try to avoid a groom-napping by the women.

"I FEEL SILLY," Shannon admitted to the kitchen full of women. They'd spent the early evening gathering the pieces for her costume, and now that she had it on, she wasn't so sure this was a good plan.

Mysterious Lady O—she'd refused to tell them what the *O* stood for—wore a black corset with white lacing and tiny, off-the-shoulder gauzy sleeves, a short black skirt slit up the side, fishnet stockings, thigh-high boots, a flat-top black hat and a short black cape.

Along with a mask, of course. All superheroes wore masks. Shannon had borrowed SuperKid's mask from her dresser for the final piece of the costume.

"You don't look silly, honey. You look sexy as hell," Lydia said.

"Mom." Bethany, the oldest daughter, rolled her eyes.

"Well, she does. When a woman is trying to entice a man back, she needs to use every weapon in her arsenal. And sex is a powerful weapon. Your brother would have to be blind and castrated to ignore her in that outfit."

Shannon's face heated while everyone else burst out laughing.

Lydia patted her cheek. "Don't be embarrassed. I've had twelve children, and contrary to what they sometimes like to believe, not one of them came from a cabbage patch."

"They're on the move," Cathy announced from the table, where she had her laptop open. "They're leaving the second bar now."

Everyone clustered around her, watching the blip on the screen. "This is great," Elke said. "We don't have to run all over Erie trying to find them. We've got to remember this GPS thing in the future."

"I don't think this will work again." Bethany shook her head. "Next time they'll be checking all the vehicles for planted bugs."

"Not if we don't tell them," Shannon said slyly. "Mysterious Lady O has superpowers—or at least really great superhero toys—that let her track the man she loves. Right?"

Lydia chuckled. "I like how you think."

"It's only a few minutes after nine." Kara, the youngest of the Hawkins clan and one-half of the twin set, pointed at the clock hanging over the doorway. "Elke, he's your groom. Do we intercept now, or let them party longer?"

"I think we can let them go a little longer. Jeremy promised me he wasn't going to drink that much anyway."

Lydia snorted. "That's what they all say. That's what your father said, and he got shitfaced. Believe me, he paid for it."

"And thus gave rise to a family tradition," Elke intoned. "The kidnapping of the groom from the bachelor party."

"Wait a minute." Cathy leaned closer to the screen. "They're heading out of town on Route 19."

"What? Oh, that's so against the rules." Lydia grabbed a pair of glasses from beside the napkin holder in the center of the table, and perched them on the end of her nose so she could see the computer.

"Those cheaters," Elke said. "I'll bet I know where they're headed. Jeremy's family has a cabin down toward Canadohta Lake."

Judy, focused on nursing her two-month-old son, piped up. "We'd have never found them there, seeing as they're not supposed to leave Erie. Good thing you're here, Shannon. They're in for a big surprise. I'm sure they think they're in the clear."

"Elke, you're staying here on babysitting duty—it's bad luck for the groom to see the bride. Judy, you get to stay and help her since you're sort of tied up at the moment," Lydia instructed.

Ryan, along with Derek's kids and Judy's three-year-old, was watching a DVD in the family room. When Shannon had peeked in before donning her costume, Katie had been snuggled up alongside Ryan, whose eyelids had been drooping.

It had been a long and emotionally taxing day for both boy and aunt.

And she still had to convince Greg she deserved another chance.

She shivered. What if it didn't work? What if she'd already lost him? What if he'd learned as much from her as she'd learned from him, and had already let her go?

No more thinking that way. You will fight until he surrenders. Life couldn't be so cruel as to only give her back half of the Super Duo who'd come to mean everything to her.

"The rest of you, let's roll," Lydia ordered. "We've got men to surprise and a groom to kidnap."

RUSTIC WASN'T THE WORD to describe Jeremy's family cabin. Though made of exposed logs with chinked walls, rustic ended there. Besides electricity and running water, the huge place had a fully furnished kitchen, satellite TV, and best of all, with the steamy heat outside—why Elke wanted to get married in the beginning of August was beyond Greg—central air.

This was Greg's idea of a cabin in the woods.

Finn pulled a glass dish of seven-layer dip from the oven and set it on the counter serving as their buffet. Several containers of wings—one garlic and butter, the other a mild version of Finn's hot wings—were already picked over.

Coolers with various beverages formed the lower buffet, lined up against the base of the counter peninsula.

The French doors that led out to the deck opened and closed on a regular basis, letting in a blast of sticky air each time.

In the living room, a bunch of guys who wouldn't have passed a Breathalyzer test were trying their skill at driving a virtual race car, with results that evoked howls of laughter from those watching.

Jeremy's brother poked Greg in the shoulder with the tip of a beer bottle. "Greg. There's a pair of masked, caped chicks at the front door, asking for you."

"Masked, caped chicks?" Greg groaned. "My stalker fans. I've got to figure out how they find me. Usually they only show up in public places."

"If these are stalkers, I gotta get me some."

Greg headed for the front door, Jeremy's brother, as well as two of his own—Finn and Hayden—on his heels.

"Ladies, come in. Don't stand out there on the porch," boomed another male voice as they approached the foyer. Jeremy's dad escorted the women in.

The cars on the screen slowed and smashed into each other as the men turned their attention to the two women in the house.

The quality of his stalkers had greatly improved, from beer-bellied frat boys to a woman who exuded sensuality.

The woman who hung back wore black jeans beneath her cape. She had a small video camera in her hand. Both of them wore masks.

But the one headed in his direction…

Thigh-high boots under a slit skirt and short cape…fishnet stockings. She kept her head down, a broad-brimmed hat hiding her face except for the tip of her chin.

She tossed her cape over her shoulders, and the testosterone level in the cabin shot through the roof. Hums of male appreciation filled the room.

Above the skirt, she wore a formfitting black corset, creating rounded swells of creamy breasts that made Greg's fingers twitch. Part of him swelled in response, triggering a wave of guilt.

But dammit, she was hot.

He was in love with Shannon, not dead. Only a dead man wouldn't respond to this woman.

Jeremy sidled up to him. "Elke's going to kill me if

she finds out we had a stripper," he whispered harshly, eyes glued on the woman's form. "And you know someone will blab. Get rid of her!"

"I didn't hire a stripper. Talk to Hayden," Greg murmured out of the side of his mouth.

"Don't blame me," Hayden said from behind him. "It's not my doing. I might bend some of the rules, but not the no-strippers rule. I like my nuts right where they are."

The woman's head snapped up, and her eyes flashed behind the mask. She propped her hands on her hips, which only drew more attention to her curves.

There was something about her…

"Oh, for crying out loud. I'm not deaf, and I'm not a stripper!"

That voice… "Shannon?" Stunned, Greg took a step toward her.

She nodded. Which made her breasts jiggle. The central air couldn't keep up with the rising temperature in the room. He wanted to tuck the cape around her, sheltering her from the predatory stares of every man in the room.

"Yes, it's me. I have something I need to tell you."

Hayden chuckled behind him. He nudged Greg. "Here comes the groveling," he said so softly Greg barely heard him. "Told you. Still, she's so hot, I might have suspended my code and gone crawling back. Way to go, Gory."

Greg swiveled to glare at his younger brother.

Shannon cleared her throat. "I stand before you a changed woman. I was wrong."

"Somebody alert the media! A woman admits she was wrong," hollered one of Jeremy's friends who'd just come in from the deck.

Someone—it might have been Derek, but Greg couldn't be sure—elbowed the guy in the stomach.

"Sorry about that," Greg said. "You were saying?"

She twisted the edge of the cape around her finger. "Without you, everything is black and white. There's no color. No joy. No surprises, no fun. No one to share my good news with. I wanted to call you today so bad when Ryan came home."

"I heard about that. Congratulations. I'm really happy for both of you." Greg's pulse pounded, and his hands grew clammy. Shannon was *here*. She'd come back to him.

"I pushed you away because I was too afraid of losing you, which was stupid. But I'd been doing it for years. And I was already hurting over Ryan.

"I guess what I'm trying to say is, I'm sorry. I'll do whatever it takes to prove that to you. I'm not going to let go, either. If I have to stalk you, hound you, dress as a superhero to get you back, I'll do it."

A lump settled deep in Greg's throat. He didn't think he could speak if he tried.

Shannon took another step in his direction. "I love you, Greg Hawkins. Will you let me be your sidekick?"

He quickly closed the gap between them. He slid the clasp down the string and removed the hat, then the mask, letting both items drop to the floor. He framed her face with his hands, holding her tight. He stared into her eyes, saw tears make the dark brown shimmer. "Is that forever I see?"

She nodded. "Yes."

He lowered his head, pressing his lips to hers. She'd never tasted sweeter.

Hoots and hollers erupted around them. "Mine," he murmured in her ear. "Mine."

"Yes," she said through laughter and tears.

Greg let her go, wrapping the edges of the cape around her and holding it shut. “Sidekick, no. But I just might be in the market for a partner.”

“Awww.” “Oh, that’s so sweet.” “Awww.” A cluster of women crowded in the front door.

Greg looked over Shannon’s head. The blonde with the camera stopped recording, pulling off her wig and mask to reveal his baby sister, Kara. Behind her stood his mother and two more sisters.

“Busted, gentlemen,” his mom said. “This bachelor party is officially over. Cathy, Bethany, gather up the unopened booze and put it in the trunk. We’ll use the leftovers for the post-reception party tomorrow night. Dump the open bottles. Shannon, since my crystal ball tells me you may eventually become a member of this family, I’m assigning you to round up the groom. Consider it your initiation. And you—” she shook her finger at Hayden “—come here.”

Hayden held up his hands, backing away as their mother advanced on him. But she reached out to grab him by the ear and tug.

Hayden bent over. “Ow, ow, Mom, come on. That hurts.”

“You were in charge of the locations, am I right?”

“Y-yes, ma’am.”

“So you broke the rules.”

“No, there’s a loophole… Erie County. We didn’t leave Erie *County!* We wanted to win this time.” Hayden’s petulant voice faded as their mother dragged him out the front door, for a lecture on cheating, no doubt.

Greg knew who’d won this time.

He had. Hands down.

Cathy and Bethany started closing the coolers, and

the men, grumbling good-naturedly, tossed empties into a blue recycling can. The bottles clanked as they landed. Finn covered up the food with aluminum foil.

"How *did* you find us?" Greg asked Shannon, who hadn't been able to attend to her assigned task because he still gripped her cape.

She smiled. "Superhero secret. We have the most amazing toys, you know."

"Forget the toys," he said softly. "I just want to know if you'll wear this costume for me one night after Ryan goes to bed." He waggled his eyebrows at her. "I'm surprised you haven't caused a forest fire out here."

She laughed. "I think we might be able to arrange a costume…party. So, I'm forgiven?"

"Absolutely. I've missed you."

"I've missed you, too. I was afraid—" her voice trembled "—afraid I'd really lost you."

"You never lost me in the first place, sweetie. Not even for a minute. I was just giving you space."

"Don't give me space ever again, okay?"

"Okay." Greg offered her his arm. The last thing he needed was her wandering unescorted through so many males who'd gotten an eyeful of her assets. "Hey, you wanna go to a wedding with me tomorrow?"

"I'd love to."

"Great. Let's go kidnap the groom. It's family tradition, you know."

"Family tradition. I like the sound of that."

EPILOGUE

Twenty-six months later

"THIS IS THE LAST ONE, right?" Ryan asked. "No more after this?"

Though the October morning had been crisp, bright sunlight streamed through the hallway windows in the Erie County Courthouse. Just outside their designated courtroom, Shannon paused. She didn't have to look as far down to meet the eight-year-old's glance. He'd grown several inches in the past two years. "Last one. After today, it's really final."

Greg held out his fist. "Final victory. Not only have we won the battle, we've won the war."

The three of them butted knuckles, then headed into the courtroom, which was already overflowing with Hawkinses, from the old to the new. Elke and Jeremy's year-old boy was being passed from person to person, everyone smooching or pinching the baby's chubby cheeks. The family, big to start with, was growing by leaps and bounds. Today they would officially add another member.

Shannon awkwardly eased herself into a chair behind the table at the front of the room, then rubbed a palm over her ribs where her own soon-to-debut Hawkins kicked her. "Settle down in there," she said. "Let's have proper courtroom decorum, if you please."

Ryan giggled as he and Greg sat beside her. "Is the baby wearing a tie, like me?" To illustrate his lame joke, he flapped the end of the new superhero tie Greg had presented him at breakfast. The old one, packed away in a memory box on the top shelf of Shannon and Greg's closet, wasn't long enough anymore. The tie tack Lloyd and Patty had sent him in honor of the day, gold, with his new initials—all *four* of them—sparkled.

"No, the baby is wearing his birthday suit." Greg leaned over to caress Shannon's distended belly. Beneath his father's hand, the baby shifted, and Greg's blue eyes lit up.

Ryan covered his mouth and giggled again.

Cathy hustled into the room, slapping her briefcase on the table. "Sorry. I got held up with another case."

"You're here now," Greg said.

And just in time, too. They were told to rise as the judge entered the courtroom. Shannon heaved herself to her feet, then sighed in relief when she was allowed to sit again.

Judge Victoria Otis, the very judge who'd awarded Ryan's custody to Lloyd and Patty oh so long ago, beamed at them from her position on the bench. "We are here today to finalize the adoption of Ryan Schaffer by Gregory and Shenandoah Hawkins."

Ryan snickered. She glared at him. He cleared his throat and straightened in his chair, and the tarnished, crooked halo she'd grown to love blinked over his head.

Greg winked at her.

It had taken several rounds of legal battles, but the State had finally terminated Trevor's parental rights.

Since he'd been sentenced to life without parole for Willow's murder, his ability to care for Ryan wasn't even a question. And it had been decided in the child's best interest to allow Shannon and Greg to adopt him.

"Both parents understand that this is permanent? Once done, Ryan will legally be your son from this day forward."

Greg took Shannon's hand. She squeezed his fingers.

"We do, Your Honor," they said in unison.

And with the signing of a few documents, and the bang of the gavel, the judge declared it so.

With everything in her, Shannon knew Willow approved.

Ryan Lloyd Schaffer Hawkins—a big name for a still-not-that-big boy—leaped from his chair to wrap his arms around Shannon's neck. She held him tightly like she'd never let go, and the baby inside her squirmed. Greg joined them in a family hug while camera flashes lit the room.

"I'm never going to let you guys go," she told them, tears spilling down her face. "Damn hormones," she muttered, struggling to wipe her tears without releasing her husband and *son*.

"Picture time!" Cathy declared. "Go on."

The three of them posed with the judge, Ryan holding the adoption certificate.

"Let's take a family picture." Lydia, camera in hand, waved people into position. By the time everyone had been wrangled into place, Shannon's feet throbbed. Lydia passed the camera to the judge, who backed against the doors of the courtroom to get the whole crew in the frame.

"Everybody smile," Judge Otis ordered. "Say family!"

Greg's arm tightened around Shannon's pregnancy-distorted waist. She leaned her head on his shoulder, filled with a sense of contentment.

"Family!" sang a chorus of voices.

They'd need a *really* big sheet of paper to sketch this group. A picture-perfect family—okay, so maybe not *quite* perfect. But warts, foibles and quirks…

They were all hers.

THEN COMES BABY

BY
HELEN BRENNA

Helen Brenna grew up in a small town in central Minnesota, the seventh of eight children. Although she never dreamed of writing books, she's always been a voracious reader of romances. So after taking a break from her accounting career, she tried her hand at writing the romances she loves to read. She'd love hearing from you. E-mail her at helenbrenna@comcast.net or send mail to PO Box 24107, Minneapolis, MN 55424, USA. Visit her website at www.helenbrenna.com or chat with Helen and other authors at RidingWithTheTopDown.blogspot.com.

For Rosalie Jensen Brenna,
the best mother-in-law in the world!

Acknowledgements

Harlequin employs many truly wonderful people and I'm proud to say that some of the best of the best are those who put their hearts and energies into the Superromance line.

Thanks to all of you who make my books possible, who answer my silly questions time and time again and who are always professional and supportive, especially Wanda Ottewell, Victoria Curran, Alana Ruoso, Megan Long, Maureen Stead, Lola Speranza, Alicia Wong and Jane Hoogenberk.

Most importantly, heartfelt thanks to my editor Johanna Raisanen for her insight, patience and never-ending faith in my stories.

I couldn't do this without all of you!

CHAPTER ONE

"DADDY, I'M SCARED."

"It'll be all right, sweetheart." Neil stood frozen, listening. "I think it's gone."

Had he caused all this? Neil wracked his brain for another explanation, but there was none. That tunnel in the Ellora caves had been sealed off for a reason, and as usual he'd ignored all the warnings. If only he could turn back the clock. If only he'd never gone to India in the first place. But this was exactly what he'd asked for, wasn't it? Excitement. The unplanned and unknown.

They both heard it at the same time, that god-awful deep-chested cat growl. Katy screamed, and Neil reacted, pumping buckshot through the bedroom door again and again. This time he had to have killed that panther demon.

Jamis Quinn's hands stilled over his computer keyboard. On rereading what he'd written, he couldn't help but chuckle. "Don't get too cocky there, Neil, buddy. Things always seem to get worse before they get better."

"Get back, Katy," Neil whispered. Nudging his daughter behind him, he went to the door. The paint-chipped, shot-up wood barely hung from the hinges. He pulled on the knob, cracked the door open. Red. That's all he could see. Red

floor. Red walls. Blood? It couldn't be. That thing had no flesh, no substance.

Then he noticed bare feet and jean-clad legs, motionless on the floor. He hadn't killed the panther demon. He'd shot— "Oh, dear God! Colleen!"

"Mommy!" His daughter darted through the doorway.

"Katy, no!" There was that growling hiss again, coming from the living room. "Get back! It's still here." He jumped into the hall, putting himself between Katy and that... Rakshasas, that's what the Hindu locals had called it.

"Katy, run! Go to the Turners!"

"But Mommy—"

"Go! I want you out of here. Now!"

She scrambled down the hall, into the bedroom and outside through the window.

Neil cocked his shotgun, pumped off several shots, reloaded and shot again before the black panther spirit leaped and engulfed him like a cool, syrupy wave. The force pushed him back against the wall, but Neil could feel it dying, feel its heat draining away. He had to do something. Before it was too late. If it consumed his energy, the damned thing would revive itself and live to kill again. That was what'd happened with Wayne.

Well, that wasn't going to fly again. Not as long as Neil had a breath in his body.

"Take this, you son of a bitch." Neil pointed the gun at his own chest and fired. He fell to the floor next to Colleen and reached for her hand. "I'm sorry, baby."

"Oops. Too bad, buddy." If he didn't talk to himself, Jamis could go weeks without hearing the sound of his own voice. "Everyone, and I do mean everyone, is fair game. That's what you get for killing your wife."

"You always said one of these days I was going to get myself into something I couldn't handle," Neil whispered. "Well, I sure as hell did it this time."

The End.

"That was a perfect scene." Jamis filled his chest with a breath of air and slowly exhaled. "A perfect ending."

He took a swig of cold, black coffee, proofread the last chapter of his manuscript, and e-mailed it off to his agent. How many books was that? Fifteen? Yeah, that sounded about right. Now what? Book sixteen, of course. But that could wait until tomorrow. He was taking the rest of the day off.

Leaning back, he contemplated the choppy waters of Lake Superior's Chequamegon Bay from the desk in his loft office. A cool, early June breeze blew in through the window he'd opened that morning, and wonderfully complete silence fell over his blessedly isolated Mirabelle Island home.

That is, until a hopeful whine escaped from the tricolored mutt lying impatiently at the top of the steps. Jamis glanced at Snickers, whose fluffy black, brown and white tail swayed tentatively. "So you think it's time to celebrate finishing the book, huh? Red wine and a T-bone? I get the steak, you get the bone. My thoughts, exactly."

So what if it was only two o'clock in the afternoon? Feeling uncharacteristically cheerful, Jamis stood and followed Snickers, who was racing down the stairs and into the kitchen. Looking at the log cabin with its marble countertops, leather furnishings and big-screen TV, it was hard to imagine the place had been built close to eighty years ago. When he'd first bought it four years ago, the roof leaked, a family of raccoons had been nesting in the loft where his office was now, and a good gust of wind would have been as likely to blow rain as snow through the cracks in the windows.

Except for the massive fieldstone fireplace, Jamis had practically gutted the entire interior. He'd hired someone to update the wiring, plumbing and insulation, but had done the majority of the finishing work himself. Though he hadn't been much of a cook when he'd first moved here, he'd never regretted adding the center island stove and countertop that looked out over the great room, the woods and the lake beyond.

He stood there now, slicing the last of the mushrooms he planned to sauté, when his phone rang. "Figures." Caller ID displayed his agent's name. "Hello, Stephen." Jamis put the call on speakerphone, cracked open a bottle of cabernet sauvignon and poured out a generous glass. "You read it that quickly?"

"What do you think? You sent me everything but the last chapter last week," Stephen said. "I had to find out what was going to happen."

"And?"

"I can't believe you killed Neil. I liked him."

"He deserved it." Jamis was normally hard-pressed to find anyone truly worthy of life, himself included.

"Why?"

"He was a selfish idiot." Jamis tossed the last mushroom toward Snickers, who snatched the morsel out of the air and gulped it down without chewing. "He should've known that killing a monster of his own creation wouldn't be easy." He took a sip of wine. *Full flavor, not overly tannic, decent finish.*

Stephen sighed. "Who am I to argue? You're on a roll. Your editor thinks this one's going to get you back on the list."

Many years ago when his career had been on the upswing, he'd hit the *New York Times* bestseller list several books in a row. But that had been before his life had fallen apart. Since then he'd done a damned good job of burning bridges and every big publisher refused to work with him. Save this last one.

"I just need to write," Jamis whispered. This crap building up inside him had to manifest itself somehow. "At the moment it seems preferable to serial killing."

An uneasy silence hung on the line. "Honestly, Jamis, sometimes I don't know whether or not you're kidding."

"It sucks to be you, doesn't it?"

"Your publisher will up your advance on your current contract if you'll come out and play."

"A signing?"

"One-shot deal. You name the time and the place."

"No." Jamis tossed the T-bone onto his stovetop grill, the mushrooms in a pan of melted butter and garlic, and flipped on the cooking fan.

"But that's—"

"I said no."

"Jamis—"

"We've been over this before." He hadn't stepped off this island in four years. He wasn't about to leave for a damned his-skin-crawled-thinking-about-it book signing.

"It'd be in your best interests—"

"It's the one thing I will not give on, Stephen."

"Well, I had to try. You're contracted to give them the next book in three months. You have to make that deadline, or else—"

"It's a wildfire, tsunami and earthquake all rolled into one. I know, I know." He'd been in this business long enough to understand that a writer's success was due, in part at least, to momentum. Lose it and you might as well give it up. Starting over was worse than never having begun.

"You going to have the next book finished by September thirtieth?"

"No problem."

The summer months were his most productive. Fall, winter and spring, he could roam Mirabelle's shoreline, even the town square, to his heart's content and rarely encounter a living soul. But from June through August, with tourists crawling all over the town, Jamis kept his in-town excursions to a bare minimum, giving him all the time in the world to sit at his desk and write.

Snickers ran over to the porch windows, jumped onto his favorite chair, an oversize corduroy-covered monstrosity, and stared outside, cocking his head. Probably a squirrel.

"You're long overdue for a vacation. Why don't you take a trip somewhere? A few weeks off might do you some good."

Vacation? He had no intention of ever leaving this island. They'd be carrying him off in a long pine box. "You want that book by September thirtieth, I gotta get to work."

"Are you cooking? I can barely hear you."

He flipped off the noisy fan and what sounded like voices and a boat motor penetrated the thick walls of his cabin. People? Here? Highly improbable. There were only two private homes nestled within the more than five square miles of undeveloped Wisconsin state parkland on the northwest side of Mirabelle Island. His cabin was one and the other was an old Victorian that had been built in the 1950s to match the quaint architecture of the rest of the island. That house, a few hundred feet away, was owned by an old woman who spent only summers on Mirabelle.

Snickers let out a short bark.

Jamis walked out onto his four-season porch, glanced out the window and down the steep and rocky hillside to the Lake Superior shoreline. Through the new spring foliage now thick on the trees he barely made out the shape of a boat. It looked as if a small barge had anchored near the shore and had swung out a gangway to the dock. Several men were carrying boxes up to the old woman's house, and by the sheer number of them, it looked as if whoever was here, was here to stay.

"Good God," he muttered.

"Jamis, you there?" Stephen's voice came across the speaker on the phone. "What's the matter?"

Snickers sat in front of him and whined.

"Looks like someone's moving in next door."

"What happened to the old woman who used to live there?"

"I have no idea."

"Well, let's hope these new people are quiet."

No one could be as quiet as the previous occupant. Jamis barely ever heard a peep out of her. Occasionally, she'd have a guest or two, and he'd hear a door slamming or a garbage can clanging, but that had been the extent of it. She'd kept completely to herself. In fact, now that he thought about it, he wasn't sure he'd even seen her last summer.

"I gotta go," he said.

"This won't interfere with the new book, will it?"

"Have I ever once missed a deadline?" Jamis disconnected the call, and shut off the T-bone and mushrooms before going out onto his deck. Snickers raced down the steps, through the yard and toward the activity next door.

The events of the past several weeks finally made sense. He'd woken late one morning to Snickers barking frantically at the door. But when Jamis had looked outside there'd been no one around, although a boat similar to the barge now anchored below had been pulling away from the shore. A few days later, coming home from a lengthy trip to town for various errands and copious amounts of groceries, he'd passed the new police chief, Garrett Taylor, on the main road. Taylor, apparently a part-time construction handyman, had been pulling a small trailer filled with tools and supplies behind his golf cart. Jamis should've guessed then that something was up.

Now he walked through the shaded woods, stepped over the poison ivy and past the heavy ferns toward the old woman's house. There had to be at least four men carrying boxes from the water's edge.

"You got that end?" one of the men hollered.

"You betcha."

"Damn, this is a steep hill."

There was no practical way to move that much stuff from Mirabelle's town center to this side of the island. The path from the main road had to be close to a mile long and barely wide enough for golf carts, the only motorized vehicles allowed on the island.

"Who's moving in?" Jamis asked one of the men passing by and loaded down with a large, cardboard box.

"Don't know for sure." He nodded toward a woman standing on the wide back porch and directing traffic. "Ask her."

"All the boxes have the rooms marked," she said to the moving men.

That spindly wood sprite was in charge? Impossible. In tight, low-rise jeans and a short-sleeved orange T-shirt, she looked barely old enough to have graduated from college.

"Bedrooms one through four are upstairs," she went on. "The numbers are on the door. Bedroom five is on the main floor." With wavy blond hair, wide, heavily lashed eyes and a tall slender frame, all that honey needed was a wand to look like a modern-day princess from a kid's movie. *Wholesome,* there was no other word for her.

"Excuse me." He stepped toward the porch. "This house belongs to a *quiet* old woman." He'd no sooner closed his mouth than he realized how odd the comment sounded, but he'd be damned before he'd explain.

"Hi," she said. Then she smiled, lighting up her face and making the deepest blue eyes he'd ever seen almost dance, and wholesome turned to lively, pretty to beautiful. "Yeah, my grandmother used to live here. Sweet, wasn't she?"

"I wouldn't know." He'd never once spoken with the old woman. "What're you doing here?"

The wattage of her dazzling smile dimmed. Much better. "Grandma passed away a few months ago, and I inherited her house." She came into the yard and Snickers raced toward her. "Well, aren't you the cutest thing in the whole wide world?" She squatted and rubbed the dog's ears.

Snickers showed his appreciation by planting a big sloppy one on her mouth. *Disgusting.* How could she let him do that?

"Is he your dog?" she asked, looking up at him.

"Yeah."

"What's his name?"

"Snickers." Was he really having this conversation?

"And you look like a candy bar, too," she cooed and scratched the dog's neck, then she stood and held out her hand. "I'm Natalie Steeger. Nice to meet you."

Feeling distinctly dazed, Jamis shook her hand before the distant rumbling of golf carts coming through the woods distracted them both.

"Oh, goodie," she said, grinning. "Here they come."

Oh, goodie. "Here who come?"

"The kids."

Kids. As in more than one?

"I know it's crazy having them come on moving day, but I wanted them to feel a part of this." She motioned to the activity around her. "You know, help with the unpacking decisions. Get vested in everything happening here."

"What, exactly, *is* happening here?"

"I'm starting a summer camp for kids."

"You're kidding." Surely, his heart stopped midbeat. "Did Stephen put you up to this?"

"Stephen who?"

Holy hell. A camp for kids.

Man, did that bring back a whole host of bad memories. That's what Jamis's too-busy-for-their-only-child parents had done to get rid of him for three of the most miserable summers of his adolescence. His mother had thought she'd been doing him a favor sending him to the plushest, most expensive camp in the country. But somehow spoiled-rotten rich kids running untamed through the woods at all hours, not to mention bullying and pranking, hadn't been Jamis's idea of fun.

This had to be a dream. His imagination often took bad, even worse turns. *Any minute now,* Jamis told himself, *you're gonna wake up and this is all going to disappear. In fact, now would be a very good time. Wake up, Jamis!*

"Are you okay?" She reached out and rubbed his arm in a comforting, soothing way.

Jamis forgot all about the noise, the movers and the cool breeze blowing up from the water. He hadn't been touched by another human being in four years. That wasn't counting the casual brushing of fingertips at the post office or grocery store, the doctor and dentist appointments.

Those were impersonal in nature and didn't matter. This contact was genuine. Her hand was still firmly on his arm. He glanced into her sapphire eyes and felt the first stirrings of arousal since he couldn't remember when.

Holy hell was right.

"Hey." She was staring up at him, concerned, yes, but aware. Aware of him, definitely, as a man.

"I'm fine." He backed away.

The disturbing moment passed as quickly as it had descended when three golf carts, loaded down with kids of varying ages, emerged from the woods and pulled into a clearing near the house. Ron Setterberg, the owner of the Mirabelle Island rental business, was leading with the first cart and teenagers, a boy and a girl Jamis had never seen before, were driving the other two.

"Isn't this great?" the princess said, smiling again. "This summer, we're starting small. Only eight kids. But next summer, who knows? Maybe twenty."

As he stopped his cart, Ron nodded at him. Jamis gave a short wave, words entirely deserting him. "Let me know if you need anything else, Natalie." Ron waited until the kids climbed off his cart and then turned and headed back to town.

"Will do, Ron. Thanks."

The kids jumped down from the other two carts. "What do you want us to do?" asked the oldest girl.

"Can you take the younger kids into the house and get everyone familiar with everything?"

"Sure," said the oldest boy as they all filed past him.

Snickers, of course, had to run up to every single one of them, sniffing and licking hands and begging for pets.

"That's Galen and Samantha." She pointed to the teenagers. "Arianna, Chase, Blake and Ella are the middle four." She put her hand on her hips when one of the boys tried tripping the young fellow in front of him. "Chase, behave, please. Ryan and Toni are the two youngest."

The littlest girl, who lifted her hands away from an inquisitive and wet-nosed Snickers and who couldn't have been more than seven or eight, was the last to walk by Jamis. She had chubby cheeks and long curly hair the color of which almost perfectly matched her big, brown eyes, just like…

No, he wouldn't—couldn't—go there. This wasn't a dream. It was an outright nightmare. Jamis shook his head and laughed out loud. He'd have been hard-pressed to write this scene better himself. It was perfect, down to every last minute detail. He deserved nothing less than this.

Welcome, Jamis, to your own personal horror story.

CHAPTER TWO

"ARE YOU OKAY?" Natalie asked. For the life of her, she couldn't figure out what this man was laughing about. The almost hysterical quality to the sound of his voice made her want to invite him in for a cup of cocoa or give him a back rub. His relaxed state of dress, black T-shirt and loose-fitting khakis belied the fact that he was obviously stressed about something.

"Wonderful. Never been better." Instantly, every speck of humor disappeared from his handsome but troubled face. His long, dark hair and scruffy beard made him look desperately in need of some grooming, but his clothes were clean, his skin was clear and healthy and she could smell the scent of some musky men's shampoo on his shiny hair. And if muscular arms were any indication, he was in excellent physical shape. "Snickers, come." He turned and headed toward the woods.

"Hey!" Natalic called. "You didn't tell me your name."

"Jamis Quinn."

The name he'd thrown over his shoulder didn't sound familiar, but there was something about the severe, angular features of his face that reminded her of someone. Her first look into his toffee-brown eyes had confirmed it, but how could she have ever forgotten that mockingly superior gaze of his?

"Wait a minute!" She caught up with him and stepped directly in his path, forcing him to stop. "My grandma was in a nursing home for a while before she died, so it's been some time since I've been on Mirabelle. Are you living in the old log cabin?" The safety of the kids was priority and this guy seemed, though attractive in a potent woodsman sort of way, a bit strange.

"Yep. Can I go now?"

That was when it came to her. "I know! You're that writer, aren't you? What's his name?" Though Natalie had never read a single one of his books, let alone watched one of the movies based on his horrific stories, a person would've had to have her head buried in the sand to not recognize him.

"Quinn Roberts," he said. "Yeah, congratulations."

Handsome, sexy even, but definitely odd. Someone who wrote such distasteful stuff would have to be somewhat touched. What she couldn't understand was why in the world so many people enjoyed his books. "Do you live out here by yourself?" she asked.

"Yep."

"All year-round?"

"Yep."

"Even in the winter?"

"Didn't I just answer that question?" He glanced down at her, his furrowed brow openly expressing his impatience.

The idea of anyone staying on this island when the windchill frequently hit twenty below zero and the only way to the mainland was by snowmobile or helicopter seemed crazy to her. Even her grandmother had always moved to her Minneapolis home during the winter months.

"I happen to like peace and quiet. Can I go now?" His left eyebrow rose in a cocky sort of way as he glared at her, and she was left with the distinct impression he'd like nothing better than for her to disappear into thin air.

"Sure. Sorry. Didn't mean to keep you." Natalie watched him stomp through the woods with his dog leading the way. He didn't seem like a very happy man. "Good to meet you!" she called after him.

"Yeah, right." He kept walking, head down.

Maybe she shouldn't have touched him. She did that all the time, touched everything in stores or outside, people and things. She couldn't help it. Most folks didn't mind, but then most folks weren't charged up like Jamis Quinn. He'd felt tense, his muscles flexed as if he were poised to run off any second. Only he hadn't wanted to run, at least not at first. Initially, she was sure he'd welcomed the feeling of her hand on his skin. There'd been something in his eyes that made her want to reach up and knead his shoulder, but then he'd pulled away.

Stop it, Natalie. Remember what happened the last time? If you're attracted to this guy, he's bound to be a loser.

"Nat!" Samantha called from an open, upstairs window. "Everyone's fighting up here. We need help figuring out the bedrooms."

"I'm coming!" Natalie spun toward the back door. It was a good thing that last week Chief Taylor had come by to make sure the house was in working order, and that the movers had brought out all the furniture and arranged everything exactly to her specifications. All she and the kids had to do was unpack boxes and settle in.

"I am *not* sharing a room." Galen stuck his head out another window.

"Who died and made you king of the world?" Sam said, tossing her ponytailed light brown hair.

"No one." Galen smirked. "I always have been."

"Hold on," Natalie said. "I've got a chart." She grabbed her clipboard and ran upstairs to find kids zipping through the halls like wild animals, yelling and fighting. "Chase, no pushing," she said. "Blake, let go of your brother's arm. Arianna, don't snap at your sister."

Everyone ignored her. She watched them for a moment, her worries building. What had she gotten herself into? She'd thought she could handle this, having worked with kids her entire adult life, first as a camp counselor in the summers during college, and then as a social worker. Maybe she'd been kidding herself. Maybe she couldn't make a difference in the world. Old tapes fast-forwarded through her mind. Maybe she wasn't smart enough, caring enough, organized enough. Maybe—

No. She closed her eyes and focused. *You will not let in those doubts.* She could do this. She *would* do this. Instead of sitting at her old social services desk day in and day out, hands tied by bureaucratic red tape, she was finally going to be directly impacting lives. She'd even gone so far as to take a leave of absence from work to bring her ideas for a baby boot camp to life. She was going to turn these kids around. They were all going home at the end of the summer feeling better about themselves and believing they could make a difference in their own lives. But first she had to get control.

She stood in the hall, put two fingers in her mouth and let a whistle rip. Everyone stopped in his or her tracks. "Attention!" She pointed to the spot in front of her. "Let's all make a circle and have a quick meeting."

"I don't wanna."

"Do we have to?"

"Where's my bedroom?"

Time to get tough. "Do I need to remind all of you why

you're here?" she asked softly, looking into each child's face, one at a time. Every single one of these kids was on track to either flunk out of school or get kicked out for disciplinary issues. Her camp was their last chance.

Finally, although the kids complained, one by one, everyone except Galen gathered around. She had to hand it to that boy. He'd mastered the sullen James Dean act to a tee, arms crossed, head tilted just so, lips curved in a sardonic smile, but Natalie wasn't about to force anything on him. He'd had enough of that in his short life. Eventually, he'd come around.

"Okay, here's the deal. All your stuff is in boxes with your name on it in your assigned room. There are four bedrooms up here," Natalie said. "Galen and Samantha are the oldest and they're camp employees, so they get the two smaller bedrooms at the back of the house." She pointed down the hall. "Galen, you're in room number three. Sam, you're in four." The teenagers each looked at the other kids with smug expressions. "Galen and Sam? Remember, this is a summer job for you two."

"I know," Sam agreed.

"Whatever," Galen said, shoving his hands inside the pockets of his baggy jeans.

"So as part of your job, you two help the other kids make up their beds, put away their clothes and then you can take care of your own rooms."

"Got it," Sam said.

Galen nodded, looking bored to tears.

"Arianna, Ella and Toni, this is your bedroom over here. Chase, Blake and Ryan, you three are over here." They started to turn. "Wait a second." She leaned in, putting her arm around Ryan's too-bony shoulder. She was going to have to put some meat on this boy before the end of summer. "What do we need to do to make this the best summer ever?"

One of them groaned. "Ah, not this again!"

The others, of course, followed suit.

"I hate this!"

"Totally lame!"

Natalie didn't care. She'd take all the ridicule this world could dish out if she could instill hope in one child. One tiny drop in a pond could make far-reaching waves. "Close your eyes," she said. "Wish it, see it, make it happen." Sooner or later, they were all going to believe. She stepped away. "Okay, let's get settled! And there's a surprise for every one of you on your beds!"

Most of them didn't have the appropriate clothing for sometimes-chilly Mirabelle, so she'd bought them all new fleece jackets, sweatshirts, tennis shoes and several outfits. Knowing the teenagers would be more selective about styles, she'd given Galen and Sam a clothing allowance when she'd first offered them the job, and they'd had plenty of time to shop before leaving Minnesota, but from the size of Galen's small pack, though, she wondered if he hadn't pocketed the money.

As the little ones raced into their rooms, Natalie grinned. "I'll be downstairs if you need me."

She bounded down the steps and stopped outside the entryway to the old-fashioned kitchen, feeling suddenly nostalgic. With the white painted cabinets, yellow Formica countertops, black-and-white checkered floor and large, sturdy oak table at its center point, the room was exactly as Natalie remembered. Well, except for the cardboard boxes stacked on every flat surface.

The first time she'd come to Mirabelle with her adoptive parents and five older brothers and sisters, Natalie had been ten years old. Those two weeks with her new family had forever altered the course of her life. She'd been able to count on a bed to sleep in at night, warm covers and, every single day, enough food to eat.

Her favorite meal had been breakfast. With all the fresh air and activity on the island, she'd wake up starving every morning. She and her new brothers and sisters would all crowd around the big oak table waiting for Grandma's secret recipe French toast. When Grandma said secret, she meant secret. Through the years, no one had managed to finagle it out of her. Before Grammy had died, though, and with her entire family encircling her hospital bed, she'd singled out Natalie and whispered, "Orange zest. And Grand Marnier liqueur."

The old woman had known the urge to pay it all back ran even more deeply within Natalie than any of the other adopted grandchildren. That's why she'd willed to Natalie this house here on Mirabelle, as well as her home in Minneapolis, and enough money to cover expenses for at least a year. Rather than feeling slighted, Natalie's brothers and sisters and their adoptive parents, all of whom still lived relatively close to one another in the Twin Cities area, had encouraged Natalie to make the best of this opportunity.

So with everyone's blessings she'd taken it from there. She'd not only put together a comprehensive curriculum and filled out mounds of paperwork in order to get this camp licensed and approved by the state, she was also working on getting donations and grants to fund future camps. It all seemed a small price to pay to give a few kids a summer to remember the rest of their lives, a summer of hope.

Natalie looked around the house, boxes stacked all around, and smiled. "Thanks, Grammy, for making my dream come true."

A few hours later, the bedrooms had all been set up with Natalie having to negotiate only two disputes, the majority of the kitchen boxes had been emptied, the kids were alternating between playing outside and making chocolate chip cookies, and a dinner of pork chops and rice was bubbling away in a large slow cooker. She stepped out onto the back porch, already on her way to being exhausted. It was both exciting and frightening. For three months, she was going to be alone with eight kids. Well, except for that strange, but ruggedly sexy man living a hundred or so yards away.

She peered through the craggy red oaks and sugar maples with their new spring leaves and discerned the outline of Jamis Quinn's cabin. He had to feel cut off out here by himself, through the long, cold winters when more than half the island headed south as soon as the last tourist left at the end of every summer. That man had to be lonely.

Okay, stop. You're taking a break from men, remember?

She had the worst luck of any woman she knew with regard to men and relationships. Every guy she'd ever dated turned out to be a total jerk.

But there was no harm in being neighborly. Right?

Grabbing a plate of chocolate chip cookies, she stepped off the porch. "Come on, kids, let's go visit our new neighbor."

"I CAN'T BELIEVE THIS is happening." With his phone on speaker, Jamis paced the floor of his kitchen, his celebratory meal completely forgotten. Except for the wine. He'd downed that first glass while dialing his attorney's number, a man who also happened to be an old friend, and had immediately poured himself another. Too bad he'd quit stocking hard liquor in the cabin after losing a couple weeks his first winter here. A shot or five of tequila would make this situation, if not acceptable, at least more palatable.

"Jamis, relax," Chuck Romney said. He might be Charles to his fellow partners in the largest, most reputable law firm in downtown Minneapolis, but he'd always be Chuck to his old college party buddies. "Maybe it won't be as bad as you think."

"She's starting a summer camp for kids."

"This is a joke, right?"

"So you had no clue this was in the works?"

"None."

"You were supposed to be watching for that house going up for sale. What happened?"

"The property never went on the market," Chuck explained. "The woman inherited the estate from her grandmother when she died. What was I supposed to do?"

"What did you do?"

"I made a few inquiries with the attorneys handling the estate, asked if the new owner might be willing to sell and got shot down."

"That's not good enough."

"If she doesn't want to sell, Jamis, there's nothing I can do."

"Then you're fired."

"Yeah, so what else is new?" Chuck said, unmoved. "I've got a novel idea. Why don't *you* move and leave this poor woman alone? There has to be some uninhabited private island in Wisconsin. You could buy your own piece of rock and never have to worry about this again."

Jamis glanced around his house and broke into a cold sweat thinking of what it would take to pack up his loft office. Every wall was lined with built-in bookcases stuffed to the gills with research books, manuals and such. When he'd remodeled this old dog of a log cabin, he'd hired electrical engineers and computer technicians to connect him to the world via satellite. Everything was wireless, including his TV, network, speakers and Internet connections. He could work on his laptop in any room in the house, out on his porch and deck, even down by the lakeshore. It'd taken him no less than a year to get this house set up so that he'd never be able to find an excuse to leave Mirabelle.

There was no good reason that woman or her camp needed to be on this island. Jamis, on the other hand, had every reason to keep himself away from the rest of the world. Away from her and her kids.

"I have a book due in three months," he whispered, his mouth suddenly dust dry. If he was late with this publisher, he'll have burned his last shaky bridge. What would he do if he couldn't write, couldn't sell his books? "She needs to move."

"Good luck with that."

"Don't people have to get licenses or something for that many kids in one house?" Frustrated, he pounded his hand onto the granite countertop. "You know like pets?"

"There are all kinds of laws that apply to organizations that care for children. If you want me to, I'll check into it and make sure she covered her bases."

"Do that. Find something that'll close her down." He took a deep breath, calming himself.

"Jamis, maybe it's not such a bad thing that you have neighbors. Maybe this is good—"

"When's the last time you read one of my books?"

There was a short pause on the line. "No offense, Jamis, but you know they're not my cup of tea."

"That's what I'm talking about. Would you want to live next to me?"

"Yeah. I would."

"You have to say that. You're my friend."

"Well, at least you'll admit to the friend part. For God's sake, Jamis, come back for a weekend at least. Let's have lunch."

How long had it been since Jamis had had a beer with a buddy at a bar? Went to a football game? Asked a woman to dance? "Can't do that, Chuck. I need her gone."

Chuck sighed. "I'll see what I can do."

Jamis disconnected the call and stared out the window toward that house. It felt strange knowing there were people, live human beings, no less than a hundred yards through those trees. Not for long, if he had anything to say about it.

His stomach grumbled and he went to his kitchen to see if any part of his meal was salvageable. The steak was tough as a hockey puck, but it'd fill his stomach. He took the plate to his computer and set to work answering the e-mails he'd left unanswered for the past several weeks while he'd finished this last book.

A strange noise sounded downstairs. *What the—?* Was that a knock? On his door? That's something he didn't hear every day. Or ever, for that matter. Could he ignore it? Pretend like he was… out?

"Hello!" a voice sounded from outside.

Dammit.

He pounded across the hardwood floor and yanked open the door. With a couple kids piled up behind her, that woman—what was her name again?—stood outside.

"We brought you cookies," she said, holding out a plate covered in plastic wrap.

"Cookies." Was she serious?

"Homemade. Chocolate chip. Can we come in?"

"No."

As if she hadn't heard him, Natalie, that was her name, took a step toward him. "Oh, goodness, look what you've done to this place." She stepped close, too close, and he was forced to back away. "This cabin used to be a ramshackle dump. My brothers and sisters and I used to play hide-and-seek in here. I can't believe the changes you've made. It's gorgeous."

While the other kids stayed outside, yelling at each other and roughhousing and jumping from one large rock to the next in his yard, the littlest girl stuck close behind Natalie and cautiously eyed Jamis with those too-big brown eyes.

"This is Toni."

Not names again. No, no, no. He really, really didn't want to know, let alone remember. "Can you just…go?"

She glanced up at him, no anger, only concern. "I'm sorry. I…"

"Look. It's not you. It's me. I came to this island for peace and quiet. Believe it or not, that's the way I like it. So…could you not…bother me? I won't bother you, either. Not a word. Pretend like I don't exist."

At first, she looked confused, then, as understanding dawned, supremely and frustratingly undaunted. "I can see you need some space."

Yeah. Try five miles of it.

She set the plate of cookies on the side table by the door. "Come on, Toni." She turned the girl around and went outside. "Kids, let's go."

Jamis watched the kids run willy-nilly through the woods, feeling something curiously bordering on regret. "I haven't always been this way," he whispered.

Years and years ago in Minneapolis, he'd lived like everyone else, worked and went to coffee shops and parties. Some people—okay, only a few—had even liked him, once upon a time. He'd been so normal, in fact, that those first years of being alone here on Mirabelle had nearly killed him. That'd been the outcome he'd been after, he supposed. Instead, he'd simply adapted over time and become comfortable with the silence. Now, Jamis couldn't imagine life any other way.

Oh, for crying out loud. His thoughts were jerked back to the present. She was taking the group straight through the poison ivy. *They are not your problem. Do not get involved.* Why should he care if every single one of them developed a horrible, itchy, miserable rash?

At the edge of the forest the smallest girl looked back over her shoulder. When she saw him watching them, she scurried forward and, apparently frightened of him, grasped for Natalie's hand. Smart girl. Kids somehow always managed to see the truth inside a person.

Something long dormant stirred inside him. Compassion, sensitivity, humanity? Impossible. Jamis no longer felt those emotions.

He glanced at the plate of cookies, grabbed one and took a big bite. Cringing, he spit the mouthful into his hand. Had the woman used an entire box of baking soda or just half?

"That has to be the worst thing I've ever tasted." He tossed the remainder of the cookie to Snickers. The dog caught the thing in midair, dropped it to the floor and sniffed at it disdainfully.

"Unbelievable." Jamis shook his head. On second thought, maybe he'd get lucky and those kids would starve to death. *Yeah, that'd get rid of 'em. Or drowning. Carbon monoxide poisoning would work, too. Aliens. Evil spirits. Water demons.*

Suddenly he realized what he was doing. Again.

Stop it! Geez, Jamis! Don't you ever learn?

I take it back. I take it all back. Every single word.

Disgusted with himself, he glanced down at Snickers. "Let's go for a run, pup. A *long* one."

CHAPTER THREE

THE NEXT DAY AROUND lunchtime, creativity having eluded him all morning, Jamis glanced into his refrigerator. Pickles, ketchup, mustard and mayo. *Yum. That'd make a spectacular meal.* Closing the door, he muttered to himself, "You've put it off long enough." He didn't relish the idea of going into town and bumping elbows with the tourist crowds, but his cupboards, too, were just about bare.

The decision made, he grabbed the package he needed to mail, his backpack, a baseball cap and a pair of sunglasses and set off on the path through the woods to the road into town. Familiar with the once-a-week ritual for groceries and mail, Snickers led the way into town until a white-tailed deer leaped onto the road and Jamis stopped. "Snickers. Sit."

The dog plopped his butt down by Jamis's side and Jamis grabbed his collar to make sure the silly mutt didn't run after the deer and get his skull kicked in. They both watched as a string of three female deer ran in front of them and disappeared into the woods. Afterward, they continued on their way with chickadees and finches chirping in the trees.

About a five-mile walk down a paved, heavily wooded and narrow road, he walked fast, considering it part of his workout for the day. It normally took him about an hour one-way. He could have his groceries and mail delivered directly to his house, but that would require conversing with these islanders, something he tried to keep to a minimum. He left them alone and they left him alone. The arrangement had worked out very well for years.

His first sight of civilization was the Mirabelle Island Inn, and as soon as its red-tiled roof became visible, his stomach took a tumble. People. Talking, laughing, breathing. This summer seemed busier than last. In fact, he had to walk on the cobblestone street to avoid the crowds on the sidewalk. The damned pool and golf course they'd built last year were wreaking havoc on his once-quiet island.

On reaching Newman's Grocery, Jamis stopped. Snickers immediately sat on Jamis's left and looked up at him, waiting. He knew the drill. Jamis hooked a leash to Snickers's collar and tied him to the lamppost. Out in the woods, Snickers could run untethered to his heart's content, but in town the leash became a necessity.

"Stay," Jamis said to Snickers, putting out his hand palm forward. "I'll be back soon."

Jamis slipped on the hat and sunglasses and walked into the store. One time, not long after he'd moved to Mirabelle, a reader had recognized him and made a fuss. "It's Quinn Roberts," she'd screamed, practically swooning. "I'm your biggest fan." Blah, blah, blah, blah, blah. Jamis had ignored the woman, but a crowd had gathered. In the end, he'd left his grocery cart and run, not walked, out of the building. He'd even skipped the post office that day, the only part of this routine he halfway enjoyed.

In the produce department, he selected his usual fruits and vegetables and glanced around. What was going on here? There seemed to be a bigger selection of items. Fresh artichokes. More varieties of chilies. Arugula. Vine-ripened tomatoes. The meat department was carrying a new brand of Italian sausage that looked amazing. Some organic selections had been added in frozen foods, so he decided to try a few things. And the variety of cheese was outstanding. There appeared to be one upside to Mirabelle's newfound popularity.

While waiting in the checkout line, several tourists eyed him, but he refused to look at them. After paying and stuffing his groceries into his pack, he collected Snickers and walked to the post office, a couple blocks inland off Main. Tying the dog to another lamppost, he entered the small brick building to the sound of a soft chiming.

The usual clerk, a woman with short salt-and-pepper hair, came to the counter, looking as cantankerous as ever. She had to be close to retirement and acted as if the event couldn't come quick enough. No matter the time or day of the week, this woman treated him as if he'd just disturbed her lunch hour. Without a word, she stared at him from the other side of the counter.

"I'm here to pick up my mail," he said.

"Your name?"

She did this every time, and every time he chose to ignore her. Today, she'd finally gotten to him. "You gotta be kidding me."

"Name."

"Jamis…Quinn," he said, punctuating every syllable.

"Identification."

He glared at her, wishing there was something, anything, he could do to mess with her, but there wasn't. He'd tried on numerous past occasions to ruffle her feathers and had more than once left completely disappointed. Nothing fazed this woman. If he didn't show her his driver's license, he wasn't going to get his mail. No ifs, ands or buts. He flipped out his wallet.

After taking her time studying his ID, she slowly walked into the back room, returned what seemed an eternity later with a stack of envelopes, papers and flyers all banded together and tossed it on the counter toward him.

"I need to mail this package," he said, setting a large padded envelope between them.

"Is there anything liquid, perishable or flammable inside?"

"What do you think?"

The only thing he'd ever sent out of this post office had been paper. Every manuscript he'd ever written he mailed to his mother. Why, he couldn't say. Although she never read any of his books, every time he finished one he had to send it to her. Most likely he was still looking for some crumb of acknowledgment from her, but he wasn't holding his breath.

The postal clerk cocked her head at him. "I think if you don't answer my question, I won't mail your package."

"No. There is nothing liquid, perishable or flammable in the damned thing."

She put the package on her scale and came up with a charge. He flipped out his credit card to pay.

"May I see your ID, please?"

He laughed. "You're funny, you know that?"

"Just doing my job."

"I already showed you my ID. Besides which, I've been coming here once a week for years picking up my mail and mailing packages, so you know very well who I am."

"Correction. You've been coming here once a week for *four* years and have never once said thank you or please."

She had him there. "What's your name?"

"Sally McGregor," she said with virtually the same intonation as he'd used with her.

"Well, Sally, you're right." He snapped up his credit

card. At this point, not drawing out his ID again was a matter of principle. "Can I *please* pay with cash?" He threw a ten spot onto the counter. *"Thank you."*

Jamis took his receipt and left the building. That had been one of the longest face-to-face conversations he'd had with any islander since coming to Mirabelle, and it was, in a strange way, invigorating.

With early summer sunshine beating down on his shoulders, he collected Snickers and headed for his next stop. He was almost there when he noticed his new nemesis, brood in tow, ready to spread her good cheer down Main Street. Damned, if Natalie Steeger didn't seem to know every single person she passed on the sidewalk. It was just his luck that she'd stopped not far from Henderson's, and he with a long list of drugstore items yet to be purchased.

Slipping his sunglasses back on, he pulled his hat lower on his brow. With any luck, he'd get out of Dodge without her noticing him.

"THIS IS PRETTY," ARIANNA announced as they approached Mirabelle's town center.

"Horses!" Toni said as an old-fashioned carriage rolled by them on Island Drive.

"I bet they have a bomb candy shop," Chase said, nudging his brother.

After morning chores and lunch, Natalie had decided to bring the kids into town to explore. A sense of community was important in a child's life, at least it had been in hers, and there was no better place than Mirabelle for feeling connected. As long as she'd been on Mirabelle, she'd never felt alone. Getting Galen involved, though, straggling as he was at the back of their pack and looking extremely disinterested, was going to take some concentrated effort.

Before reaching Main Street, she'd noticed the town was much busier than she remembered the last time she'd visited her grandmother, so they'd parked their bikes and walked. Now, as the children followed her down the cobblestone street, she realized not much had changed in the two years since she'd been here, although everything looked somehow brighter and fresher.

Whether it was new coats of paint or changes in colors, she wasn't sure, but the green and white striped awnings marking most businesses looked new and fresh. The American flags hanging from every other old-fashioned black lamppost and the gold and black signs on every street corner listing the shops on the upcoming block were nice new touches.

"It feels like we're in an old movie," Toni whispered to Sam, who was holding hands with her and Ryan.

"Weird," Sam murmured, looking around. "There really aren't any cars?"

"Nope," Natalie said. "Except for the emergency equipment."

Ryan picked up a penny lying on the sidewalk and quietly stuffed it in his pocket.

"Can we go sailing sometime?" Blake asked as they passed by the marina.

"Sure," Natalie said. "The plan is to take in everything Mirabelle has to offer at some point during the summer. Kayaking, windsurfing, horseback riding. We're going to work hard and play hard."

That met with murmurs of approval. Galen appeared to be keenly interested in the sailboats, kayaks and windsurfer boards in the bay, and Natalie smiled to herself. He'd get there.

As they continued down Main, Natalie glanced up a side

street and noticed a man leaving the post office. The way he moved, with purpose and confidence, felt familiar, although a baseball cap and dark sunglasses shaded his face. Then she saw the dog tied to the lamppost and knew she'd been right. Her new neighbors, Jamis and Snickers, had also come to town.

She was about to head toward them, when she met up with her first islander. "Hey, Doc." She waved as she approached Doc Welinsky, a tall, always jovial fellow who seemed much older than she remembered.

He pulled up short and studied her. "Well, if it isn't little Natalie Steeger. Only you're not so little anymore. How the heck are you?"

"Very well, thank you."

His smile disappeared. "Sorry, about your grandmother."

"Thanks, but if I live to ninety-seven, I'm going to guess I'll be ready to go. We can't all live forever." In her peripheral vision she noticed Jamis slinking into the drugstore, obviously hoping to avoid her.

"Ain't that the truth?" Doc turned pensive. "I've actually been thinking about retiring."

For as long as Natalie had been coming to the island, he'd been Mirabelle's only doctor. "What'll they do without you?"

He shrugged. "Time for some new blood."

A tourist bumped her shoulder and passed on without pardoning herself. "Why is it so busy in town?" Natalie asked.

"We put in a golf course and a couple swimming pools up on the hill."

"No kidding?" The pool would be another activity for the kids. "Doc, I'd like to introduce you to my summer kids." She went down the line, introducing everyone. "This is Doc Welinsky."

"Hey, kids." He gave them all his thumbs-up.

"I've set up a camp at Grandma's house."

"Yep, I remember hearing about that." An oddly concerned look had passed over his features as the kids moved down the street and stopped in front of the drugstore to pet Snickers. "There was quite a discussion at the town council meeting when you first applied."

"There was?"

"Oh, yes. There were a few folks who weren't too sure about opening up the island to…" he said, pausing, "an undesirable element."

"Undesirable? These kids?"

"Well, they come from some pretty tough neighborhoods, don't they?"

"Yes, but none of them are troublemakers." Yet.

"Well, it'll probably take some time to convince some of the more stubborn islanders, but I wish you the best of luck, Natalie."

"Thank you," Natalie said, but Doc's comments had definitely colored the day for her. She'd had no idea that some of the islanders had been against her camp.

She rejoined her kids and they all went into the drugstore. Bob Henderson was standing at one of the cash registers. He glanced up and opened his arms and hugged Natalie as if she were a long-lost child. "Natalie! It's so good to see you."

"Good to see you, too, Bob."

"We heard through the town council that you were opening a camp for kids out at your grandmother's place," Bob said. "Boy, that created quite a stir."

"That's what I've heard."

"Well, you know how some of the Mirabelle folk hate changes." He smiled and whispered, "But I thought I'd better give you fair warning."

"Thanks. But Doc already beat you to it."

"He did, huh? Well, I'm gonna guess he's looking out for you, too. How's it going?"

"So far, so good. Let me introduce you to everyone. Kids, this is Bob Henderson. I worked for him and his wife every summer all through high school and college."

"And she spoiled us, she did. Haven't found as good a clerk ever since."

Galen picked up a magazine off the rack and pretended to be flipping through it. With Sam craning her neck down the makeup aisle, it was clear even her attention was wandering. "Everyone up for some ice cream?"

"Yeah!"

"Sweet."

"I'll meet you kids at Mrs. Miller's ice cream and candy shop, 'kay? Galen and Sam, you guys are in charge. Keep everyone together." She handed them some cash.

"Will do," Sam said.

After they'd left, Bob said, "That crew looks like a lot of work."

"They're all good kids at heart. They'll be working a lot this summer, but should have plenty of fun times, too. I think the time away from the city will do them all some good."

"If you need any help, you let me or Marsha know." A customer came to the register. "She'll be disappointed she missed you."

"I'll be here all summer." Natalie turned to go and spotted her new neighbor in the hair care aisle, head down and searching the shelves. He was a tall man and in surprisingly good physical shape for a writer. She would've expected someone who made up stories all day at his computer to have rounded shoulders, pasty white skin and a potbelly.

Wearing sunglasses and a hat, even inside the store, Jamis appeared to be hiding. She flashed on his reaction yesterday when she and the kids had brought him cookies. *Pretend like I don't exist,* he'd said. As if. The man had a presence that simply couldn't be ignored, despite being either totally antisocial or extremely shy. Good thing she was neither.

She spun around and meandered toward him, flashing her brightest smile. "Fancy meeting you here."

Jamis glanced up, but wouldn't hold eye contact. Not that she could see much of his eyes through the dark lenses of his glasses. "Yeah," he said, sounding infinitely bored. "What do you know?"

"We missed you at our campfire last night," she said, hoping to start a normal conversation.

"I doubt that." He tossed a bottle of shampoo into his basket and then moved to the first-aid aisle.

"We'd love for you to join us some time. Really," she said, trailing after him and grasping for common ground. "S'mores. Popcorn. Hot dogs. You name it, I'll make sure we've got it for you."

Ignoring her, he grabbed several items off the shelf, tossed them into his basket and moved to the next aisle, passing a section of books and magazines.

Books. That was the ticket.

Searching amidst the varied covers, she spotted his name toward the bottom of the display. "I've been thinking I should read one of your books." She picked up a cover that caught her eye. "How 'bout this one?"

His gaze swung toward her. "Um. No. You won't like that one."

"What about this one?" She grabbed the next paperback in line and held it out.

"You do know I write horror stories?"

She nodded. "It'll be good for me to expand my horizons." *In more ways than one.* Her gaze automatically flew to his mouth. She'd never kissed a man with a mustache, let alone a beard. *Stop it, stop it, stop it!* As if reading her mind, he reached up and ran a hand down his cheek, smoothing his whiskers. Would they feel as soft as they looked?

"Yes," he whispered.

Startled, she sucked in a breath and blinked up at him. "What did you say?"

"I said, yes. On second thought, maybe you should read one of my books."

"Oh." She swallowed, relieved that her thoughts hadn't been quite so transparent. "Then which one would you recommend?"

As he studied her, she couldn't be sure, but it seemed the barest hint of a smile worked the edges of his mouth. "This one." He picked up the title *Lock and Load* at the end of the row. "Knock yourself out." That time, the smile on his face and in his voice was unmistakable, and it was a surprisingly pleasing sound.

"Thanks."

"No problem." He headed to the checkout counter and without so much as a backward glance was out of the store within minutes.

By the time she'd finished with her own purchases and went outside, both Jamis and Snickers were long gone. More than a little disappointed, she moved on to her next stop, Mrs. Miller's ice cream and candy shop. "Hi, Mrs. Miller!" Natalie sailed through the front entrance with a smile on her face. "I see you've met my camp kids."

"So that's where these kids came from." Mrs. Miller frowned.

"I'm sorry. Have there been problems?"

"No, not yet, but maybe next time you should all come in together so you can keep an eye on them."

"All right, I'll do that." She turned to her kids. "Well, guys, if you know what you want, tell one of the clerks." There were several college-aged kids behind the counter scooping up ice cream.

Every one of her kids hesitated. A couple dug into the pockets of their shorts. "And I'm buying!" Natalie quickly added. "So get whatever you want."

While the younger ones were ordering, Galen and Sam were talking to several teenagers, both boys and girls, sitting near the far corner. "Come to the pizza place Friday night," one of the boys said. "Hang out. Play some foosball."

Yes! Natalie did an internal happy dance. Sam and Galen were already making friends. This was working out perfectly.

After they left Mrs. Miller's, Natalie said, "Last stop is the gift shop." She wanted to touch base with the owner of the store, a very nice young woman who had agreed to take on consignment everything they made at her camp. Natalie had spoken with her on the phone several times and met her once or twice while visiting her grandmother. They'd connected immediately.

Walking a couple of blocks down Main, she stopped outside the gift shop's interesting window display. Instead of the standard Midwestern collection of painted wooden loons and coatracks made out of deer hooves, there were candles and incense, handmade jewelry, books on astrology and tarot cards and new age CDs.

"Last stop, guys," Natalie said. "You can come inside if you promise not to touch anything. Okay?"

Their mouths full of ice cream, they all nodded or murmured in agreement. A soft chime sounded as she opened the door to Missy Charms's shop and everyone filed inside. A row of wind chimes for sale tinkled in the warm breeze blowing in from outside. The scent of something spicy and warm hit Natalie's nostrils and she noticed a stick of incense burning at the front counter. There were tourists in the store, a mother and daughter, flicking through a stand of T-shirts.

A sign up front declared customers could Buy with a Free Conscience. Every product in the store was guaranteed as either free trade or made in the U.S.A. Natalie loved this place.

With the sound of beads parting, a young woman's familiar face appeared from the back room. "Natalie! You're here!"

"Hey, Missy!"

Galen came alive the moment Missy appeared. But then with curly blond hair, green eyes and the angular face of an elf princess, there probably weren't many men who didn't immediately notice the woman.

"I see you brought your whole group with you." Missy glanced around.

"Yep."

"Well, I need to meet them." She charged up to each child and introduced herself. At least Missy didn't have any reservations about these kids. "You guys need to get cracking. It's been so busy already this summer that my inventory is flying off the shelves."

"We've started the ball rolling and should have something for you by next week. Right, kids?"

"Right," everyone except Sam agreed.

She was enthralled with a stand of necklaces on the front counter. "Missy, can I make jewelry for you?"

"Boy, can you ever. Hold on a minute." Missy went into her back room and came out a moment later with a small box. "Here are a few samples and all the supplies you need to make bracelets, necklaces and amulets." She leaned toward Sam and whispered, "If Natalie ever gives you some free time away, I'll teach you how to bless the feathers."

"Awesome," Sam whispered, putting the box in her pack.

The younger kids were getting restless. "We need to get going." Natalie turned. "See you next week, Missy."

As the kids all filed outside, Missy grabbed Natalie's arm. "You got a sec?"

"Sure," Natalie said. "Sam and Galen, why don't you two go get the bikes and take the younger kids back to the house? I'll catch up with you in a few minutes, okay?"

"Come on, guys." Sam led the way for the younger kids and, with a last glance at Missy, Galen took up the rear.

The moment they were out of earshot, Missy said, "Call me sometime soon. You can come into town and have dinner with me and a couple of friends."

"Oh, I don't know." Natalie shook her head. It wouldn't be right for her to just take off. "I should be with the kids."

"Twenty-four-seven out on that lonely end of the island with eight kids and no adults to keep you company? You're going to burn out, honey."

That's something Natalie hadn't given a lot of thought. "You're probably right."

"You're paying Sam and Galen, aren't you? Let them take care of the kids now and then. You're going to need some adult time."

"But you're forgetting." Natalie grinned. "I've got Jamis Quinn for company."

Missy laughed.

"What do you know about him?"

"Very little. He's a tough man to read."

"He seems very private. And quiet."

"So unlike you."

"Seriously. You must know something about him."

"I've never talked with the man." Missy sighed. "But I hear things about him and the blue aura I see around him when he comes to town is quite an enigma."

"Why?"

"Blue usually signifies a person who's extremely balanced and relaxed."

"Doesn't sound like the Jamis I've met."

"Exactly."

"So tell me—" Natalie smiled at Missy "—what color is my aura?"

"Mostly turquoise. Dynamic, energetic. People want to follow you, Nat. You're perfect for these kids." She squeezed Natalie's hands and then grinned. "And now that I think about it, blue goes awfully well with turquoise."

"Oh, no." Natalie shook her head.

"I thought you liked flings. Minimum time commitment for maximum fun? Three months and you'll be leaving Mirabelle. Doesn't get any better than that."

Leaving the fling before the fling could leave her. That was—used to be—right up Natalie's alley. "I've sworn off all men."

"I'll believe that when I see it."

"I'm serious. I haven't dated anyone for…three whole months."

Missy laughed.

"Okay, so I'm trying. You would, too, if you had the kind of luck I do with men. Things will be going fine and then all of a sudden a major deal-breaker pops up out of nowhere." She shook her head. "I just want to be friends with Jamis. Nothing more. Nothing less."

"Then you'd better watch out for that gray shadow I sometimes see surrounding him."

"Meaning?"

"He has an unpredictable dark side," Missy said. "I have a feeling a friendship with Jamis might get you more than you bargain for."

CHAPTER FOUR

AS THE SUN DIPPED lower on the seemingly endless Lake Superior horizon, Jamis paddled his kayak to Mirabelle's rocky shoreline. He'd circled one of the outer lying Apostle Islands before heading home, so it'd been an acceptable workout. Stowing the kayak away, he headed up the steep hill to his cabin. After a shower and a cold beef sandwich, the silence was getting to him. He put on an alternative rock CD and, with Snickers close on his heels, went out onto his deck, cold beer in hand.

He wasn't entirely comfortable relaxing after having had, so far, such an unproductive writing week. Unproductive? It'd been disastrous. With all the comings and goings next door, he hadn't written anything except e-mails. But he needed to unwind and the beer tasted good on this warm evening.

Doing his best to ignore the Victorian, he took a swig from the cold bottle, followed quickly by two more and glanced out over the lake to watch the sun sink below the horizon. Quickly now, it slipped lower and lower still until finally disappearing completely. Dusk, quiet and heavy, settled over the lake. From here he could see for close to five miles on a clear night. Most nights he contemplated the serenity of the uninhabited islands to the north, but tonight it was the flickering lights of the mainland that grabbed his attention.

Lights from homes and businesses where life was taking place. People making dinner. Running children to various activities. Reading. TV. Talking. Laughing.

As if he'd conjured the images in his mind, voices low and indecipherable came to him on the light breeze. But these were real. He glanced toward the sound and saw fire-light flickering in the distance. Miss Camp Director and her rug rats were having another campfire.

Snickers glanced up at Jamis as if asking permission to join the group. "Sorry, Snicks. Not our game."

Closing his eyes, Jamis listened to his music and let his mind wander. Ideas for a new book were bound to come to him. Any time now. Now would be good. Perfect setting for creativity to burst forth. *Right…hold it…hold it…now!*

A little squeak of a whine pierced his thoughts. Next a tail swishing on the surface of the wood deck. Then a whimper.

Jamis opened his eyes. The dog immediately stood and pawed at Jamis's leg, clearly hoping for an invitation. "Okay. Up you go."

He jumped onto Jamis's lap and settled. Jamis scratched under the dog's collar and behind his ears and Snickers threw his head back onto Jamis's chest and breathed a heavy and contented sigh.

"Tell me something, Snick," Jamis whispered. "Do you ever miss them?"

As if the memories were too much for him, the dog hopped back down to the deck and wagged his tail expectantly. "All right. Fine. Go." Jamis nodded toward the woods. "Go on. Get out of here."

The dog scampered quickly down the steps and trampled through the woods. Jamis knew the moment he'd reached them.

"Snickers!" It was her voice, Natalie's, filled with

sincere joy. "Isn't he the cutest thing? Watch out for the fire. His tail!"

Then it seemed as if the whole group joined in squealing, talking, laughing.

"Snickers, lie down."

"His nose is wet."

"And cold."

"Kisses. Kisses." Natalie blubbered on and on. "I love you, too. Yes, I do. Lie down. Good boy."

Jamis would've bet anything Snickers was lying at Natalie's feet, but he wondered if the little girl was still frightened of the dog. Curiosity getting the better of him, Jamis moved silently through the forest until he could see them and make out the quieter bits of their conversation. The moment he saw Natalie's face lit by the fire, he stopped. He wouldn't have thought it possible. He'd thought sunlight and blue skies would put her wholesome beauty at its best advantage. But he couldn't have been more wrong.

She might look like an angel in daylight, but at night with golden firelight flickering in her eyes and shadows dancing around her, that innocent angel had turned into a sultry and mysterious she-devil. The angles of her face. The shape of her shoulders. Her lips.

Five long years he'd been without a woman. For the first year after Katherine had left him, he'd been sorely tempted by anything with long legs, but hadn't wanted to add any more fuel to her flame. These past four years, he could not have cared less. He'd seen women in town, some pretty, some gorgeous, some on the beach in bikinis baring a lot of skin, but not once had he regretted isolating himself. Not once had he imagined touching a woman's skin, her lips, her waist, her…

With a hard-on pressing against his jeans, he closed his eyes. *You have no right to step into her world. Your touch would at best taint her, at worst destroy her.* But he could watch, couldn't he? From a distance.

He leaned up against the nearby tree. She'd made a fire pit, arranging a ring of rocks around a nice-size blaze and a couple of fallen logs for seating. Although he was just out of the ring of light, he could see their faces, illuminated by the red-orange glow of the fire. It was chilly tonight and they all sat close. All of them except for the teenage boy.

Snick was indeed at Natalie's feet, but she was sitting on a log and out of reach. The youngest girl, on the other hand, was sitting on a folded blanket, her legs crossed. She was inching away from the dog, but the more she tried to get away from him, the more pathetically he begged for her attention. First a nose to her hand. Then a lick on a finger. Then a whole head nudged slowly under her arm.

He rested his chin on her leg and waited, his tail thumping expectantly every time she glanced down at him. Finally, she tentatively touched his forehead and Jamis could've sworn he heard the dog sigh with delight.

"So where were we?" Natalie asked. "Oh, yeah. Highs and lows this week. Arianna, it's your turn."

"My grandma gave me and Ella both ten dollars for spending money," the one who must be named Arianna said. "She's never given us money before."

"That's pretty exciting," Natalie said.

"But," the girl went on, her voice a little sad, "it has to last for the whole summer."

"I didn't get any money," said one of the boys.

"Me, neither."

"Who's got the chocolate chips cookies?"

"You've already had two."

"So?"

"Hey, hey. I made them for everyone. Pass them around." That was Natalie. "As for money this summer, you'll all have the chance to earn some when we sell our crafts in town. The nicer they look, the more money you'll make. It'll be your money. You'll get to decide how much to save and how much to spend."

What kind of camp was this?

"Toni, how 'bout you?" Natalie asked. "Is there anything you'd like to share?"

"Hmm." The little girl made a small sound. "I guess my high was coming here. And my low." She paused. "I don't know."

"It couldn't have been easy leaving another foster home," Natalie said, nudging her.

Foster home?

"I'm used to it," the little girl said.

The circle around the fire fell silent.

"Anyone missing home yet?"

"Are you serious?"

"As if."

"Galen? Do you have anything you'd like to share?"

"No."

"You sure?"

"Trust me. No one around this fire wants to hear what I have to say."

"Get off it, Galen." That sounded like the teenage girl. "Every single one of us was handed a shitty deal. What makes you think you're so special?"

The circle around the fire turned quiet again.

"Okay. You want to hear my high for the week?" He paused. "That was when my mom kicked me out of the house. She locked all the windows and put chains on the doors. I had to break one of my bedroom windows to get some clothes for this stupid camp."

He threw a piece of wood onto the fire. "By the time I get back from this camp, I won't have anything to come back *to.* Even if she is still living in that dump, she'll have sold all my shit. You know what happened to that money you gave me for some clothes, Natalie? My mom stole it." He looked away. "That enough sharing for you guys?"

Great. This was a camp for disadvantaged kids. Just what Jamis needed next door, a do-gooder and her do-goodees.

"Galen," Natalie said. "For the summer you can forget about what's happening at home. What's important for you right now is what's happening here."

The boy grunted and looked away. "Whatever."

"I'd like each of you to think about what you'd like to get out of this summer," Natalie said. "You don't have to share it with me or anyone else, but after you've spent some time thinking about it, I want you to visualize those hopes coming true." She closed her eyes and Jamis couldn't keep from staring at her face, at the conviction and determination lit by the flames of the fire. "See it. Wish it. Make it happen."

Holy hell. She believed. So many people dallied with the concept of making your wishes come true, but Natalie truly believed. She understood.

"This summer is going to change all of us," she whispered. "I believe."

He'd never told anyone what he'd done. He'd simply packed up and left, holing himself up in his cabin on Mirabelle and letting Chuck handle everything else, selling his furniture, art, cars and houses. Suddenly, Jamis felt chilled, as if his heart had stopped pumping warmth to every extremity.

He didn't belong out here at their campfire. He didn't deserve to be sharing this night with good and decent people.

As quietly as possible, he turned to head home. Snickers, naturally, chose that moment to hike into the woods and head directly for Jamis. The moment the dog found him, he barked and jumped up.

"Jamis?" Natalie said. "Is that you out there?"

Jamis froze and waited.

"What if it's a wolf," one of the younger boys said, his voice laced with a wickedly mischievous undertone. "Or a bear?"

"Stop it, Chase," Natalie said. "Snickers? Who's out there?"

"Do raccoons eat dogs?" the littlest girl asked, nervously looking over her shoulder.

"Could be a coyote," another one of the boys teased.

He had to show himself, or risk scaring the whole crew. "It's me," Jamis said, moving through the brush and stepping into the firelight. "Sorry to interrupt. I was looking for the dog."

"Jamis!" Natalie said. "Join us. We have more cocoa." She held up a thermos.

"No, that's okay." Suddenly, he wished he was alone out here with Natalie. The firelight, the moon, the stars. Talk about a glutton for punishment.

"Jamis, are there wolves here?" the littlest asked, looking up at him.

Her small voice clutching at his emotions, he refused to let her name settle in his mind, let alone his heart. "No," he whispered. "No wolves or bears on the island."

"You sure?" asked one of the older girls.

"Positive. We only have deer. There's nothing in these woods that would hurt you." As far as he knew. Wolves and bear had been known to cross the ice during the winter looking for food, but since there'd been no sightings all these years there was no point in frightening the kids.

"Sit down. Join us." Natalie smiled at him. "I'll make you a s'more."

He glanced around at the young faces illuminated in the flickering firelight and felt something chip away at the frozen shell of his heart. There seemed to be no turning back. "A s'more sounds nice." He sat on the ground next to Snickers.

"Why do you live out here?" one of the boys asked. "All alone?"

"Because I like it." Jamis watched Natalie put a marshmallow at the end of her stick and set it over the fire.

"Don't you get lonely?" the girl next to him asked.

"I've got Snickers."

"Jamis is a writer." Natalie turned the marshmallow.

He wished she hadn't said that.

"What do you write?" the oldest girl asked, suddenly interested in the conversation.

"Books."

"What kind of books?" the little girl asked.

"They're…horror stories."

The boys grinned and nodded.

"Dude," one said.

"Sweet," said another.

"Any of them ever been made into movies?" the oldest boy asked.

"Yeah. A couple."

"No shit? Which ones?"

"I don't remember."

"How can you not remember?"

"I know," Natalie said. *"Bring the Night. Nothing to Lose. Lock and Load."*

"You're Quinn Roberts!" said the oldest boy. "Awesome. I've read most of your books."

The marshmallow Natalie roasted was a toasty brown. She stuck it between two graham crackers and chocolate and handed it to him.

"Suddenly, I'm not very hungry." He held it out.

"I'll take it!" One of the younger boys reached out his hand.

"Why did they change the ending on *Lock and Load?*"

"No spoilers!" Natalie announced. "I plan on reading the book."

He was counting on it. That story was just what she needed to put him in perspective, and then maybe she'd rethink having her camp next to a madman. He glanced at the teenager. "I don't know. Never saw it."

"You don't watch your own movies?"

He shook his head. "Don't read my own books, either." Once he sent the manuscripts off to his agent, he never wanted to revisit those characters or their pathetic lives again.

"Where do you come up with your ideas?" the teenage girl asked.

He didn't want to talk about this. Him. His books. "I don't know. They're just there. In my head." Except for now. Now he could really use an idea.

"I've read your books, too," the girl said. "There's almost a spiritual quality to some of them. Like your last one, *House of Reign.*"

Spiritual quality? He almost laughed. *That was a good one.* Across the fire he caught Natalie's gaze and he quickly looked away. Writing about a man whose life was destroyed even as his every wish came true had damned near killed Jamis.

"You know it's getting late," Natalie said, glancing at her watch. "Time for bed, guys."

A few of the kids groaned. A few yawned in quiet acceptance. The little girl glanced at Jamis. "Will you and Snickers walk us up to our house?"

The request took him by surprise, and before Jamis could refuse, Snickers was already following the other kids. Now he had no choice. "Yeah, I'll walk you up," he said, standing. "Snickers needs to stretch his legs before we go to bed." His heart almost stopped when the girl reached out and laced her small fingers through his. The small hand. Warm and soft. He looked down at her and immediately regretted ever having come outside in the first place tonight.

While he was pulled along down the path, Natalie put out the fire. By the time they reached the steps of the Victorian, she'd caught up with them. As all the kids ran into the house, she called, "Everyone brush your teeth and get ready for bed. I'll be up in a minute to say good-night."

The interior lights flicked on and footsteps pounded up the stairs as she turned to Jamis. Suddenly his hand felt empty and cold. He shouldn't be here, in the dark with a beautiful woman. Not with the yearning for simple touch he felt coursing through him. The need. The want for her warm hands on his skin. He should've been turned off by her too-good-to-be-true nature, instead he couldn't seem to tear his eyes away from her lips.

Go, Jamis. For her sake. Get as far away as you can.

"Good night, Natalie." He spun away. "Snickers, come."

"Jamis?"

He turned, held himself back. One of his favorite smells, wood smoke, emanated from her hair along with something else, something sweet like chocolate. He wished he could bury his face in the long blond curls and breathe her in.

"Why are you hiding on Mirabelle?" she whispered.

No one had ever asked him that. He supposed everyone had assumed he was despondent after the accident. He had been, but there was a bigger reason. A reason he wasn't sure he could share. Not now. Maybe not ever. "Who says I'm hiding?"

She came down the steps and met him in the grass. "Me."

"I'm not a nice man, Natalie. The world is a much better place with me out of the way."

"I think you're wrong. I think inside here," she said, pressing a fingertip to his chest, "there's a good man hiding away."

It was all he could do to keep from stepping forward and leaning into her touch. He grabbed her fingers and held them for a moment before noticing a face, one of the kids, peering out from the window and watching. Slowly, he pushed her hand away. "You might know what's inside most men, but not me," he said softly. "Have you read my book yet?"

"No."

"Do it. Then you'll get a glimpse of the real Jamis Quinn."

And then you'll despise me, want nothing to do with me, and the world's balance will be set right again.

JAMIS'S BOOK SAT ON Natalie's bedside table, as yet unopened. Every night since she'd started this camp, thoroughly exhausted, she'd all but collapsed onto the bed. Tonight, though, curiosity had kept her awake. She sat up with her laptop in front of her and stared at the newspaper headline on the screen, tears pooling in her eyes.

Author Quinn Roberts's Wife and Children Killed

Having searched and pored through everything she could find on the Internet regarding Jamis after she'd gotten ready for bed, she'd finally found details of a horrific car accident in an old online article. Now that she read the headline, she remembered all those years ago having heard something about the incident, but not bothering to pay attention to the details.

Now she read that his children, Caitlin and Justin, ages three and one, had been killed at the scene. Their mother, Katherine, had made it to the hospital before succumbing to her extensive internal injuries. Jamis had suffered a concussion as well as a broken arm and leg, three broken ribs and a lacerated liver. His children had been little more than babies.

Although no charges were expected, sketchy accounts claimed icy road conditions may have played a role in a semitrailer carrying heavy equipment broadsiding the Quinn vehicle in the middle of a busy intersection. The truck driver had walked away with only minor injuries. The only survivors from the Mercedes had been Jamis and a lucky little puppy, a tricolored mutt.

Snickers.

Oh, Jamis.

Flicking off the lamp, she snuggled under the covers and glanced out the open window and through the woods. A lone light shone through the trees. He was still awake. Instinct had her wanting to run over to his cabin right then and there to comfort and heal him. Make that damaged man whole again. Only she had to admit, if only to herself, that there was something else going on inside her, something not entirely altruistic.

When she'd touched his chest earlier that night after

he'd walked them back from the fire, the urge to kiss him had welled up from some deep and primal place inside her and that urge had little to do with taking care of Jamis and nothing at all to do with wanting to be neighborly. She could feel it, her own heavy yearning. She wanted Jamis for herself. She wanted to feel his hands on her body, his mouth on her lips. Closing her eyes, she sighed.

A girl couldn't be all good all of the time. Apparently, Jamis wasn't the only one with a dark side.

CHAPTER FIVE

"OKAY, DAD." CHASE groaned into the phone after dinner a few nights later. "Yes, we're behaving. I swear. Ask Natalie."

Natalie stood by the sink helping Ella dry the dishes Arianna was washing and listened to the one-sided conversation in case there was anything with which the boys might need help. Both boys looked forward to what they'd hoped would be twice-weekly conversations with their dad over the summer, but after a few minutes they were antsy to get moving. Arianna and Ella, on the other hand, had proved they could stay on the phone for hours in their conversations with their grandmother.

"Okay. Okay. Here's Blake." Chase handed the phone to his brother.

"Hey, Dad, how's it going?" Blake leaned up against the wall. "I'm good, good." Then he went into a long and excited explanation of everything he'd been doing since their last conversation.

"Your dad doing okay?" Natalie asked Chase.

"Yeah. He's mad at himself."

She nodded, understanding. After two DWIs, their dad had stayed sober for more than five years, then he'd fallen off the wagon at a buddy's wedding and got his third offense and a ninety-day jail term. The wedding had been no excuse, and losing his boys for the summer was, hopefully, going to be what it took to keep him on the straight and narrow. At least Natalie prayed it would be enough, given the boys' mother was no longer involved in their lives.

"Nat," Chase said, "can I have something to eat?"

"We just finished dinner." Natalie put a stack of clean plates into the cupboard.

"I'm still hungry."

"All right. Something healthy. Grab the grapes leftover from lunch."

He dug around inside the refrigerator for a few minutes and then wandered into the living room, passing Sam and Galen on their way into the kitchen. They hung around, looking as if they were at loose ends. Finally, Galen said, "It's Friday."

"Yes, it is." Natalie glanced at them. They seemed to be waiting for something. Then it hit her. "Oh, goodness! I almost forgot our agreement. You guys have the night off, and I need to give you paychecks!"

"Yes!"

"Cool!"

Galen and Sam connected fists in the air.

Natalie ran back to her bedroom, grabbed the two payroll checks she'd left on her desk by her laptop, and hurried back out to the kitchen. "Okay," she said, handing them envelopes. "The kitchen is clean and the supper dishes are done. You two are on your own."

The teenagers glanced at each other.

"Want to go into town?" Galen asked.

"Totally! Let me change first." She took off upstairs and came down a short while later. "The sink is clogged again."

"I'll take a look at it," Natalie said, studying Sam. Something had changed. Clothes? No. Hair? Yep, that was it. She'd forsaken the ever-present ponytail to let her light brown hair hang long and straight halfway down her back. And she was wearing makeup. With hazel eyes and pleasing features, Sam was naturally pretty, but the mascara, blush and lip gloss, not to mention a full, almost womanly figure, made her look easily several years older than Galen, despite the fact that she was actually a couple months younger than him.

Even Galen had done a double take when Sam came into the kitchen. "Dustin and Chad said they'd be at the pizza place," he said, recovering quickly.

"Sounds good."

"Blake's off the phone," Arianna said. "Can we call Grandma now?"

"Absolutely. And then when you two are done we're going to have some popcorn and watch a movie."

As Galen and Sam shot through the back door, Natalie followed them outside, not a little envious of them having a night without a single responsibility. They'd been here less than a week, but the concentrated time with eight kids was forcing Natalie to accept that Missy had most definitely been right. She was going to need a break every now and again.

"Hey, guys!" she called. "Be home by eleven, okay?"

"Whatever."

"No, not whatever, Galen. Eleven. And take the golf cart, so you can see your way home in the dark."

"Good idea."

"Do you have your cell phones?"

They both nodded.

"And one more thing." They both looked up at her, clearly anxious to be on their way. "Have fun."

Feeling an odd mixture of both excitement and apprehension, Natalie watched them drive the cart out of the yard and disappear within minutes on the path through the thick woods. *Don't worry,* she reassured herself. Sam and Galen are from a big city. What trouble could befall them on Mirabelle?

"QUIT KICKING ME!" The next morning Arianna glared across the kitchen table at Chase.

"I'm not even touching you!" Chase said.

"There!" she said. "What was that?"

Day and night. Night and day. The kids were constantly after each other, and Natalie could feel her normal patience waning more and more every day. "Blake?" she said softly.

The other twin, looking innocent as all get-out, glanced at her. "What? I'm not doing anything."

She'd been up and about since the crack of dawn getting organized for the day. There wasn't much these kids were going to sneak by her. "Keep your feet to yourself, Blake, or you'll be doing the breakfast dishes alone this morning."

"Fine," he grumbled, apparently unconcerned about having gotten caught attempting to get his twin in trouble.

"Um, Natalie?" Toni said. "Is there any cold cereal?"

"You don't like the pancakes?"

Quietly, the little girl shook her head.

A quick inspection of the table showed Galen, Blake and Chase in various stages of devouring everything on their plates, Samantha forsaking everything else for a yogurt and apple, and Arianna and Ella picking at the food on their plates. This scenario had been virtually the same for most of their meals this past week as they set about establishing routines and getting settled. In the past, Natalie had managed to survive on her own without being much of a cook, but things were different now that she was responsible for all these kids.

"Okay," she said. "I can see things are going to have to

change. After breakfast, I want each of you to write out three suggestions for meals and set them on the counter by the phone."

"Why?"

"Do we have to?"

"If you want food you like to eat, yes," Natalie said. "And I can see we need a rule about meals."

Everyone groaned except for Galen. That boy had been nearly impossible to awaken that morning and with his longish black hair still sticking out this way and that it was obvious he'd merely thrown on jeans and a shirt before stumbling down the stairs.

"Not another rule," someone murmured.

"If you don't like what's being served or are still hungry after a meal," Natalie said, glancing in particular at the growing boys, "the options are cold cereal or PB and J, but you have to prepare it yourself. You don't like the rules, you can go home. Anyone want to go home?" She looked at each and every one of them.

Everyone except Galen shook his or her head.

Going home for the twins, Chase and Blake, meant dealing with a father in jail. For Arianna and Ella, it was a mother who couldn't be found and a grandmother who was going through drug and alcohol treatment. Toni, Ryan and Sam would be going back to foster care homes. And for Galen, it meant a mother with unacknowledged substance abuse problems.

Natalie had painstakingly selected every one of them from a group of more than fifty applications, looking for kids whose profiles implied a high risk for problems, but a probability for success with the summer program she'd outlined. While Natalie was loathe to send any of them back before she'd gotten a chance to instill a small amount of hope in each one's heart, she wasn't going to sacrifice the success of the entire camp for any one individual.

The only one in the group who hadn't matched her profile was Galen. His school counselors, principals and teachers had all told her he wouldn't make it. They saw a young man with a bad attitude who was going to end up in trouble with the law, just like his mother. Natalie saw a boy with a possible learning disability trying desperately to find his way, a boy who hid his frailty behind a mask of defiance. Somehow, she had to find a way to get through to him.

"Okay, let's review the schedule we developed these past few days," she said. "Breakfast is at eight every morning, lunch at noon, dinner at six. Lights out at nine for everyone except Sam and Galen. After breakfast is chore time."

Because of their home lives, all of these kids spent far too much time alone. The more life skills she could instill in them, the higher their self-esteem and the better they'd fare once they went back home.

"After chores, we'll do some sort of fun activity and then free time until lunch. After lunch, we'll be making crafts to sell at the gift shop in town, and, if everyone behaves, we'll be taking in all of Mirabelle's charms over the course of the summer."

"What does that mean?" Arianna asked.

"Well, this summer isn't going to be all work and no play. We'll be making field trips into town at least once a week, and taking advantage of all that Mirabelle has to offer. Horseback riding, sailing, fishing, golfing."

"Horses!" the girls squealed.

"Fishing. Cool," was the consensus from the boys.

"All kinds of fun stuff." Natalie smiled. "So let's all work together this summer, and if you're ever not sure what you're supposed to be doing, look at the whiteboard on the pantry door. I'll do a new one every week with rotating chores and activities."

Toni raised her hand.

"Yes, Toni?"

"What's a pantry?"

Natalie was explaining it was the room next to the stove where their food was stored when the phone rang. Sam hopped up to answer the call. "It's for you, Natalie."

She stood and took the phone, and the boys finished with breakfast and wandered toward the living room. "Ah, ah, ah!" she said, covering the mouthpiece of the phone. "After meals, no one leaves the kitchen without first taking his or her own dishes to the sink. And then chores, people."

Another round of groans sounded, but the boys turned back. She pointed to the pantry door. "When in doubt, refer to the whiteboard."

"Ha-ha, Chase. You have to wash dishes," Blake taunted.

"So! You have to wash tomorrow."

"Yeah, but—"

Deciding to let them hash it out themselves, Natalie went inside the pantry with the phone and closed the door. "Sorry about that. Natalie here."

A man chuckled over the line. "It's Roger." Her grandmother's longtime attorney and now Natalie's. "Sounds like you have your hands full."

"We're still ironing out some details. We'll get there."

"I thought you might want a heads-up on something."

"Shoot." She leaned against one of the shelves and felt it wobble. The board was warped. That was going to have to get fixed.

"I got wind of someone making inquiries with the city

of Mirabelle and various departments with the state of Wisconsin with regard to the filings for your camp."

"Who?"

He sighed. "An attorney here in town who just happens to represent your neighbor."

"Jamis? Why would he care?"

"If I were to guess, I'd say he's looking for a way to shut you down."

"Well, that's just sil—" She stopped. "You're right. He's not at all happy about our presence on this end of the island. Can he make us leave?"

"All the proper paperwork has been filed and approved, but, in my experience, if a person looks hard enough, he can usually find some kind of loophole, especially if he has a good attorney. Jamis Quinn could make your life miserable."

He could try. "Thanks, Roger. Let me know if anything else comes to your attention."

"By the way, we filed those grant requests for you."

"Oh, good. Do you think I'll get enough to fund this camp for next year?"

"I think you've got a good chance, Natalie. There are several agencies very excited about what you're doing. But it wouldn't hurt to solicit some private donations. Send me some information and I'll get it out to our list of donors."

"Thanks, Roger." She hung up the phone. So Jamis wanted her and the kids gone, huh? Well, there was only one thing for it. She was going to have to change his mind.

NADA. ZIP. ZILCH.

Jamis stared at his blank computer screen. This morning and every morning since Miss Chipper had taken over next door, he had nothing. Normally, starting a new book was a piece of cake. Long before he typed the words *Chapter*

One a concept for a story would have effortlessly laid itself out for him. Sometimes in a dream a fully formed opener would come to him. Other times, a kernel of a scene would hit him while he was running or lifting weights. He could be brushing his teeth and a line of dialogue would hit him. Cooking a pasta dish he might feel a character's name hot on his tongue. Or out on the water kayaking, an overall concept would come to him, giving him something to work out in his mind as he worked out his body.

Unfortunately, the only story his brain seemed receptive to developing these days was a bloody mass murder at a small-town orphanage. And for good reason. Natalie seemed to have made it her personal mission to feed him.

Earlier in the week, she'd brought over a hunk of cake, undercooked and mushy in the center. Jamis had gone back to his computer in the hopes of starting his new book, but it wasn't happening. He'd finally surrendered and had put on his wetsuit, dragged his kayak down to the frigid water and paddled his way around several of the islands as fast as he could.

A few days later, it was homemade ice cream she and her kids had churned by hand in her grandmother's machine. That particular treat hadn't tasted half-bad, but how could anyone screw up sugar, strawberries and cream? Again, after attempting unsuccessfully to return to work, he'd finally gone outside and chopped half a cord of firewood.

After she'd needed bay leaves for a soup he could only hope he wasn't going to have to sample, he hadn't bothered returning to his computer. He'd gone straight to his workout room and pumped weights until every single one of his muscles had failed.

The biggest problem was that as that woman grew more irritating, she also seemed to grow more beautiful.

She would stand on his porch with sunlight glinting off her hair, a bright smile on her pretty pink lips, and a twinkle in her sea-blue eyes. In spite of everything, there was something indomitable about her that he couldn't help but respect. What in the world had possessed her to organize a summer camp for kids? What was the point? What made her tick? And why in God's name did she give a rat's ass about him?

He glanced at his watch and was surprised she hadn't been over to his house yet today. *Great.* He shook his head, disgusted with himself. Now he was actually waiting for her to make an appearance on his doorstep.

Snickers whined.

"What?"

The dog's ears arched expectantly.

"No." Jamis scowled. "You cannot go over to her house."

Another whine, and this one was accompanied by a swish of the tail.

"It's *not* Snickers time. Snickers time is *after* lunch."

Resigned, the dog laid his head on his paws. He continued looking up at Jamis with those forlorn brown eyes, and the memory of the morning Snickers had come into his life came back to Jamis in a rush. The smells, the sounds.

"Daddy, that's him," his three-year-old daughter, Caitlin, had declared in her sweet little voice. "He looks like a candy bar." She'd stuck her chubby fingers through the cage at the pound and singled Snickers out from a litter of puppies.

He'd tried steering her toward a tough pit bull, a Rottweiler, even a lab mix, but no. She'd wanted this puny mutt. A scruffy-haired mishmash of white, black and caramel, the animal folk had guessed he was part hound and part Border collie. When they'd gotten him out of the cage, Justin, not quite a year, had toddled over, grabbed the puppy by his ears and planted a sloppy wet kiss on his furry forehead, and it had been a done deal.

At the time, Jamis had thought it would help his children with the rough patch they were going through with the impending divorce. Instead, Snickers had been the reason for yet another fight, another bargaining point for the lawyers, another excuse for Katherine to wheedle more money from Jamis. Now the poor dog served only as a constant reminder of the two lowest points in Jamis's life.

"Come here, Snick." Jamis patted his lap. The dog hopped up and Jamis scratched him good and hard on his neck and ears. "Good boy." He kissed his forehead and let him hop to the floor. Snickers's ears perked up and he cocked his head toward the window.

"No!" The sound of a girl's voice came through the open office window. "I'm not going to ask him. You ask him."

"No way." That was a different kid, a boy.

Snickers ran down the steps and, without a single bark, sat at the door, waiting.

"This is so jacked." That voice belonged to an older boy, perhaps the teenager.

"Then you ask him."

A knock sounded on the front screen door.

"Unbelievable." Shaking his head, Jamis pushed away from his desk yet another time and went slowly down the steps. The outline of several heads standing on his porch took shape. He opened the solid oak door and stood in front of the screened storm door, not bothering to invite them in. "What?"

Snickers pawed excitedly at the door as several of the camp kids of varying ages and sexes stared up at Jamis. "Do you have any marbles?" asked the littlest girl.

Was this a joke? Jamis stared at each one of them, in

turn, debating. No, they were serious. "Why?" He heard himself asking the question as if disembodied from the idiot he'd suddenly become. What purpose could possibly be served by engaging them in conversation?

"We're on a scavenger hunt," said the middle boy who looked to be about twelve. "The first team to get all the items on Natalie's list gets breakfast in bed tomorrow morning."

So Miss Chipper had started up with her camp activities, huh?

"The other team is beating us," said the youngest girl.

Jamis glanced at the teenage boy, who was shaking his head and rolling his eyes. "Yeah, I got marbles. Come on in." He'd gone nuts. Certifiably so. All this time alone on this island had finally done the trick. "How many do you need?"

He opened the door and Snickers happily scurried around the kids, sniffing every one of them and pushing his wet nose into their hands. The kids stepped inside, the littlest one keeping her cautious eyes on the dog. One look at the big-screen TV and the teenager's attitude went from bored to calculating in seconds. Jamis could practically see his wheels turning looking for the angle that would get him viewing time on that screen.

"Just two," said the teenager.

Jamis went to a vase on the table by the window, pulled out the arrangement of dried grasses and dug out a couple of the clear acrylic marbles at the base used to hold the arrangement in place. "Will these do?"

"Sure. Why not?" The oldest boy took them. "So...do you have satellite?"

"Yeah."

"Sweet."

Shoving the dried grasses back into the vase, Jamis set it down. "Yeah, it is. You can go now." He ushered them outside and closed the door while they were still standing on his porch.

He'd taken several steps up to his computer when his doorbell rang. He paused, considering his options. Would they get the hint if he didn't answer? Snickers whined and his tail swished back and forth on the rug. The bell rang again and was followed by a quiet knock.

He spun around and threw open the door. "Now what?" He'd barely kept himself from yelling.

This time Miss Chipper herself was standing on his porch. "Hi, Jamis."

Today, her hair had a brighter honey-gold sheen, as if she'd been in the sun, and her lips looked wet, as if she'd just licked them. And if that wasn't enough to tempt him, there was always the way that strappy tank top clung to her too-full-for-that-body set of breasts. From nowhere, he was struck with the sudden urge to pull her into his arms and kiss her senseless, but then he'd more than likely end up senseless as well, and where would that leave them?

"We'd like to invite you over for dinner tonight." She bent and scratched Snickers behind the ears. "And you, buddy."

"He has other plans. So do I."

"Tomorrow night?"

"Plans."

"Any night work for you?"

"I'm a very busy man."

"Okay. We'll keep trying." The ever-cheerful Natalie looked a bit perplexed. "We'll be having campfires off and on. You're welcome to join us at any time."

"Well, Sunshine, I'll keep that in mind."

Studying him, she stepped back. "Okay. Have a good day." Off she marched with her pesky kids in tow, and there she went again directly through the poison ivy.

"Hey, hey, hey!" he called before he thought to stop himself. "Do you see what you're walking through?"

She glanced toward the ground and pointed out the offending plant to the children. Then she lifted the littlest girl onto her back and waved at him. "Thanks!" she called, as if they were now the best of friends.

Dammit. "Snickers, come." The moment the dog made it inside Jamis shut the door and leaned his forehead against the cold hard wood. Life, in the form of a beautiful young woman, was literally knocking on his door, and God help him but a very big part of Jamis was ready to invite her inside.

"Oh, no, you don't," he said loudly, clearly, hoping to get through that thick skull of his. *You gave up the right to a life four years ago, you son of a bitch.* "Don't even think about it."

Enough was enough.

CHAPTER SIX

RUNNING A FINGERTIP along her lips, Natalie stared out of the porch windows contemplating Jamis's house the next day and wondering what he was doing at this exact moment. No matter what she did or didn't do, she couldn't seem to get the man out of her mind. Somehow, someway, she had to find a way to break through his sturdy armor. A tug on her arm pulled her away from her thoughts and she glanced down.

Toni was standing next to her. "I'm sorry, honey, did you need something?"

"Do they need to be all the same size?"

Without a word, Ryan looked up, the same question burning in his young, oh-so-sincere eyes.

"I don't think so," Natalie said. "They should be kind of small, though. Think about what size you'd want to put in your pocket, and then make some slightly bigger for adults."

It was after lunch and everyone was working on projects to sell at the gift shop in town. She'd gotten a lot of questions about this part of her baby boot camp curriculum until she'd explained the kids would keep every cent earned from the sale of their respective crafts and would be allowed to save or spend as each saw fit, thereby teaching them the beginnings of fiscal responsibility.

Natalie had turned the front porch into a craft room.

Two long, narrow tables with comfortable chairs had been set on either side of the room. Shelving lined the walls and housed various storage baskets, buckets and drawer filled with supplies—glue, beads, ribbons, feathers, paints, frames, envelopes, card stock. If the kids needed something for a particular project chances were Natalie would have it. She'd been ordering and accumulating supplies for months.

The youngest of her kids, Ryan and Toni, were making pocket stones, flat coins of clay stamped with various inspirational words. Although Natalie had over twenty stamps made for them, they got to pick which words to use.

Her four middle-schoolers, Arianna, Ella, Chase and Blake, were making bookmarks with ribbons and beads and choosing their own color combinations from a selection Natalie had ordered in preparation for this camp. She was surprised by how calming these craft afternoons seemed to be for both Chase and Blake.

"Is that a necklace or a bracelet, Sam?" Natalie smiled at the young woman who was busy concentrating on her latest creation. She'd used a Chinese coin, this one with a hole in the middle, wrapped one end in leather bands, strung beads along the leather and was now tying off the ends with some kind of closure.

"Either one." Sam focused on tying a knot. "It'll bring confidence to the person who wears it."

"Why is that?"

"Missy told me that this coin is supposed to attract good fortune. In everything."

Galen grunted with disbelief from where he sat staring out the window at the next table.

"And what are you going to make, Galen?" Natalie turned her attention toward him.

He didn't respond, merely sat back and kicked his feet up on the nearest bookcase.

"I'll tell you what," she said. "You don't want to make any extra bucks this summer, that's your business, but don't complain when everyone else gets the money they've earned from sales at Missy's shop."

The sound of pounding drew her attention to the woods between her Victorian and the log cabin. She caught glimpses of a black T-shirt amidst the green trees. Jamis was out there doing something, and her curiosity was piqued. "Galen, your turn to help the kids," she said, heading for the door.

"Whatever."

"I'll be right back." She went outside, down the path between the two houses, and found Jamis, hammer in one hand and several red and white no-trespassing signs in the other. The implications didn't immediately register, but once she understood his intentions she couldn't help but feel slightly offended. "Where did you get those?"

"Went in to town yesterday afternoon."

"I suppose they're for us."

"You'd be supposing correctly."

"Why?"

He glared at her. "You really don't know?"

"Well…"

"Cake, ice cream, bay leaves, scavenger hunts. Sound familiar?"

Apparently her plan had backfired. "I'm sorry. I didn't mean—"

"Explain to me why you're doing this." He spun around and faced her.

"Pardon me?"

"This camp?"

She thought for a minute. "Because I can."

"No." He shook his head. "There's more to it than that."

"My grandmother left me this big house here and another one in Minneapolis and a lot of money. What else would I do with it?"

"I can think of all kinds of uses for that house. Sell it. Use it as a vacation home. Rent it out. Let it rot." He walked toward her. "For some reason, a camp for kids is the last thing that comes to my mind." He stared at her, waiting.

"I do this because…I've been where these kids are. I know what it's like to feel as if there's no one in the world who cares whether you live or die. I know what it's like to live without hope."

He said nothing for a moment, only studied her, but she had the distinct feeling he knew exactly what she was talking about. "Go on. There's more, I'm sure."

She'd never talked to anyone about this. Her family had known her story, so there'd been no point in sharing it with others. Truthfully, she didn't like rehashing the past.

"I'm waiting," he said, his gaze piercing.

"Let's just say my early childhood experiences were less than ideal. In fact, the only pictures I have of my mother are police mug shots." She glanced at him, expecting to hear some sarcastic response. Instead, he was still waiting, listening, an unreadable expression plastered on his face. "Until I was adopted at ten, I didn't have much hope for my future. But hope is what changed my life. These kids all need hope that things can be better in their lives. I think they'll find it here on Mirabelle."

"What's the point? You've got eight kids here. There are millions out there in the same if not worse shape. You're not going to change anything."

"One child at a time." She took a deep breath. "If this

summer experience gives one of these children hope where there was none before, then I've succeeded. Every child needs hope to be able to dream, and they need to dream to believe anything is possible."

"And when they all return to the same old same old at the end of the summer, then what?"

"They'll go knowing their lives can be different. Better."

"You're setting them up for disappointment."

"I've worked in social services for a long time." She shook her head. "There have been so few true successes along the way. My grandmother gave me the chance to do things my way, to try to make a difference in the lives of these kids." She studied his face, decided it was time for a question of her own. "Do you believe in wishes coming true?"

His eyes turned dark and he clenched his jaw. She'd hit a nerve.

"Well, I do," she said, taking his reaction for skepticism. "These kids need to believe they can make changes in their lives. They need to feel empowered. I want them to know that dreaming is okay, dreaming is important. But we can't just sit back and let things happen to us. *We* have to make things happen in our lives. Wish it, see it, make it happen."

He looked as if she'd punched him in the gut. "Unbelievable." He shook his head.

"I've seen it happen. Dreams and wishes, changing lives."

"You're such a Pollyanna."

Oddly enough that hurt. If he only knew how hard she'd worked to turn her life around. "Wishes do come true, you know," she whispered.

"Yeah. I know," he growled, spinning away from her. "That's why you'd better make sure you tell every single one of your charges to be very, very careful what they wish for."

Talk about hitting nerves. "What did you wish for,

Jamis, that went bad?" She reached out and touched his arm. "Tell me."

"Our little heart-to-heart is over." He shrugged her off and picked up another sign.

She didn't like leaving things like this, but she knew from the look on his face he was all done sharing. "Can you just skip the signs? Please?"

"I have a September deadline and because of the constant interruptions haven't been able to even start the book."

"What if I promise to leave you alone?"

He raised an eyebrow at her. "You expect me to believe you can control yourself?"

"All right, I'll make a deal with you," she said. "One week. If I can go that long without bothering you, will you forget the signs?"

He studied her face, seeming to weigh his options. "Why should I?"

"Simple neighborly courtesy."

"I have absolutely no interest in being neighborly."

She grinned. "Maybe you'll get lucky and get the satisfaction of saying I told you so."

His dark eyes flickered with interest. "Throw your kids into the bargain and it's a deal."

"Deal." She put out a hand.

He glanced at her for a moment, and when he finally reached out, his touch was surprisingly soft, warm and strong. "Deal."

"Wonderful."

He turned around, placed one of the signs against the nearest tree and pounded it in at eye level. Then he turned around and smirked at her.

"But I thought..."

"Sunshine, you won't last three days."

EVERY SPARE MOMENT SHE had the next day, Natalie found herself glancing out her windows toward the log cabin, wondering, imagining, obsessing over that man. What was it about him? Then again, it wasn't entirely his fault. Natalie had never been one to take no for an answer. Tell her she couldn't have something, and that something was all she'd want. In this case, something was Jamis Quinn.

He'd lost his entire family, Natalie reminded herself. The guy was bound to have issues. Trying to put him firmly out of her mind, Natalie went back to the craft room with the rest of the kids after breakfast and helped them with their projects. Galen, once again, chose to not involve himself in a craft.

Natalie glanced at the clock. "Galen, why don't you come help me with lunch." She started toward the door. When he didn't move, she turned around. "Work on a project or help me with our meal. It's your choice."

With a sullen look, he stood, noisily pushed in his chair and followed her out the door.

"You set the table and I'll get out the lunch meat."

He leaned against the counter, crossed his arms and made no attempt at complying.

"You know, Galen, some people make the mistake of assuming that I'm a pushover," Natalie said, needing to clear the air. "This camp is important to me, and I don't want you to ruin it for everyone else."

"You gonna make me go home?"

She opened the refrigerator and set lunch meat, condiments, milk and cheese on the counter. "Not if you don't break the rules."

He glanced over at her. At close to six feet with broad shoulders and shaggy stubble, this fifteen-year-old could pass for a man. If only he'd lose the attitude.

"Galen, there are some choices you need to make this

summer." She shut the fridge door, turned around and faced him head-on. "You have an opportunity to make some changes in your life, but those changes aren't going to happen on their own."

"What difference does it make?"

"It's your choice. Your life."

"What do you know about my life?"

More than he realized.

"What's your story, anyway?" He pushed away from the counter and paced along the other side of the big, oak table, as if to put some distance between them. "Why are you doing this camp, anyway? Why do you care?"

She hesitated. "My childhood wasn't all that different from yours."

"Bullshit." He crossed his arms. "You come from a rich family. Your grandmother even gave you this house."

"I didn't always live with this family."

"So what? You still don't know anything about me or my life."

She set the deli slices of meat and cheese on the table and washed bunches of red and green grapes in the sink. "Some things are different."

"See?"

"For one thing, I didn't live with my mother." She brought the grapes to the table and studied him. "She gave me up when I was two and I never saw her again. She was murdered a couple years later."

He looked away.

"Actually, my story's more like Toni's. Moving from one foster home to another."

She hated dwelling, let alone thinking, about the first ten years of her life. What was the point? What was done was done. So what if she'd never stayed in any of her foster homes more than a year? None of those people who'd sent her packing as if she'd been no more than an outgrown pair of jeans had really cared about her, even if she had come to care for them.

"I was adopted, Galen," she added. They were the only family that mattered now. If not for the Steegers loving her as if she was their own flesh and blood, there was no telling where Natalie would've ended up. "My grandmother knew I wanted to do something like this, that's why she gave me the house."

The kitchen was silent as she took some plates out of the cupboard and held them out to Galen. He only glared at her.

"I know you feel as if you have to be tough," she said softly. "That you have to shield yourself from the world." Though Natalie tended to overcompensate and open herself up to the world, she still struggled with this issue. "But there's no one here in this house who wants to hurt you."

He made no movement to take the plates.

"This summer is going to be what you make of it. Do you want to stay?" She waited and waited.

Eventually, he nodded.

"Then all I ask is that you try."

Finally, he took the plates from her and set them out on the table.

She took out the silverware and handed it to him. "Maybe it would be best if you don't think about the end of the summer."

"Easy for you to say." He threw the forks onto the table. "When this camp is done, you go back to your regular happy life. Me? I go to that place I'm supposed to call home. Square one. As if I was never here to begin with."

"Only if you let it."

"If *I* let it?" Angrily, he pushed one of the chairs away

from the table. "I'm only fifteen. I don't have a choice. My life's not my own."

Suddenly, she wasn't sure how to refute that. Every response she formulated in her mind seemed pat and idealistic.

"My mom was right." He pushed over a chair. "You do-gooders are all alike. The only reason you're having this camp is so that you can pat yourself on the back and tell yourself, tell the world, that you tried to do something good for someone else. You don't care about any of the kids here. You don't really care about me."

All sorts of challenges to his comment were at the tip of her tongue, but as he stalked out the door Natalie couldn't help but accept that a part of what he was saying was true. At the end of summer, she *would be* returning to her nice cozy life, and these kids would be going back to what they'd left behind.

Chase, Blake, Arianna and Ella had homes waiting for them. They weren't perfect family situations, but there was someone home in Minneapolis who truly seemed to love each of them. Chase and Blake's dad would be getting out of jail at the end of summer. Arianna and Ella's grandmother would be out of treatment. In fact, those four kids would be going home a week earlier than the rest of them, their caretakers wanting to prepare them for school starting.

Toni, Ryan, Sam and Galen would be returning to the Twin Cities with Natalie. They had no one in their lives who truly cared. Was this camp fair to them? Jamis's accusations came back to her. Was she setting them all up for disappointment?

Wish it, see it, make it happen.

Somehow, she had to make it happen.

DRUMMING HIS FINGERS ON HIS desktop, Jamis stared at the blinking cursor on his blank computer screen. Had he really called Natalie a Pollyanna yesterday when they'd argued over the no-trespassing signs? God, he could be such an asshole. So what if she got some kind of crazy thrill out of doing good? As long as she didn't mess with him, her issues were none of his business. But, then, that was exactly what he was worried about. Her turning him into one of her pet projects.

A noise on his front porch that sounded distinctly human distracted him. "I knew it. She didn't even make it twenty-four hours." Dreading the prospect of having to look and not touch the slightest inch of skin on that gorgeous woman, Jamis took off down the stairs, wanting to get his dose of daily torture over and done with.

"What now?" he said, yanking open the door.

Instead of Natalie, the teenage boy stood there shuffling his feet. "Hey," he said, his bangs, far too long, hanging in his eyes.

"What do you want?" Jamis glared at the gangly kid, not wanting to remember his name. Galen. It popped up anyway. *Dammit.*

"Um. I was just... I was wondering." The kid looked away. "Do you think I could watch some TV? Here at your house?"

He couldn't be serious, could he?

But then Jamis understood. All those kids. The noise. The constant activity. What normal person wouldn't go positively insane living in that Victorian? Still, there was no way this boy was stepping foot in this house.

"I mean," the kid said, "if it's not too much trouble... I just... Oh, forget it." He turned to leave. Hanging his head, the boy stepped off the porch and absently kicked a rock into the woods. There was something about how his feet seemed too big for his body that reminded Jamis of how awkward his own teenage years had been.

Hell, here I come.

"Hey, kid," Jamis said. Someone else's spirit, a much more kindhearted and compassionate one, must have taken over Jamis's body. "I was just leaving to go into town. You can watch TV while I'm gone." He'd have to give Natalie a pass on their deal for this one.

"You sure?"

"Do you want to, or not?"

"Totally." The relief in Galen's eyes was almost tangible. "I can't tell you how sick I am of watching stupid cartoons and girl shows. They don't have video games. Or even a DVD player over there."

Yeah, life was tough all over. Jamis showed him how to use the remotes. "Do they know where you are?"

He looked away. "Not really."

"How old are you?"

"Fifteen."

Old enough to be gone for a while without Natalie calling Garrett Taylor.

"I kinda had a fight with Natalie," the kid explained.

No way was Jamis getting drawn into this discussion. "Yeah? That sucks."

"She just drives me crazy, sometimes," Galen said, the frustration almost palpable. "You know? All that cheery ass positive thinking bullshit."

"Yeah. I know." Okay. So it wasn't another human that had taken over his body. It was aliens.

"What does she think is going to happen?" He shook his head.

Jamis might have been wrong, but he could've sworn he saw tears gathering in the boy's eyes, and the kid wasn't too happy about it, either. "Okay." He cleared his throat. "Well, this is where I cut out." He gathered up his grocery list, backpack and a package he should've mailed out yesterday and headed for the door. "Come on, Snick. Let's go."

The dog hesitated, glancing from the boy to Jamis and back again before running outside.

"And, hey," Jamis said, pausing on the porch, "this is a one-time deal, dude. And don't you dare tell Natalie or any of those other kids you've been here."

"I won't. Thanks, man."

Jamis shut the front door behind him, closed his eyes and took a deep breath. It was debatable whether or not he'd managed to dodge that bullet, but he certainly stepped directly in front of the next one. When he got to Main Street, the town was crawling with tourists. He glanced at the package in his hand. There was nothing for it. His editor needed this paperwork by tomorrow, and he was not going home to hang out with that kid.

"Come on, Snick. Gotta do it." Avoiding Main, he took a side street to the post office. Breathing a sigh of relief, he stepped inside the cool, quiet building and went to the counter.

A young man appeared. "Can I help you?"

For four years he'd been coming to this post office on a regular basis and for four years there had been only one person who'd ever assisted him. "Where's the regular postal clerk?"

"She's on medical leave."

"Sally? For what?"

"I don't know." The guy squinted at him. "But even if I did, I couldn't tell you that. It's private."

"When will she be back?"

"Don't know."

"Is she okay?"

"Don't know."

"Do you know anything?"

"Look, buddy. They told me to fill in, so that's all I'm doing. Filling in."

"You're not from Mirabelle, are you?" If he'd been an islander, he'd know what was going on with Sally.

"No. Like I said. Just filling in."

He shouldn't care. Really, he shouldn't. Jamis mailed his package and left the post office only to have bright sunlight hit him square in the face. He flipped his sunglasses on, untied Snickers and stood there, debating. Sally McGregor, as gruff as she'd been, had been the only human contact Jamis had had through the years. It seemed strange and unlikely, but he already missed her.

With Snickers by his side, he walked down the street, feeling at a loss. He stopped at Newman's, filled his grocery list and was standing in line behind several people when a store employee, an older man with glasses that Jamis had seen nearly every time he'd been in the store, walked by him.

"Excuse me," Jamis said out of the blue.

"Yes, sir, what can I do for you?"

"Do you know Sally McGregor?"

"I do." His expression turned instantly somber.

"Can you tell me what's wrong with her?"

The man studied him. "I don't know—"

"I'm Jamis Quinn."

"I recognize you, but…"

"I live on the other side of the island. Quinn Roberts?

The writer?" At that several strangers spun around, stared at him and whispered amongst themselves.

"Oh, yeah. Quinn Roberts. I'm Dan Newman."

Absently, he shook the other man's hand. "I'm sorry we haven't met before now…"

A small crowd gathered around them.

"Mr. Quinn," someone said, "could you autograph this receipt?"

Jamis glanced at the woman. There were others looking for pens and paper.

"Why don't you come to my office?" Dan took him by the arm and drew him into an office near the front of the store and quickly closed the door.

"Thank you," Jamis said awkwardly. "The man at the post office said Sally was on medical leave. Do you know if she's all right?"

He studied Jamis. "Well, I suppose there's no harm in telling you. The way the gossip circuit works around this island, all you'd have to do is ask any islander and they'd likely be able to tell you." He sighed. "She was diagnosed with cancer."

"What kind?"

"Pancreatic."

"What's the prognosis?"

"From what I hear, not very good."

"Is she still in the hospital?"

"As far as I know."

"Thank you." Jamis turned to go, feeling oddly disoriented. When he opened the door, a small group had gathered, each person holding pen and paper.

"There he is."

"It is Quinn Roberts!"

They asked him to sign books, papers, T-shirts, hands. Resigned, he quietly went from one person to the next.

A short while later, the storeowner came to him with his groceries bagged. “You better take off.”

He reached for his wallet.

“Don’t worry about it.” Dan waved his hand. “This bag’s on me.”

CHAPTER SEVEN

ONE DAY DOWN IN HER deal to stay away from Jamis Quinn. Only six more to go. The nighttime hours, especially those after the kids had gone to bed, would be the worst, so Natalie decided it was time to take Missy up on a girls' night out.

Having left Sam and Galen in charge of the rest of the kids for the first night since they'd all arrived on Mirabelle, she now sat at a table in Duffy's Pub with Missy and a couple of her friends, Sarah Marshik, the flower shop owner and wedding planner, and Hannah Johnson, one of the island's elementary school teachers.

Over wine and pecan-crusted fish fingers and stuffed mushrooms, she laughed until her stomach ached at the story Missy was telling about doing tarot card readings for a group of hard-core FBI trainees when she'd lived near the training base in Quantico.

"So I'm flipping over the cards and knives and sword are showing up everywhere," Missy said, pausing. "And I said to the guy, 'I hate to say this, but there's blood in your future.' He looked up at me with this deer in the headlights look and said, 'From what?' I looked at him and said, 'Dude, you're an FBI agent. What did you expect?'"

"He wasn't serious, was he?" Natalie chuckled.

"Totally," Missy said. "Turned out he was an accountant. He was working computer fraud cases and hated guns."

Natalie had so needed this night, needed to get away from the kids and the house, and a wonderful meal cooked up by Garrett Taylor's new wife, Erica, had been an unexpected bonus.

"I can't believe you take care of eight kids all day every day." Sarah shook her head. "One child is enough for me."

"Hey, what about me?" Hannah said. "I have more than ten kids in my classes. All day long."

"Yeah, but you have the summer off. And during the school year you get to go home every night. Alone."

"Don't remind me." Hannah downed the last of her chardonnay and then thrust her hand out across the table, palm up. "Missy, read my love line."

Missy chuckled. "Why?"

"I want you to tell me if I'm ever going to get married."

"It's not like that, honey."

"Then what good is it having your palm read?"

"Not much. All I can tell you is pretty much what you already know about yourself." She grabbed Natalie's hand, flipped it over and studied her palm. "Take Natalie for example. See her very strong, deep line," she murmured.

"What is it?"

"Your heart line." Missy ran her index finger along the line running mostly horizontally below Natalie's fingers.

"What does that mean?"

"The ability for strong and deep devotion." She glanced up at them. "Anyone surprised by that?"

"About a woman running a summer camp for disadvantaged kids?" Sarah chuckled. "No."

"Then again." Missy pointed to a spot in the middle of her palm. "That could be him."

"Who?"

"The love of your life." She grinned conspiratorially at Natalie.

Natalie grabbed Missy's hand and studied her palm. "What does yours say?"

"One true love for my entire life. And I already met him."

"You did?" Sarah said.

Hannah's jaw dropped. "You've never told us."

"What happened?" Natalie whispered.

"Didn't go so well." Missy's expression turned somber as she twirled the straw in her Black Russian. "He died. In an FBI training operation. A helicopter crash."

"I'm so sorry," Natalie murmured.

"Don't be."

"But you said he was the love of your life."

"He was. That doesn't mean we were right for each other." Missy chugged the last of her drink. "I loved him. He loved his job. No getting around that one."

"So that's it? You're done?"

"With anything serious. Most likely." She pointed at each of the other three. "But you guys aren't."

"The only problem is that there aren't any eligible men on Mirabelle," Hannah grumbled.

"You got that right. And the last one was snapped up so fast by Erica, everyone's heads were spinning." Sarah glanced up and noticed Garrett Taylor sitting in the booth next to them with Herman Stotz, his deputy, and Jim Bennett, the ex-police chief. "Hey, Garrett," she called.

He glanced up.

"You got any brothers?"

He grinned and held up three fingers.

"Yeah, but are they single?"

His smile broadened and he continued holding up two fingers.

"So when are they coming to visit?" Missy said, laughing.

"I'm not sure either one of them is Mirabelle material," Garrett said, shaking his head.

All four women returned to their drinks, decidedly more serious than before. Natalie took a big gulp of her Cabernet. "I know an eligible bachelor on the island. And he's very attractive."

"Who?"

"Jamis Quinn."

Sarah put down her martini and leaned forward. "He's come into my flower shop a couple of times. Sent flowers to funeral homes. An office once for someone's birthday. I'll tell ya, he's an odd one."

"Well, if he showed even an iota's worth of interest in me," Hannah said, "I'd be all over him."

Natalie couldn't imagine this woman all over any man. She looked every inch the elementary schoolteacher. Too sweet for Jamis, that was for sure.

Where did that leave Natalie?

"Turquoise and blue," Missy said.

"What's that?" Sarah asked.

"Our auras," Natalie explained.

"Perfectly matched." Missy grinned. "Only Natalie, here, has sworn off all men forever."

"Uh-uh," Natalie objected. "Only until my luck changes."

"Bad luck with relationship, huh?" Sarah asked.

"Don't get me started." Natalie shook her head.

Hannah chuckled. "Must be contagious."

"Like a virus," Missy added.

"WELL, I HATE TO TELL you this, Jamis," Chuck Romney's voice came quietly over the phone, "but Natalie Steeger has done a very thorough job in preparing for this camp. She obtained approval from the Mirabelle Island council and has complied with all the state licensing requirements for this type of facility."

Jamis still hadn't started a new book. Even a realistic idea for a story hadn't revealed itself, preoccupied as his thoughts were with the bustling activity on the other side of the trees bordering his property.

"You're sure?" he asked. "You didn't find anything?"

"I took it apart. Piece by piece. You have no grounds to shut her down."

He paced in his kitchen. "What about trespassing?"

"Jamis, give it a rest. Is she truly that bad?"

"You have no idea."

"Do you have no-trespassing signs up identifying your property line?"

"I put them up the other day."

"All right. Well, there's a process to these things. Eventually, you'll have to file a complaint with the police." He sighed. "You sure you want to go that route?"

No. He wasn't sure, but he was getting desperate. "What about buying her out?"

"You have enough money for that?"

"I'll figure it out."

"You go that route and you can forget about getting rid of her before the end of summer."

He sighed, resigning himself to that fact. "Not having to worry about her returning next summer is better than nothing."

"Do you want me to make her an offer?"

"Yes."

"I'll talk to her attorney again, but I'm not expecting to make any headway. That man's made it very clear that she doesn't want to sell, and from the information I've gathered about her she doesn't have to. Along with the house on Mirabelle, she also inherited another house in Minneapolis and a big chunk of change from her grandmother. She's soliciting donations and grants for the future, but with or without outside funding, she can keep this summer camp running for several more years."

"You need to talk to her directly, Chuck." This was for her own good. "Tell her I'll buy her something in town or on one of the other islands. I could give her a donation for her camp on the condition she moves. Do whatever it takes to get her off this island."

"Whatever it takes. All right, I'll give it a shot."

Jamis hung up the phone and immediately became aware of a presence outside in his yard, and it wasn't as innocuous as a squirrel. He glanced out the kitchen window and there climbing around on his rocks was that little girl with the curly dark hair. *No, Jamis. You are not going out there. No way. No how.* That teenage boy was one thing. This little bundle of wide-eyed innocence was an entirely different matter. The kid could putz out there all day long for all he cared, and Natalie was not going to get a pass for this one. Their deal was over, fair and square.

The kid picked up a stone and threw it into the woods. Then she wandered a few feet away, bent down and studied, presumably, an insect crawling through the dirt. Next, she picked a wood violet and another and another, starting a tiny bouquet in her little fingers.

He couldn't keep his eyes off her. Every step. Every movement. She did exactly what Caitlin would've done. His heart twisted inside out as memories of a different little girl in a different, happier time popped into his mind one after another. Caitlin's first steps, her first words, the way her fingers felt on his arm as he read her to sleep, the way her arms felt around his neck as she hugged him with all her might. Little girls. Were they all exactly the same?

Oh, God. He sucked in a quick breath and pushed the memories back where they could cause no further pain. Then she set her bouquet down, reached for the lowest branch of a small pine, and hoisted herself up. She was a good little climber, but every time she reached higher, Jamis cringed. One branch led to another and in no time, she was halfway up the tree, a good fifteen feet off the ground. If she fell—

He caught himself holding his breath. That was it. Yanking open the front door, he stepped out onto the porch and crossed his arms. "Hey, kid. Get down from there. Now."

She glanced over at him with a face as innocent as a bunny rabbit's. "Why? I'm not going to fa—"

"I said get down!"

She frowned, but did as he'd asked, scrambling quickly down the tree trunk. "I've climbed lots of—"

"What are you doing over here?"

She glanced up. "Nothing."

"Then go do nothing in your own yard."

She didn't move. Instead, she whispered, "I thought you reminded me of my daddy, but I guess not."

"Definitely not."

"He died."

Shit. Shit, shit, shit. Jamis swallowed as if the words stuck in his throat. "I'm sorry, but I'm not your dad."

Bending down, she picked up her violets and gathered them back into a bouquet. "Why do you try to be mean?" she asked without looking at him.

"Try? *Try* to be mean?"

She nodded.

And he couldn't do it. Just couldn't. Another pass for

Natalie. Taking a deep breath, he stepped out onto the porch and sat on the top step. "What's your name?"

"Toni."

He felt the name poke at his heart like the tip of a dull knife. "Well, Toni, you remind me of my daughter. And it hurts."

"Did she die, too?"

He nodded. "And my son."

"That's sad."

"Toni!" The call came from next door. "Dinner's ready!"

"Coming!" She glanced up at Jamis. "Here." Tentatively, she offered him the flowers. "I picked these for you."

Unable, unwilling to move, Jamis stared at the little hand.

Before he could step out of her reach, she thrust the flowers into his hand. "I gotta go!" she said, running away. "Want me to come back later?"

"No!" Jamis called, flicking the flowers into the woods. "Please," he whispered after she disappeared into the old Victorian.

If only he could put a no-trespassing sign on his heart.

NATALIE AWOKE AT HER usual early hour, but the kids got to sleep in late this morning. Weeks ago, she'd established the routine for the summer weekends. Saturdays were cleaning days. Saturday nights were pizza and a movie in town. And Sundays were play days all day long. She padded into the kitchen, made herself a pot of coffee and would've given anything at that moment to have an adult conversation. Unfortunately, the only adult within a five-mile radius was a certain grizzly bear of a man who'd made it very clear with or without his no-trespassing signs that he didn't want anything to do with her.

The clear call of a cardinal pierced the quiet of the morning, and she cracked open the window to listen. At that moment, the sound of Snickers's bark joined that of the bird's call, and she noticed motion on Jamis's deck. Curiosity getting the better of her, she snuck outside and into the woods for a better look. She hunkered down and peered through the branches to see Snickers chase through the trees after a squirrel, and grizzly bear Jamis standing near his deck rail. He was holding what appeared to be a steaming cup of hot coffee as he searched the branches, presumably for the bright red feathers of the male bird that was singing his solitary, melancholy tune.

Natalie was dying to stand up and walk over there with her first cup of coffee and talk. "No can do," she whispered. Thanks to that silly bet. *Two days down, five to go. Five? Whose idea was this, anyway? Oh, yeah. Mine.*

All she could do was watch as he sipped from his mug, closed his eyes and put his face to the sky. His longish hair was rumpled as if he'd just rolled out of bed. He was wearing flannel pajama pants and a fleece pullover, as if chilled, but he was barefoot.

What a paradox, that man. There was something so elementally virile about him, but it didn't make any sense. A writer? Virile and sexy? An attractive, intelligent man all alone in the woods? He shouldn't be alone. That man needed a woman. Not just any woman. He needed someone strong and compassionate, someone who could take him in stride.

Someone like her.

She imagined waking up naked in his arms, sliding over his tall, tense frame, and desire sung through her swiftly, cleanly, undeniably. Where was this coming from? Normally, she liked reserved and patient men. Jamis was neither. He was about as tentative as a bullet. He wouldn't ask for what he wanted. He'd take it.

Almost intuitively, his gaze traveled from the water

toward Natalie's house and back out to the trees as if he could sense her there. She squatted farther down and out of sight. *Stop it, Nat. Even if you hadn't sworn off men, you're too busy this summer for a relationship.*

Snickers started sniffing the edge of the woods in front of her and she held her breath. If he came running toward her, she'd die. Die.

"Snickers, come," Jamis called, and the dog quickly ran back to the cabin.

Natalie breathed a sigh of relief. Jamis and the dog headed back inside and then, resolutely, she put the slightly damaged but very sexy Jamis out of her mind, slinked back to her kitchen and focused on her plans for the day. Grabbing the whiteboard, she mapped out cleaning duties and started a load of laundry.

Gradually, over the course of the next couple of hours, one by one, the children wandered into the kitchen looking for something to eat. It was no surprise that Galen was the last one to the breakfast table. The previous night, he and Sam had gotten home only a few minutes past eleven, but she'd heard Galen up and about for some time before she'd drifted off to sleep.

She'd let them all watch some TV while she cleaned up from breakfast and then went into the living room and shut off the TV. "Time to get moving, guys."

Groans all around.

"Cleaning day. Remember? Top to bottom."

Major groans.

"Then tomorrow we're heading to the beach for sailing and kayaking. And today, the sooner we get done, the sooner we can head into town for pizza and a movie!"

That announcement was met with a resounding round of approval, and Natalie assigned chores. Another glance out the open kitchen window gave her an idea, and she grinned. After opening several more windows throughout the house as wide as they would go, she dropped a disk in the CD player and cranked the volume as high as it would go. She might not be able to go over to Jamis's, but their agreement didn't preclude him from coming over here.

JAMIS DRUMMED HIS FINGERTIPS on top of his desk as the sax solo for Ricky Martin's "Livin' La Vida Loca" pounded through the previously quiet forest. He'd already closed all of his windows, but Miss Not-So-Innocent-After-All had the volume so loud he swore the leaves on the trees were vibrating.

"The little vixen." He caught himself smiling.

This wouldn't be such an untenable situation, except for the fact that he was actually, almost, starting to like the woman.

With Snickers taking the lead, he strode to her house and pounded on the back door. When no one answered, he let himself into the kitchen and several heads turned toward him. One kid was scrubbing out the sink. Another was sweeping. Another washing the cabinets. One was vacuuming the living room. Another one dusting.

He had to give the woman credit. This was nothing like the posh camps he'd attended as a kid. He'd more likely have gotten breakfast in bed than be assigned chores. In any case, he walked past them all, found the CD player and flicked it off.

"Hey!" Natalie, holding a toilet brush in her hand, came out into the hallway from what must've been the bathroom. Goddamn, she looked gorgeous. In jeans shorts and a tank top with her hair up in a messy ponytail. Her skin glowing with a honey-gold tan. "Who shut off the music?"

"It's only considered music when listened to at reasonable decibels," Jamis said. "Otherwise it's nothing more than noise."

She spun toward him, put her hands on her hips, nice, curvy, luscious-looking hips, and raised her eyebrows. "Oh, so you can come over here, but I can't come over to your house?"

He laughed. She'd done this on purpose. Well, two could play that game. "Deal's off." He strode outside.

"Wait a minute!" She ran after him. "I'm sorry. I am."

"No, you're not."

"I am. Honestly."

Refusing to stop and discuss this with her, he stalked through the woods. She, predictably, followed. Within seconds he was standing in front of his house and she was close behind him. He spun around. "See? I was right."

"About what?"

"You couldn't even make it three days." He grinned. "This is where I get to gloat and tell you I told you so."

"What?"

"You, Sunshine, are trespassing."

Her mouth gaped open, showcasing pretty pink lips and a delectable tongue. "You did that on purpose!"

"So what if I did?"

"Of all the—"

That was it. He couldn't take it anymore. Striding toward her, he grabbed her around the waist, pulled her flush against him and kissed her. He'd only intended—Who was he kidding? He hadn't intended on touching her at all, but once he'd started he didn't want to stop. Neither did she. A harmless peck on the lips turned into open mouths, tongues clashing and hands groping. Her hands were on his chest, his neck, diving through his hair. Before he knew what he was doing, his fingers had found their way under her shirt and were making their way up her side toward her breasts.

Then a rap song suddenly sounded from Natalie's house, piercing the air and snapping Jamis back to reality. He stepped back and swallowed, feeling slightly stunned.

Natalie's eyes drifted open. "What…what was that for?" she whispered.

"I've been wondering what you'd taste like." She was a minty orange flavor he had a feeling he'd end up craving for a very long time.

"And?"

He might try to tell himself he didn't enjoy her company, her conversation, her presence, but the truth was he enjoyed her far too much. And he sure as hell didn't deserve to be enjoying much of anything.

"Now I really don't want you on my side of the trees." He stalked into the house, grabbed a few more no-trespassing signs and nailed them up between their two houses on every single tree he could find sturdy enough to hold them. By the time he was done, Natalie was nowhere to be found and the northwest corner of Mirabelle had fallen eerily silent.

CHAPTER EIGHT

SILENCE. A FULL SUNDAY'S worth of it and Jamis had managed to eek out only a chapter. As if a dam or a maze had been constructed in his brain, words were piling up inside him, making it impossible to release them in any coherent form. If they didn't come pouring out fairly soon, he might just explode. But at least he'd started the damned book. Sort of. He had no clue where this story was going. All he knew was that it was finally going somewhere.

Around suppertime, he called it a day. The scene wasn't turning out exactly as he wanted, so he'd have to hammer it into shape another time. As he was checking e-mails, a note came in from his agent. "I'm out next week. Forgot to tell you. How's the book coming?"

He typed back, "It's not."

"What's the problem?"

A woman. And her kids. "Writer's block." He had a block all right. He couldn't seem to think of much outside of Natalie and her lips, the way her skin had felt, like the petals of a wild trillium.

"It's the kids' camp, isn't it?"

"Yes." As he typed, he heard Natalie and her crew returning from wherever they'd spent the day. Snickers barked to go out and rather than argue Jamis left his agent's e-mails and went downstairs to open the door. The dog ran through the trees and up to each child. "Snickers!" they each called, in turn.

They were carrying beach towels, coolers and picnic baskets. A day at the beach—with people, laughter and games, hot sun, cool drinks. Surprisingly, it sounded like a nice way to pass a summer day.

Not gonna happen. Not in your lifetime.

He went to his office to turn off his computer and found another e-mail from his agent. "You going to meet the deadline?"

"No," he typed.

A few moments later, the phone rang. Jamis picked it up and walked across the room. "Yes, Stephen."

"You've never missed a deadline before."

"You think I don't know that?" He glanced out the window.

From this high up, the second floor of his house, he could see Natalie and the kids fishing at her dock. She had her hair up in a ponytail and was wearing a baseball cap. In jeans shorts and a red shirt, he wasn't sure he'd ever seen her look sexier. What would she look like in a bikini?

He closed his eyes and imagined her skin bared, soft and supple. Warm, the way her hand had felt on his neck yesterday, her fingers in his hair. She'd wanted him as much as he'd wanted her. A man didn't have to be a rocket scientist to figure out what might've happened between the two of them if those kids hadn't been next door. His thoughts quickly tracked in that direction. He imagined himself over her, moving with her, making love with her.

"Jamis? Jamis!"

He'd completely forgotten his agent was on the phone. "What?"

"You've started the book, though, right?" Stephen asked, not quite pulling Jamis back to their conversation.

"I have one chapter of a story. Not quite sure what it is yet." He went out to the porch for a better view of Natalie. "What's going on?"

"I don't know." She bent over, picked up something from the dock and laughed as she threw it into the water. "Too distracting around here, I guess."

Stephen held silent for a moment. "She's pretty, isn't she?"

"Uh-huh."

"Are you looking at her now?"

"Mmm-hmm."

Stephen laughed. "How long since you've been with a woman?"

"None of your business."

"Since Katherine, right?"

Jamis refused to answer that.

"You need to get laid."

"Oh, that'd solve a lot of problems." But there was no doubt that all these years without sex, without human touch, was taking its toll on Jamis.

"You'd be surprised."

No, he wouldn't. He was quite sure that a quick, noncommittal romp under the sheets with Natalie would do more than free his mind.

"You miss this deadline, Jamis, and this last publisher will not only close the door in your face, they'll drop all the publicity they've planned for the book you just turned in."

"You think I don't know that?"

"I'll call them. See what I can do."

As Jamis disconnected the call, the sight of Toni sitting with her feet dangling off the end of the dock caught his eye. She reminded him so much of Caitlin. The color of her hair. The curls. That sweet voice. He missed his children. And suddenly he realized the memory of their faces was beginning to fade.

Before he could think better of it, Jamis went to his office and pulled out the bottom drawer of his credenza, a drawer he hadn't opened since a box had been placed inside the day he'd moved into this cabin. He flipped open the flaps and there on top staring at him was the last picture he'd ever taken of his daughter and son. God, it was good to see them again. He picked up the frame and studied their smiles, their bright eyes. Finally, he could look at their beautiful faces without breaking down.

Jamis had taken them to a carnival by himself because it was the type of thing Katherine had hated. He'd loved doing things with the kids. On the merry-go-round, he'd put Justin in front of Caitlin and snapped off a picture.

Justin's dimples brought a smile to Jamis's face. With eyebrows heavier than most babies and a distinctive jawline, people had always commented on how much Justin had looked like Jamis. Caitlin, too, with her dark hair and big brown eyes. Katherine, as much as their marriage had been a sham from her standpoint, had given him two beautiful children.

Katherine.

He should've known better when she'd seemed attracted to him. An ex-model, Katherine had the body of a goddess and, on top of that, an electric personality. It hadn't made sense that such a woman would've been interested in him. Too bad he hadn't listened to his instincts all those years ago. He could've saved himself a helluva lot of heartache.

Well, Jamis was listening this time. He set the picture of his children back down into the box and closed the drawer. Natalie Steeger, a children's camp director and all around do-gooder, could only be interested in him for one thing. She wanted to fix him.

Boy, was she in for a big surprise.

AFTER THAT KISS, NATALIE vowed to give Jamis some breathing room.

For the first day or two that wasn't all that difficult. She and the kids stayed busy. But as the week wore on, Jamis and his kiss seemed to be all she could think about. The unexpected softness of his beard, the strength of his arms, the solid breadth of his chest—he'd taken her completely by surprise and kissed her as if he wasn't sure the sun would rise in the morning. The fact that he'd stated very succinctly that he still didn't want her on his side of the trees confused and confounded her. Maybe it was the way he called her Sunshine. She wasn't silly enough to think the nickname was meant in a kind way, but when he said the word there was a distinctly endearing quality to his voice.

Somehow, someway, she was determined to break through to that man. But how?

Already, it was Friday night and after dinner Galen whipped through his chores as if Arlo Duffy, the town carriage driver, was cracking a horsewhip on the boy's behind. Natalie chuckled to herself as he came speeding downstairs, smelling heavily of cologne.

"Can I go now?"

"Just a minute." Natalie took a box out of the pantry, wanting to catch all the kids before they all wandered away. "I have something for everyone!"

The kids all glanced at her expectantly as she set the box on the table. "What is it?" someone asked.

"Candy?"

"Ice cream."

"Journals!" She beamed, pulling out various shapes and sizes of decorated books filled with nothing except blank pages. She'd hoped this would help them with the dreams and wishes side of this camp. "You don't have to write in them if you don't want, but I'd like each of you to take one and think about it."

"Diaries are for chicks," Blake said.

"These aren't diaries," Sam said, picking up a red silk-covered book heavily decorated with beads. "They're journals."

"This—" Chase picked up a lavender book with tiny pink ribbons glued to the front and held it out "—is a diary."

"Maybe, dude." Galen held out a leather-bound book. "But this is a guy's book. You could use this to draw comics."

"Exactly!" Natalie said, smiling at Galen. Since their talk several weeks ago, he'd been making a marginally better effort to engage in activities and in helping with the kids and household responsibilities. Slowly, but surely, he'd been coming around. "I'd like you to write all your dreams and wishes in here, but they're your journals, so you can use them for anything. Jokes, stories, pictures."

Chase shrugged and took the book out of Galen's hands. Blake grabbed one of the other leather-bound books while Ryan found one covered with sports pictures. Arianna and Ella each picked out books covered in bright, fuzzy fur, but chose different colors. Toni took the lavender book Chase had discarded. "I like this one," she whispered.

"It's yours," Natalie said.

Each child thanked her as he or she wandered into the living room. Sam, though, hung back, glanced at Natalie and raised her eyebrows.

"I know. I know," Natalie said, pulling out another box

from the pantry that had been delivered that afternoon. "I have something else for you, Galen."

"What is it?" he asked.

Sam grinned. "Open it up and find out."

Natalie watched him tear back the cardboard flaps, feeling amazingly unsure for the first time around a kid. "If you don't like it, it's all returnable. I found what looked like a trendy online site and Sam helped me from there."

Sam shrugged. "I tried, anyway."

His face turned serious as he pulled out three sweatshirts and several T-shirts. He glanced up at Sam and a slight blush washed her cheeks.

"I'll let you know how much you can spend and you can order some jeans or shoes, but…" Natalie trailed off. "Is this stuff okay?"

"Okay?" He glanced up at her, and his sullen and disgruntled demeanor disappeared. "Um. Yeah, this stuff is way okay. Thanks."

He hugged Natalie, and by the time she pulled away Sam had disappeared into the living room. "Cool. I'm glad you like it, but Sam is the one who picked everything out."

He got a funny smile on his face. "So she doesn't really hate my guts?"

"No. I'm sure she doesn't."

He shrugged out of his old sweatshirt and into one of the new ones. "See you later." He ran toward the door.

"Isn't Sam going with you?"

"She didn't want to tonight. Can I still go?"

"Sure."

"Thanks again, Natalie. For everything." He paused at the door. "And I'm sorry for being such a jerk. I'll try to do better." Then he rushed outside and disappeared.

Her work with Galen wasn't finished, but they were

making headway. She wandered into the living room to find out what was up with Sam. She'd gone into town with Galen every Friday since they'd arrived on the island and seemed to have a good time. The younger kids were lying on the floor or lounging on the couch. Sam was sitting off by herself in a corner chair, looking bored. "Hey." Natalie nudged her on the shoulder. "You didn't want to go into town with Galen?"

"No, those guys are tr—" She stopped and looked quickly away. "I don't feel like going out. Kinda tired. In fact, I'm going upstairs to my room to read." Taking her journal with her, she disappeared up the steps.

Natalie watched her and wondered what those islander teenagers were getting into, but she couldn't ask Sam to snitch on Galen. *Galen, let's hope you have your head on straight.* She did not want to have to send him home.

"Anyone for a game?" she asked.

"Yeah!" came the resounding response followed by every kid calling out his or her favorite board game.

Several hours later, after a night of playing board games and having stuffed their stomachs with popcorn and soda, the kids all went to their respective rooms and promptly went to sleep. Natalie cracked open Sam's door to see if she wanted to watch a movie and found her sound asleep, her new journal open in front of her. Natalie hadn't planned on spying, but the one line Sam had written was as clear as a bell.

I wish I could stay here forever.

Oh, Sam. Natalie wanted to brush back the long strands of hair that had fallen over the girl's face. *I hope this summer is everything you need it to be.*

Natalie switched off the bedroom light, snuck quietly downstairs, and wandered into the kitchen. She paced in front of the sink, feeling a bit like a caged animal. After debating all of thirty seconds, she scribbled out a note for any one of the kids who might come looking for her.

"Kiss or no kiss, it's time we cleared the air." She grabbed a bottle of wine from the top shelf in the pantry and two glasses and took off through the woods. On reaching Jamis's yard, she noticed him on his deck, Snickers asleep near his chair.

Wearing a black fleece jacket, his feet propped up, his long, jeans-clad legs stretched out in front of him, he glanced up from the book he was reading the moment she came into the clearing. "You're trespassing," he said, frowning.

She held up the bottle. "But I come bearing a gift." Snickers hopped up and ran to greet her and she patted his head.

Jamis snapped the book closed and folded his arms across his chest. "What is it going to take to get you to leave me alone?"

"Come on, Jamis. Our houses are the only ones on this end of the island. Can't we be friends?"

CHAPTER NINE

"FRIENDS?" JAMIS SAID, a note of disbelief tingeing the sound of his voice. "Not possible."

"Sure it is."

"You don't give up, do you?"

"Nope." Natalie opened the bottle, poured him a glass and held it out.

He glanced first at her, then the wine and then back again. As clear as the full moon glowing high in the sky, she could see the memory of their kiss skittering through his mind, but then he seemed to lock it up and put it away. He shook his head and reached for the glass. "All right, Sunshine, but if we're going to do this, I want some honesty. And none of this 'the world is a perfect rainbow of happiness' bullshit, either."

"Okay." She leaned against the deck rail. "Honesty. Why do you—"

"Oh, no. We're going to talk about you." He pulled his feet off the chair and stood. Holding the glass of wine, he studied her. "Starting with what do you want from me?"

She shrugged. "I told you. To be friends."

"See, that's not good enough." Studying her, he slowly moved toward her. "I think this camp isn't enough for you. I think you want to turn me into another one of your projects. I think you'd like nothing more than to be my savior."

"I'm not trying to be anyone's savior."

"Sure you are. You'd save the entire world if you could manage it." He shook his head and chuckled. "I'll bet anything that you've spent your vacations building, painting or repairing houses, haven't you?"

"A couple."

"Ever work in a food bank?"

"Several times a year."

"Give blood?"

"Just got my five gallon pin."

"Women's shelters?"

"I used to answer the phones once a week."

"Figures." Scoffing, he shook his head.

"What does?"

"Neck deep in one crusade after another."

"When you put it that way, it sounds rather pathetic." She set her wineglass on a nearby deck table. She didn't mind standing up for her camp. She'd been doing that for months while getting approvals and licenses, but this personal attack was something altogether different. "You think all I am is a Goody Two-shoes, don't you?"

He said nothing.

"Well, I got news for you, there's more here than meets the eye."

"That I'd like to see." His gaze turned smoky and disconcerting.

"What's so wrong about helping other people?"

"Nothing. As long as you're not using all those activities to avoid your own issues."

"Which are?" She straightened her shoulders.

"I don't know. You tell me."

"I don't have any issues."

"Sunshine, we all have issues."

"Maybe I've dealt with mine."

"Right." He looked her up and down. "Fresh out of college? I don't think so."

"As a matter of fact, I just turned thirty. Thank you very much."

He looked surprised and possibly relieved. "Survived a big one, eh? So why aren't you married?"

She took a fortifying gulp of wine. "Who says I'm not?"

"No man in his right mind would let you out of his sight for three months." He paused and gazed at her. "Smart. Caring. Sexy." His eyes were dark and getting darker. For a moment, she thought he might reach for her. "What's the catch, Natalie?"

Cocking her head, she whispered, "Can't cook."

He chuckled, and it was one of the most fascinating sounds she'd ever heard, full of nuance and suggestion. She tilted her head upward and though she hadn't moved, the distance between them seemed to close. "It so happens I haven't met the right man."

"I don't believe you." He was going to kiss her. Almost sure of it, she quickly turned away, breaking whatever spell had overtaken him. "So that gets us right back to where we started. What do you want from me?"

"I told you. I could use a friend."

"You haven't dated many men, have you?" he asked.

"Plenty. Trust me."

"That many, huh? What's the longest you've been with one guy?"

She didn't like feeling cornered. "That's not relevant."

"Bet it wasn't very long—"

"What is this, an inquisition?" She crossed her arms.

"You're the one who wanted to be friends."

"You going to take down the no-trespassing signs?"

"Maybe."

She considered him for a moment and realized she had nothing to hide. "I've had a streak of bad luck with men. That's all."

"Bad luck. Right." He stared her down.

"All right. Fine. The longest I've ever dated a guy was three months."

"That's not very long. Who was he and why did you break up?"

"He was a coworker's brother," she said, picking up her wine and turning away. "Owned an excavating company. Came from a family of ten kids, but didn't want any of his own."

"And it took you that long to figure that out?"

"He *claimed* he'd made that clear right up front, but I don't remember him divulging that key piece of information." She felt herself getting slightly miffed at Jamis for bringing it all back up. When she'd broken up with Chad, he'd literally fallen apart and blamed it all on her. "How could anyone not want children, anyway?"

"Fatal flaw, huh?" He stepped in front of her, forcing her to look at him. "The one before that?"

"Teacher. Liked kids so much, he wanted—"

"Let me guess. Six."

"Eight." And was so convinced she was destined to be the mother of his big brood that he wouldn't accept the breakup. He'd turned stalkerlike within a week.

"I'll bet you even dated one who was too much like a child himself."

Carl. Now she was getting angry, angrier than she'd been in a very long time.

"I'm sure there were more. Keep going."

"No."

"So now you're pouting."

She glared at him. "There was a personal trainer who couldn't stop looking in the mirror. The perpetual student who never wanted to get a full-time job. The DJ who so much liked the sound of his own voice—"

"—he couldn't stop talking long enough to listen to you." He shook his head. "Why are you always picking men with these glaring flaws?"

"Well, I certainly don't know they have them right away."

"Sure you do. I'm guessing you've known instantly about every flaw of every man you've ever dated."

"That's just..." She stopped.

"Not bad luck, that's for sure. You knew nothing would come of any of those relationships. They were all doomed before they'd even begun."

She backed away from him. "And you're such an expert on relationships?"

"Not even close. But I was married for four years, and filing for a divorce wasn't my idea. At least that tells you I'm not afraid of commitment."

What an infuriating ass of a man. "I'm not afraid of commitment!"

"No. You're afraid of being abandoned. That's why you always pick men with no possible future with you."

Furious now, she didn't—couldn't—say anything.

"You like to fix things, don't you?"

"What does that have to do with anything?" she threw back at him.

"Because all the men you choose are fixer-uppers." He studied her, as if he was working something out. "It gives you an easy out."

She felt tilted off center. Leave them before they could leave her. Dammit, but he could be right.

"What about me?" he whispered. "Am I just another man you want to fix?"

"No. It's not that, it's—"

"What do you want from me, Natalie?"

"Nothing, I—"

He tucked a strand of her hair behind her ear. It seemed an innocent enough gesture, except for the fact that his hand lingered near her neck. "You don't get it, do you?"

"What?" she whispered.

"I don't want you here."

"I think you've made that perfectly clear." He'd been nothing short of attacking her. Maybe it was time to return fire. "Why don't you give me a little honesty? Tell me why you don't want me here and I'll leave you alone."

"Because you came over here tonight thinking if you share a glass of wine, some conversation, then wave your magic wand over me all would be well. You want to fix me just like you've tried to fix all those other men."

"No, I—"

"Only I don't need fixing, Natalie."

"You're wrong. You do. You lost your wife, your children—"

His gaze swung toward her. "Be very careful what you say."

"I wanted to understand why you were here, so I looked up some old online articles. But it doesn't make any sense. It was an accident."

He clenched his jaw and looked away.

"Why do you hate yourself so much?" She put her hand softly on his arm. "It wasn't your fault."

He glanced down at her hand and his mouth parted. "I haven't been with a woman in five years, Natalie. The next time you touch me, you'd better be ready to be touched back."

Five years. That was a long, long time for a man. For some crazy reason his admission felt more to her like a challenge than a warning. She trailed her hand up his arm, over his shoulder and through the locks of soft, curly hair on his neck. His face was only inches from hers.

"I'm warning you," he whispered. "Unlike the rest of your fatally flawed men, I happen to like myself the way I am."

"No, you don't. You just think you do."

Like a wild animal sniffing out its territory, he leaned closer, smelling her neck, then her hair. "You willing to take that risk?"

She closed her eyes and kissed him.

He stood still, ramrod straight as she peppered his mouth with the lightest of touches. But when she lingered a moment, her lips opened and felt his tongue with the tip of her own, his breath left his body. "Okay, Sunshine. You want it, you got it." He dragged her close and held her against him.

As his tongue brushed against hers, something fired to life inside her. This. This is what she wanted from him. *To feel him.* She ran her hands up and along his side. *To touch him.* His back muscles were tight and tense. She'd never kissed a man built so perfectly. He was so strong and demanding.

As if to prove it, his hands dipped under her shirt, traveled up her bare back and flicked the clasp on her bra. He cupped her breast and she shivered. He pulsed his hips toward her and his erection pressed against her, feeling at once wrong and right, startling and bone melting. She wanted her clothes off. She wanted to feel his naked skin next to hers. She wanted—

He pulled back and dropped his hands to his side. "That's what you want from me, isn't it?"

She swallowed.

"Well, I'm not available."

"You are, without a doubt, the most infuriating man I know."

"Well, you know what you can do about that."

"Of all the..." Clenching her teeth, she spun around and ran down the steps and across the yard.

"Don't bother coming back," he called after her. "I am not the broken man you think I am!"

DON'T COME BACK HERE. *Don't ever come back.*

Jamis watched her stalk away, feeling intense sensations of both relief and regret.

A part of him hadn't wanted to be so damned right about her. A part of him had wanted to be no more than a simple, uncomplicated summer diversion for her. So what? Who could blame either one of them? Neither of them was wet behind the ears. They both understood the consequences to that kind of impulsive behavior. There was nothing wrong with no-strings-attached sex.

But he had been right. Jamis was no more than a summer project for her, like her camp. She planned to fix him and move on, get what she needed from him—the satisfaction she took from helping another human being, or whatever else she got out of it—and then disappear from his life. Just like Katherine.

Jamis closed his eyes. He could taste Natalie, the wine on her tongue, the heat of her mouth. On his lips. He could feel her. On his hands. This was one raging hard-on he wouldn't be willing away all that easily.

Gulping down what was left of the wine in his glass, he immediately filled it again. *You're an idiot.* He'd thought he'd scare her away, make her keep her distance and all he'd accomplished was heightening the tension between them.

She was angry at him? Thought *he* was out of line? He shook his head and laughed. Before the summer was over he had a sick feeling that woman was going to bring him to his knees.

At the sound of the knock, Bradley opened his hotel-room door and in sauntered that woman from the bar. Her lusty gaze settled on his groin.

"Don't do it, Bradley," Natalie whispered into the quiet stillness of her bedroom. "You don't have to do it."

As if he were no more than a piece of meat to be chopped up and fried, she licked her lips. Thought she was hot shit, didn't she? Most of them did. She had no clue what she was getting herself into.

Natalie glanced at the clock. Three o'clock in the morning. She'd started reading Jamis's book after all the kids had gone to sleep more than three hours ago and couldn't seem to put it down. Quickly, she turned the page and kept reading.

He waved her forward with a flick of his fingers. She came to him, knelt before him, and unzipped his fly without a moment's hesitation. When he came in her mouth she didn't even pause to swallow, simply let his fluid drip from her lips.

Scanning to the end of the chapter, Natalie cringed as the man brutally murdered the woman.

She was nothing. Nothing. He watched her eyes dim, reveled in her mounting fear. Too scared to scream.

Natalie slapped the book closed and set it on her bedside table. How could he write about a man ruthlessly killing one person after another? Where did it come from? Even more amazing was how he'd brought her almost to the point of empathizing with the murderer. Worse were the eerie parallels between the killer and the cop chasing him. No wonder they'd made a movie from this story. Jamis was an incredibly skilled and gifted writer, and it was the kind of over-the-top story of conflicted, damaged characters that Hollywood loved.

Not a broken man? Like hell.

The urge to do something for him coursed through her like a river through a wide-open dam and she grew frustrated with herself. Was he just another mission for her? Was she afraid of abandonment? Could he be right on every single count?

She couldn't deny that there was some measure of truth in what he'd said. From the time she'd been adopted, she'd felt the need to pay back what she'd been given. It seemed she had to always be doing for others in order to feel right about herself. That couldn't be good, even if good was being done.

As for men, she'd broken off almost every single one of her past relationships. But that was in the past. There was something different about Jamis. He was strong, despite the fact that he was hurting inside. He made her laugh, sometimes want to cry, and always, always made her want him. And that was, perhaps, the sexiest thing of all about Jamis. He didn't need her. He wanted her.

CHAPTER TEN

"NATALIE! TELEPHONE!"

When someone called from the living room, Natalie was throwing another load into the washing machine from the seemingly endless pile of dirty clothes eight active kids seemed to generate. "Coming!" She threw in some detergent, started the wash cycle, and then took the phone from Chase. "This is Natalie."

"Miss Steeger, my name is Charles Romney. I'm an attorney in Minneapolis."

"Hello, Mr. Romney. What can I do for you?"

"You're a very difficult woman to get ahold of."

"I am, huh?"

"Has your attorney relayed my offers?"

"Nope."

"That's unfortunate. I believe you're missing an opportunity."

At that her warning flags were raised and she kept her mouth shut.

"You recently inherited a home on Mirabelle Island and I represent a party interested in acquiring that property."

Confused, his comment didn't immediately register. "It's not for sale."

"Well, before you immediately discount the possibility

I think you should be aware that money is of little importance in this situation."

She waited.

"My client is prepared to pay you three, four times the current market value of your property. You name the price. It's yours."

Jamis.

Most of her life she'd taken criticism for trying to stay positive in dismal circumstances. She thought she was used to it, immune to its inherent negativity, but this hurt in an unexpected, but no less devastating, way. "He's that desperate to have us gone?"

"I beg your pardon?"

"You can tell Jamis Quinn that I have no intention of selling my grandmother's house. He's stuck with us, Mr. Romney. Goodbye."

"Wait! Natalie!"

She held the phone.

"You want to help kids. I get it, I do." Regret filled his voice. "But eventually your inheritance and your personal savings are going to run out. You may find it extremely difficult to raise funding for your project."

"I already have several donors interested."

"Things can change."

Had she heard correctly? "Are you threatening me?"

"No. Not at all. But I think you should consider that Wisconsin is full of lakes and lake homes that would suit your purposes. You should think about how many more children you could help with that additional funding."

He was right, but so wrong. "Mr. Romney, you probably think you know a lot about me, don't you?"

"Well, I—"

"I'm going to guess you know I was adopted." She took

a deep breath. "So to say that my ancestors built this home generations ago would be a lie. You probably also know that I came to live here when I was ten." She paused, stuffed her shaking hand into her jeans pocket. "What you can't find in any court documents or social services records and the reason why my attorneys refused to bring your offer directly to me is because they understand that Mirabelle Island was a dream come true for me."

Now it was his time for silence.

"I will get funding to continue this program in my grandmother's house if it's the last thing I do. This home is going to continue being a dream come true for a lot more kids. For years and years to come. I will never sell this house."

"You're sure about that?"

"As sure as I am of anything."

"I'll relay your answer to my client."

"Don't bother. I'll tell him myself." She slammed down the phone.

Angry as she could ever remember being, she marched out the door. The sharp sound of Jamis chopping wood filled the air as she charged through the woods to his house. The moment she rounded the corner and found him, his back to her as he worked his way through a pile of wood, she stopped.

Oh, crap, he isn't wearing a shirt.

Mesmerized by the sight of the flexing muscles of his bare back, she could only watch. His biceps pumped with every swing. His leg muscles worked to stabilize his body with every thrust. Her mouth grew dry, her cheeks turned flush. Air didn't seem to be making it past the lump in her throat. She wanted that body, naked and next to her. She wanted to touch and taste and feel. This ache for Jamis seemed to be destroying her from the inside out.

Wait a minute. She was angry with him. Wasn't she?

JAMIS SET THE LOG ON the chopping block, heaved the ax behind him and swung, splitting the wood in two. Keeping half on the block, he swung again, quartering the original piece. Another piece of wood. Another swing and a chop. Again. Again. Hard. Harder. As hard and fast as he could.

After having spent several ineffective hours at his computer, he'd finally given up and come outside to let off some steam. He was letting off steam all right, but his head wasn't any clearer than when he'd begun. He set another log on the block and grabbed his ax handle.

The softwoods, birch, cottonwood and ash weren't cutting it. Today, he needed hardwoods, oak and maple, to work off his demons. He had a damned book due by the end of the summer and he'd barely gotten past the first chapter. He could blame it on the kids distracting him, but that was nowhere near the truth.

It was Natalie. If it wasn't her smile and lighthearted laughter washing away the built-up grime on his soul, it was the look of her long legs in short shorts stirring things up inside him. It was the way she looked in the moonlight pulling him toward her. It was those lips beckoning to be kissed.

The woman was killing him. Even now, it was as if he could smell her on the slight breeze. He stopped swinging his ax in midair, closed his eyes and took a deep breath. She was here. He spun around to find her motionless and staring at him. Sunlight streamed through the trees and lit the soft glints of gold in her hair, but it was the want he saw mirrored in her eyes that sent a jolt to his groin, giving him an instantaneous hard-on.

After a moment, with only the sound of a chickadee piercing the silence, he whispered, "You shouldn't be here."

"I..." She blinked, as if coming to her senses. "I need to talk to you."

"Not now." He turned away from her and set another piece of wood on the chopping block.

"Yes. Now," she said, sounding distinctly irritated.

This time when he glanced back at her, her hands were on her hips and a scowl covered her face. She looked as worked up as he'd ever seen her, and, by God, still all he wanted to do was kiss her.

"I'm not selling my house."

"Good for you."

She didn't seem to know what to say about that. "Are you going to try to tell me that Charles Romney isn't your attorney?"

"No."

"So he is?"

"Yep."

"You are the most infuriating man." She looked perplexed, and he couldn't blame her. She had that exact effect on him. "Do we drive you that crazy that you can't coexist with us?" she asked.

He dropped his ax and walked toward her. "Day and night, I hear children laughing, talking, fighting. Playing." He ran his hands through his hair. "And when I don't hear them, I'm expecting them. To knock on my door. To bring me cookies. Invite me to the fire. Ask if they can watch—" He stopped and spun away. Dammit, he wasn't supposed to say anything about that.

"Watch TV?" she asked. "Is that what you were going to say? Someone came to your house and asked to watch TV?"

He kept his mouth shut.

"Galen?" She shook her head. "I'm sorry. I didn't—"

"No. You didn't." He glared at her and felt something

inside him give way. "But it's not only the kids. It's *you.* You have no clue what you do to me." *You drive me crazy. Thinking about you. Wanting you. I can't get you out of my mind.*

Her mouth parted and she seemed to lean toward him, as if the exact thoughts were running through her mind.

"I came to Mirabelle for peace and quiet, Natalie. You and your kids disrupt my world. I want to be alone."

"And you'll do whatever it takes to get me off this island?"

"Something like that."

"Even if it means blocking the possibility of obtaining future funding for my camp?"

"I don't know what you're talking about."

"At least I'm trying to make a difference, which is more than I can say for the people who hole themselves up in their homes, or their minds, or their islands, all alone insulating themselves from the rest of the world so they don't have to face reality."

"Is that what you think I'm doing?"

"You sit here day in and day out feeling sorry for yourself because you've lost your family. You went through a big trauma. I'll grant you that. But we all have heartache. We've all lost things. The difference between you and the rest of the world is that you're stuck in the past, and the rest of us have moved on."

"You finished?"

"Not even close." She stalked toward him. "You think you're the only one who has bad days? Nasty, depressing thoughts? Well, I've got news for you." She jabbed her finger into his chest. "You're not so special or unique. I have plenty of bad days. Some nights I cry myself to sleep. There are even times when I think maybe life would be easier if I shut myself off from the world and go hide on an *island* somewhere."

He clenched his jaw and waited.

"But I don't do that. You know why? Because I'm not going to give up. I refuse to go down waving a white flag. I'd rather be a Pollyanna any day than a coward."

Her words hung for a moment in the still air between them.

"That's what you think I am?" he whispered. "A coward?"

"Yes." As if someone had tossed water on her angry fire, she seemed to sputter out. Her shoulders drooped and her brow furrowed. "I thought you were a decent person, Jamis. Inside. I thought…we'd made a bit of a connection. I was wrong. So, so wrong. I can't believe you'd stoop so low as to try cutting me off at the knees."

He wanted to object, defend himself, but he kept silent. It would be better for them both for her to continue thinking so little of him.

"We'll leave you alone, Jamis." She turned and stalked away. "From now on, you can go ahead and rot in your own personal hell!"

Jamis watched her march off into the woods. "It's about time," he said aloud. "Good riddance to you. And your kids."

She'd no sooner gone into her house, letting the porch door slam behind her, than she was stalking back outside carrying a hammer.

Now what was she up to?

A moment later, he had his answer. She ripped every one of his no-trespassing signs off his trees and pounded them into her trees, facing his property. Angrily, he swung his ax, splitting the log in two with one strike. Who did she think she was? And had she really called him a coward? Went to show what she knew and understood about him. There was nothing wrong with wanting to be left alone.

But he hadn't wanted it to be at her expense.

Son of a bitch. He stalked into his house and dialed a number on his phone.

"Romney, here."

"What did you say to her, Chuck?"

"Hello to you, too, Jamis." He sighed. "I told her to name her price and it was hers."

"And?" Jamis paced by his kitchen counter.

"She turned it down."

"So you countered with?"

"I told her it might be difficult for her to raise funding for next year."

"And what exactly did you mean by that statement?"

"You told me to do whatever it takes."

Jamis ran a hand over her face. "Did I say that?"

"Yes. You did."

He could've. He *would've.*

"So I did some digging to find out how she's funding this," Chuck went on. "Her inheritance and personal savings will last a year or two. After that, she'll have to finance this deal with donations and grants. I've got a list of the people and organizations she's soliciting."

"You haven't done anything yet to sabotage her obtaining that funding, have you?"

"No. I was just throwing it out there to see if we could get her to take an offer. You say the word and—"

"No." Jamis closed his eyes. "Drop it. Right now. If anything, put in a plug for her *and* her camp."

"Jamis, what's going on?"

"I was wrong. Simple as that. Make an anonymous donation to her camp from my account." He looked around his cabin, a stronghold and prison all rolled into one. "And find me a private island for sale. Anyplace but here!"

"JUST IN TIME!" MISSY exclaimed the moment Natalie and her kids entered the gift shop. "Everything your kids are making is flying off the shelves. I hope you've brought more inventory."

"We certainly did," Natalie said.

Almost a week had passed since Jamis's attorney had called and their resulting argument outside when he'd been chopping wood. Since then, she'd vigilantly kept the kids on their side of the tree line. The result had been some very productive crafting sessions. Galen set a box full of their wares on Missy's counter, and Natalie handed her an itemized list of what they'd brought this time.

"Looks good," Missy said, handing Natalie a check and a statement. "And here's the payment for everything I've sold so far."

Natalie scanned the list of what Missy had sold and the amount due each child. "Woo-hoo, Sam! You topped out at a hundred and twenty-five bucks."

Sam grinned. "That's how much I made?"

"Yep."

"What about me?"

"And me!"

"Me, too."

One by one, she relayed how much each child had made from the sale of their crafts. Galen was the only disappointed one in the crew, but that was to be expected since he'd dragged his feet up until the past week or so. "You'll do better next time," Natalie offered.

"I know," Galen said. "It's my own fault." He'd begun making key chains and wristbands using leather products and had cut and burned his own designs into the smooth tanned surface.

As the kids filed out of Missy's store, Missy held Natalie back. "You okay? You look tired."

"We've been busy."

"You need a break."

"No, I can't—"

"One entire night alone."

"I don't like to be al—"

"I'm not taking no for an answer." Missy stuck her head outside and called out to the kids, "Who wants to go camping tonight with me?"

"You mean sleep in a tent?"

"Yep." Missy nodded.

"Yeah!"

"Cool!"

"I'm in!"

Every single one of the children was excited, even Galen.

"There. Done." Missy turned back to Natalie. "Relax tonight. Glass of wine and a movie. A full night's sleep. Tomorrow, you'll be a new woman."

Knowing Missy wasn't going to budge, Natalie accepted the fact that she needed a break. After they left Missy, Natalie cashed the check at Mirabelle's little corner bank and doled out cash to each one of the kids.

"Let's go to the candy store!" Chase exclaimed.

"Totally!" agreed Blake.

"Are you sure that's what you want to do with your money?" Natalie asked.

The kids glanced at each other.

"You can save or spend, it's completely up to you, but it might be wise to decide on how much you want to spend before you go to the store. That way you won't eat into the amount you want to save."

There were nods all around, and she took them to Mrs. Miller's candy store. They'd all agreed to spend no more than five dollars each, except for Sam and Galen. They both swore they were saving every penny of their earnings.

"How are you doing today, Mrs. Miller?" Natalie said, going to the front counter.

"I'm good, Natalie." Mrs. Miller was watching all the kids as they wandered around the store, suspicion clouding her eyes as her gaze settled on Galen.

"Is it bothering you that I bring the kids here?" Natalie asked.

"It's nothing against you, dear," the woman whispered. "But I did hear a rumor about your older boy causing some trouble."

Natalie tried to stay calm, but this prejudice against her kids was bothering her more than she'd expected. "Are you referring to Galen?"

Mrs. Miller nodded.

At the mention of his name, Galen moved a little closer to Natalie and seemed to tune into their conversation.

"Can't be too careful these days," Mrs. Miller went on. "Honestly, I'm not sure Mirabelle is the right place for your camp."

"Kids!" Natalie called. "Pick out what you want and come on over here and pay for it. It's time to go." She leaned toward Mrs. Miller and said softly, "After today, we'll take our business to the other candy store." It would be a bit longer of a walk toward the other end of town, but they might be more welcoming.

As soon as they got outside, Natalie turned to Galen and whispered, "Do you know what Mrs. Miller was talking about?"

"No." Galen shook his head. "I swear I haven't done anything wrong."

Natalie watched him walking away with the rest of the kids and kept her fingers crossed he was telling the truth.

CHAPTER ELEVEN

"TEN THOUSAND DOLLARS?" Standing in the kitchen later that night, Natalie almost dropped the phone. Missy had no sooner collected all the kids for their campout at the state park on the island than her attorney had called to give her the good news. "Someone donated that much to my summer program?"

"No strings attached," her attorney said.

"Who is it?"

"That particular one was anonymous, but there are several others who've promised some fairly substantial amounts."

"Why all of a sudden?"

"Someone, somewhere put in a good word for you."

Jamis. He had to be behind this.

"I thought you'd be more excited."

"Oh, I am. This is great. Thanks." She hung up the phone and glanced out the window toward Jamis's cabin. Oddly enough, she missed the sound of his voice, his sardonic looks and even his sarcastic comments, and this big house seemed awfully quiet without the children.

No, you are absolutely not going over there!

She ran a bath and threw in some scented salt. Next, she lit a candle, turned on some soft music and got ready for a night of blissful peace and quiet.

JAMIS LAY ON HIS SOFA with Snickers stretched out alongside him. He stared up at the knotty pine ceiling absently petting the dog's head. Jazz played softly. The only light in the room came from a dim lamp in the corner and a small blaze burning in the stone fireplace. It was exactly the kind of idyllic, quiet night Natalie might intrude upon and ruin. Not that he wanted her to. It just made sense to brace for a possible attack.

Then again, he hadn't seen her since that day she'd called him a coward and told him to rot in hell. He still couldn't believe she'd had that in her. He deserved everything she'd said, but that didn't make it any easier to swallow.

A tap sounded on the patio door. Snickers perked up and raced across the room. Then the door slid open. "Hey, Snick."

He glanced over to see Natalie patting the dog's head. She was in a sweatshirt and sweatpants and her hair was wet as if she'd just stepped out of the shower. She smiled uncertainly. "Want some company?"

"Do I have a choice?"

At first she didn't say anything. "I've been thinking." She stayed where she was, the door cracked open behind her. "We started off on the wrong footing."

"You think?"

"Can we back up?"

"Why? What's the point?"

"I'll leave if you really want me to."

He hesitated. God help him, but he wanted her to stay. "There's a bottle of wine up on the counter. Help yourself."

She slid the patio door closed, kicked off her flip-flops and went barefoot into the kitchen. He heard her moving from cupboard to cupboard. He would've told her where to look for a glass, but there was something comforting about the sounds of someone, another body, a real live person rummaging around in his house.

A moment later, she came back into the great room, set the bottle of wine on the coffee table and sat on the other half of the oversize sectional sofa. Snickers jumped up next to her and rested his head in her lap. For an instant Jamis imagined her fingers on *his* head, smoothing back his hair.

"I'm sorry," she whispered. "For all those harsh things I said to you the other day when I was angry. About you being on this island. And being a coward."

"Everyone has a right to their opinions."

"Having them is different than voicing them."

"I deserved it, didn't I?" He shrugged, sloughing it off, though for some reason, her opinion of him was beginning to matter. "If not for that, surely for something else."

"I started reading *Lock and Load* the other night."

He said nothing.

"You're an amazing writer." She took a sip of wine. "I couldn't put the book down for hours, but it was a little like a train wreck."

"That's life, isn't it?"

"Don't you ever write anything…nice?"

He just stared at her.

"Isn't there enough pain in the world already?"

"When people read my books, their own pain seems less significant."

"So is that why you write?" Disbelief tainted the sound of her voice. "To help people?"

He sat up, took a sip of wine and cocked his head at her. "I think you know the answer to that question."

"Then why *do* you write?"

"Because I have to." He was quiet for a moment. "These stories hit me, take over my mind and it seems the only way to get rid of them is to write them down. I can't… I don't know what I'd do if I couldn't write."

"That sounds as if you don't enjoy writing."

"Most of the time, I do. It can feel good to lose myself for a while. Building worlds and immersing myself in them." His gaze turned intense. "I like stepping into other people's lives and knowing what's going to happen. I like the sense of control. I can stop things from happening. Or make things happen. What I say goes."

"Your characters don't do anything you're not expecting?"

"Never."

"What about if—"

"Why did you come over here?"

"The kids are gone. Camping with Missy Charms for the night."

"And you were bored."

She looked away. "I don't like to be alone."

"Why does that not surprise me?"

She shrugged. "I ate dinner, then primped and pampered myself until I couldn't stand it anymore. Now here I am."

All primped and pampered. Her face glowed as if she'd scrubbed it with some mask. If the fresh coat of pink polish was any indication, she'd given herself a manicure and a pedicure. She'd probably even shaved her legs. He closed his eyes against the images of lots of bare skin flashing through his mind.

Oblivious to his thoughts, she stood and walked around. "I can't believe you did all the work on this house yourself."

"The winters here are quiet. And last a while."

"How long did it take?"

"Two years."

She raised her eyebrows.

"It's not such a big deal." He swung his feet down off the couch and watched her. "I had a lot of time on my hands, and I needed the physical and mental outlet."

"Interesting."

"What?"

"Other than these landscapes." She pointed to a set of four pictures he'd taken of the seasons on Mirabelle. "You have no photographs. Anywhere."

"So?"

"Your children?"

"It's…still painful to look at pictures of Caitlin and Justin."

Her expression softened. "Nice names."

He looked away and gulped down some wine.

"What about the rest of your family? Your parents?"

"We're not very close." That was putting it mildly.

"Where do they live?"

"In Minneapolis." He refilled his wineglass. There probably wasn't enough left in the bottle for this turn in the discussion.

"And they never visit?"

"Good God, no."

"Don't you keep in touch with them at all? Even with phone calls?"

"I haven't talked to my dad in…at least six years. He was in China, arranging some buyout or something and didn't bother coming to the funeral for his own grandchildren. That's the last time I saw my mother. She phones occasionally, but all she does is drone on and on about a particular charity drive she'd organized or some society event she and my dad had attended. She's a cliché."

"That's cruel."

Silently, he studied her for a moment. "She was a cruel mother. I have a memory or two of her being relatively attentive when I very young, but for most of my life, she was absent, apathetic or in one way or another disinterested."

"I'm sorry."

"Why? My poor little rich boy childhood can't possibly be worse than yours."

"Strangely enough, sometimes bad attention is better than none. You have no siblings to commiserate with?"

He shook his head. "I don't think my mother and father ever intended on being parents, and they had no clue what to do with their strange, introverted and grossly shy son who didn't fit their lifestyle." He took a sip of wine. "My father couldn't relate to me, so he didn't bother, and my mother, quite simply, rejected what she couldn't understand."

"How did you do at school?"

"Teased, ridiculed. As a nerdy teenager, I disappeared into my stories."

"Did you always write?"

He chuckled. "I wrote my first book when I was eight. It was a short story, only about twenty pages, but by the time I was sixteen, I'd written five complete novels. They weren't half-bad, either. Sold a couple of them later with a few rewrites. College was actually a relatively peaceful time in my life. Had my first date when I was a junior. That was interesting."

"So you were twenty before you had your first date?"

"You're too good-hearted to see the truth, but people don't like me, Natalie. Especially women. At best, I'm strange. At worst an outright asshole. Either way, I'm not a nice person."

"That's not true." She shook her head, releasing the minty smell of her shampoo. "You've just been telling yourself that for so long, you don't see the Jamis you've matured into. The Jamis I'm coming to know is an articulate, confident, fascinating and…handsome man."

He wanted to believe her, but the last time he trusted a woman who was attracted to him he not only had his heart broken, Katherine might as well have run it through a shredder, poured gasoline over the remains and tossed a match. "I'm no different today than I was all those years ago."

"Then maybe your perception of who you were then is shaded, as well."

A truce was one thing, but he didn't like this turn in the conversation. Or his thoughts. He spun away from her, went into the kitchen and poured himself a glass of water, hoping to clear his head.

She studied the landscape photos he'd framed. "Did you take these?"

He nodded. "Here on Mirabelle."

She pointed. "I like the winter picture."

He remembered the morning he'd taken that shot. A heavy, wet snow had settled on the trees and rocks. It was difficult to tell the cloudy sky from the ice-covered lake, the lake from the rocks. The world was white.

She pointed to the storm, lightning and rain, hovering over the water some five miles away while the sun beamed down on Mirabelle. "Is this in the summer?"

"August three years ago." Back when he'd still marveled at Mirabelle's beauty. He walked toward her.

"I can't tell spring from fall."

"Spring." He pointed to the one with tall waves crashing against the shore.

"Is that ice?" she asked, leaning in for a better look.

"There and there." He reached over her shoulder, pointed at the waves, and the scent of her skin, clean soap and warmth, distracted him for a moment. "Those chunks are huge, but you can barely see them." He closed his eyes and breathed her in.

"So that's fall, then," she said, indicating the photo of the ferry loaded down with tourists leaving the island. "Why?"

He looked down at her profile, curious and beautiful. "I look at that when I need to remind myself that the madness of summer tourist season will eventually end."

She chuckled. "Oh, Jamis."

"You think I'm kidding?" And that was when he knew that he would feel differently about this fall because this time around she'd be leaving with all those annoying tourists.

She looked up at him with that wondrously warm smile on her face and stared into his eyes. When she reached out to trail her fingers down his cheek, he froze. Her smile slowly dimmed as heat filled her eyes.

"Natalie, don't—"

She wrapped her hands around his neck, reached up and kissed him. Backing him against the wall, she pressed into him. "I've been wanting to do that all night," she murmured.

He held completely still for a heartbeat, two at most, and then as if a cord finally snapped inside him he drew her into his arms. His answering kiss came hard and fast. There was nothing tentative in his touch. He'd crawled through a four-year desert and she was a cool spring rain waiting for him on the other side.

Lifting her onto the countertop, he stepped between her legs and bracketed her head with his hands, holding her there, devouring her. Then he trailed his hand along her neck, over her breast and dipped his fingers under her shirt.

"It's not enough," she whispered. "More."

He flicked the clasp on her bra and cupped her breast.

She shuddered and groaned beneath his hand. "More, more, more." She dragged his shirt up and over his head, than splayed her hands over his chest. "This is crazy," she whispered. "I want you so badly."

When he dragged his hand along her stomach, she pulsed toward him and he inched beneath her waistband. She groaned and shifted, putting his fingertips only inches from her sweet warmth.

"Touch me." She pressed his hand lower, and lower still.

He shuddered at the first feel of her, swollen and wet and wanting him to take her, right then and there. "You feel like…" He sucked in a ragged breath and stopped. Clenching his jaw, he pushed away from her. "I don't have a right to this," he whispered. "I don't have a right to you."

She opened her eyes, looked dazed from his touch. She wanted him. He wanted her.

"Jamis—"

"Son of a bitch!" He raked his hands through his hair. "All these years alone." He closed his eyes and turned away. "You make me want to live again."

"Is that so bad?" She reached out to caress him.

"Damn right, it's bad!" He spun away. "Before you came here, I was fine. Resigned, if not entirely content. You're here a month or so and you and your kids are messing with me. Making me feel things I haven't felt in years. Making me hope. Making me dream. Making me… want." *You.*

"Jamis, I'm not asking for forever. I'm not even expecting tomorrow. I just want tonight."

She made it sound so harmless, so perfect. And with everything in him he wanted to believe it was okay. One night. Hadn't he suffered enough? She moved toward him, and from there it all happened so fast, he wasn't sure if it was real or a dream. One minute they were in each other's arms again and they were kissing and the next Natalie was naked on the floor and he was driving himself into her as if a demon was chasing him.

He looked into her eyes and felt a connection with her that he'd never felt with anyone. Then she groaned and shifted her hips to meet him. One more thrust and he felt her orgasm pulsing around him. And that was all she wrote. Like Lake Superior waves crashing against the rocky shore, they collided, came together in one violent upheaval.

A few moments later, as residual tremors faded and sanity returned, he rolled off her. "Holy hell," he whispered. He hadn't even paused long enough to take off his pants. Confused and even slightly disoriented, he zipped back up. "That wasn't supposed to happen."

"Not that fast, at least." She sat up.

"Not ever." He sucked in a shaky breath. *Dammit all. Damn Natalie. Damn this island. Damn this life.* He'd fucked up everything. His marriage. His children. Why him? Why, why, why?

"Jamis, are you—"

"You need to leave." He stood.

"Why?"

Keeping his eyes averted, he gathered up her sweats and held them out to her. If he saw her naked beauty again, there was no telling what might happen.

She took her clothes and he could hear her dressing. "Can we talk about what just happened?"

"A mistake happened." He couldn't look at her face, couldn't bear to see the hurt he heard in her voice. "Nothing more, nothing less."

"It didn't feel like a mistake to me."

"Natalie, leave. Before we make this night any worse."

"Why are you closing yourself off from the world? Protecting yourself so fiercely?"

He looked at her then, and he'd never seen a more tragic sight. Her hair mussed. Her lips slightly swollen from his kisses. Her neck reddened by his beard. Her eyes clearly showing her vulnerability. She'd been marked by him and he damn sure didn't have a right to claim anyone. "It's not me I'm protecting."

"Then who?"

"You."

"From what?"

"Me." He gritted his teeth, knowing he had to shut her down. "Tonight was about one thing and one thing only. Sex. Don't read anything more into it than it deserves."

"You're wrong," she whispered.

"Am I?"

Suddenly, she didn't look so sure.

"You're a woman," Jamis said. "And you were here. That's all there is to it."

"This isn't over," she said, slowly backing toward the door.

"Yes. It is." Fighting the urge to withdraw everything he'd said, Jamis turned his back on her. As the patio door slammed shut behind him, he smelled her sweetness on his hands. "For your sake." Then he reached for a bottle of wine, hoping to wipe the memory of her naked and beneath him completely from his mind.

NATALIE'S CHEEKS BURNED with humiliation as she ran through the woods. The possible physical complications of no protection didn't bother her overly much, given it was the wrong time of the month by at least a few days. She was safe and healthy, and Jamis having had no sex since he'd come to Mirabelle meant he was most likely safe as well. But how could she have let tonight happen? How could she have gotten carried away by a man's touch to the point of losing all sense of reason?

Because Jamis's touch *had* carried her away. Their encounter may have been a record quickie for her, but it was the most satisfying orgasm she'd ever experienced.

And what had it all meant to Jamis? Had it been simply a mistake? Spontaneous, earth-shattering and over far too quickly, yes, but a mistake? If not a mistake, had it truly been just about sex? Then why ask her to leave?

Feeling confused and raw to the bone, she stopped and glanced behind her, panting for air. Dim light spilled out through Jamis's windows into the night. He was in his kitchen, pacing and drinking wine straight from the bottle. Suddenly, he stopped, slammed the wine down on the counter and covered his face with his hands.

No. Tonight was not a mistake. And he knew it.

JAMIS AWOKE THE NEXT morning to the shrill sound of his phone ringing. He held his head as a raging pounding shot through his skull. A hangover. Damn, it'd been a long time since he'd had one of those. In an effort to stop the noise, he grabbed the phone. "What?"

"Good morning to you, too." It was Stephen. "Worked things out with your publisher. They're giving you another six weeks. That's the best I could do. The book is now due November fifteen. You gotta get it done before Thanksgiving. Can you do it?"

Did he have a choice? "Sure."

"Jamis—"

"I said no problem."

"My, but you're crankier than normal this morning. Hangover?"

"Screw you, Stephen." He hung up and tossed the phone onto the bed.

After dragging himself to the bathroom, he puked all but his guts out. On standing up, he caught his reflection in the mirror and stared. Who was that man with his scraggly beard and too-long hair? He looked nothing like the image in his mirror for most of his life, nothing like the clean-cut man on the back cover of his books. *I look like a freaking wild man.* How had that happened?

"Well, I've had enough of you." He grabbed a pair of scissors and a razor and chopped, trimmed and shaved. By the time he was finished, aside from a few more wrinkles and severely bloodshot eyes, his reflection looked damned close to the old Jamis. Then he crawled back to bed, covered his head with a pillow and passed out again.

CHAPTER TWELVE

AMIDST THE CHATTER OF eight children finishing breakfast, Natalie stood at the counter making a last batch of waffles, lost in thought. More than a week had passed since that fateful night at Jamis's house, and she still couldn't get the feel of him, or the way he'd made her feel, out of her mind. Being with him had felt so perfect, so right, it was hard to feel any degree of shame over what had happened. What would an entire night with Jamis be like?

But that wasn't likely to happen. Even if she managed another night alone this summer, Jamis would never let it happen. Why did he feel the need to protect her from him? What had he done? And why was she so bound and determined to break through to him?

The waffle iron started steaming. "Okay, who wanted more?"

"Me," Chase said.

"And me." Blake raised his hand.

She split the waffle between Chase and Blake. As she headed back to the counter, she glanced up through the kitchen window hoping to catch a glimpse of Jamis through the trees. No such luck. Either he'd barricaded himself in his cabin or he was doing an awfully good job avoiding her.

The sound of a golf cart drew her gaze to the path through the woods only a moment before the island's chief of police, Garrett Taylor, drove into her yard. "I'll be right back." She set the waffle iron down and went outside. "Hello there, Chief Taylor. It's good to see you again."

He stepped from the cart and shook her hand. "Natalie, you gotta start calling me Garrett."

"Hard to do with you looking so official in your police uniform, but I'll try to remember." When Natalie had discussed the minor renovation work she'd wanted him to do on the house, he'd been wearing jeans and a faded work shirt. "By the way, congratulations on your marriage."

He grinned and ducked his head. "Thank you." For such a big tough guy, he certainly looked whooped.

"But you didn't come all the way out here for small talk, though, did you?"

"I'm sorry, no." His smile disappeared. "Last night there was a break-in at the Hendersons'. A bunch of movies and CDs were stolen along with several hundred dollars from a bank deposit bag."

Natalie's brain started buzzing. "And?"

"One of your camp kids, Galen, was seen heading through the woods not far from the store about the time of the theft."

"What time?"

"Around midnight."

"But he was home. In bed."

"You know that for sure? You saw him?"

She thought back. As usual, she went to bed around eleven after checking on the younger kids. But she'd passed on Sam and Galen, thinking they had a right to some privacy. Had he snuck out sometime during the night? "No, I didn't see him here at midnight." She had to be honest, no matter how protective she felt toward her kids. "You need to talk to him? See if he was there and saw anything?"

"Please."

"Do you want to come in?"

"I think it'd be better if he came out here."

That didn't sound good. "You don't think he did it, do you?"

"Just have him come out, Natalie, please."

"I'll get him." But when she turned around Galen was already stepping out onto the porch. Sam stood in the doorway with the younger ones filling in behind her.

"What's up?" Galen asked, glancing warily at Garrett.

"Could you come out here, please?" Natalie watched Sam's reaction. The teenager shook her head and rolled her eyes as if she'd expected this outcome. "Sam, can you take the kids inside and start cleaning up from breakfast?"

"Come on, guys." Sam closed the door.

Natalie shifted her attention back to Galen. "Chief Taylor would like to talk with you."

He came toward her, but his gaze turned guarded. "Yeah? What about?"

As Garrett glanced at Galen, his demeanor changed from pleasant handyman to suspicious cop in seconds flat. "Were you hanging out downtown last night?"

Galen glanced at Natalie.

"Tell him the truth," she said.

Galen hesitated. "Yeah. I was."

So he had snuck out of the house. Disappointment washed over Natalie, but she struggled to stay objective. This didn't mean he'd committed a robbery.

"Who were you with?"

Galen crossed his arms over his chest and that old, sullen look passed over his face.

"Galen," she said, "you snuck out of the house, so you know you're in trouble, but don't make this worse. If you don't have anything to hide, then there's no reason to not cooperate with Chief Taylor."

"I was with Dustin and Chad," he said. "And a couple of girls."

"What were you doing?"

"We played some foosball and pool and then we hung out in the woods for a while. Built a fire. Talked."

"Were you drinking?"

Galen didn't say anything.

"The truth," Natalie urged. "Lying will only make your situation worse."

"No," Galen bit out. He glanced at Natalie. It was clear her opinion was more important to him than Garrett's. "I was not drinking."

Garrett studied him. "Then why did we find empty beer cans and liquor bottles at your fire pit?"

"First off, it's not *my* fire pit, okay?"

"Relax." Natalie touched Galen's arm, but he shrugged her off.

"And the empty cans and bottles weren't mine."

"You telling me the others were drinking, but you weren't?"

"I got nothing else to say to you." He turned to go into the house.

"Friends don't give up friends, huh?" Garrett said. "Were you aware the Hendersons' store was broken into last night?"

Galen stopped, kept silent.

"There was a theft."

"Great. Just great." Galen shook his head and paced. "You think I did it, don't you?" He glared at Garrett, but when he turned his gaze to Natalie, a look of intense betrayal and hurt filled his eyes. "You can't do this to me," he yelled. "This isn't fair."

"Galen, settle down—"

"No, Natalie! I snuck out of the house, that's it. I didn't do anything else wrong."

"Garrett, have you talked to Dustin and Chad?" Natalie asked.

"Yep." Garrett kept his eyes on Galen. "They're both claiming that it was Galen's idea. That he's the one who broke the rear window and snuck inside." He paused, waiting for a reaction. "What do you think of your friends now?"

Galen looked away.

"If you didn't do it, then who did?" Garrett asked. "Did you see anyone else?"

At first, Galen didn't answer. Finally, through clenched teeth he said, "No. I didn't see anything."

"You're sure?"

"Positive."

Natalie took it one step further. "Do you know anything about the robbery? Anything at all that might help Chief Taylor?"

"No!" he yelled at Natalie. "Can I go now?"

She glanced back at Garrett.

"At the moment," he said, "that's all I need."

Without another word, Galen stalked back into the house. Natalie turned to Garrett. She was going to trust there was a wealth of compassion under that hulky, formidable exterior. "I think you should know that if Galen is charged with theft, the rules of my camp require he be sent home to Minneapolis immediately."

Garrett considered her. "That's a good rule."

"I have a zero tolerance policy with regard to breaking the law."

"Does he like it here? At your camp?"

Natalie felt her protective instincts kick into high gear. "He pretends not to, but I think he does."

"What's waiting for him back home?"

She sighed and rubbed a hand across her forehead. "A drug-addicted mother who steals from him and kicks him out of the house."

Garrett nodded. "Do you think he's telling the truth?"

Natalie paused, giving the question fair consideration. "Yes." She nodded. "I do."

"We lifted a couple prints off the scene," he said. "If Galen comes in on his own to get printed, that'll say a lot."

She nodded. "I understand."

"I'll do some more digging."

After Garrett left, Natalie went into the house. Sam had taken all the kids into the craft room and had gotten them all working on their projects. "Where's Galen?"

"Upstairs." Sam came out of the porch and dragged Natalie into the living room. "What happened?" she asked.

Natalie explained the situation.

"Those losers!" Sam crossed her arms. "I knew something like this was going to happen."

"Is that why you wouldn't go with them the other night?"

She nodded. "They're bad news."

"Sam, I need to talk to Galen. You got things under control down here?"

"Sure."

Natalie went upstairs and knocked on Galen's door. "Can I come in?"

"No."

"For sneaking out last night without permission, you're

grounded next Friday night." She waited for a protest, but nothing came. "I have something more important to say, and I don't want to say it from the hallway."

The door cracked open to show a defiant young man standing with his arms folded across his chest. "I might as well just pack my bags now, huh? Is that it?"

"No." She glanced into his face and her heart ached for all the pain, frustration and insecurities she saw there. "I wanted to tell you that I be—"

"Screw it!" He turned his back on her. "I'm just going to pack—" He stopped, spun around and stared at her. "You do? You believe me?"

She nodded.

"Why?"

She shrugged. "It's not that I don't think you're capable of stealing. In fact, I'm sure you are. Most people are. And I'll tell you something I've never told anyone else. I stole something from the Hendersons' store when I was about thirteen."

He was listening, studying her.

"A tube of mascara that I really, really wanted." She walked into his room and was happy that he didn't try to stop her. "My mother found out and made me go back and apologize. I felt ashamed about it for years."

"You still went to work at that store anyway?"

She nodded. "Bob and Marsha are good people. Working for them helped me get over a lot of guilty feelings." She tilted her head at him. "Kids steal for a lot of reasons. Attention. Sense of entitlement. For the fun or adventure. Every once in a while, they steal because they have to."

"Maybe I just wanted to impress someone," Galen said, trying to stay tough.

"No." She shook her head. He was testing her and she

understood. "I know, in my heart, that you didn't steal anything from the Hendersons. Because I know, in my heart, you wouldn't risk having to leave this island."

The sullen tough guy disappeared as he hung his head and looked away.

"Chief Taylor said they found some prints at the scene of the robbery. He said that if you go in to get fingerprinted that would send a strong message that you were innocent."

"I am innocent! I shouldn't have to prove it. It's supposed to be the other way around."

"Galen—"

"No, Natalie! If Chad and Dustin go in to get printed, then I will, too."

How could she argue with that? "The only problem is that if Chief Taylor believes there's enough evidence to charge you with this crime, then regardless of what I believe you'll have to go home."

"I get that," he said, pushing past her and down the hall. "I'll figure it out."

"Galen," she said, "you don't need to figure this out all alone."

"Yes. I do."

Much to Natalie's dismay, Galen refused any further discussions on the matter. The next time they went into town rumors of Galen having been involved in the robbery at Hendersons' had spread like wildfire. Missy had told her there'd even been a special town council board meeting to discuss whether or not her camp license would be renewed for next summer. By the time they were finished with their errands, Natalie had had enough.

"I'm sorry, Natalie," Galen said as they left the gift shop. "But I didn't do it. If they close down your camp, that'd be so unfair."

"Galen, you and I need to stop at the Hendersons'."

"You sure that's a good idea?"

"Bob's on the town council. I need to know what he's thinking." Natalie turned to the group.

"I'll get everyone home," Sam said.

"Thanks." Natalie sent her an appreciative smile. "We'll catch up in a few minutes."

"Come on, guys." Sam led the way to where they'd parked their bikes.

Natalie went into the Hendersons' store first and noticed Galen hanging back. She spun toward him. "Do you have anything to apologize for?"

"No."

"Then we need to explain that to these people and clear the air." She was glad to find Bob and Marsha together restocking one of the aisles. "Hey there, you two."

"Natalie!" Marsha hugged her. "It's so good to see you again." But her smile turned down when she noticed Galen's sullen expression. "Marsha and Bob, this is Galen." Natalie tugged him forward. "He has something to say to you."

Neither of the Hendersons said a word.

Slowly, Galen looked up from his study of his tennis shoes. "I didn't… I think you should know…I wasn't the one who broke into your store."

"There are a couple of witnesses who say otherwise," Bob said.

"They're lying," Galen said, his eyes turning angry.

"Do you know who did it, then?" Marsha asked.

Galen looked away.

"Whoever broke down the back door, stole a bunch of stuff and made quite a mess of things in here."

"I'm sorry, but it wasn't me," Galen said, crossing his arms.

"Why should we believe you?"

"You don't have to." He turned and headed toward the door. "Doesn't make any difference to me."

Bob sighed and glanced at Natalie. "There goes one stubborn young man."

"Do you believe him?" Marsha asked Natalie.

"I do." She nodded. "I don't know these other Mirabelle kids that are involved, but I know enough about Galen to know he's telling the truth."

"Those other boys got into some minor trouble last summer," Bob said. "Honestly, though, we don't know who to believe."

"You trusting him is enough for us, dear," Marsha said.

"Well, I don't think it's enough for the rest of the town." Natalie sighed. "I've heard there's a town council board meeting scheduled to talk about not renewing my camp application for next year." She glanced at Bob. "Is that true?"

Bob nodded.

"Are you still on the board?"

He nodded again. "The council will hold off on any final decisions until the police get to the bottom of this. I'll talk to Garrett and see if he can speed things up."

"I don't think anyone was too keen on having us on the island even before the robbery."

"You're not going to let that stop you, now, are you?" Bob asked with a smile.

As she caught up with Galen and the rest of the group, she noticed a somber mood had settled over every single kid. By now they'd all heard about what was happening with Galen, and were very likely aware of how some of the islanders were shunning their business.

She couldn't shake the feeling that Mirabelle may not have been the best place for this camp after all. Even worse, maybe camp alone wasn't enough to make a difference in the lives of these kids. Every single one of them needed a safe home and loving care all year-round. How could she ever trust another person to care for these children? How was she ever going to say goodbye? But what else could she do?

Her thoughts flashed on the house she'd inherited from her grandmother back in Minneapolis. It was big enough for four, maybe even six kids. She'd been planning on selling it to provide more funding for her summer camp, but maybe that wasn't the answer. Maybe the answer was a year-round group foster home.

Her stomach fluttered at the thought. She'd already gotten cleared as a foster parent during the licensing process for this camp, so that wouldn't be an issue. But what about the job she'd taken a leave of absence from for this summer? What about all her other commitments? What about her future plans for this camp?

How far would she go to make her dream happen?

BY THE TIME JAMIS BECAME fully aware of what he was doing, he'd not only made a huge batch of chicken noodle soup, he'd also cooked up two small pans of lasagna and a batch of tuna casserole. For some reason cooking had seemed like a reasonable outlet for all the pent-up frustration he was carrying around.

Almost two weeks had passed since he and Natalie had been intimate—the term *sex* seemed too cut-and-dried and the phrase *making love* inaccurate—and while he'd actually gotten some writing done, he'd been distracted. Five years without sex and he'd managed okay. One night, or should he say five minutes, with Natalie and he couldn't get the woman out of his mind.

Normally, he'd freeze all this food, but a better use

suddenly came to mind. By the time he'd split the food into individual serving containers and set off for town, it was after four o'clock. With Snickers on a leash by his side, he queried the first islander he recognized, Jan Setterberg. "Excuse me," he said.

She stopped and glanced at him, surprise mixed with wariness registering on her face. "Yes?"

"Can you tell me where Sally McGregor lives?"

"Why?" she asked, understandably suspicious of him.

"Because…I wanted to take her some meals."

"Seriously?"

He nodded.

She studied him another moment. "You are a very strange man."

"I'm aware of that."

"Big yard behind the church—1215 Maple."

"Thank you." He walked past the church and found Sally's house, a redbrick French Colonial with white trim and a green shingled roof, and headed up the sidewalk, carrying his pack filled with food. He knocked on the door and waited. Through an open upstairs window, he could hear movement, someone coming down the stairs.

She opened the door. "What the—?" She stopped, blinked, took a moment to recognize him, clean shaven as he now was. "What are you doing here?" she asked, self-consciously running a hand over her bald head.

"I…heard you were sick."

"So?"

"So I made you some meals. Just in case you're too tired to cook for yourself."

Staring at him as if a bug-eyed green alien had just burst out of his chest, she tightened her pale blue robe.

"Look, I know it seems odd, but we all know I'm

an…odd kind of guy. So here." He unzipped his pack and held out several of the containers. "Take these."

She glanced at the offering, then up at him and backed away from the door. "Why don't you come in, Jamis?"

Surprised, he stood there, unsure.

"Have you eaten dinner?" she asked.

"No."

"Then why don't we share something you brought?"

"That wasn't… I didn't mean…"

"Please." She paused. "More than the food, I could use the company."

Funny, so could Jamis. He stepped inside and closed the door behind him.

"So what did you make?" She walked toward the back of the house. "I hope it isn't stew. After the mediocre batch Lynn Duffy brought over the other day, I don't care if I ever eat stew again as long as I live."

He followed her into the kitchen. "Chicken noodle soup. Lasagna. Tuna casserole."

"Well, I've never been much for tuna. You can take the casserole home with you." She turned around and then awkwardly said, "I'm sorry. I didn't mean—"

"You don't need to be sorry."

"I offend people. Seems I've gotten worse since my husband died some years ago."

"You don't offend me. I like the way you talk. I feel comfortable around you."

"Then we're a couple of sorry excuses for humans, aren't we?"

He nodded. "Sit. You look like you might fall down." He heated up one serving each of chicken noodle soup and tuna casserole in the microwave, dumped the contents into a couple of bowls and joined her at the table. This was the first time Jamis had shared a meal with a live human being in four years. For him, it felt strange and awkward.

They sat eating in silence for a short while. Finally, Sally said, "I see you've shaved and cut your hair."

"Yeah." He ran his hand along his smooth cheek. "Guess it was time."

"How's that kids' camp going?"

"Noisy."

She grunted. "If it's any consolation, I didn't want her on the island, either."

He glanced up. "Either?"

"There was quite a heated debate at the town council meeting when she first applied for that camp."

He'd probably gotten notice in the mail and had, as he did most things, tossed it out without reading. "They're good kids."

"Got you hoodwinked, anyway. She must be pretty."

He cocked his head at her.

"She is, isn't she?" Sally chuckled. "Do you like her?"

"She's…different."

"Well, that isn't saying a whole helluva lot, now, is it?"

Natalie's scolding that afternoon when he'd been chopping wood about him being stuck in the past, about him being a coward, hit him again, and again he found himself curiously offended. Why should he care what the woman thought of him?

"I'm planning on leaving Mirabelle," he said.

She glanced at him.

"As soon as I finish this next book and can find another place."

"Because of the camp?"

Because of her. "It's best I'm left alone."

"I hear the council's already considering not renewing her license for next year. You complain and—"

"No." He shook his head.

"It wouldn't take much. Not with people thinking that oldest boy of hers robbed the Hendersons."

"What? Galen?"

She filled him in on all the details.

"I can't believe he'd do that." He shook his head when she'd finished.

"This island's no place for that camp."

Jamis frowned and looked away.

"You disagree?" Sally asked.

He glanced up at her. "I don't know what I think."

She considered him for a moment. "Hmm. Interesting."

They finished the rest of their meal in silence. She never commented on the food, but he could tell the soup had met with approval. After they'd finished, he suggested she relax in the living room while he picked up the kitchen, put away the clean dishes in her dishwasher and loaded it with the dirty dishes in the sink.

After he'd finished, he found her sitting in an old and frayed easy chair in her den off the rear of the house. Her eyes were closed and her breathing even. Unsure what to do, he glanced around. Much to his surprise, bookcases lined every wall in the room, and it appeared she read everything from classic literature to genre fiction, including mysteries and romance. The books appeared alphabetized by author—popular, big names and more than a few surprises. There was even a row and then some of Quinn Roberts's books. He looked through the titles and it appeared she had every single book he'd ever published.

"I think I liked your last one the best."

He spun around to find Sally awake and watching him. "Why?"

She grunted. "The ending. Kinda left a reader guessing."

"Ha! My editor hated that ending, but I refused to change it." He'd gotten a lot of disgruntled reader letters over that one. "What did you think of *Harry Stone?*"

"Eh." She shook her hand in a so-so motion. "Not your best work."

He laughed.

"Not sure I'll be around to read your next one."

He fell quiet, considering her. He hadn't wanted to bother her with questions about her prognosis. What was the point? Pancreatic cancer seldom had hopeful outcomes. "I could print the manuscript off my computer. Would you like to read it now?"

"You know what I'd like even more? For you to read it to me." She paused, a scowl on her face. "My eyes aren't what they used to be."

He nodded. "I can do that."

The doorbell rang, and Sally scowled. "What is this, Grand Central Station?" When she opened the door Doc Welinsky was standing on the steps and holding a plastic container filled with what looked like food. "Willard," she whispered. "What are you doing here?"

"I thought you might be too tired to cook." He looked a little uncomfortable as something almost intimate passed between them.

A slight pink flush rushed to her cheeks. "Well, come on in then."

He stepped inside and pulled up short on seeing Jamis. "Sorry, Sally, I didn't know you had company."

"Doc has been administering my chemo treatments," she explained to Jamis.

He'd been wondering how she was accomplishing that on an island this size.

"You were getting ready to leave, weren't you, Jamis?"

"What?" Jamis was taken aback, until he noticed the look passing between Doc and Sally. "Um, yeah, I was about to leave." He took his cue and went out the front door. *Well, I'll be damned.* Maybe gruff old Sally wasn't as lonely as he'd thought.

CHAPTER THIRTEEN

NATALIE AWOKE AROUND midnight feeling as if she was going to die. Staggering to the bathroom, she barely made it to the toilet before vomiting violently. Even after her gut was empty, dry heaves racked her body. Finally, exhausted, she rinsed out her mouth and glanced in the mirror, expecting to find a rash covering her face. This felt like her allergy to shellfish, but there was no rash. She glanced down at her arms and her stomach. No rash there, either. A new kind of food allergy? Or food poisoning? No, the kids would be sick, as well. Had to be the flu.

As she opened the bathroom door the knob fell off in her hand. Great. If it wasn't one thing it was another. Then she heard the steps creaking. She walked down the hall but stopped when she noticed movement on the stairs, a figure sneaking up the steps.

"Galen?" she whispered. "What's going on?"

He spun around. "I was…outside…going for a walk."

"After midnight?" She took a deep breath, steadying her stomach. "Are you lying to me?"

He clenched his jaw. "I went to talk to Dustin and Chad."

"Why?"

"Because they lied to Chief Taylor."

"You don't need to do that. Garrett will get to the bottom of this." Although he hadn't sounded too positive when

Natalie had called to inform him that Galen refused to be fingerprinted unless the other two boys came in, as well.

"And what if he doesn't? Then what?"

She held her stomach.

"You look sick," he said. "Are you okay?"

"There must've been something we ate at dinner that I'm allergic to. Either that or I've caught a flu bug."

"Do you need anything?"

"Yeah. To be able to trust you. To not have to worry about you sneaking out at night anymore." She held her stomach as another wave of nausea rolled over her. "To not have to worry about whether or not you're doing your job of taking care of the younger kids while I'm sick in bed tomorrow." And she was going to be sick, very likely for a couple of days.

"I'm sorry, Natalie," Galen whispered. "I'll let Sam know what's going on. We'll take care of everything. I promise."

She wobbled to her room and collapsed onto the bed.

AFTER A RESTLESS NIGHT'S sleep, Jamis had gotten up and gone straight to his computer to write a scene that had come to him in a dream. He'd made breakfast and, on a roll of sorts, returned to his office. He sat in front of his computer now, frustrated that he couldn't get this scene perfected. Something wasn't playing out properly and he couldn't figure out the problem. Deciding to break for a while, he went to the kitchen and made himself a roast beef sandwich.

It'd been close to three weeks since he'd seen Natalie, giving him a glimpse of what it would be like around here come September. Quiet. Peaceful. Back to normal. And incredibly lonely. The house seemed, somehow, too quiet, so he went outside onto the deck. A fragrant summer breeze met him the moment he stepped through the patio door, but there were no sounds of children playing, laughing or fighting. In fact, now that he thought about it, he'd heard nothing from Natalie and the kids all day. Everything was too quiet, and it wasn't even Sunday.

He took a few uneasy bites of his sandwich. Something wasn't right. "Come on, Snick. Let's check it out." Within minutes, he was knocking at the back door of the Victorian. "Natalie?" He could hear the TV blaring inside the house, but it seemed to take forever for someone to answer the door.

"Hi," Sam said, holding a dishrag in her hand. "What's up?"

"I haven't seen anyone out and about today." He stepped inside the house to find Galen ineffectively cleaning a kitchen in a state of total disarray. "What's going on?" Stacks of dirty dishes filled the sink and counter, and sticky pots and pans covered the stove. A kitchen chair was pushed up against the counter as if someone short had needed to reach a high shelf.

He stalked into the living room to find couch cushions dislodged, every table littered with dirty cups, cans and bowls, and the younger kids watching TV. "What's going on here?"

The kids shot out of their respective seats, as if caught in some wayward act. Someone reached for the remote and lowered the sound on the TV. "Umm. Nothing," Ella said.

"We were just watching some TV," Arianna added.

He glanced from one face to the next.

"I'm hungry," Blake said.

"Me, too," his brother, Chase, agreed.

"You guys just ate," Sam said, disgusted.

"Where's Natalie?" Jamis asked.

"Sick," Galen answered from where he was filling up the dishwasher.

"With what?" Jamis walked into the kitchen.

"Some kind of food allergy or the flu."

"Since when?"

"Last night."

"Where is she?"

"Sleeping in her bedroom."

"Which is?"

Sam pointed. "Down the hall."

Getting oddly angrier by the minute by their obvious lack of concern, Jamis walked toward Natalie's room. He passed a bathroom and another room that appeared to be a laundry room and knocked on the only closed door at the end of the hall. "Nat, are you in there?"

A low groan was the only response. On opening the door, he found the shades drawn and the room dark and cool and a figure balled up under the covers. He sat on the edge of the bed and brushed the hair from Natalie's face. Her skin pale, she lay on her side. "Jamis, is that you?" she whispered, reaching up to touch his cleanly shaven cheek. "You shaved and cut your hair."

"Yeah."

"Why?"

Because he was sick of himself, only cleaning himself up hadn't changed much of anything. "Needed a change."

"I'm sick."

"I can see that." He felt her forehead. She didn't have a fever. *But, dammit, why wasn't anyone taking care of her?* He searched the room, found a heavy blanket in the closet and folded it over her prone form. "Have you eaten anything today?"

"No, my stomach is too queasy. There must've been some type of shellfish in something I ate," she whispered. "Maybe it's the flu."

"Do you need me to get Doc Welinsky?"

"No, it's all out of me by now." Her smile was weak. "And I used an emergency shot of antihistamine to be on the safe side. I'll be better tomorrow."

Tomorrow. And in the meantime?

"Are the kids okay?"

"They're fine." But they needed supervision and he wasn't going to be able to walk away from this one with a clear conscience. "I'll keep an eye on them until you're better."

"You don't have to do that. Sam and Galen will take care of things." She closed her eyes and fell back asleep.

He pulled the blanket up to her chin and brushed a lock of hair from her face. The indomitably positive force of Natalie Steeger felled by a little shellfish. "Amazing." He quietly closed the door on his way out of her room.

On reaching the living room, he grabbed the remote and flicked off the TV.

"Hey!"

"Turn it back on."

"Who did that?"

"I did," Jamis said. "And if you ever want to see this remote again, you're going to have to get your butts in gear." He glanced at Sam and Galen as they came in from the kitchen. "Natalie put you two in charge, correct?"

They nodded.

"Then what are these guys supposed to be doing?"

"Helping us clean the kitchen," Sam said, glaring at all of the younger kids.

"But they kept ignoring us," Galen added.

"Well, the party's over, little ones," Jamis announced. "Get up and get moving."

His order was met with sighs and groans, but Sam and Galen did indeed take charge. Jamis supervised as dishes were washed, counters were wiped down, beds were made and laundry was done. He marveled at the bulletin board Natalie had prepared for the week, outlining not only a daily menu, but everyone's duties and responsibilities.

"Does this thing actually work?" Jamis asked Sam as she came into the room for cleaning supplies.

"Surprisingly, yes."

Today they were supposed to be having macaroni and cheese for lunch. He found the supplies in the cabinets, and an hour later the kids had been fed, the kitchen cleaned and the whole gang, per the chart, was outside for their daily dose of fresh air before craft time.

Jamis retrieved some chicken noodle soup from his freezer, heated it up and carried it in to Natalie along with a stack of soda crackers.

She cracked open her eyes. "What is that?"

"Chicken soup. Can you eat?"

"Probably not. Even the smell is making me nauseous."

He set the bowl on the bedside table, reached under her arms and lifted her up. His palms brushed the edges of her breasts, and the only thing stopping him from letting his hands linger for a while was the fact that she was as limp as one of the noodles in the soup.

"Try one of these first." He handed her a cracker.

She nibbled on an edge and then ate the rest. "That's sitting okay."

"Try some soup." He put a spoonful of broth to her lips.

She swallowed.

"Still okay?"

"So far so good."

He gave her another few sips and waited.

"Thank you," she whispered.

"This is a one-time deal," he grumbled. "Don't get used to it."

"THERE. THAT SHOULD DO it," Jamis said to Galen as the teenager tightened the washer on the new heavy-duty garbage disposal they'd installed under Natalie's kitchen sink. "What do you think?"

"Thanks for showing me how to do that." Galen slid out from under the sink.

"No problem."

Refusing to get involved in all that crafty business happening out on the porch, Jamis had figured he'd work on a few things around Natalie's house. Galen had chosen to help him. While Sam kept an eye on the younger kids, Galen and Jamis had spent the day fixing the doorknob on the main-floor bathroom, replacing a warped shelf in the pantry, unclogging both bathtub drains, fixing the basement stairs railing and installing a metal hose on the washing machine. The old rubber one had been cracked, the sure sign of a flooded floor waiting to happen. While there was a host of other projects to be done, one day wasn't enough for him to take care of anything more than the most pressing.

As they were putting tools away, steps sounded on the porch. "Hello in there," Garrett Taylor said through the screen door.

"Hey." Jamis opened the door for the police chief. "What can I do for you?"

Taylor eyed Galen as he stepped into the house. "Natalie here?"

"She's sick. A food allergy. Can't get out of bed."

"So you're helping with the kids?" He looked surprised.

For some unknown reason that irked Jamis more than it should have. He shrugged. "Neighbors helping neighbors, you know?"

"In that case, can I talk to Galen?"

"What do you need him for?" Jamis asked, feeling oddly protective of the kid after what Sally had told him.

"It's personal, Jamis. Galen, can you come outside?"

"No," Jamis said, stepping in front of Galen. "Either you tell me what you want, or you can come back another day when Natalie can be present."

Taylor glanced at the teenager. "You okay with me telling him what happened?"

The boy shrugged. "Whatever."

Jamis wanted to hear Taylor's side of the story, so he kept silent as the man relayed the details of a robbery of cash and hundreds of dollars worth of CDs and DVDs at Hendersons' and the allegations thrown at Galen.

Jamis glanced at the boy. "Did you have anything to do with the robbery?"

He shook his head. "No."

"Dustin and Chad said you threatened them the other night," Taylor said. "They claim you promised to kill them if they didn't lie for you."

"I never said that!" Galen's face turned red. "I told them to tell you the truth or I would."

"Galen," Taylor said. "What is the truth? You don't tell me, and all I've got to go on is their word."

Jamis put his hand on the boy's shoulder and held his gaze. "These guys aren't your friends, man. Your friends are here in this house. Tell Taylor the truth."

Galen hesitated. "I don't know for sure who robbed the Hendersons' store, but while we were around the campfire, Dustin and Chad started talking about raising some hell. The girls got up to leave, not wanting anything to do with their bullshit, and I left with them. And came home. That's all I know."

Taylor shook his head. "That's more than I had before."

"It's enough," Jamis said.

"Anything else you can remember?"

He shook his head. "No."

"There's one more thing to think about," Jamis said to Taylor. "Why would Galen steal a bunch of movies when they don't have a DVD player here?"

NATALIE CRACKED OPEN HER eyes to find her room pitch-black. She'd slept all afternoon and night had fallen. Before getting up, she munched on a couple of crackers Jamis had left on her bedside table. Feeling rather disoriented, but physically much better, she swung her feet down to the floor and stood. Most of the nausea had passed. Feeling a bit wobbly, she walked into the hallway. Except for soft light coming from the living room, the house was dark.

Only a few steps down the hall, she heard the steady sound of a deep, resonant voice. She paused and listened. Jamis was reading aloud from a popular young adult novel. The inflection in his voice was perfect for the dialogue, and his narrative intriguing and entertaining. Sneaking quietly toward the living room, she peeked around the corner.

Galen was lying on the floor with his eyes closed, but awake and quite likely listening. Snickers was snuggled up alongside Galen, sound asleep. Sam was sitting with her chair pulled up to an end table and using the bright lamp-light to illuminate the necklace she was making. Chase and Blake were lying on the floor on their stomachs, their chins in their hands, staring at Jamis. Arianna and Ella were curled up next to each other in one of the oversize chairs. What surprised Natalie more than anything were Ryan and Toni. They sat on either side of Jamis on the couch, snuggled into him as if he were a cuddly teddy bear.

They'd never even done that with her. Of course, she

may very well have discouraged it, not wanting them to get too attached. But look at him. Big, gruff Jamis, connecting effortlessly with all eight of her camp kids. If she hadn't seen it with her own eyes, she may never have believed it. And he seemed to be enjoying himself.

She watched his face, his smile, his eyes twinkling as he read to her kids. She wouldn't have thought it was possible, but he was even more handsome without the beard. Despite her weakened condition, arousal stirred low and deep. She wanted him again, fixer-upper or not.

Jamis glanced up, caught her gaze and suddenly looked a bit self-conscious. "Hey. You're alive."

All the heads in the living room turned toward her.

"How are you feeling?" Sam asked.

"Good." She stepped into the room. "I'm actually hungry."

"I can get you something." Galen stood, his hands stuffed in his pockets. "Jamis made tacos for dinner and there were some leftovers."

"Too spicy." She glanced at Jamis. "Is there any of that chicken noodle soup you gave me at lunchtime?"

"It's in the fridge, Galen. That blue container I brought over from my house earlier today."

"I'll heat some up for you." Galen disappeared into the kitchen. He was probably sucking up in the hopes he wouldn't get into too much trouble for sneaking out, but it still felt nice to be waited upon.

"I should probably go." Jamis shut the book.

"No!"

"Just one more chapter!"

"Please, Jamis?" Toni held his arm.

"Don't leave on my account." She plopped into one of the chairs so she could watch Jamis as she listened to him. "You have a very soothing voice."

"All right. One more chapter. And then from the looks of Natalie's chart, it'll be time for bed, but let's wait for Galen."

Galen brought in her bowl of soup and Natalie quietly sipped away as Jamis read another chapter. Like the kids, she felt as if she could've listened all night to him. By the time he'd finished, all of the kids looked sleepy.

"Bedtime." He closed the book.

This time without any grumbling, they all stood and started toward the stairs, even Galen and Sam.

Ryan straggled behind the rest. He turned on the first step. "Jamis, will you read again tomorrow night?"

Natalie felt her eyes grow wide. Ryan had actually spoken when he hadn't been spoken to.

"I'm not sure, Ryan. We'll see."

After the kids had gone upstairs, Jamis headed for the door. "I need to get home."

"Thanks for holding down the fort," she said. "You must have made quite an impression on Ryan. I've never heard him say more than one or two words at a time."

He opened the door and hesitated.

She didn't know what to say, how to be, at least not after everything that had happened between them this crazy summer.

His gaze skittered self-consciously away from hers as if he knew what she was thinking. "Snick, come on."

The dog had roused from his sleep, but sat in the living room staring at Jamis as if to say, "Do I have to?"

"Come, Snickers." He whistled.

The sight of the dog walking toward the back door was nothing short of comical. Head hanging low, he walked as slowly as he thought Jamis would tolerate.

"He liked being with the kids today," Jamis explained.

"Looked like you did, too."

"Me?" He shook his head. "I can't wait until September when you'll all be gone."

September. It was about a month away. Not long ago, Jamis had thought the end of summer couldn't come soon enough, but now he knew it would come too soon. Natalie—and the kids—would be leaving before the end of August.

Yellow light glowed from the windows of that big, old Victorian, beckoning him. In the shadows of the woods, he stopped and glanced back to see the lights on in the kids' bedrooms. He imagined them smiling, joking, talking, interacting with one another. Jamis had no more wanted to leave that house or the comfort of Natalie's presence than had Snickers. He wanted to be in that big, old house, with all those noisy kids, with her. Somehow, someway, the thought of leaving Mirabelle once Chuck found him a private island for sale didn't bother him nearly as much as the thought of being without Natalie.

CHAPTER FOURTEEN

SUNLIGHT HIT HER FULL in the face. That was strange. Natalie rolled over and glanced at her clock. Nine? In the morning? How in the world had she slept so late and why hadn't anyone woken her?

She sat up and nausea swept through her. Again. She'd been battling this flu for a couple of days. Running to the bathroom, she slammed the door behind her and vomited. For a moment, she felt better and then another wave of whatever the heck it was went through her. Brushing her teeth and rinsing out her mouth, she looked for the emergence of any kind of rash. Still nothing. She was positive she'd eaten nothing that normally caused her an allergic reaction. And as for the flu, it was odd that none of the kids had gotten sick—

"Oh, my God," she whispered to her suddenly pale reflection in the mirror. "I…can't be." How could she not have been paying attention? Because she'd thought she'd been safe. Her last period was—she counted back on the calendar. If she ovulated earlier than most women by several days, she could be. "Pregnant."

You don't know that. She put her hands on either side of the sink and waited out another wobble in her stomach. *Get through this morning. Get to the drugstore in town as soon as possible. And then everything will be fine.* She put on a pair of sweats and a T-shirt and found the kids in the kitchen cleaning up after breakfast.

"Ryan and Toni, it's your turn to wash and dry dishes," Galen said as he wiped off the countertops.

"I get to dry," Toni said.

"All right," Ryan murmured.

"I'll sweep," Sam said.

"And I'm taking out the garbage," Galen offered.

"Well, look at this," Natalie said. "Running like a smoothly oiled machine."

They all turned to look at her leaning against the door frame.

"Are you okay?" Galen asked.

"I couldn't get you to wake up," Sam said.

"You look sick," Toni said.

"Yeah, I'm not feeling very well this morning."

"More food allergies?"

"No. It's the flu. I'm going to run into town quick and get some medicine."

"I can go," Galen offered.

"Thanks." She smiled weakly. "But the fresh air might do me some good." She headed for the door and turned. "And thanks, Sam and Galen, for taking care of things. All of you, thanks."

As she glanced into each and every kid's eyes, a sense of overwhelming pride filled her. The summer was winding down, and they'd done okay. Every single one of them had grown these past couple of months. She felt herself getting emotional and quickly grabbed a baseball cap and headed out the door. "I'll be back in half an hour."

She glanced at Jamis's house as she pulled the cap low on her brow and kept her fingers crossed that she wouldn't run into him until she could reconcile herself one way or another to what would be. Not up to biking, she grabbed a golf cart and headed into town.

Breathing a sigh of relief that a college kid she didn't know and, more important, didn't know her, was manning the front cash register, she bought a pregnancy test and snuck out of town. The kids were busy on the porch with their respective projects when she made it home. She ran to the bathroom, followed the directions on the packaging and waited for the results.

She paced in the little room. When the designated amount of time had passed, she glanced at the finished test stick and a dizzy spell hit her. Sitting on the toilet seat, she put her head between her knees. *Pregnant.* She had a baby growing inside her. She touched her belly. Could she—should she—be a mother? The very limited options ran through her mind and she quickly eliminated all but one.

But can I do this?

Yes. This summer, with these kids, had taught her at least that. She was capable of having and supporting this child, and that's exactly what she was going to do. She was going to be a mother. She was going to have Jamis's baby.

LOST IN THE MIDST OF writing another chapter—apparently sex had done wonders to unblock him—Jamis was completely unaware of his surroundings. Until Snickers came and pawed his leg, he'd had no idea someone was outside. A moment later, a quiet knock sounded on the front door. Jamis crossed through the great room, opened the door and stepped back the moment he saw Natalie. Her expression was serious and determined. There was no point in fighting her. If she wanted in, she'd get in, one way or another.

Without a word, she came inside and glanced around. "Are you alone?"

He raised his eyebrows. "You seriously need to ask that?"

"I need to talk to you."

Something was wrong. "Okay." He shut the door.

She walked around the house, paced was more like it, from the great room into the kitchen, then out onto the porch, back into the great room. Jamis stayed where he was and waited. When she didn't seem to be able to start the conversation, he said, "Natal—"

"I'm pregnant." She stopped moving and stared at him.

He stared back at her, her words not completely registering. "With a baby? You're going to have a baby?"

"Yes."

Holy hell. Relax. Get the facts. He took a deep breath. "Don't take this the wrong way. I'm making absolutely no judgment, but could you have been pregnant when you came to the island?"

"No."

"Has there been any other man other than me?"

She shook her head. "No."

"So you think..." Could she be lying to him? Could another man be responsible? The way Katherine had used and manipulated him ran through his mind.

"Jamis, I know," she whispered. "You're the father."

He glanced into her face, her eyes, and knew she wouldn't lie to him. This was Natalie not Katherine, so it had to be true. He'd fathered a child. A child. *Good God.* The room around him seemed to almost tilt as if on an axis.

He imagined Natalie pregnant, her belly growing round and beautiful. He imagined her giving birth, him holding a tiny bundle. He'd love everything about being a father. The baby-soft skin. The gurgles and gummy smiles. The bedtime rituals. Those wide, dark eyes looking into his soul as if in that moment nothing, no one else on earth, mattered. Even the diapers.

And he'd miss it all. He just couldn't be a father again, not after messing it up so horribly the first time. "I can't be. Natalie…I can't be."

A sad, melancholy sound escaped from her throat. "We had unprotected sex several weeks ago. You are this baby's father."

"That's not what I meant. I believe you." Jabbing his hands through his hair, he paced as panic set in. "I… I…can't be a father."

Silent, she studied him.

"Don't you get it? I had two children, and I lost them. I don't deserve a second chance."

"Jamis, you're wrong. Every person deserves a second chance."

For a moment, he let himself believe what she said was true. He let himself imagine. Was she carrying a boy or a girl? If only he could— *No. No, no, no. Don't you dare think for one damned minute that you can have anything to do with this.* "Not me." He turned away from her. "Not after what I've done."

She quickly grabbed his arm, made him look at her. "What did you do, Jamis? What?"

She needed to know. She deserved to know. He shrugged away from her. "Years ago, I met a woman, Katherine, at a nightclub."

"Your wife."

He nodded. "My career was skyrocketing. I'd just signed the biggest contract I could imagine and was celebrating with a group of friends." He stepped away from her. "Katherine, I thought, was the icing on my cake. Sexy, sultry, mysterious. My limited experience with women made me, I guess, an easy mark. We were married six months later. A month after the wedding, despite all our talk about spending a few years alone before starting a family, she got pregnant. I remember being upset. All our plans would change. This would curtail our travel, our fun."

Afraid if she uttered one sound he might stop, Natalie bit her tongue.

"But when Caitlin was born, I took one look at my daughter's beautiful face and everything changed for me. I know it sounds corny, but she became the light of my life." He smiled. The curve of his lips was so tender, yet so filled with agony, it was all Natalie could do not to reach out and hold him. "So when Katherine got pregnant again within the year, I was happy. A boy. Justin. Those chubby cheeks and legs. Those blue eyes. I was so delighted, I was blind to what was going on."

"What was happening?"

"Katherine filed for a divorce a day after Justin's first birthday."

She sucked in a breath. That had to have crushed him. "Why?"

"She'd never loved me." He shook his head and paced. "Even admitted it privately. She was too old to model, so she'd married me and had two children merely to secure her financial future. It was as simple as that. She smeared me in court, using my books as evidence that I was an abusive husband and an even sicker human being."

How could anyone be so cruel? Her heart ached to comfort him, but she held back, waiting, knowing there was more.

"Like an idealistic idiot," he went on, "I fought what was happening. We argued. Incessantly. Then finally, on Caitlin's birthday, in the midst of nasty custody proceedings, I gave in. I went to the house. There was a winter storm that day, and the roads were icy, but I'd promised Caitlin we'd all go out to dinner together, like a real family. Before we left, I took Katherine aside. I offered her every penny I owned, every home, every car, everything in return for full custody of the children." He covered his face with his hands. "Even that wasn't good enough. She said the kids guaranteed her future child support payments. She would never, never give them up." He ran his hands through his hair. "Two minutes later, we got into the car to go to dinner and that's when I made the biggest mistake of my life."

She held her breath.

"I made a wish." He looked away, wouldn't hold Natalie's gaze. "I put every ounce of energy and hope and emotion I had in that one wish. I wished Katherine would just die, then my nightmare would be over. I wanted it so badly for her to simply go away. I even envisioned ways it could happen."

Wish it, see it, make it happen. Natalie cringed inside.

"She could fall in the shower," he continued, "and crack her head open. She could choke on one of her low-cal, high-fiber wrap sandwiches. She could slip down a flight of stairs. An elevator could crash. Lightning. Flood. Earthquake. Aliens. Ghosts. You name it, I pictured it. Including a car accident." He spun away from her. "A minute later, I skidded through an icy intersection and we were broadsided by a truck."

"Oh, my God," she murmured, unable to imagine what he must've gone through. The guilt and shame. The agony.

"Everyone died, except for me."

"And Snickers," she whispered.

He glanced at her and the anguish in his eyes made her chest ache. "He was just a puppy. He was thrown from the car and landed in a pile of fresh snow in the ditch."

"I'm so sorry." She felt tears gathering, tears of sadness and understanding.

"Don't look at me like that." He glared at her. "I don't deserve your empathy. If you'd seen my babies after that accident, you wouldn't be so quick to make excuses for me. Justin. My sweet, chubby son took the brunt of the force. His body was barely recognizable. Caitlin. My beautiful little girl. Looked like she was sleeping. Sleeping. Except that the back of her head was smashed in and caked with blood. Me? I walked away without much more than a scratch."

That wasn't true, but Natalie imagined that for Jamis anything less than his own death was mercy he didn't deserve. She brushed away the tears streaming down her face.

"I never deserved those children."

"Jamis, it was an accident. You didn't mean for that to happ—"

"Doesn't matter! I wished it. I saw it. *I* made it happen."

"But you didn't—"

"You believe. I know you do. That wishes can come true. How many times have you told your kids 'wish it, see it, make it happen'?" He stepped toward her. "Natalie, I was driving. Sure the roads were icy, but I was distracted by my anger, by making that damned wish. I was the one who went through the red light. Not the truck driver. Me. How can you tell me that I didn't make *my* wish happen?"

JAMIS HAD FATHERED another child. Of all the stupid, short-sighted, selfish things he could've done, this was the worst. Not even bothering to try to write, he sat at his desk and stared off into space. At the distinct sound of a child humming outside, Jamis glanced through his open window. Toni was sitting on the bottom branch of his maple, swinging her legs and peering innocently through the windows of his house. Her concentration was focused on his first floor, so she didn't notice him upstairs.

She peeked through the windows and sighed. Swung her legs and hummed a little louder, clearly trying to get his attention. He tried to summon some anger, or at least a little agitation, but all his steam seemed to have blown off when he'd spilled his guts to Natalie. He just didn't have it in him anymore. It wasn't Toni's fault she reminded him of Caitlin. It wasn't her fault he missed his children.

Caitlin and Justin. And an unknown, a boy or girl growing inside Natalie. He desperately wanted to be a part of that baby's life, but somehow it didn't seem fair to go on without Caitlin and Justin as if they'd never existed. It was time he accepted that there was no wish, no magic spell, no fairy dust he could sprinkle to get them back. He swung around, opened the bottom drawer of his credenza, and pulled out that last picture he'd taken of his children. Reverently, he ran his fingers over the smooth glass and then set it on his desk, near the screen, so he could see them as he worked. Then he pulled out everything else he had in the drawer and walked around his house displaying the items.

Clay figures Caitlin had made with him on a lazy Sunday in winter, he set on his desk. Several photos he arranged in his kitchen and great room, his favorite on his bedside table. He'd framed a couple of the pictures they'd drawn, so those he hung on a wall downstairs. He could never forget his children—didn't want to even try—but at least for today he could remember them with a smile in his heart.

As Toni watched him through the window, he walked over to the front door and stepped out onto the porch. She straightened and smiled hopefully. "You again," he said, trying to sound gruff. "You know you shouldn't be in that tree."

"But I'm a good climber."

"Even the best fall. Don't you think Natalie would be sad if you got hurt?"

She grimaced. "Oh, all right." Swinging down from the branch, she jumped the remaining few feet to the ground.

"I've got an idea."

"What?" She glanced up.

"How 'bout I make you and the other kids a simple tree house? In your yard?" It would only take him a few days and give them a fun way to end the summer.

"Really? You could do that?"

Nodding, he smiled. "If it's okay with Natalie."

When Natalie came back to Mirabelle next summer, Jamis would be gone. He had no other option. A tree house wouldn't be much, but it'd be something to remember him by.

SHE SHOULD'VE SAID NO.

Natalie had known she'd made a mistake within a few hours of agreeing to let Jamis build that damned tree house for the kids. For three days, she'd watched him through the kitchen windows, measuring, planning, sawing and hammering the wood. And for three days, she'd been nothing short of tortured, watching the concentration on his face and his strength as his muscles flexed and released. She wanted him even now. But this was her body reacting irrationally, and her body had gotten her in enough trouble already.

How could she reconcile in her mind the cranky man she'd met on move-in day what seemed a lifetime ago to the quiet, peaceful man who'd read aloud to her kids when she'd had her first massive bout with morning sickness? How could a man put up no-trespassing signs one day and a few weeks later build the very same people he'd tried keeping off his property a tree house? If that wasn't enough, the patience he'd showed over and over again with Galen these past three days, who'd adamantly insisted on forgoing craft time to help construct the tree house, had been nothing short of admirable. But how could she put aside his wish about Katherine, without bringing into question and discounting everything she believed? Her conviction that wishes came true was the entire reason for this camp.

Natalie was in the kitchen folding clothes when she glanced outside to gauge progress on the tree house. About eight feet above ground in a mature maple in the backyard, the tree house sat on a large platform that Jamis had first built supported by two large branches. He'd then secured a tall railing around the edges, foregoing solid walls. Natalie's only condition was that she be able to see the kids at all times to be sure they were safe. Jamis and Galen were now putting the finishing touches on the roof when she saw Garrett pulling into the yard on a golf cart.

Immediately, she dropped the clothes and went outside. "Hey, Garrett."

"Hi, Natalie." He stepped off the cart and looked up into the tree. "Sweet tree house. Who's building that?"

"Galen and Jamis."

"Jamis?" Garrett said. "First he was babysitting and now this."

"I know. Strange."

Garrett shrugged. "I came out to give you and Galen some good news."

"Yeah?"

"Dustin and Chad confessed to robbing Hendersons'."

"They did?"

He nodded. "When I found out you guys didn't have a DVD player, I put some more pressure on the girls who were with the boys that night. Turns out their stories pretty much matched Galen. After I told Chad and Dustin's parents what was going on, they decided to search through the boys' rooms and found the DVDs. It's a done deal. They've signed confessions."

"So Galen wasn't involved at all?"

Garrett shook his head. "Not at all."

"Does the town council board know?"

"They will, Natalie. I'll make sure of it."

"Thanks, Garrett. For getting to the bottom of it."

"That's my job." He glanced back up into the tree. "Tell Galen I hope there's no hard feelings."

"Oh, I think he'll just be glad it's over."

Galen glanced over the edge of the tree house railing just as Garrett hopped back onto his golf cart and drove away. "What did he want?" he called down to Natalie.

She smiled at him. "I'll tell you when you get down."

"We're almost finished."

Then as if the word *finished* had echoed all the way into the house, Toni came running outside, followed closely by Arianna and Ella. Ryan, Chase, Blake and Sam weren't far behind the young girls. "Are they done yet? Are they done?" Toni asked excitedly.

"Almost."

"Can we go up and see?"

"Not yet," Natalie said. "They'll let us know when it's ready."

Toni and the kids stood there for a few minutes before Toni called out, "When can we come up?"

"In a minute," Jamis called back. "We're putting the last board on the roof and then it's all yours."

A drill sounded, some pounding, and then a moment later Jamis climbed down the ladder with a load of tools and scrap wood. His feet had no sooner touched the ground, than Toni ran to him, throwing her arms around his waist.

"Thank you, Jamis!" She grinned.

"You're welcome," he said, ruffling her hair and stepping back. "Now up you go!"

One by one, the kids all scrambled up the ladder.

"Galen!" Jamis called up to the tree house.

"Yeah?" The teenager stuck his head out over the rail.

"Show them how to lock the gate, so you all stay safe up there."

"Will do."

Jamis glanced at Natalie and asked quietly, "How are you feeling?"

"All right." She crossed her arms, hugging herself. "I've been keeping soda crackers by my bed and pop a few in my mouth before I get up. Eating more often, smaller meals. It's all helping."

He looked away. "Good."

"Thank you, Jamis. For the tree house. You and Galen did a beautiful job."

He glanced back at her and his eyes were filled with so many emotions Natalie couldn't name them all. Quickly, he looked away. "I hope they like it."

"Are you kidding? I won't be able to get them down from there." All eight kids fit with plenty of room for more. "Next summer, we'll have to put in a swing set and other play equipment."

Jamis was silent.

"Maybe you could help?" she asked, holding her breath. She wanted him to at least see his child so he'd know who he'd be turning his back on.

"Next summer." He nodded at her, but she couldn't read what was going on inside his head. "Right."

She watched him walking slowly away, confusion rattling her thoughts. Who was Jamis Quinn? Really? There was something he wasn't telling her, something she hadn't figured out.

"What did Garrett Taylor want?" Galen had climbed down from the tree house and his shoulders looked tense, his expression worried.

She grinned. "Chad and Dustin confessed." She relayed everything Garrett had told her.

Galen relaxed and smiled. "Sweet."

"I didn't even think about telling him we didn't have a DVD player. How'd he find out?"

"Jamis told him."

"Jamis?"

"That day you were sick."

"He did?"

Galen nodded. "Turns out he's pretty cool."

Yeah, he was. Natalie looked out through the woods and barely made out Jamis heading into his house. They should've never made love without protection. It had been totally irresponsible. Even so, she couldn't help wanting Jamis's baby with all of her heart.

IT WAS A GORGEOUS, LATE summer afternoon. Preoccupied as he was about Natalie and her pregnancy, Jamis had all but given up writing this damned book until September when he figured he'd be able to concentrate. He pulled on his wet suit, hiked down the hill and dragged his kayak to the water's edge.

"Hey." The voice came from behind him, down the shoreline.

He spun around and found Galen sitting on a large flat boulder nestled on the hill.

"Going kayaking?"

Wet suit. Paddle. Kayak. A smart-ass comment came to mind, but Jamis didn't have the heart today. Especially not after having spent three days working side by side with the kid making that tree house. The boy had proven to be not only a hard worker, but also smart and good with tools. "Yeah, I'm going kayaking."

The kid threw a rock into the water. "Can I go with you?"

Spend some guy time with a kid and all of a sudden we're best friends. "Dude, do you see another kayak around anywhere?"

Galen threw a couple more rocks into the water. "I could rent one in town. If you wouldn't mind waiting for me."

Jamis looked away. "Something happen between you and Natalie?"

"No, we're cool." He shrugged. "Chief Taylor got those townie jerks to confess, so I'm in the clear. Thanks to you telling him we didn't have a DVD player."

"That's good. So what's wrong then?"

The kid shrugged again. "Nothing."

"Bullshit."

"Guess I just don't want the summer to be over."

"Don't want to go home?"

The kid didn't say anything.

Jamis took a deep breath and against his better judgment caved. "All right, Galen. Get up and get moving. I'll meet you in town at Setterberg's Rental. If you're not in a wet suit and on the beach waiting by the time I get there, I'm leaving without you." It was an empty threat, but the kid didn't need to know that.

Before Jamis could climb into his kayak, Galen had already set off running through the woods. In truth, Jamis didn't mind spending time with the boy. It made him wonder what Caitlin and Justin would've been like had they lived to become stubborn, know-it-all teenagers. It made him wonder what it would be like to be a father again.

CHAPTER FIFTEEN

A CRACK OF THUNDER, deafening in intensity, jolted Jamis from a sound sleep. Lightning flashed, illuminating the rain pouring into his open bedroom window. He jumped out of bed, cranked the window closed, and noticed the electricity had gone out. He was wiping up the wet sill and dabbing at the carpet when a loud pounding sounded on his front door.

Snickers barked and ran downstairs.

He trailed after the dog and swung the door wide to find Natalie standing on his porch. He hadn't seen her since he'd finished the tree house more than a week earlier and he had to admit pregnancy was looking damned good on her. Dressed in only pajama pants and a very wet, clingy T-shirt, the fact that she wasn't wearing a bra became immediately apparent, and it was all Jamis could do not to stare.

"Can you please come to the house?" she asked, shivering, her wet hair flattened to her cheeks.

He almost went with her, no questions asked, until his sanity returned. "What for?"

"It's Toni. The storm." As if just now becoming aware of the wet state of her dress, she crossed her arms over her chest. "She woke up screaming and keeps calling your name."

"*My* name? You're joking."

"Please, Jamis. I know you and I have issues, but all the kids are scared. Toni's upsetting them even more."

"Why me?"

"I don't know." Natalie shook her wet head. "You must make her feel safe."

Him? The king of horror? He made a child feel safe? What a crock. "I'm not… I don't—"

"She wants you, Jamis. Not me."

He looked away and swallowed the sudden lump in his throat.

She shivered and her shoulders sagged. "Well. If you change your mind, you know where to find us."

"Fine," he said. "I'll come." He grabbed his slicker off the rack and handed it to her along with a flashlight.

"I'm already wet," she said. "You—"

"I'll be all right. Come on, Snick."

After grabbing a couple more flashlights, he followed Natalie as she raced down the path between their two houses. Every window was dark in her house. Candlelight illuminated the shapes of kids looking through the windows. The moment they entered the house, he heard the screaming.

"Is that her?"

Natalie nodded. Either her face was wet from the rain, or she was crying, probably both. She grabbed a bath towel off the top of the dryer and handed it to him. "Go, please. I'll take care of Snickers."

After rubbing the towel through his wet hair, he stepped into the kitchen and found all of the kids loitering around, a couple of them holding their hands to their ears. The only light came from several candles on the table and counters. The littlest boy, Ryan, was crying, but Jamis guessed Natalie could handle him.

"Where is she?" he asked.

"Follow the screaming." Galen pointed upward.

Sam glared at Galen. "I'll show you."

Jamis followed her up the stairs.

"In here." She stopped outside an open door. "Toni? Jamis is here."

The screaming continued unabated.

Jamis entered the bedroom and glanced around. It was a pretty girly-girl room with a fluffy multicolored shag rug, pale pink walls and white furniture, including two sets of bunk beds. A lantern-style flashlight on the bedside table provided the only light in the room.

Another jolt of lightning and a crack of thunder and he saw Toni huddled in the corner on one of the lower bunks. "Toni?" He sat on the bed and reached for her. "Hey, it's okay. Nothing's going to hurt you." He reached out to touch her arm and she jumped.

He waited, rubbing her back in a soothing motion, but when her cries didn't subside he gently picked her up and pulled her onto his lap. Still hysterical, she flailed in his arms, kicked, scratched and swung her head.

"Shh, shh, shh. It's okay." And like that, it all returned to him, what he was supposed to do and say to calm a little child. "Sweetheart, you're okay. Toni, shh, shh, shh."

He rocked her, kissed the top of her head, patted her back and smoothed her curls away from her tear-streaked face. He did everything he could think of, every trick he'd used years ago on his own two children, to calm her. Within a few minutes, her high-pitched screams fell to a loud wail, then her body, tired and stressed, shuddered in relief.

She turned her face into his chest and her little hand gripped his arm, and it was all Jamis could do to keep his own tears at bay. What had happened to this child to frighten her so badly?

"Is…Snickers…here?" Her words came out in a choppy cadence.

"He is. Do you want me to get him?"

"No! Don't leave!"

"I'm not going to leave." Standing, he carried her to the door. "Snickers, come!"

The dog bounded up the stairs and flew into Toni's room.

With Toni on his lap, Jamis sat on the bed, and together they petted the dog's head.

"Can he sleep with me?" she asked.

"Absolutely. Come on, Snick, up."

The dog jumped onto the mattress and licked Toni's tear-salted cheek. She hugged him and kissed him back.

"If you lie down, I'll bet Snickers will cuddle right up with you."

Clearly exhausted, she fell onto her pillow. "I don't want you to go."

"Then I won't." He sat on the floor and held her hand. "I'll be here until morning."

"Promise?"

"Promise."

Jamis leaned back against the mattress, kicked his legs out in front of him, and listened to the sound of her breathing. If Caitlin had lived, she'd have been around Toni's age. He turned his head and glanced at the little girl, her eyes closed, her mouth slack, her small form moving slowly with each breath. He had the strangest feeling Natalie was carrying a girl. A girl. What would she name her daughter? The thought of her giving birth and raising a little one without him twisted his stomach in knots. He was going to miss out on so much.

All at once, the joy and pride Jamis had experienced in the very short time he'd been a father came back to him in a rush. He'd probably spoiled both his kids, but considering how awful his own parents had been at the job,

Jamis had done all right. Until the end. He'd be paying for that one wish the rest of his life.

IT TOOK FOREVER TO GET the kids settled. Eventually, they all fell back into peaceful slumber, the boys and Sam in their respective rooms and Arianna and Ella in Natalie's room downstairs. After changing out of her wet clothes, Natalie silently crept upstairs, poked her head into Toni's room and was relieved to find the girl sound asleep with Snickers snuggled in front of her. What gripped her heart was the sight of Jamis asleep sitting on the floor, one arm resting on the bed and Toni's doll-like hand swallowed up by his big mitt. For all his blubbering to the contrary, Jamis had a heart of gold, coming over here in the pouring rain and helping a child for whom he wasn't the slightest bit responsible.

His eyes cracked open and he spotted her at the door.

"You don't need to stay," she whispered. The worst of the storm had moved southeast of the island, and the rain had slowed to a steady pitter-patter.

He carefully disentangled his hand from Toni's and came out into the hall, pulling the door nearly closed behind him. "I promised her I'd stay until morning," he whispered. "If it's okay with you, I'll sleep on the other bunk, so if she wakes she'll see me there."

"Are you sure?"

He nodded and looked away, uncertain.

"What's the matter?"

"Why?" he asked. "Why was Toni so frightened?"

"Kids get scared in storms—"

"No, she wasn't just scared. She was hysterical."

Natalie wasn't supposed to share private information, but Jamis deserved an explanation. "Let's go downstairs, so we don't wake the kids." Using a flashlight, she went into the kitchen. Thunder rumbling in the distance and steady rain beating against the window over the sink made the room seem cozy.

"Toni's parents were killed about a year ago. She was in the backseat of the car when the vehicle got stuck on a railroad track. There was a bad storm that night. Like tonight, it was raining, lightning and thundering when the train hit the car, killing her parents."

Jamis looked down. "And Toni?"

"She was in the hospital for several weeks with a concussion and a broken leg." Natalie rested her hand on his arm. "She has no relatives that could take her. She's been bouncing from one foster care home to another since she got out of the hospital."

"I suppose every kid here has a similar story."

"Some have it a little tougher than others, but, yeah, not one of them has had an easy life."

"I was wrong, Natalie. What you're doing here is important."

She couldn't have been more shocked by his humble admission. "Thank you." The moment turned awkward, as if neither knew where to go from there. "Your shirt is still wet from the rain," she said. "I think I've got something that might fit you." She went into the laundry room and found a T-shirt she'd bought for Galen that had come a size too big. "Here. This might fit."

"Thanks."

Natalie hadn't intended on watching as he shrugged out of his wet shirt, but from the moment she caught sight of his bare chest and the mat of dark, curly hair, she couldn't peel her eyes away from him. He drew the dry shirt over his head, caught her gaze, and quickly looked away. "Now where's your fuse box? I'll see if I can get the electricity going again."

"In the basement." She cleared her head, grabbed a flashlight and opened a door next to the pantry. "I've never done this before, so can you show me?"

"Sure."

She went down the basement stairs. The old-fashioned fuse box was located toward the far end of the room, so with Jamis following, she walked across the cool and dank room on the uneven cement floor. Aside from the beams from their flashlights and the faint light coming from the top of the stairs, the basement was pitch-black. "Here it is."

She stood beside him while he showed her how to tell which fuses had blown and how to replace them. She'd never noticed before how comforting his voice could sound when he wasn't being sarcastic. No wonder Toni had asked for him. After a few moments, she shivered with the chill in the air. Heat emanated from him, and she found herself inching closer to his tall frame.

"There. That should do it." He turned, bringing them mere inches from each other. He smelled fresh, like the rain that had dried on his skin. "We should go."

"Do we have to?" she whispered.

He was silent for a moment. "Yes. Now." In the darkness with shadows all around, she couldn't see his eyes, but somehow she sensed his arousal.

Her knees turned weak at the thought, and he reached out to grab her. "I'm having a hard time forgetting our night together," she whispered. "You should know that kind of thing has never happened to me before. You know…sex… just like that."

He said nothing. Only the sound of his breathing turning

quick and raspy gave any indication he'd heard and been at all affected by what she'd said.

She closed her eyes and leaned toward him and his mouth slowly descended toward hers. The first touch of his lips was soft and slow, exploring and testing. Tentative. Not at all like the other night when they'd made love, but then she reached for him, felt the muscles of his chest and shoulders, and a whimper of pure, unadulterated appreciation escaped her throat.

Then everything happened almost at once. His kiss went from gentle to insistent with one thrust of his tongue. "You're killing me," he whispered, pressing her against the wall. And then his hands, his touch, seemed everywhere at once, from her neck to her breasts, her stomach to her butt, thrusting under her shirt, dipping just below the waistband of her shorts.

She was no better, gripping, groping and scratching him. She couldn't be sure, but she may have even bit his lip. "What is it with us?" she murmured against his lips.

"Put a man who's only had sex once in five years in close proximity to a beautiful woman and he's going to…"

"Is that all this is?"

"No." He buried his nose in her hair. "I've never… You're the only woman I've ever… Hell, I don't know."

"I know I want you." She leaned into him, pulsed her hips against him.

He groaned as if in pain. Then he stepped back and threw his hands in the air. "No. This is wrong. Haven't we done enough damage already?"

"A baby is not damage. At least not as far as I'm concerned."

"Natalie, we're moths to the flame, you and I. You don't want me. Not really. I may have fathered your child, but that's not going to change anything. As far as you're concerned, I'm just another man that you want to fix. And as soon as things get too messy, you'll find some fatal flaw in me and then move on to your next project."

"You think, huh?" she murmured.

"I know. I'm doing us both a favor."

She held his arm as coherent thought returned. "There was some truth to everything you said about me being afraid of abandonment, but I swear, Jamis, you're different. I'm not sure how, but you are."

"I'm unavailable. That's the difference." He pulled away and stepped back.

"I leave to go back to Minneapolis in a little more than a week. How can you turn your back on this? On your child? You were a good father. I know you were."

"This is your baby, Natalie. I'll provide whatever financial support you want, but it'll be *your* child. Not mine. I can't—won't—be involved in any way other than to pay bills. I lost my family. I don't deserve another one." He grabbed his flashlight and went upstairs to Toni's bedroom.

LYING ON HIS BACK, Jamis slowly opened his eyes. If the wedge of sunlight streaming from the edges of the window blind was any indication, it was already midmorning. He glanced up to find cutouts of magazine pictures plastered overhead. Ella or Arianna must've taped them onto the bottom of the top bunk. Rather than a collage of fanciful pictures, it was more like a photo layout. Most of the cutouts were of models, but whoever had done the cutting had obviously decided she could do better than the original designers.

In paper doll fashion, a scarf and a pair of shoes had been glued over one model. Pants and a jacket onto another.

A dress, made from a mishmash of clippings, had been taped or glued onto a third. A coat and hat onto a fourth. A necklace, earrings and purse onto the last.

"You're sleeping in my bed." The little girl's voice coming from the other bunk was soft and sleepy.

So Toni was the wannabe fashion designer. He glanced over at her. Other than her eyes being slightly puffy from crying, she looked no worse for wear. "It's very comfortable. Why aren't you in it?"

"It's by the window."

The lightning last night during the storm. "Oh." Not wanting to embarrass her, he wasn't sure what else to say.

"Thanks." She stared at him, and without uttering another word, he understood how grateful she was.

"Why me?" he asked, needing to know. "Why did you ask for me last night?"

"'Cause I was right the first time. You do remind me of my daddy."

"You mean I look like him?"

"No. You…feel like him."

He *comforted* her? How was that possible? This was a crazy damned world, and he'd never understand it.

"You hungry?" His stomach felt like a gurgling pot of acid.

She nodded.

Chairs scraped and cupboards closed in the kitchen below them, signaling breakfast time. "Then let's go get something to eat. Natalie does feed you, doesn't she?"

Toni made a face. "She tries."

Jamis laughed and smoothed her hair.

Toni swung her feet out from under a pink, green and white quilt. By the time they got to the kitchen, the rest of the kids were dressed and sitting around the table and Natalie was dishing up French toast. "Well, good morning!"

He glanced at her. With the sun streaming through the window behind her, she looked almost angelic. “Morning.”

They’d set a place for him at the table and everyone appeared to be waiting for him to sit. A family. What would it feel like to have one again?

“Will you stay for breakfast?” Toni asked.

He was getting in deeper by the minute, but how could he refuse that sweet face? Taking a seat, he forked a piece of French toast as the plate was passed around, squirted on a blob of syrup, took a bite and nearly gagged. “Did you make this?” he asked Natalie. As if there was any doubt.

“Mmm-hmm.” She nodded. “It’s my grandmother’s secret recipe.”

Almost as bad as her baking soda cookie, this concoction was so orangey and rich he barely choked it down. “What’s in it?”

“Well, if I told you it wouldn’t be a secret.”

Too bad the recipe hadn’t died with the old woman.

And you’re such an ass, Jamis.

He glanced at the faces of the children around the table. “Do you kids like this stuff?”

No one said anything.

“I know.” Natalie sighed. “Mine never seems to taste quite like Grammy’s.”

“May I try?” he found himself asking, suddenly remorseful over the nasty thought about her grandmother.

“Go for it.”

He went to the counter and threw the rest of her French toast into the sink.

“By the way, thanks for installing that new garbage disposal,” Natalie said, coming to stand by him. “We really needed it.”

Well, there was a big surprise.

"Can I help?" she asked.

His instinct was to keep her as far away from the stove as possible, but her expression was so earnest it was impossible to not concede. "Crack the eggs." She couldn't screw that up, could she? Apparently, he was wrong. After scooping out a few tiny shells Natalie had missed, Jamis scrambled the eggs, added milk, vanilla and cinnamon. "This your secret ingredient?" He held up the bottle of Grand Marnier liqueur.

She nodded.

"A little of this stuff goes a long way. Like vanilla." He poured a small amount into the egg mixture. Five minutes later, he was piling hot French toast onto a platter. "Dig in, guys."

Natalie took a bite and closed her eyes. "Mmm. Now that's just like Grammy's."

Syrup clung to her lips and Jamis resisted the urge to lick it off. She opened her eyes and caught him staring at her mouth. Instead of looking away, their gazes locked and held. *This was complete craziness.* And he couldn't believe it was all going to be over in a little more than a week. Then he could go back to being completely and miserably alone.

CHAPTER SIXTEEN

ANOTHER FEW LONG, slow days passed during which Natalie had neither seen nor heard from Jamis. Although Snickers made several visits a day to her house, he would merely appear and then disappear without a sound from his master. The summer was almost over and Natalie felt as if her world was unraveling.

Arianna, Ella, Blake and Chase were going home today. Natalie and the other kids would be following a week later. Although Ryan and Toni hadn't yet grasped the ramifications of the four middle kids going home, Galen had barely said a word all morning, and Sam was sniffing back unshed tears. As they left the house and went into town to catch the Mirabelle ferry to the mainland to meet Arianna and Ella's grandmother and Chase and Blake's father, the mood of the group was a jumbled-up mess of excitement, sadness, joy and resignation.

The closer they got to the mainland, the more the homebound children got excited. Suddenly Arianna screamed, "Grandma! Ella, there she is." She pointed toward the pier and jumped up and down, waving.

"Do you see Dad?" Blake asked Chase.

"Not yet," Chase said.

"He'll be there," Natalie reassured them. "I talked to him on the phone last night, and he's all ready for you guys."

"You sure?" Chase asked.

"Positive."

"There he is!" Blake called as the ferry pulled up to the pier and docked. "Dad!"

"Dad!"

The ferry gate no sooner opened than the four children raced onto the pier. Sam and Galen helped Natalie carry off the luggage and Ryan and Toni followed, suddenly dragging their feet. After the girls were finished hugging their grandmother, Natalie shook hands with the older woman and then hugged each girl tightly. "We're going to miss your girls," she said, standing.

"Not as much as I missed 'em." The woman wiped tears of joy from her cheeks. She looked a bit on the haggard side, but clean and sober.

Blake and Chase's dad turned to Natalie as soon as he extricated himself from the boys' arms around his neck. "Thank you, Natalie." The man looked tired and drawn, but overjoyed to see his boys. "You turned what would've been a horrible summer for these boys into something they'll never forget."

"It was my pleasure." She hugged both boys.

Natalie could barely watch all the kids saying goodbye. By the time the rest of the kids and Natalie returned to the ferry for the return trip to Mirabelle, there wasn't a dry eye on the pier. No one said a word on the windy trip home across the water. She had no clue how she could possibly say goodbye to these last four children. Not these kids. For the first time Natalie could ever remember, three months was feeling to her as if she was just getting started.

Maybe a foster home wasn't such a bad idea. Maybe it was time for her to make a commitment to something even more important than this camp. Maybe she needed to make promises to these kids that went beyond summer care. It was so much more than she'd bargained for when envisioning this camp, but somehow it was starting to feel more right than anything Natalie had ever set out to do. The big question was would they want her?

By the time they got back home, it was late in the afternoon. Knowing their big old house was going to seem mighty quiet without the four middle kids, Natalie had invited Missy, Sarah and Hannah over for dinner and a campfire. Late that night, after the kids had gone upstairs and were settled in bed, she and the other women walked the path to the fire pit.

"So that's where the beast lives," Missy murmured, pointing to Jamis's log cabin.

"Shh," Natalie said. "He'll hear you. Voices travel at night out here in the woods." They all helped build a small fire and then poured out a few glasses of wine and sat back to stare into the flames and talk. Rather than risk possible questions, Natalie simply didn't drink the wine.

"Well, I for one can't believe that jerk tried to close you down."

"But he didn't. That's all that matters."

"You're awfully forgiving," Sarah said.

"He's not as bad as you think."

Natalie threw a stick onto the fire.

"Why are you making excuses for him?"

"I don't know. I like him."

"Why?"

"He's interesting. And funny. And compassionate."

"He's hot," Hannah said. "I'll give him that."

"But have you read anything he's written?" Sarah asked.

"His books aren't anything like him."

"There has to be some screw loose for him to come up with that stuff."

"Can we not talk about Jamis anymore?"

The other three women glanced at Natalie, Missy for a particularly long time.

"So who's met the new doctor helping out Doc Welinski?" Sarah asked.

"I have," Hannah said, smiling. "Dibs!"

JAMIS LAY IN BED WITH his windows wide-open. He was about to drift off when soft voices came to him on the cool night breeze. Feminine sounds, giggles, laughter, conspiratorial whispers. It might have been a comforting way to fall asleep had he not been able to make out so much of their conversation. As it was, though, at least half of what they said was easily decipherable. And they were talking about him.

Surprisingly, most of what they said cut more deeply than he'd expected. He'd always known the world looked upon him as an oddity, but it was different to hear people he knew being so blunt and honest. At least he could easily tell Natalie's voice from the others, could hear her defend him in a way. Maybe that was the most surprising part of it all. Would she go so far as to tell them she was carrying his child? He didn't care what the islanders thought, but he hoped Natalie understood his decision.

"Can we not talk about Jamis anymore?" Natalie said.

Thank God. Now he could fall asleep. They murmured about this and that, most of it mundane chick-speak.

"You okay with this camp coming to an end?" asked one of the women.

Jamis stilled.

"Actually, I'm thinking about being a foster parent for Galen, Sam, Ryan and Toni."

What? His breath hitched in his throat. Emotions, left and right, assaulted him. Concern. Was she ready for that, especially with a baby coming? Regret. Had he spurred her on somehow by claiming she lived in fear of abandonment? But mostly there was envy. She was moving on with her life, a life that would no doubt be rich and full even without him.

ONLY TWO MORE NIGHTS left on the island. After Toni and Ryan had gone to sleep, Natalie stood in the kitchen thinking she'd do more packing. Instead she found herself gazing out at Jamis's house. Every day, since the four middle-schoolers had left, Natalie had felt a sense of almost panic rising higher and higher inside her. By now, she'd hoped to have come to some resolution regarding Jamis, but there seemed to be no clear direction.

Although questions had plagued her for days about Jamis's true character, she was finally content with the belief that no matter what Jamis wanted the world to think, he was an inherently good man. He was a good man who'd not only been betrayed by the woman he loved, he'd lost his children. Natalie refused to believe that was the price he'd paid for a terrible wish. The world couldn't possibly work that way.

Somehow, someway, she had to convince Jamis to be a part of her life and their child's life. Leaving Mirabelle without him was going to be the hardest thing she'd ever done.

Sam came into the room, went to the refrigerator and poured herself a glass of milk, then grabbed a couple cookies. She leaned against the counter. "You okay?"

"I'm fine. Just thinking."

"About what?"

Natalie glanced at Sam's earnest, innocent face, thought about how much this young woman had grown through the summer. Not long and she'd be an adult. "Do you believe wishes can come true?" Natalie asked.

"With all your talk about *wish it, see it, make it happen,*" Sam said, smiling, "you expect me to answer that?"

Natalie chuckled. "Not fair of me, I know, but I'd appreciate your honesty."

Sam took a bite of cookie and washed it down with a gulp of milk. "Well, *honestly,* I don't know if I believe in wishes coming true. But I can tell you that no matter what happens when I go back to Minneapolis in a couple days, I don't think my life will ever be the same."

Natalie desperately wanted to tell the kids about her idea for a foster home, but she couldn't. Although she'd made the necessary calls to check into fostering all four kids and faxed in all the appropriate forms, final approval hadn't been given. "So you don't think your life will be the same. How so?"

"Well, I may not be able to change what my foster family believes or what they do or how they act, but I can feel a change inside myself. I believe I can make a difference in my own life."

"Yes!" Natalie closed the distance between them, hugged the young woman and then stepped back. "That's it! That's what I'd hoped you come to understand before the end of summer. It's that make-it-happen part that brings it all together. I'm so happy for you!"

Sam shrugged, but the brightness of her eyes belied her seemingly nonchalant attitude and Natalie hugged her again. As she stepped back and looked into Sam's eyes, something hit Natalie. There it was. The key. "The make-it-happen part," she whispered. "That's it."

"What's it?" Sam asked.

Natalie looked up, her thoughts racing. "Oh, just something I've been thinking about."

"Well, I'm going to bed," Sam said.

"G'night, Sam." She couldn't let things sit the way they were between her and Jamis. She had to try one more time to convince him to come with her. To ease his fears and change his mind. Before she could second-guess herself, Natalie picked up the phone and dialed. "Missy? I know it's late, but could you do me a really big favor?"

THE NIGHT HAD TURNED CHILLY and Jamis had made a fire inside. The flames, though, had made him think of Natalie, so he'd come outside. With a blanket wrapped around his shoulders he now stood on his deck and stared at the moon in all its full and bright and magical glory. Occasionally, leaves rustled quietly in the woods, signaling a raccoon, perhaps, or a deer on its nighttime search for food. In the distance, an owl hooted his intermittent and mournful song.

Come to me. One last time, come to me.

Weak man that he was, Jamis closed his eyes and put the wish out there. Sick of hating himself. Sick of the self-loathing. Sick of his pathetic, solitary existence, he wanted Natalie. He wanted to taste her. Touch her. Love her.

"No," he whispered to himself. "I take it back." *For her sake.*

Lost in thought, he didn't hear the footfalls until they landed on the steps behind him. He turned. There she stood, her face and hair pale in the moonlight, shadows making her eyes unreadable. Was she nothing more than a figment of his imagination, a dream?

Without a word, she moved toward him, but it wasn't until her hand rested on his chest that he knew she was real. "You came. Why?"

"Because I want you. More than anything in the world, I want you."

"You, of all people, should hate me for what I've done."

"I could never hate you, Jamis. I needed time to think to—"

"Find a way in that great big heart of yours to forgive me?" he said, unable to keep the scorn from his voice.

"No." She held his gaze. "Jamis, there's nothing to forgive."

"I killed my family."

"You didn't. You haven't done anything, thought anything, wished for anything worse that most people in this world. We've all had moments where we've wished ill on someone."

"Not you."

"Trust me. I have. There's a big surprise, huh? I'm human, like you. But unless you took steps to actually make that car accident happen, it wasn't your fault."

"Wish it, see it." He glared at her. "*I* made it happen."

"I hate to break it to you, Jamis, but you're not that powerful."

He looked away. She didn't get it.

"I know what you're thinking, and you're wrong. I do get it." She touched his arm. "Our dreams and wishes breathe inside *us*. Help us to make changes inside us. Wishing something and visualizing alone isn't enough. Nothing happens until we take steps to make it happen. Our wishes don't change the world or other people or their lives. They change *us*. You didn't kill Katherine and your children because you didn't take any purposeful steps to make it happen. You didn't intend for anyone to die."

What she said made sense, but he didn't know how to let go. "Why then? Tell me why they're all dead?"

"I don't know, Jamis." She reached out and caressed his cheek. "But I do know that with or without you and your wish the accident would've still happened. I do know that you need to forgive yourself and step out into the world. Because I know the world will be a better place with you out there muddling through it like the rest of us." She wrapped her hand around his neck and kissed him.

He held her away from him. "I can't do this," he said softly. "Touching you is killing me."

"That's because you want more and so do I. If I have to leave without you, give me one night. Tonight, let's—"

"No—"

She took his face in her hands and kissed him, deeply, honestly. It was the sweetest sensation Jamis could remember, but he pulled back. "You're leaving." It was a lame excuse, he knew it, but he'd throw out anything he could to make her keep her distance. "What's the point?"

"I want to do it right this time. I want to know what could be."

"You shouldn't do this," he whispered, grasping again. "Your kids?"

"Missy's staying the night. In my room. I have no place else to go."

With a frustrated groan, he turned away. He felt her warmth as she wrapped her arms around him. She splayed her hands against his chest and he threw his head back, looking to the stars and refusing to move. "Natalie, don't."

"A woman throws herself at you and you remain unmoved."

Oh, he'd been moved all right.

"What are you afraid of?"

Jamis said nothing, just stared.

"Jamis, please."

"Please what?" he groaned. "Nat, what do you want from me?"

"I want tonight. I want to make love with you. That's all." She made it sound so harmless. So safe.

Safe. He almost laughed out loud. What a word. He wasn't safe from her. From this night. From his own devastating wants and needs. From the feelings he had for her. But in two days she was going to be gone. Gone. Out of his life. Forever. He wanted this, too.

"Tonight," he whispered. "That's all I've got to give."

"I'll take it."

He took her hand and drew her into his cabin. The moment the door closed behind them, she unzipped her jacket and shrugged it off. Next came her shirt, then her jeans, her socks. He stood there watching, frozen, just a man wanting a woman. When she reached behind her to unsnap her bra, he came to life. No more fear. Not tonight. Tonight, holding nothing back, he wanted to make love.

"Wait." He stilled her hands. "Let me look at you." He trailed his fingertips along her collarbone, her arm, her waist, then back up to rest on her lips. She looked like an angel, pale and perfect. Even her bra and thong were white, almost virginal. Goose bumps broke out on her skin. "You're cold."

"No."

He entangled his fingers with hers, unsure of how to proceed. Although once upon a time, he'd gained confidence and proficiency in pleasuring women, he'd never been close to a ladies' man. Suddenly, he felt awkward and clumsy as if this was the first time.

"Jamis?"

"I—"

She silenced him with a kiss as soft as it was sweet, as slow as it was warm. A touch of her tongue. Her hands kneading his chest, his shoulders and instinct took hold. He unsnapped her bra, tore off her thong with a quick tug and devoured the sight of her. The curves of her hips, her breasts, even the angle of her shoulders.

Reverently, he touched her, savoring every one of those curves, from breasts to bottom, from waist to face, from neck to back and all over again. Then he couldn't stop himself. He reached lower and touched the wet, swollen spot between her thighs. He groaned and sucked in a breath. "So very, very sweet."

She pulsed against his fingers and let out a shaky sigh, and then she took her turn discovering him. Her hands took over, on his stomach and chest, his arms and his neck. Anxious and needy, she worked the fly on his jeans. She pushed away the knit fabric of his boxers and cupped his erection.

"No," he groaned and jerked away. "You touch me and it'll be over."

She pulled him down to the rug in front of the fire and then pushed him onto his back. That's when the virginal angel turned into every inch the wanton devil. Naked, she straddled his waist. He closed his eyes, hoping to contain himself. Then she kissed him, moved over him and before he understood her plan, she eased down on him with her wet warmth and took him inside.

"Oh, Natalie." He jerked and moaned. "Stop. Don't."

She moved, slowly, purposefully in a primal rhythm, and when he opened his eyes, took in the sight of her, mouth slightly parted, eyelids heavy with lust, breasts moving with her every thrust, he was lost. Pulling her hips down to meet him, he thrust hard inside her one last time, in a pulsing, thorough, complete release.

She ground against him, dragging out the agonizingly sweet intensity until he thought he'd go mad. "Nat, stop," he rasped, putting his hands on her hips and holding her still as he caught his breath.

He opened his eyes and looked into the face of a triumphant woman. "You planned that, didn't you?"

She smiled, a leisurely curve of kiss-reddened lips, before smoothing out his brow. "I wanted to do that for you."

"I've told you over and over," he murmured, "I am not a man who needs to be fixed. I'm not a charity case. Don't get me wrong. That was…amazing, thrilling and damned hot, but not what I wanted for you."

"No?" She grinned at him.

"No."

"Then show me."

He lifted her off him and grabbed a heavy blanket and lay back down with her in front of the fire. Now that his urgent need had been satisfied, he could take his time. He leaned over her and kissed her. He lingered at her mouth, her lips. Trailed his tongue down her neck and stopped at her breasts. "This is what I want from you."

She moaned and arched toward him as he took first one breast then the other, drawing her nipples into his mouth. All the while, he felt tension mounting inside him. By the time he moved past her stomach, he was hard again. Spreading her knees, he lingered between her legs, licking, sucking, dipping his fingers into her heavenly wetness. And loved her. In only a moment or two, she was squirming. Over and over she whispered his name.

"Come," he whispered.

"No. You. Inside me."

The need to own her coursed through him. He fought it and failed. Moving up and over her, he entered her slowly, deliberately, lovingly. He moved with her until she whimpered and moaned as momentum gathered for them both.

She wrapped her legs around him, gripped him and he watched her sweet, beautiful face as she flew apart around him. "Jamis!" she cried.

But he wouldn't let himself go yet. Not yet. He took her again, watched the desire spiraling within her and then, and only then, he came inside her. A moment later, nearly spent, he collapsed over her, his lips at the hollow beneath her ear, his fingers entwined with hers above her head.

"Was that more of what you had in mind?" she whispered, a smile in her voice.

"We're getting there." He kissed her. "But I have one night to make up for five long years, and if I can help it I'm not wasting a minute of it sleeping."

FINALLY, JAMIS HAD FALLEN asleep. Curled next to him, Natalie studied his profile backlit by the red-orange flames in the fireplace. Without a single worry line on his face, he looked almost happy. Surely, he appeared peaceful and satisfied, not at all the tortured soul he was when awake. She barely kept herself from outlining his lips with a fingertip, from running her hands along his soft cheek, from entangling her fingertips in the mat of hair on his chest, a chest that rose and fell in a contented rhythm.

What in the world did you do, Natalie?

Again, she'd miscalculated. She'd come here to make love to Jamis, hoping against hope she might bring him back to life. Instead, he'd turned the tables. He'd made love to her, lifted her up and rocked her world. He'd filled a hole in her heart, a hole she'd never before admitted to herself that she'd had. He'd been right. He didn't need to be fixed, and she could see herself wanting much, much more than three months of Jamis.

As she tucked herself next to him and closed her eyes,

she realized she loved every crazy thing about him. His intensity, his sardonic grin, that look in his eyes that always made her wonder what he was thinking, the curiously easy way he had with her kids. Even his sarcasm. There was no doubt about it. She'd fallen in love with Jamis. Easily. Effortlessly.

So where was the fatal flaw?

Could it be there wasn't one?

CHAPTER SEVENTEEN

NATALIE AWOKE TO A stream of harsh sunlight hitting her in the face. Shielding her eyes, she rolled over to find Jamis gone. As memories of last night returned, she stretched and smiled. "Jamis?" she called. "Where are you?"

Snickers ran down from the loft, came to her side and licked her hand. As she petted the dog's head, she heard a cabinet closing only a moment before Jamis came downstairs. He was dressed in running clothes, and she wanted nothing more than to run into his arms.

"What do you need, Natalie?"

The instant the impassive look on his face registered, her heart sank. Last night's magic was as cold as the ashes in the fireplace. "I wanted to see you." Wrapping the blanket around her naked body, she stood. "To talk about last night."

"There's not much to talk about, is there?"

"I wanted to make sure we were okay."

"We're fine. Why wouldn't we be?" He spun away from her and put his coffee cup in the sink.

"Jamis, don't do this."

Leaning against the counter, he crossed his arms over his chest. "What is it that I'm doing?"

She stomped into the kitchen and glared at him. "You can't pretend that last night didn't happen. That it wasn't completely and wonderfully amazing."

"Last night was last night. And, yes, it was amazing. But you did your thing, Sunshine. You waved your magic wand over me. Voilà. I'm fixed. All better. Now you can go back to Minneapolis tomorrow with a clear conscience. Okay?" He glared at her. "You even got a baby out of the bargain."

"Wha— Oh!" She growled. "You're such an asshole."

"Really? Here I thought I was stating the facts."

"That's not fair. I wasn't trying to get pregnant the first time, and last night wasn't about me trying to fix you."

"Then what do you want? A long-distance affair? Phone sex and e-mails? Happily ever after? I'm confused."

"I want you. For me. And this morning—"

"A lot of things become clear in the light of day."

"I want to keep seeing you. I want you to be a part of our baby's life. Part of *my* life. I want to find out where this goes."

"I can tell you right now where we go without all the hassle of tears and fights and broken hearts. I've made my situation perfectly clear to you. Why is this a problem?"

She closed her eyes. "Because you…you can't just walk away."

"I'm not the one who'll be doing the walking," he said, leveling his gaze on her. "You will be. That's been your plan all summer long. Last night changed nothing. Nothing!"

It had changed everything, but she had a sick feeling in her gut that there wasn't anything she could say that would make him admit to it. "So that's it? You're just going to hide away here on Mirabelle forever?"

"Actually, no." He looked away. "I'll be gone before you return next summer. As soon as I can find my own island, I'll be moving."

Anger built inside her. How could he simply throw away what they might have together? How could he *do* this? "You know if you didn't have any feelings for me," she bit out, “I’d be okay with this, but you’re lying, Jamis. To me. To yourself. I know what I saw in your eyes last night when you touched me. When you kissed me. When you came inside me. That look was not the look of a man merely releasing pent-up *sperm*.”

That was when it came to her. What this was really all about.

“You’re afraid,” she whispered. “Afraid you might want me too much. Afraid to feel. Afraid you’re going to fall in love with me. Then what? I’ll hurt you, right? The way Katherine did? The way Caitlin’s and Justin’s deaths did? Do you think I’m going to die? Leave you? Use you?”

He spun away, refusing to look at her.

“This isn’t one of your books, Jamis. Neither of us knows what’s going to happen next. You think I’m not scared? You think this is easy for me?”

“A helluva lot easier for you than for me,” he ground out. “I’m just another fixer-upper to you. You’ll just screw around with me until you think I’m all better, claim I have some flaw that’ll make it impossible for you to commit to me and then toss me out the door.”

She was right. He was scared to fall in love again. She walked toward him. “Not this time, Jamis. You’re different.” She stroked his cheek. “Because I love you.”

He groaned as if a jagged knife was cutting him inside out. “Well then, there’s your fatal flaw.” He stepped back. “I can never love you back.” He took off for the door. “Snickers, come!” he called. When the dog didn’t budge, Jamis took off running through the woods without him.

AFTER HAVING RUN ALL the way around the island, Jamis stopped on the side of the dirt road by his house and bent to catch his breath. He’d run so fast and so far that his lungs were burning and his legs nearly gave out from under him, but he couldn't run away from the memory of Natalie's expression when he'd told her he could never love her back.

She couldn't have looked more hurt than if he'd sucker punched her. Her skin had turned ashy white and her lips parted as if she might gag. It'd killed him to see her reaction, but he'd had to say it. For her sake. Now she could leave, move on and raise her baby with a clear conscience and without him.

"This is for her," he whispered. "For her."

IT WAS THEIR LAST FULL day on Mirabelle. As Natalie and the kids readied for their departure, cleaning and packing things away, a curious mix of emotions swirled through the house. Sam, Ryan and Toni fell quiet and seemed sadly resigned to the end of summer. Galen, on the other hand, was angry. He didn't show it. He didn't speak about it, but Natalie could feel it like a river's current under layers of ice.

Late in the afternoon, Natalie had gotten a call from the social services department back home, letting her know she'd been approved as a foster parent for Sam, Ryan and Toni. Galen, though, was going to be a problem as his mother had clear custody and she wasn't about to relinquish her rights. On the bright side, he turned sixteen in a month. His age, coupled with the fact that his mother was on probation for dealing drugs, might be enough to convince a judge that Galen would be better off with Natalie. While she was excited about the news, she was also nervous about how her foster home idea would be received.

A somber mood had settled around the less than normally hectic dinnertime and had only grown heavier as the night progressed. "I think we should have one last campfire," Natalie said, putting thoughts of Jamis firmly out of her mind and focusing on the kids. Everything was packed and ready to go. In the morning, they'd have breakfast and head to town to catch a ferry to the mainland. "What do you say?"

"Yeah!" Toni said.

"Okay," Sam and Ryan said in unison.

Galen glanced at her.

"Come on, guys. Let's go." She took off outside and headed for the fire pit.

By this time, they all knew the drill. Once the blaze was going, Natalie poked the fire with a stick. Had she done the right thing? Had this camp accomplished its objective? For Sam, it seemed as if it had, but what about the others? She glanced at each one of the faces illuminated by the flickering firelight and was happy to see Ryan had put on some weight.

No one seemed to want to talk, but, regardless of what their reactions might be, she had to throw her foster home idea out there. "I have a question for you guys," she said. "What did you think of this summer? What did you think of living with me?"

Sam glanced up and frowned. "I had a good summer. I'm glad I came. I'll miss you."

"Same," Toni said, her voice small.

"Same." Ryan threw a handful of leaves on the fire and they crackled and exploded into flames. "But I don't want to go home. I want to stay here. With you. All of you."

Everyone stopped what they were doing and stared at the little boy who'd rarely spoken more than a handful of words all summer long.

"Galen? What about you?"

He picked up a rock and threw it into the woods. "I don't want to go home, either."

Natalie took a deep breath. "What if…none of you had to go back to the places you were living before we started this camp?"

All four heads turned in her direction, but no one said anything for several moments.

"Do you mean stay here?" Sam asked.

"I mean…coming to live with me in the house my grandmother left me in Minneapolis," Natalie said tentatively. "You wouldn't have to if you don't want to. It's just a suggestion. I have enough room. It's a big house."

"Like a foster home?" Sam asked.

"Yes," Natalie said. "If you want, I could be your foster mom."

"All of us," Toni asked.

"Even me?" Ryan said.

Galen looked away. He was old enough and smart enough to understand it wasn't going to be so easy for him.

"Well," Natalie said, careful with her response, "Sam, Toni and Ryan have already been approved. Galen's situation is a little more complicated."

"My mom will never let me go," he said, his anger apparent.

"But if you can prove you're better off without your mom, you may have grounds for what's called emancipation of a minor," Natalie said. "And then you can decide for yourself where you want to live."

For the first time all day, the worry lines on his face cleared, his anger dissipated. "Do you really think that'll work?"

"I do, Galen. And if you want to live with me, I'll fight for you," Natalie said. "So do you guys want me? Or not?"

"I want you." Toni came toward her and hugged her around the neck.

"Same," Ryan said, coming to her other side.

Sam's eyes glistened with unshed tears. "Yeah. You can foster mom me any time you want, Nat."

Everyone turned to Galen.

"Are you kidding?" He shook his head and grinned. "What do you think I've been wishing for *and* visualizing all summer long?"

All five of them fell into a group hug. The news of a baby on the way would wait for another day, but she had a feeling they would all make wonderful foster siblings.

"What's going to happen between you and Jamis?" Sam asked.

"What do you mean?" Natalie said, feigning innocence.

"You know what she means," Galen said.

Boy, am I in for trouble, Natalie thought ruefully. "I don't know yet, but I can tell you there's something I'm wishing for and visualizing on top of fostering you kids. I'd love for Jamis to be a part of our lives." But it was going to have to be up to him. "That okay with you guys?"

"Yeah," Sam said.

"He's cool," Ryan said.

"Totally," Toni said.

Galen nodded, as if he understood better than any of them the possibilities. "You say when, though, and I'll take him out."

YESTERDAY, JAMIS HAD watched the activity taking place next door. From the sounds of the music blaring through the open windows, there'd been cleaning and packing going on all day long. Now this morning, boxes and suitcases were being stacked on the porch. Natalie was sending a message, loud and clear. She and what was left of her crew were leaving today.

He spun away from the sight of the Victorian and

covered his face with his hands. He'd been unable to sleep more than an hour or two last night. All morning, he hadn't been able to eat. His gut was a nauseous mess, his brain a disconnected stream of thoughts. He should go over there. No. He couldn't. He should say goodbye. But how? And with what words? Even Snickers wasn't himself. The way a dog knows something is going on, he'd been running back and forth between their two houses all morning, anxious and watchful.

When a knock sounded on the cabin door both Jamis and Snickers jumped. Snickers whined and glanced up at him.

"Let's get this over with." He opened the door and Galen and Toni stood on the porch.

"We're leaving now," Galen said. "We'll be catching the next ferry."

Jamis nodded.

"We wanted to say goodbye," Toni said, her eyes watering.

"And thanks," Galen added. "For everything you've done for us this summer."

"This is for you." Toni held out an envelope with his name scrawled across the front in childish print.

Jamis nodded and took the card. Still no words.

Awkward silence filled the next long minute.

"Well." Galen held out his hand. "See ya."

Jamis shook the young man's hand and that motion seemed to shake him from his stupor. "Galen, good luck with school." *Good luck in life.*

"Thanks."

"Goodbye, Jamis," Toni whispered, her voice cracking.

"Bye, Toni. You have a good year at school, too, okay?"

She nodded.

Galen turned and reached out for the little girl's hand. "Come on. We have to go."

Toni let her hand get swallowed by Galen's, but kept her eyes on Jamis as they walked down the porch steps. When their feet reached the ground, Toni stopped. "Wait." She tugged free, raced back up the steps and launched herself at Jamis. "Goodbye," she said in a choking voice.

Jamis knelt down and wrapped her in his arms and did everything he could to keep from falling apart. "You're going to be all right," he whispered in her ear.

She sniffed. "But I'll miss you. And Mirabelle. And Snickers." She wrapped her arms around the dog's neck. Snickers licked every last salty tear away, and then she spun around and ran to Galen.

Before Jamis knew it, the kids were climbing onto the golf carts. They'd be gone in minutes. Panic nearly immobilized him, but he had to do this. "Come on, Snick." He followed the dog's well-worn path. By the time he reached Natalie's yard, she was stepping off the porch.

She stopped when she saw him. When hope filled her eyes, he regretted this decision, but again this wasn't for him. It was for her. "I came to say goodbye," he said, setting her straight right away.

"Don't. Please." She shook her head, her eyes bright.

"It's for the best."

"No, it's not." She came to him. "You should be coming with us. You still can."

He glanced into her eyes. She loved him. That, he didn't doubt. But as his gaze slipped to her stomach and he imagined that sweet, innocent little life growing inside her, he knew he had no other option. "You're better off without me—"

"I don't want to hear more of that. It's not true."

"It is, Natalie. You'll be a wonderful mother. I know it. You're all that child needs. I'd only mess it up."

"You're wrong. More wrong than you've ever been in your life." She stepped toward him, her face set with determination. "But I want you to know that the love I feel for you isn't going to change. I'll still love you in four months, two years, ten years, until the day I die."

"Good luck with that."

"You're such an asshole." She shook her head and smiled. Smiled. "When you change your mind, I'll be waiting."

"I wouldn't do that if I were you."

"Well, you're not me." Without another word, without a kiss or a touch or a backward glance, she climbed onto a golf cart and left.

As they drove away, Snickers looked from Jamis to the kids and back again and barked his head off. He wagged his tail, barked some more and made it very clear he was all ready to go with Natalie and her crew.

"You want to go, then go." Jamis forced the words from deep in his soul. "Go, Snick, go on. You'd be better off without me, too."

Snickers looked after the quickly disappearing golf carts and whined. Then he quietly lay down, rested his head in his paws and sighed.

Stupid, stupid dog.

Yeah. And Jamis was such a genius.

FROM THE FERRY, NATALIE watched Mirabelle's shoreline grow more and more indistinct. With every cold wave hitting the side of the massive boat, her sense of panic escalated.

No, no, no. She hugged herself, holding herself together. *He's not leaving you. You're leaving him. And oddly enough, this time it's the right thing to do. If—when—if he comes to you, it'll be what he wants. It'll be his choice.*

"Choose me, Jamis," she whispered, closing her eyes and turning her face into the warm, late-summer sun. "Choose me. And our baby."

CHAPTER EIGHTEEN

"THE VICTORIAN IS for sale."

On some level, the words Chuck was speaking over the phone registered in Jamis's brain, but he couldn't seem to make sense of them. "What did you say?" He sat back from his keyboard. For the past two months, the pages of his latest book had been flying off his fingertips and he was close to the halfway point. He'd refused to stop writing. When he did, thoughts of Natalie flooded his every sense.

"Natalie Steeger is selling her grandmother's house."

The possibility that she might not come back had never occurred to Jamis. She swore she'd never sell her grandmother's place. This was what he'd done to her. She was doing this for him. She didn't want him to move.

Jamis glanced at the dust-covered envelope Toni had given him just before they'd all left the island. Unopened, he'd set the card on his desk that morning after they'd gone and hadn't touched it since. He couldn't bring himself to open it. "Is Natalie buying another place on Mirabelle?"

"There's nothing else for sale. Except for your cabin once you decide on the island you want. You did get the realty information I sent, right?"

"Yeah." He'd gotten the listings of private islands for sale in both Minnesota and Wisconsin, but he couldn't seem to make himself look at them.

"What do you want to do?" Chuck asked.

"Buy the Victorian," Jamis said without a moment's hesitation. "Do whatever it takes. I want that house."

"I take it that means you're not moving."

"I don't know what I'll be doing, but there is no way I'm letting anyone else get Natalie's house."

He hung up the phone and stared at the page full of words on his computer screen. The horror story he'd been trying to write all summer long had fallen by the wayside within a few days of Natalie's departure, and he'd started a new book, something different from anything he'd ever written. The entire story had been nearly fully formed in his head. All he had to do was get it down on paper, but just now, that didn't seem important. He yearned for the sound of children's laughter out his window, the sight of Natalie, her voice, her touch. Her. Just her.

Pushing away from his desk, he grabbed his coat and walked with Snickers into town. The fall colors had long since disappeared from the treetops and bare branches swayed in a wind that held the promise of an early snowfall. He walked down the sidewalk and glanced around, needing…something. It was late in the afternoon, almost dinnertime. Main Street was deserted, many of the residents having left for their winter homes. The off-season had once been his favorite time on Mirabelle. Now he couldn't seem to stand the quiet.

As he walked by Duffy's Pub, the sound of laughter and music made him stop and glance through the window. A young woman he'd never seen was serving a nearly crowded bar. Feeling so distant from the world, he sat on the nearest bench, closed his eyes and listened.

"You look like you could use a beer."

He knew that voice. Jamis opened his eyes and found Sally standing in front of him.

"Come on. It's two for one. Happy hour."

"No, I don't think that's a good idea."

Sally sat next to him. "So she's gone, huh?"

He nodded.

"Why didn't you go with her?"

He could find no words. He might have been able to type them on his computer, but nothing that made sense was going to come out of his mouth.

"I'm dying, Jamis," she said.

Startled at her being so blunt, he glanced up at her. Her hair was growing back and she looked at if she had energy again. "But you look good—"

"I stopped the chemo treatments." She took a deep breath and looked down the street.

"Why?"

"Because I knew they weren't going to work."

"You could extend the time you have left. Who knows what could happen in the field of cancer treatments?"

She shook her head. "I'm old. I've done what I've wanted to do. It's my time. I don't have any regrets."

"Postmaster on Mirabelle? That's it? That's all you want out of life?"

"I was born on Mirabelle. Never had any interest in going anyplace else. These people know me. Accept me as I am. It's not glamorous or exciting, but I've been happy."

"So you're just going to quit? It's over."

She nodded. "You should know what that's like. You've done the same thing."

He studied her face.

"At least I have an excuse," she said. "I'm old. You? You're a young man, and you've already given up."

"This isn't about me—"

"Oh, yes, it is. I have terminal cancer. Stepping off the merry-go-round is allowed for me. What you've done is a travesty. A waste of four years of life. Four years you can never get back." She tilted her head at him. "So your wife and kids died. So you feel partly responsible. Get over it, Jamis. Get over yourself. You've wallowed on Mirabelle long enough. A life without pain is a life without joy."

"I know that."

"Then start acting like you believe it." She stood, went to the door to Duffy's and glanced at him. "It's time, Jamis, don't you think?"

Jamis didn't know what it was time for, but a beer or two had never hurt anything. Then again. "I can't leave the dog out here for very long."

"Ah, bring him in. Anyone gives you guff, I'll tell 'em where to go."

Jamis stood, held the door for Sally and then followed her inside. Heads glanced up from the bar and the few faces he recognized looked surprised, but no one said a word about Snickers.

"Sally!"

"How you feeling?"

"Good to see you here again."

"Ah, quit making a fuss," she said, sitting next to Doc Welinsky at the bar. "Well, I owe my friend here a drink. Everyone, this is Jamis Quinn. He's the oddball who's been living in that log cabin at the other end of the island."

Jamis took the open seat on the other side of Sally, next to Garrett Taylor. "Hello, Garrett."

"Jamis." Garrett nodded and proceeded to introduce the residents lining the bar. Jamis had heard most of the names, Setterberg, Henderson, Newman and so forth, but had previously met only a few of them. "And this is my wife." Garrett's eyes softened as he indicated the bartender. "Erica."

"Hey, Jamis." Erica reached out and shook his hand. She was noticeably pregnant and the sight of her, the shape of her, made it hard for Jamis to breathe. "This is our nephew, Jason." She indicated a young boy sitting near the end of the bar drawing pictures with markers.

"Hi." Jason glanced up at him and smiled.

Jamis, unable to find his voice, could only nod in response. He never would've believed how much he could miss the sight and sound of children. He cleared his throat and glanced at Erica. "When is your baby due?"

She locked gazes with Garrett. "February twenty-fourth."

"I'm going to have a cousin," Jason said, grinning.

"Congratulations."

"Thank you," she said.

The love passing between those two was palpable, and immediately Jamis regretted his decision to come to town. There was so much life in this bar he was nearly choking to death. He was about to push back his chair and hightail it out of there when Sally's hand came down on his arm.

"Well, for crying out loud," she said, tightening her grip and holding him there. "What's a person have to do to get a drink around here?"

Erica brought Jamis a mug of beer and Sally a gin and tonic.

"So where the heck are Arlo and Lynn?" Sally asked.

"Went to visit their boys for the holidays," someone said. "Then they're spending a month in Florida."

"No kidding?" Sally said, glancing at Doc.

He shrugged. "I suppose this is as good a time as any to tell everyone."

"You tell them," Sally said.

Doc cleared his throat. "Sally and I are both retiring, and then we're heading to Arizona."

"Together?" someone asked on a note of incredulity.

"Together," Sally said.

"Well, I'll be damned," someone murmured.

"Good for you two."

"Miracles never cease."

"What are we gonna do for a doctor?"

"He's already here," Doc said. "That young man who's been filling in for me here and there has decided to stay."

Amidst the sound of questions erupting around the bar, a slow, romantic song played on the jukebox. Sally turned to Jamis. "I'm thinking I'd like to dance."

"You asking?"

She grabbed his hand. "It's time for you to start living again, Jamis. Don't you think?"

He'd been dead so long, he wasn't sure he remembered how to live.

"You'll remember how to dance, Jamis. Put one foot in front of the other. It's as easy as that."

CHAPTER NINETEEN

SHE WAS GONE. CALEB couldn't blame her for leaving. Not after what he'd done. "I wish..." He stared into the bitterly cold night sky. "For Susan...to have a happy life."

"That's because you're a sap." Jamis's hands stalled over his keyboard. He took a deep breath and quickly exhaled. "But a nice sap. After what you've been through, you might actually deserve her."

He heard a sound behind him and turned. "Susan."

"There's only one person," she whispered, "who can make that wish come true."

He didn't dare hope, didn't dare dream.

"You, Caleb. There's no happy life for me without you."

The End.

There. Done. Another perfect ending even if it was happily ever after. Once upon a time, Jamis wouldn't have believed he could write such an ending, but now? Now he would've given anything to roll the clock backward and write his own ending to this past summer. It certainly wouldn't have involved Natalie leaving Mirabelle.

He e-mailed the last chapter of this latest book to his agent, turned off the computer and glanced out the window.

Without realizing it, he'd written through the night and finished only a week past his deadline. At least it was done. With an unseasonably cold November wind whipping up the light dusting of snow that had fallen last night, the sun rose over Lake Superior. Through the bare tree branches a brilliant sun dog lit the ice crystals in the air, creating an early winter rainbow of pale oranges and reds.

Snickers whined and Jamis glanced down at him. "Bored, aren't you? Well, don't look at me. You had your chance to escape, dude. You snooze, you lose."

The dog swished his tail.

"All right. Up you go." Jamis patted his lap and Snickers joyfully jumped up and rested his head on Jamis's chest.

Absently, Jamis rubbed the dog's ears and patted his head. It was Thanksgiving weekend. Almost three miserable months had passed with excruciating slowness. There'd been no children's laughter and no outside sounds of running feet. In all that time, Jamis had never once turned on the TV. All he'd done day and night was write. He had nothing to say to anyone, and no one had anything to say that he wanted to hear. Except for that day he'd gone into town and Sally had convinced him to go into Duffy's.

He frowned, remembering the obituary he'd read in the town flyer in his mail the other day. Sally had died, less than a week ago while in Arizona with Doc. He couldn't believe she was gone. Just like that. The way four and a half years had slipped away from him. Some of the last words she'd ever spoken to him thrummed through his memory. *Put one foot in front of the other.* It was time.

"I'm sorry, Katherine," he whispered suddenly. "I wish things had been different. I wish you, Caitlin and Justin were alive. I wish I could've seen my children grow." He paused. None of those wishes were going to come true. "I wish there was peace on earth. I wish for food on every table. I wish…I wish she was here." None of those things was going to happen, either. He could wish and wish and wish, day and night, night and day, and none of them would come to fruition.

Snickers hopped to the floor and lay down at the top of the stairs.

Could we change the course of other people's lives? Yes. No doubt. By things we do or don't do. Natalie had proven that to him. Every one of those kids that had stayed with her for the summer had gone back with a vision of a better life. But she couldn't have made those changes by simply wishing for them. His wish, as fervent as it had been, hadn't killed his family. The semitrailer truck had killed them. And he could finally accept that.

So what was he still doing on Mirabelle?

Apparently, Natalie had called it. He was frightened. Scared to immobility of losing what he loved. And he loved Natalie. But how could he—Jamis Quinn, odd man extraordinaire—have done something as stupid and naive and honest as fallen in love?

Since the first moment he'd laid eyes on her on moving-in day all those months ago, he supposed, these emotions had been struggling to take root inside him. From her terrible cookies to her bright smile, once she'd made a crack in his veneer he hadn't a chance of fighting her. His feelings for her had taken off like a weed, nearly choking him.

The love he'd felt for Katherine paled in comparison to what he felt for Natalie. He knew it. He could feel it. When Katherine had asked him for a divorce, he'd been hurt and angry. His heart had cracked that day there was no doubt, but the truth was he'd rather cease to exist than live without Natalie. He was scared, scared of how much he loved her, scared of how much he was going to love their child, scared of falling in love with Toni, Galen, Ryan and Sam. And, ultimately, frightened beyond even his own comprehension of losing them all.

But if he stayed on Mirabelle wouldn't he lose them anyway?

Reaching for the envelope Toni had given him that last morning, he carefully opened it and extracted a handmade card. On the front, she'd drawn a colorful picture of the tree house with the kids inside, smiling and waving from up high. Two other figures stood next to each other near the base of the tree. The one with the beard was clearly Jamis, and the other with her long and curly yellow hair had to be Natalie. Inside, Toni had written in her childish hand:

> My Daddy was a good Daddy. That's why you remind me of him.
> Love, Toni
> XOXO

Jamis wiped away the lone tear trickling down his cheek. He had been a good father. He'd tried his best as a husband. He deserved another chance. But how could a man put one foot in front of the other when he'd completely forgotten how to walk?

His phone rang, startling him. When the sound of his agent's voice on the answering machine registered, Jamis reached across his desk and picked up the call. "Stephen. Hey."

"Jamis. Holy shit, man. This is the best book you've ever written."

Honestly, he didn't care. It was out of him. That's all that mattered.

"The only problem is that it's nothing like your other books."

"So?"

"They can deal with it being a week late, but your contract with the publisher calls for another horror story. This is a freaking romance."

Jamis laughed. "Weird. I know."

"You don't happen to have a spare horror story lying around the house, do you?"

"Sorry, no."

Stephen sighed. "Well, I'll have to send it to them anyway and we'll take it from there."

"Whatever."

There was a short pause on the line. "Jamis, are you all right?"

"No." He glanced again at the tree house picture Toni had drawn for him and at the sight of the curly-haired stick figure an ache spread through him. "I did a really, really stupid thing, Stephen." He set the card on his desk and looked away. "I fell in love."

Stephen was silent for a moment. "That's good, isn't it, Jamis?"

Jamis walked outside and took a deep breath of cold morning air and knew exactly what he had to do. The only question was whether or not Natalie would have him. After almost three months without so much as a phone call, she'd have every right to slam the door in his face. Then there was the not-so-little matter of her most likely fostering four kids. And a baby. His child. The thought of being a father again scared him witless. But he had to try. He closed his eyes and imagined Natalie saying yes. He imagined himself being a loving husband and father. He imagined himself stepping off the shores of Mirabelle.

"Jamis?" Stephen's voice pulled him back. "I'd like to help."

"Then find me Natalie Steeger's address and the quickest way to Minneapolis."

Stephen chuckled. "How does a helicopter sound?"

"Not fast enough, but it'll have to do." He was about to hang up, but had one more thing to say. "Stephen?"

"Yeah?"

"Thank you. For everything you've done over the years."

"I'm glad you're back amongst the living, my dear friend. It's about damned time."

NATALIE PLUGGED IN THE last string of lights on the Christmas tree. Continuing with her family's tradition of getting a tree on Thanksgiving weekend, she'd taken the kids out that morning. "Okay. It's all yours."

With holiday music playing in the background, Ryan, Toni and Sam dug into the ornaments and began hanging their respective favorites. Galen cocked his head. "I've never seen that many lights."

"The more the merrier. As it is with so many things in life." She grinned, elated that she'd decided to go one step beyond being a foster mom. Social services had just that previous week approved her requests for adopting all four kids. She swung an arm around his shoulder and squeezed, and he surprised her by not pulling away.

"Thanks for taking a chance on me," Galen said. "I promise I won't disappoint you."

As they'd all expected, Galen's mother had put up a stink over the whole fostering thing, but the moment Galen had turned sixteen and filed a petition requesting emancipation, the woman had huffed out of the courtroom swearing that she'd never take him back. Once he'd joined them at the house, the decision to adopt them all had been a no-brainer for Natalie.

"I'm already proud of you, Galen," she said. "Be proud of yourself."

"I'm getting there."

She smiled, but it was hard to completely disguise the deep sadness in her heart. All the kids understood she missed Jamis, and every change her body went through as a result of the pregnancy only made her miss him all the more.

"You know you don't need him," Galen whispered.

"I know." She only wanted Jamis with an ache as deep as Lake Superior. "Go," she said. "I'm okay."

He joined the other three kids hanging ornaments on the tree, and Natalie watched them. There was only one thing that could make this moment more perfect. Her smile slowly disappeared. "Anyone for some cocoa?" she asked, hoping to keep the mood light.

"Yeah!"

"Sounds good."

"Can we help?" Sam asked.

"No, no," Natalie said. "That's one thing I can't screw up." Barely stifling the tears, she went into the kitchen. After putting a kettle of water on the stove, she wrapped her arms around her waist and collected herself. If any of the kids saw her like this, it would ruin their nights, especially Galen's. He'd been so protective of her lately.

The doorbell rang as she was pouring boiling water over cocoa mix into five mugs.

"I got it," Galen called.

There was a moment of silence, and then the sound of a dog barking, the younger kids screeching with excitement, and then muffled voices that got louder and more vehement with every word.

"I like you, man," Galen said. "But you need to go away."

"I get it. I do."

Jamis. Running into the living room, she stopped at the sight of him standing on the front doorstep with Snickers jumping from one child to the next and wiggling ecstatically.

"Snickers remembers us," Toni said, grinning.

"How could he ever forget?" Jamis murmured, his tall frame outlined by Christmas lights strung around the entryway. Big, fluffy snowflakes fell slowly in the darkness behind him. Part of Natalie was elated to see him. The other part felt every second of every day of the past three months like pinpricks to her skin.

Galen was blocking his path into the house. A concerned look on her face, Sam was holding hands with Toni and Ryan. Jamis glanced up and his gaze locked with Natalie's, but his expression was unreadable.

"Galen, it's okay," Natalie said. "You guys keep decorating the tree. I'll go outside." Grabbing a jacket out of the front closet, she went out into the chilly night air, closing the door behind her. She crossed her arms in front of her. It wasn't that cold outside, but it gave her hands something to do when all they wanted was to hold him.

"How are you feeling?" he asked, glancing quickly at the small bulge in her sweater.

"Good. The morning sickness is completely over." She tightened her arms around herself. "How are you?"

"Been better. Only one other time I've been worse." He backed up a step, giving her some space. "I've discovered I can survive without you, but it's not very pretty. I guess I did need fixing. I needed you."

Unable to help herself, she smiled. "Oh, Jamis."

"I'm sorry it's taken me so long to come to you. I guess

I needed some time to clear my head and figure things out. If you don't want to see me, I understand."

"That depends on what you have to say."

"I know why I want you, Natalie. You brought me back to life. Gave me hope. Make me think anything is possible. Make me *feel* like a better man than I am. You truly fill each and every one of my days with sunshine." He paused, reached out but then stopped.

"But?"

"Why in God's name do you want me?"

"I love you," she said.

"Why? What could you possibly love about me?"

"Oh, Jamis." She reached out and caressed his cheek. "I love you because you make me look at the world differently. You made me see myself. You make me laugh and think. You're caring and passionate. You believe in wishes coming true. And you're a good cook." She smiled. "But mostly, your flaws fit remarkably well with mine."

"You sure? Because a three-month stint isn't going to be enough for me. I want a helluva lot more from you."

"I'm sure." She nodded. "A three-month stint wouldn't be enough for me, either."

"Natalie." He fell to his knees in the snow. "Will you marry me?"

"Are *you* sure?" she whispered, unable to catch her breath.

"I am."

"There's something else you need to know, though. You'll be getting quite a handful in this bargain."

"I know. You're fostering Toni, Ryan, Sam and Galen. I think it's a great idea."

"That's not exactly it," she said, shaking her head. "There's more."

"If you love me half as much as I love you, nothing else will matter."

"You can be such an ass." A tear slipped down her cheek. "I love you…more than you could ever imagine. More than you could ever dream. More than you could ever, ever *write*."

"Nat—"

"I'm adopting all four of them."

"Adopting them?" His stunned gaze flew to the window. They were, all four children, looking outside the window. Along with Snickers.

She put a hand low on her sweater and wished she could take it back. She shouldn't have told him. Not yet. Not like this. If the adoptions cost her Jamis, her heart would break all over again. "It's all right if you change your mind. I know…I know it's a lot to take in. You probably didn't plan on being a father of so many so quickly…"

He looked away, clearly overwhelmed. "I don't—"

"Oh, Jamis, don't say it." She cupped his face in her hands. "You'll be a wonderful father. A wonderful husband. This baby deserves you. So do those four kids in there. And me. You're who we want. No one else."

Could he live up to her image of him? Could he be the man she believed in? What would Caitlin and Justin say?

The image of his daughter swam in front of his eyes. His baby son, chubby and perfect. He'd done his best to never fail them. That was what they'd say. He deserved a second chance to get this family thing right. "I will give you everything I have to give." He held her face in his hands. "Marry me, Natalie, and I will do the best I can to become the man you think I am."

"You already are." She kissed him to the sound of hoots, laughter and whistles coming from inside the house. "The man I've been wishing for my entire life."

"I love you." He leaned in and returned her kiss.

Snowflakes fell on their cheeks, their lips. They both looked to the window and found all four kids standing just inside the house watching and smiling. Snickers had his front paws on the sill as he stared at Jamis.

"Come on in and help us decorate the tree," she coaxed. "The only thing this house has been missing is you."

As she drew him inside her home, her life, Jamis realized even he could never have written a better ending to his story. This was perfect. Thanksgiving. A Christmas tree. Big, fluffy snowflakes falling gently in the night.

Then again, there was always making love on a warm, sunny beach with palm trees blowing in a soft breeze. He smiled inside. No. Those things didn't matter. Sunshine, rain, clouds, snow, Mirabelle, Minneapolis. As long as Natalie was with him, every scene in Jamis's life—the good, the bad and the sexy—was going to be absolutely and perfectly…real.

EPILOGUE

"SEAN, EVERETT, Vincent and Gregory!" Natalie pointed to the upstairs boys' bedroom. "You guys are in that room."

"Ashley, Kally, Lindsey and Sarita." Sam spread an arm toward the girls' bedroom. "You, young ladies, are in here."

"And you guys, Erin and Matt—" Galen walked to the end of the hall to show the two teenage summer helpers to their respective rooms "—are down here."

"Cool."

"I get the top bunk."

"No, I do."

"I *want* the bottom."

"Well, good for you."

"I get this dresser."

"Oh, no, you don't."

"I hate pink."

"Don't touch me."

"Don't touch *me*."

"You started it."

"I did not."

It was the first day of summer camp and the previously quiet northwest end of Mirabelle Island was bustling with activity. Apparently, mayhem and unbridled energy were the rules of the day. What could be better? Snickers, of course.

He chose that moment to scamper up the steps, race

from one room to the next and jump from bed to bed. Kids were screeching and laughing, and the dog was ecstatic to be back on the island. No more fenced-in yards or leashes. He could go where he wanted, when he wanted.

This was going to be a great summer. Maybe Natalie's best ever. "Okay, kids," she said to the new campers. "Unpack your stuff. You'll see I left a fun surprise for each and every one of you on your beds." New sweatshirts and more. "And then meet me outside in the yard."

She glanced at Sam and Galen, her oldest daughter and son. She loved thinking of the two teenagers that way. Her son and daughter. "Well," she said, "what do you guys think?"

Sam grinned. "I'm glad to be back on Mirabelle."

"Galen?"

"Ten kids this summer? I think you're nuts." He shook his head and smiled. "But I'm glad to be a part of it. Even more glad to have graduated to the log cabin this time around."

Natalie had hired a head camp counselor who would be staying in the Victorian with the camp kids. Natalie, Jamis, Sam, Galen, Ryan and Toni would be living at Jamis's log cabin. The quarters sometimes felt a little tight, but they were managing.

"Let's go see what the others are up to." Natalie hooked her arms through Sam's and Galen's and tugged them down the stairs and out into the yard.

The sight that greeted her the moment she stepped onto her grandmother's back porch made her heart flutter. Holding a little pink bundle, Jamis sat on one of the swings of the play equipment he'd built when they'd first arrived back on Mirabelle last week. He was busy gazing into the face of their baby, rocking her gently and nuzzling her cheek. Toni and Ryan were hanging out in the tree house tower high above Jamis's head.

Jamis glanced up as they stepped out into the yard. "What's going on up there, World War Three?"

"Isn't it great?" Natalie smiled. "They're settling in well."

"Oh, goodie," he murmured.

Galen laughed and held out his arms for the baby. "Can I have her?"

Reluctantly, Jamis handed her over.

She fussed a bit with all the jostling. "Shh, Anna, shh," Galen whispered in his sister's ear and patted her back.

"I get her next," Sam said.

"Then me!" Toni called.

"And me," Ryan added.

Natalie held back tears of complete and unadulterated joy as Jamis wrapped his arm around her shoulder. They'd been married since early December, and she couldn't imagine a day without him. "I love you," she whispered into his neck.

"I love you, too." He rested his forehead against hers. "But you need to quit avoiding the discussion about how many babies we're going to have."

"Shoulda gotten that firmed up before you said I do." She chuckled. "Coulda used it as the fatal flaw."

"Need I remind you, Sunshine, the log cabin has only three bedrooms?"

"Well, then, it's a good thing you're so handy with tools."

He sighed and glanced at their kids, his family. "Your mother is something, you know that?"

"Yeah," Sam said with a smile. "We know."

Anna started crying and Galen handed her over to Natalie. She brought her daughter up close and kissed her soft cheek. "Shh, Anna." She glanced up and caught her husband watching her, the look in his eyes filled with so much love, Natalie felt as if she might burst. Her husband.

He sighed contentedly. "I gotta get to work."

He was writing so much these days that chances are the words wouldn't fly off his fingertips quickly enough. His last book had placed third on the *New York Times* bestseller list and had hung in the top ten for four months. They were expecting his romance due to be released any day now to do even better.

"What are you writing this time?" she asked.

"Could be a romance. Or a horror story." He grinned, that sardonic twist of his lips that had captured her heart. "I'm not sure yet."

The new camp kids came running out the back door of the house and into the yard, yelling, laughing and jostling one another. Jamis took one look at them and pulled a set of earplugs out of his pocket. After brushing Natalie's cheek with his fingertips, he headed toward the log cabin.

"Jamis?" She reached out and touched his arm. "Will you join us this one time for a huddle?"

He glanced at the faces of the children, debating. Then he shook his head and put the earplugs away. "One time, Nat. That's it. I'm serious."

"I'm sure you are."

He scowled at her.

The new kids were running this way and that. "Let's gather together!" she called. Amidst a lot of groaning and moaning, they all, including Sam, Ryan, Toni and Galen, eventually gathered around Natalie. Glancing into Jamis's eyes, she leaned in. "What do we need to do to make this the best summer ever?"

"This again?"

"Oh, great."

"Get used to it," one of her kids muttered, probably Galen.

"Close your eyes," Natalie said. "Everyone." But she kept hers focused on her husband's clear and loving gaze.

"Wish it, see it," Jamis said, loud and strong. "Make it happen."

* * * * *

'0710/23a

SPECIAL MOMENTS™ 2-in-1

Coming next month

DADDY ON DEMAND by Helen R Myers

Left to raise twin nieces by himself, millionaire Collin Masters turned to Sabrina. She accepted his job offer and found herself falling for the reluctant father!

DÉJÀ YOU by Lynda Sandoval

When a blaze sparked memories of a life-changing accident, firefighter Erin DeLuca ran to the arms of a mystery man. But that one night had far-reaching consequences!

A FATHER FOR DANNY by Janice Carter

Samantha finds things for a living and she's been hired to find a missing person! Someone has to tell Chase Sullivan that he has a son – who needs him desperately.

BABY BE MINE by Eve Gaddy

Tucker wants his best friend Maggie to be happy, even if that means a fake union so she can foster a baby girl. Until he discovers he wants this marriage to be real.

THE MUMMY MAKEOVER by Kristi Gold

When Kieran offers to help Erica get her life back on track, he finds himself willing to break the first rule of personal training – no fraternising with the clients...

MUMMY FOR HIRE by Cathy Gillen Thacker

Grady McCabe isn't looking for love – just for a mother for his little girl. But when matchmaking Alexis tries to change his mind, he starts to relent...and fall for *her*!

On sale 16th July 2010

Available at WHSmith, Tesco, ASDA, Eason and all good bookshops.
For full Mills & Boon range including eBooks visit
www.millsandboon.co.uk

Single titles coming next month

THE PREGNANT BRIDE WORE WHITE

by Susan Crosby

When Jake McCoy came home to Chance City, he found a whole new family waiting for him. Was the adventurer ready to become an honest husband?

SOPHIE'S SECRET

by Tara Taylor Quinn

For years it's suited Duane and Sophie to keep their relationship a secret. Then Sophie becomes pregnant – and Duane proposes. Are they ready to make their private affair public news?

HER SO-CALLED FIANCÉ

by Abby Gaines

What possesses Sabrina to tell everyone she's going to marry Jake Warrington? She's sure her ex hates her! Sabrina needs Jake's help – and he might give it. But it comes with some conditions attached...

DIAGNOSIS: DADDY

by Gina Wilkins

Connor Hayes had just started to pursue his dream of being a doctor when he found out he was a father. Mia wanted to help, but was she up to multitasking as best friend... nanny...and love of Connor's life?

On sale 16th July 2010

Available at WHSmith, Tesco, ASDA, Eason and all good bookshops.
For full Mills & Boon range including eBooks visit
www.millsandboon.co.uk

0410_S0ZED

2 FREE BOOKS
AND A SURPRISE GIFT

We would like to take this opportunity to thank you for reading this Mills & Boon® book by offering you the chance to take TWO more specially selected books from the Special Moments™ series absolutely FREE! We're also making this offer to introduce you to the benefits of the Mills & Boon® Book Club™—

- **FREE home delivery**
- **FREE gifts and competitions**
- **FREE monthly Newsletter**
- **Exclusive Mills & Boon Book Club offers**
- **Books available before they're in the shops**

Accepting these FREE books and gift places you under no obligation to buy, you may cancel at any time, even after receiving your free books. Simply complete your details below and return the entire page to the address below. You don't even need a stamp!

YES Please send me 2 free Special Moments books and a surprise gift. I understand that unless you hear from me, I will receive 5 superb new stories every month, including a 2-in-1 book priced at £4.99 and three single books priced at £3.19 each, postage and packing free. I am under no obligation to purchase any books and may cancel my subscription at any time. The free books and gift will be mine to keep in any case.

Ms/Mrs/Miss/Mr ________________ Initials ________________

____

Surname ______________________________________

Address _______________________________________

____

______________________________ Postcode ____________

E-mail ____

Send this whole page to: Mills & Boon Book Club, Free Book Offer, FREEPOST NAT 10298, Richmond, TW9 1BR

Offer valid in UK only and is not available to current Mills & Boon Book Club subscribers to this series. Overseas and Eire please write for details.. We reserve the right to refuse an application and applicants must be aged 18 years or over. Only one application per household. Terms and prices subject to change without notice. Offer expires 30th June 2010. As a result of this application, you may receive offers from Harlequin Mills & Boon and other carefully selected companies. If you would prefer not to share in this opportunity please write to The Data Manager, PO Box 676, Richmond, TW9 1WU.